S0-AAE-707

Elizabeth Ridley was born in Milwaukee, Wisconsin in 1966. She has a degree in journalism from Northwestern University and a MA in creative writing from the University of East Anglia. In 1994 she was a recipient of a Hawthornden Fellowship. Her earlier works include two novels, *Throwing Roses*, published in the USA in 1993, and *The Remarkable Journey of Miss Tranby Quirke*, published by Virago in 1996. She lives in London.

Praise for *The Remarkable Journey of Miss Tranby Quirke*:

'Humour, historical flavour, political astuteness and a style which affords the reader a pleasure akin to that of watching a bird in flight . . . a love story of unusual beauty' *The Times*

'A refreshing and beautiful novel' *Literary Review*

'[Possesses] the power to make us think about an entire generation of women in a way we may never have done before' *Independent on Sunday*

'A gas-lit melodrama that wears its learning, and its strangeness lightly' *Independent*

By the same author:

The Remarkable Journey of Miss Tranby Quirke

RAINEY'S
– LAMENT –

Elizabeth Ridley

A *Virago* Book

First published in Great Britain in 1998 by Virago

Copyright © 1998, Elizabeth Ridley

The moral right of the author has been asserted.

*All characters in this publication are fictitious and any resemblance to real
persons, living or dead, is purely coincidental.*

All rights reserved.
No part of this publication may be reproduced, stored in a
retrieval system, or transmitted, in any form or by any means,
without the prior permission in writing of the publisher, nor be
otherwise circulated in any form of binding or cover other
than that in which it is published and without a similar
condition including this condition being imposed on the
subsequent purchaser.

A CIP catalogue record for this book is
available from the British Library.

ISBN 1 86049 412 9

Typeset in Weiss by M Rules
Printed and bound in Great Britain by
Clays Ltd, St Ives plc

Virago
A Division of
Little, Brown and Company (UK)
Brettenham House
Lancaster Place
London WC2E 7EN

Thanks to Stephen Finucan, Jonny Geller, Thomas L. Ralston, Alan Samson and Erik Skuggevik. Special thanks to Jan and Trevor Johnson for their unfailing love and support, and also special thanks to my mother, Marcia Ridley, without whom this book never would have been finished.

For Sophie,
Who Will Never Know Why —

'But I have that within which passeth show,
these but the trappings and the suits of woe.'
— *Hamlet*

RAINEY'S
– LAMENT –

– PART 1 –

1 9 7 0 – 1 9 8 0

Thanksgiving Day 1970
Owauskeum, Wisconsin

We're just kidding ourselves when we imagine the earth is one place, one big old ball zooming through the universe, thinks Mary Jane McBride, *because really the world is made up of two places, two separate rooms – one for people who know grief, and the other for those who still haven't found it, a place for those who haven't yet opened that door.*

In the ten months, three weeks, and four days since she entered that other room, she no longer remembers anything about the fifteen years that she lived in the first. Her head spins, her world breaks open like a cracked skull full of blood. She sometimes wakes up in the morning and asks herself, *Was there ever a time before Michael died?*

Today is Thanksgiving Day, a day to come together with family in the spirit of peace and goodwill. But Uncle Jens won't have Mary Jane at the table, he refuses to sit down with someone who, in his words, 'has brought such shame and disgrace to the Svensen family name. In the Old Country, you'd never get away with what you've done – pregnant at fifteen! We had a word for girls like you.'

'Damn your Old Country, you live here now,' Mary Jane says to herself, standing alone, round-shouldered and barefoot, exiled to the cool solitude of the living room. The smell of turkey, stuffing and pie torments her from the dining room, and she listens for the hungry noises; the symphony of knives and forks and spoons. She shivers through the thin fabric of her embroidered peasant blouse. 'Damn you all to hell,' she says. She feels a knotted paradox rise inside her as she gazes down at her five-month-old daughter, Rainbow, sleeping on the sofa next to baby Andy. Mary Jane knows it is her own sin, her shame, which gave birth to something so beautiful. Mary Jane lifts the baby to her shoulder, pats her on the back, and tries to capture the frantic, pedalling feet. 'My baby, Rainbow Planet, loves to eat spinach. Her chins wiggle and her feet curve inwards. I sometimes think she's cross-eyed.' Mary Jane repeats the words like a prayer; she engraves them on her heart, in order to invoke them later to make her peace, her penance. 'Forgive me, my daughter. Forgive what I'm about to do.' The baby blows a bubble which breaks against her mother's ear.

Rainbow Planet is getting heavier, too heavy to lift sometimes, and with that weight comes the added responsibility, which is already too great for Mary Jane to bear. Her ears ring all day and night with Mama's constant scolding:

'Åh, nei, nei, nei. That's not how you feed a baby. Lift her head and shoulders and keep them straight. No wonder she gets gas.'

'Not so much water in the bathtub, you could drown the baby that way.'

'Mary Jane, don't let her play with your necklace. Take that away from her right now. If it breaks in her mouth, she could choke on the beads and die.'

Mary Jane was horrified. Danger lurked in places she had never considered before; in a drop of water, in the fold of a blanket, in the collapsible leg of a card table. There were a million ways this child could be lost. In the first few months after Rainbow was born, Mary Jane used to sneak the baby into her bed late at night. She had wondered what the baby did when everyone else was asleep, and she learned that Rainbow Planet gurgled and laughed, talked to herself, and liked to play with her toes. These warm, gentle evenings were perfect bliss, until Mary Jane realised she might turn over in her sleep one night and hurt the baby, might accidentally crush those tiny bones. It was at that moment she first decided to run away with Carlos, run away and leave Rainbow behind. 'I'll come back when I'm older,' she promised. 'When I'm grown up enough to take care of you, then I'll come back.'

Mary Jane has sworn to remember everything in her exile, but already she is forgetting; so much is already gone, and more disappears everyday. *There's not enough in this world to hang on to,* she thinks. Mary Jane's soul belongs to Carlos Espinanza with all the sixteen-year-old certainty of a girl who knows she'll never suffer through another Wisconsin winter and she'll never have to do algebra again. Every time she looks at Rainbow, she feels herself in the presence of a great mystery – *I carried this baby inside me for nine months and didn't even know she was there. When she was born, it hurt so bad. But when it was over, I didn't remember giving birth.* She remembers when she feeds the child, but forgets again every time she lays her down.

The other baby still nestled on the sofa stirs and sneezes. His thin arm with its tiny fist reaches out and struggles to punch the space beside him.

Sissel. Mary Jane thinks. *My stupid cousin Sissel. She's always had to do me one better. I had a baby, so she has one two months later. Only for her it's OK, because she's twenty-one and married to some rich guy she used to work for. Sure, everybody's happy for her.* Mary Jane sticks out her tongue at the pale little boy. *Well, Sissel can have her prissy little Andy, my Rainbow is the biggest and brightest baby in the whole wide world,* she thinks. A bruising joy briefly lifts the curtain of her grief but, as quick and hot as sunlight, sorrow shoots her down. *What does any of it matter? My baby may be beautiful, but my brother is still dead. Dead as he was yesterday, dead as he'll be tomorrow, dead forever, dead from now on.*

The pale little boy stops crying and falls asleep. Tomorrow baby Andy will return to his bronzed nursery with his starched sheets and expensive toys. At the same time, Mary Jane's Rainbow will be on her way to the Milwaukee County Courthouse, where $5 and the signature of Mary Jane's parents will change the baby's legal name forever, from Rainbow Planet to Rainey Astrid McBride.

'Rainbow Rainbow Rainbow,' Mary Jane sings to the smiling baby. 'Mama and Pop never let me get my way. But I'll always know your birth name. Your *real* name. Rainbow Planet. Rainbow Planet. Rainbow Planet. That's what I'll call you when I talk to you in my heart, when I tell Carlos all about you as we're driving down that long and dusty highway.'

Outside the snow begins to fall, and a low wind in the distance rises to a moan, making Mary Jane shiver. She holds the baby close, so close she can feel the baby's breath against her neck, and the honeysuckle shape of those tiny lips. Mary Jane watches the snow slowly falling, filling the corners of the fields as it fills the rim of the windowpane, each little flake pressing flat as an opened palm against the glass. She surveys the broad field, row after row of stunted corn stalks and dusty brown cabbages, all the dead things left to wither in the dirt. Abandoned farm implements stand like sentries, hunch-backed and gnarled, wearing soft pads of snow like saddles on their backs. She has learned to see loneliness in a landscape which used to seem friendly, that had once been full of warmth and joy. But now her eyes search for and find the barren scarecrow, the bent weather vane. The cows further a field huddle together for warmth. *Winter,* she thinks, *time to escape.*

Mary Jane sees in the window the reflected outline of her face, her own gypsy prettiness; a Norwegian-Irish gypsy, with long black hair, pale freckled skin and vivid green eyes. She plays up this image with gold hoop earrings and long strings of beads, loose gauzy skirts that drape to the floor, tickling the tops of her bare, narrow feet. But she no longer believes in her own beauty. She no longer believes in God, no longer believes anything her parents have told her, ever since they lied about Michael coming home from Vietnam. Rainbow Planet squints and blinks and rattles; her lip quivers, but this child never cries.

Mary Jane hears an after-dinner argument rising from the dining room – Uncle Jens has forgotten her for now, and has turned his anger to cousin Erik, who is running away to Canada to avoid being drafted.

'How can you leave the country that's been so good to us?' Jens demands.

Not this again, Mary Jane thinks. They were in their Old Country, the old, dead, dried-out country, so cold and stern and faraway, but she was on her way to a new life with Carlos in a warmer, drier climate; a land full of fruit trees and a high, forgiving sky.

'*Fanden ta deg! Hvordan kan du? Din feiging.* Your mother would never forgive you for this. How can you do this to her? You might just as well go spit on her grave. We sacrificed everything to come here, we sacrificed everything for you.'

Mary Jane closes her eyes and rocks back and forth. 'Rainbow, Rainbow, Rainbow,' she whispers in the baby's ear. This is as close as she comes to praying now days. She lets her body feel the fullness of the child, confident she won't forget anything about her this time. She rocks back and forth until she is satisfied that each of her bones has registered Rainbow's weight – it is imprinted on her breasts and in the folds of her elbow; the skin of her stomach is quilted with the memory of these little kicks. 'I'll think about you every day,' she promises her baby, kissing the top of her broad, bald head. 'Every morning, every night. And that will be my punishment. Punishment enough.'

Voices rise again from the dining room and reach Mary Jane's ear. 'Erik, God help me, if you weren't so damn big, I'd take you out to the shed and thrash you within an inch of your life. What shame you've brought on us.'

Mary Jane holds Rainbow as tightly as she can and tries to still her own quivering body. She presses the baby to her chest, covers the exposed ear with the cup of her hand. 'Shhh,' she tells her. 'Shhh. That's my baby. There's my girl. Don't listen to that racket, don't listen to them.' She doesn't want Rainbow to remember the angry, quarrelling voices of this evening, their last night together; she wants Rainbow to remember only the sound of her mother's heart.

An hour and a half later, Mary Jane goes to check on Rainbow one final time. In the past fifteen minutes, she has forgotten the curve and tightness of her baby's clenched fist; even while everyone else ate their pecan pie, and Erik sat stewing in front of the television set, and his sister Ingrid, in the corner, wiped away her silent, silver, unacknowledged tears.

Mary Jane hurries down the corridor and stumbles into Aunt Ingebjorg, radiant with a baby in either arm. Rainbow is on the left side, her face squeezed and feverish, barely visible in the folds of Ingebjorg's hefty elbow. On the right side is Sissel's pale little Andy with his sticky eyelids and his feeble cough. *Just look at these two babies! There's no contest at all – my child is much more wonderful!* Mary Jane thinks, then feels the familiar corkscrew of pain twisting inside her, turning and burrowing deep into the pit of her stomach.

'I know what Farfar Jens says,' Ingebjorg tells Mary Jane, bouncing the babies up and down as if judging their relative weights, 'and I suppose he's got a point. You're way too young to be raising a baby by yourself! What about your education, think of that. You haven't even finished high school. And after everything your parents went through.' Ingebjorg softens, then sighs. 'But babies are wonderful,' she admits. 'All babies come from love. I'm sure it will work out in the end.' Ingebjorg kisses the babies' heads in succession; first one, then the other, then the first again. She rubs her nose against their scalps, breathes in their essence, nibbles their ears. She consumes the smell and touch and texture of them with her ravenously hungry love. 'Åh, de er så søte, så søte. I know it's time for you to feed her, but just let me hold her a little longer. After all, I only get to see her twice a year, but you'll be her mother for the rest of your life.'

TWO

The First Day of Junior Kindergarten
Harry S. Truman Elementary School

M i l w a u k e e ,   W i s c o n s i n
S e p t e m b e r   1 9 7 4

Rainey McBride, having reached the age of four years old, is now red-haired, square-shouldered and solidly built. She stands next to Mormor, holding her grandmother's hand as a door in her mind blows open. She hears a dozen voices crying 'Mommy' and sees a stream of anxious, dimpled fists and terrified faces. *Mommy. I have no Mommy. Rainey has no Mommy.* The thought is thrilling. The classroom is dizzy with children, so many children dip and dance and dart around her. Rainey had no idea there were so many other children in the world. The busy, noisy room is filled with plastic farm animals, an old piano and coloured numbers and letters lining the walls.

The tables and chairs are all my size! There's a little kitchen with a Styrofoam fridge. Please let me stay here forever! Rainey thinks. She stamps her feet in anticipation of playing in the little kitchen.

Mormor squeezes Rainey's shoulder. 'I'm leaving now, and if you cry at all, I won't come back,' she says. Her eyes are icy. Rainey's upper arm remembers to hurt where Mormor pinched her for not getting dressed fast enough.

Cry? Why would I cry? Rainey thinks. *Go away, Mormor, I want to play with that make-believe fridge.* Rainey looks down at the pleats of her frilly pink dress and her polished black patent-leather shoes. She shakes the silver charm bracelet around her wrist, feels the ribbon itching in her hair, and she knows this is not her true self; the real Rainey is a tomboy and doesn't wear these girlish things.

Tomorrow I'll wear my boy clothes, she thinks. *I don't care if Mormor pinches me or not.*

'Where are the child's parents?' asks the nice lady whose name is Mrs Schiefle and who smells like lemonade and gingerbread.

'We're her legal guardians, my husband and I,' Mormor answers.

'And who are you?'

'I'm Sonja McBride. I'm Rainey's grandmother and I'm here to register her for school.' Mormor squeezes Rainey's shoulder, looks down at Rainey and purses her lips.

'This is unusual.' Mrs Schiefle licks the tip of her pencil and scribbles in a big red book. 'Rainy? R-a-i-n-y like the weather?'

'No, R-a-i-n-e-y. It's a family name,' Mormor says impatiently. 'My husband's mother's maiden name, if you must know.'

'I see.'

Go away, Mormor, Rainey thinks, tearing her hand away from her grandmother. *I want to stay with this lady with the silver curls and a gold key around her neck. She has pockets full of lollipops, and crayons, and plastic soldiers.*

Mormor leans down and looks Rainey right in the eye. 'All right, Rainey, I'm going home now. If you're a good girl, you can have braunschweiger for lunch. Remember to tell Mrs Schiefle if you need to go pee-pee.'

Go away, Rainey thinks, but she says nothing, only nods her head yes. She grabs Mormor's leg to say good-bye. Mormor touches Rainey's head for a moment, then pushes her away. Mrs Schiefle leads Rainey towards a circle of children singing a song:

'The wheels on the bus go round and round; round and round, round and round.

– 10 –

The wheels on the bus go round and round, all through the town.
The driver on the bus goes, talk talk talk, talk talk talk. Talk, talk,
talk.
The driver on the bus goes talk talk talk, all through the town.'

The song continues. The children twirl in a circle, picking up
speed.

Mrs Schiefle holds out her hand. 'Come on, Rainey, please join
in,' she says. 'Join in the fun.' The circle keeps turning. Rainey
begins to feel dizzy, the children arch backwards and continue to
spin. A gap in the circle opens up, ready to pull her in. But she steps
away from the circle instead, keeping herself upright while teeter-
ing on the brink of some unknown thing. *No, I don't want to join in,*
she says to herself.

'Who are you?' someone asks. Rainey turns around and sees a
small, brown-eyed girl standing before her. 'My name is Jenny. Do
you want to be my friend?'

'No, I don't,' Rainey tells the girl. Rainey looks up and the sky
seems to break open. Something dazzles her for an instant, then
tumbles down. The words strike her upturned face as cold and
sharp as September raindrops. *I am myself, my self alone, my thoughts
belong only to me. I am Rainey, Rainey is me.*

The bliss she feels at that instant lasts well into the afternoon.
Years later, she will remember this as the moment she first believes
in God, the first time she feels the touch of His hand against her
forehead. But for now she plays by herself in the toy kitchen,
thrilled with the little fridge which squeaks when it opens and
closes. She tries to make ice in the back of the freezer, cracks open
the plastic eggs, turns all the multi-coloured milk bottles upside
down. *I am Rainey, Rainey is me,* she says to herself. The other girls
make faces at her, sitting on the edges of the table and kicking their
white-stockinged legs.

'Don't you want to share those toys with the others?' Mrs
Schiefle asks helpfully. 'I think Donna and Debbie would like to
try the mix-master. And Annette would like to use the Easy-Bake
oven.'

Rainey shakes her head. 'No, I don't want to share with anybody,' she answers confidently, measuring out the ingredients for her imaginary chocolate cake. She has discovered a whole new room inside her head where she is free from Mormor, a place where she can stand beside herself and know for the first time, absolutely, she is loved.

THREE

Thanksgiving 1979
Owauskeum, Wisconsin

Five years had passed since she first started school, and Rainey, at the age of nine, had become fascinated with the news account of her entry into the world. Lying on her stomach in the attic, torch in hand, she slid the yellowed newspaper out of the envelope and carefully read the front page of *The Milwaukee Journal*, from 1 June, 1970. She skimmed over the report about the munitions depot blast that had rattled Saigon, and the advertisement for pantyhose on sale at Gimbels, three pairs for $1.50. Her gaze slid down to the report at the bottom of the page that announced her birth. She read aloud, pausing at the end of each sentence. She wanted each word to rise from her lips, float through the roof of the small wooden blue bungalow and spread throughout the dusty neighbourhood that in summertime smelled of tar, burning rubber and hot ham sandwiches.

HIGH-SCHOOLER GIVES BIRTH AFTER PLAY-OFF GAME
Mary Jane McBride, 16, of Milwaukee, gave birth last night to a healthy 5lb, 4oz baby girl, fifteen minutes after helping her basketball team, Emmanuel Lutheran High School, to a 115–89 victory

over Our Lady Queen of Peace in the Southeastern Wisconsin Parochial Schools All-Girls Championship League semi-finals.

'I didn't know I was pregnant,' McBride said. 'I had a cramp at half-time, but I just thought I was dehydrated or something. Because I was tired, Coach only let me play ten minutes of the second half, but I still managed to score 12 points. After the game I was chang-ing in the locker room and I felt like I was going to faint. Then something busted inside me, and I said, "Oh my Gosh! There's a baby coming! Somebody help me, quick!"'

An ambulance arrived within minutes for a trouble-free delivery. Mother and child are both reportedly doing well this morning at Mount Sinai Hospital.

Officials at Emmanuel Lutheran High School have made it clear that they will not allow McBride to return to classes as a junior this fall. 'We do not want to appear to be condoning lascivious and promiscuous behavior by allowing such a student to return to our school. We want to send a clear message – premarital sex among our students will not be accepted,' Principal James Howard said.

Having won the semi-finals, Emmanuel Lutheran will meet Gethsemane Lutheran in the finals next Saturday in Oconomowoc.

Rainey tried to recall that moment she thought she remem-bered. Bouncing around wildly in the hour before her birth and feeling the burn of her mother's struggling muscles, she pictured herself breaking free in a rush of water, sliding out on to a cold linoleum floor, opening her eyes and staring up into the faces of sixteen good Lutheran girls in their numbered jerseys, many of whom were unfamiliar with the facts of life, but all of whom must have gazed in wonder at her arrival. It didn't matter who called her a bastard, Rainey told herself, and it didn't matter if Mormor referred to her as a punishment, because this newspaper story was further proof that she was special, that she was loved by God.

Rainey examined the fading photo of her mother which accom-panied the story. She paid particular attention to the long, dark hair framing the bright, angelic face, the broad mouth with its dimpled smile, and the freckles that seemed to leap from her skin. Mary Jane looked triumphant, as she must have been. After all, this was the second time she had succeeded in surprising Mormor. Mary Jane had first surprised Mormor by daring to look so Irish, so much the image of her father, with none of the Scandinavian stamp of Mormor's family – the thin lips, the high-bridged nose or the long, pale, jutting face.

What had happened between the time of the newspaper article and five months later, when Mary Jane fled Milwaukee with a Cuban man named Carlos whom she met at the Greyhound station? What had Mormor done to hurt her daughter so deeply? For clearly, it was Mormor's fault. Mary Jane McBride was not one to abandon a five-month-old baby, that much was evident from the photo. Rainey was sure her mother had meant to take her along, meant it with all her heart, but at the last minute she must have changed her mind. It was a supremely sensible thing to do, Rainey had to admit that much. Mormor and Garth could give Rainey a roof over her head, food on the table, stability, good schools, a college education. *All the things we left the Old Country for*, in the oft-repeated family mantra. Mary Jane would have an uncertain future full of tortillas, piñatas and grimy bus depots. Rainey saw that her mother had made a great sacrifice in leaving her behind. Mormor often said to Rainey, 'Your mother didn't want you, so she ran away with some Spic.'

'No she didn't,' Rainey would answer her defiantly. 'I know she's coming back for me someday.'

'Rainey, are you dressed yet?' Mormor called up the stairs, breaking Rainey's meditation. The door to the attic steps was open, and in wafted the familiar smell of coffee and curling irons that sent chills down Rainey's spine. Burned hair, burned beans and pies baking in the oven – the odours of stoicism which heralded holidays and family events.

'I'm almost ready,' Rainey called back, sticking her head through the hole in the floor.

'Hurry up, we got a long drive ahead of us, and we don't need you slowing us down.'

'I'll be ready in a few minutes,' Rainey said, more to herself than to Mormor, who had already shut the door. Rainey pressed the photo to her lips and tasted the bitter black ink. 'Happy Thanksgiving, Mommy. I know you'll come back for me someday,' she said, then slipped the clipping back into the envelope and replaced it in the box under the armoire, where Mormor mistakenly believed it to be well hidden.

Rainey tiptoed down to her bedroom and stood in front of her mirror. Carefully lifting the blue and white pleats of her excessively frilly winter dress, she strapped the vinyl holster around her waist and let her toy gun rest squarely against her hip. She was wearing underpants, bloomers, a petticoat and a pair of white tights, but even so, the metal felt cold and sharp against her skin. She pressed it into her flesh, right to the bone, and revelled in her toughness. 'I'm bringing Little Joe,' she said to the pale, freckled face in the mirror. She called it Little Joe after her favourite character on *Bonanza*. 'We might just run into Injuns on the way to Owauskeum,' she reasoned. 'And make no mistake – just because I'm wearing a dress doesn't mean I'm a cry-baby girl.' She smoothed down the top layers of her clothing so the gun and holster were well hidden under the flouncy fabric of her skirt.

'Harald and Eve won't be there,' Mormor was saying.

'They might be,' Grandpa Garth offered.

'No. They won't. I'm sure they won't,' Mormor said with certainty. 'And just where have you been?' she asked as Rainey came into the kitchen.

'Nowhere,' Rainey answered, slouching towards the kitchen chair. Grandpa Garth was busy braiding Mormor's long swath of iron-grey hair while she used the curling iron to curl the fringe away from her forehead. Mormor rarely wore make-up, but today she wore dark eyeliner around her eyes and a coral lipstick which cast a pallor around her mouth. Her few faded freckles had been dusted with ivory powder, which stuck in the creases of her eyelids and gave her a blurred, uncertain quality that did not fit the intensity of her expression. Everyone said that Mormor had once been beautiful, but that was a long time ago now.

'What were you doing upstairs all that time?' Mormor asked.

'I was working on my book report about the Pilgrims,' Rainey said.

'Liar!' Mormor shouted, and struck Rainey across the mouth with the back of her hand. Rainey tasted the cold metal of Mormor's wedding band right between her teeth. 'That report is on the table in the den, where you left it last night. Don't you go lying to me, young lady. Now what were you doing?'

'I was watching the Macy's Day Parade on TV,' Rainey mumbled, secretly pleased to be exchanging one lie for another. Tears tickled the rims of her eyelids, but she refused to weep. Crying was only for cry-baby girls. Her fingers pressed against the numbness of her mouth, hoping to discover blood, but there was none. Mormor knew how to hit so it would never split a lip, never bruise the skin, even though the pain could reach deep into the bone and settle there, echoing for hours. 'I'm sorry. I won't do it again,' Rainey said, quivering.

'Make sure that you don't,' Mormor said as she folded up the curling iron and got ready to leave. 'You take the pumpkin pie,' she instructed Rainey as she gathered up the food and the extra dishes. 'Pa, you take the cherry one.' Mormor went out to load the car while Grandpa Garth and Rainey put on their coats and boots.

Just before they walked out the door, Grandpa Garth turned around to face Rainey. 'I think there's something in my pocket,' he said, lifting his arms. She reached in and took out a Mallow Mint, cool and shiny in its bright green wrapper.

'Eat it quick before Mormor sees it,' he said and winked. As they were leaving, Rainey stopped in the doorway. She stared at her speckled face in the mirror, blotchy with shame and happiness and swallowed pride, and felt the red pressure of weeping behind her eyes, which she would not release. There was a thrill of pleasure in her chest as she pressed the toy gun secretly into her skin. *I don't like Pilgrims anyway*, she told herself, biting through the Mallow Mint's crisp chocolate coating and hitting the soft creamy middle inside.

As they began the slow drive to Owauskeum, Rainey bit her lip bloody but still she did not cry. Milwaukee faded from view, and she pretended she would never see home again. They were heading north towards Sheboygan, hugging the coast of Lake Michigan but far enough inland to be deep into farmland, and Rainey imagined she was discovering the rich countryside for the very first time. Pressing her face up against the frosty window, she could be a Nicolet, Juneau or Champlain; an explorer charting prairie and moraine. Instead of billboards, barns and silos, she saw teepees, circled wagons and Indian burial mounds.

'What will we say if Harald and Eve are there?' Grandpa Garth asked. 'I mean, it's bound to be awkward if . . .'

'They won't be there,' Mormor said. 'I'm sure they won't.'

'Still . . .'

'They won't.' Mormor settled back into the seat, then looked over her shoulder. 'Don't breathe on the glass, you'll smudge it up,' she said, but Rainey was far too engrossed in fantasy to hear what Mormor had said. The car was unbearably hot. The heater had been turned up to ten but Mormor and Garth still shivered in the front seat. The car smelled of stale tobacco, Ben-Gay and hot water bottles; odours of old age. Although her grandparents were only in their late fifties, they moved and spoke and spent their days preparing to be much older.

'Do the animals get cold in winter, Mormor?' Rainey asked, looking out at the fields dotted with cows.

'No.'

'How come?'

'They've got hair on them,' Mormor answered tediously.

'No they don't. Not really,' Rainey insisted, suddenly feeling a stab of sympathy for the beasts who stood bravely at their troughs, huddled in wreaths of steamy breath with only their broad black-and-white backsides as protection against the wind. 'If I had a barn, do you know what I'd do? Do you know, Grandpa Garth? I'd build them a fire and put blankets on 'em, and maybe, maybe let them wear sweaters. Look, Mormor, do you see that horse over there? Can I get a horse?' Rainey went off on a flight of sympathy and wishes, in love with the rural world she rarely saw at home.

Suddenly the copper-coloured Oldsmobile wheezed asthmatically, then jerked and pitched forward as Grandpa Garth guided it slowly towards the side of the highway. Other cars honked and angrily sped past them.

'Dang it all anyway,' he said, and his stout neck flushed with colour as the car ground to a halt and steam poured from under the bonnet.

'Now look what you've done,' Mormor said to Rainey. 'You've gotten his Irish up.' They climbed out of the car and on to the shoulder. Grandpa Garth popped open the bonnet, took out his red-and-white checked handkerchief and motioned for Mormor to hand him the water bottle out of the back seat. They both stood peering into the inner workings of the Oldsmobile, sizing up the situation with grim faces and hands on chins, pretending they understood the inner workings of the engine.

'Let's flag down someone to go get help,' Mormor said.

'We don't need to do that,' Grandpa Garth insisted.

'*Uff!* We'll never get there,' Mormor said glumly, plunging her hands into the deep pockets of her old felt coat.

Rainey turned away from her grandparents and away from the highway to face the broad field with its row of evergreens deep in the background and a pencil-thin silo off to the side. In front of her was an undulating spread of alfalfa, soy bean and dead cabbages, their heads dusted with snow like frozen green roses. She stamped her feet for warmth, but her patent-leather shoes offered little cover as the cold wind sliced through her tights and nibbled her ankles and the tops of her feet. She drew her arms into her chest and buried her chin deep into her fake-fur collar, wincing in pain when the cold zipper brushed her lip. Wait a minute! She had let her guard down! The cold had made her drowsy and inattentive, and now she was vulnerable to attack! Quickly, she tossed up the folds of her skirt, reached under her petticoat, into the holster and drew out Little Joe. She fired at the encroaching Indians who slid silently on their hard brown bellies through the frozen rows of cabbages.

'Bang Bang Bang!' The gunpowder stung her nose and lifted into the chilly air. One, two, three, the Indians arched up briefly in spasms of death, and she watched them fall back into the fields as a lone imaginary arrow wavered in the air and landed in the gravel at her feet.

'If you don't behave, we'll drop you off at the reservation,' Mormor threatened, glaring at Rainey from the front of the car.

'Can you?' Rainey asked, intrigued.

'Sure, if you'd rather live with Injuns than with us,' Mormor replied.

'I would,' she said defiantly, as Grandpa Garth closed the bonnet of the car and motioned for them to climb back inside. He hadn't actually done anything, but seemed convinced that the engine had cooled enough that they might make it to Owauskeum.

'Fine. If that's what you want, I'm not complaining,' Mormor said as she slammed the door and sliced the seat belt across her body. 'Let them feed you, and send you to school, and buy you all those nice things you never appreciate, and listen to all your damn fool bellyaching.'

'I want to go,' Rainey said confidently. 'Can you drive me to Oneida? I'd rather go there instead of Black River Falls.' She was proud of the research she had done about the various reservations. Grandpa Garth guided the Oldsmobile back on to the highway, joining the cortege of over-full Fords and Chevys heading north for the holiday.

'The Injuns will scalp you, won't they, Pa?' Mormor said slowly.

'I 'spose so,' he answered.

Suddenly the idea seemed to take flight in Mormor's imagination. 'They'd like your red hair, hanging from their belt,' she began. 'I bet that'd fetch a good price, a nice head of strawberry-blond.'

Rainey blanched, imagining the crown of her skull hollowed out and hanging limply from an Indian's belt. Her head would be a ruby in a row of dusty blond- and brown-coloured pebbles, quivering in the light as the Indian's tan arm drew back an arrow. 'We could leave next Tuesday,' Rainey offered, very quietly. 'I don't think we should go before then. I got a math quiz on Monday. And Gretchen Stegner owes me fifty cents because I gave her my eraser.' Her scalp prickled and needles tickled her hairline. Nausea swelled in her stomach as a wave of hot, sour air pumped through the car. Rainey imagined a knife slicing through her forehead, and blood dripping on to her blue and white dress. She closed her eyes and fought the burning in her throat, knowing if she vomited on the vinyl seats, Mormor would slap her again.

'Now she's quiet. You've scared the poor girl,' Grandpa Garth said, pushing his hat further back on his head. His voice revealed nothing, neither sympathy nor satisfaction.

The old Svensen family homestead, built in 1940 by Mormor's father and his three brothers, was located a few miles north of Owauskeum, and situated in such a way that it was impossible to pass anything remotely interesting while driving towards it from any direction. The whole family resented the house for being so far from where most of them now lived, and this, combined with the general lack of scenery, guaranteed a sour arrival for everyone. The last town they passed before reaching the house was Owauskeum itself, and that was even more desolate than Rainey remembered it. It had once been a thriving paper-mill town, but the mill had closed a generation ago, taking with it all signs of life and liveliness, reducing it to a desert of sheet metal, concrete and quarry stone. All that remained of the mill was the looming brick smokestack and the strange scent like a honey-roasted ham, which hung in the air on humid days as a bittersweet reminder of the town's past prosperity. What was left of the grass was perpetually overgrown, and even the bent mailboxes and twisted laundry lines had faded from the years of dust, salt and sun. As they drove through town, Rainey imagined the ghosts of Thanksgivings past, when packs of immigrant families would have gathered here to celebrate, and the streets and porches and doorways would have been warm and bright with handshakes, pine fires and thick winter coats.

Turning off the main road, Grandpa Garth manoeuvred on to a gravel track marked with a small sign that read 'CCC' and led into a field. Stalks of dying corn shrivelled and swooned on either side of the car, and Rainey felt closed in by the dry rustle of leaves, reaching out to touch her like so many pleading fingers. She leaned her shoulder against the seatback and looked out the back window and up into the clean, drained sky which was scrubbed of all cloud cover. It was certain to snow. She was proud of knowing that, of her ability to feel the shift in the wind. Explorers had to be able to anticipate the weather. Autumn moved to winter very quickly here, once the smell of burning leaves filled the air, and hard things – pumpkins, squash, and knotted gourds – sprouted from the frozen ground. Something crackled in the distance as cold things broke, and Rainey thought she could hear the sap hardening in the veins of the trees and taste the phantom flavour of Christmas' maple-sugar candy.

The dead field split open as the car broke free of the corn. They drove up to the house, which was an old-style Victorian homestead, ornate and artificial, with whitewash windows and spiked gingerbread trim. A dozen cars were parked haphazardly around the perimeter in a broken circle of broad-backed Fords and Buicks, ranging in colour from tan to brown to mustard yellow.

'I see Ervald bought himself a Cadillac,' Mormor said. 'Where he got the money from, I just don't know.'

'Maybe he won it playing Bingo,' Grandpa Garth said, in his usual inscrutable voice.

'Could be,' Mormor admitted.

'He does like to gamble,' Grandpa Garth offered.

'*Uff!* He only goes so he can socialise with Catholics,' Mormor insisted.

'Well, they do have better parties,' Grandpa Garth replied. Mormor shot him an angry glance, while he winked at Rainey in the rearview mirror.

Rainey couldn't wait to get out of the car and into the house. She thrilled at the thought of the upper room at the top of the old staircase, a place of mystery and possible sin. Every year she and her cousins would climb the creaky wooden stairs and play in that room for hours, hypnotised by the heady incense of attics, old aunts and hat boxes.

'Be careful with those pies!' Mormor said as Rainey opened the door and a pie slid down the seat. 'Rainey, you better behave this year or else,' Mormor warned.

'Or else what?' she asked defiantly, although she knew full well what Mormor meant. On Thanksgiving of the previous year, Rainey had argued with her cousins, the twins Katrina and Karina. 'My mommy says your mommy is a fly buzzing in hell and all the other flies are eating her right now,' Katrina had taunted Rainey while they played in the upper room.

'They are not,' Rainey insisted.

'Are so,' said Karina.

'Are not.'

'Are so.'

'Oh yeah?' Rainey said, rising to the challenge. 'Well, if my mommy is in hell then your dolls are going to be in the sewers.' She grabbed Katrina and Karina's matching Baby-Burps-And-Wets-Alot dolls and ran down to the bathroom, where she held the dolls' plastic heads under the water while she flushed the toilet again and again. When the twins told Mormor what Rainey was doing, Mormor ran upstairs and grabbed Rainey, slapping her hard behind the knees, and then marched her downstairs, soggy dolls in hand, to apologise to everyone for ruining the twins' Thanksgiving. The worst part was not the apologising, but the inevitable whispers that followed her the rest of the evening. 'What do you expect? She's her mother's child through and through.' 'Pity the poor girl. She deserves pity, not scorn.'

But Rainey had held her head high even as she felt Mormor's handprint darken and swell on the skin behind her knees. She would not give anyone the satisfaction of seeing her cry, even though her eyes pinched and her throat ached as if she had swallowed an apple whole and it had lodged halfway down to her heart. Instead she got her revenge after supper by kicking Katrina and Karina under the table, and when they began to wail, she gobbled up their slivers of sweet pecan pie.

'You'll behave, young lady, or else you'll be sitting out in the car eating Thanksgiving dinner all by yourself,' Mormor warned, holding Rainey hard by the wrist, and Rainey, although unwilling to make any promises, nodded her head yes.

'Sonja, Garth, Rainey, welcome. Happy Thanksgiving,' Aunt Ingebjorg said jovially as she answered the door and ushered them inside. They stepped into the foyer and were immediately swallowed up in a hub of noisy activity. Plates, pots and dishes danced from hand to hand, chairs squeaked and slid across the waxed wooden floor, and red-cheeked children unrolled balls of tinsel while a litter of striped kittens darted from lap to lap. The house was densely humid and all the windows had been opened, in spite of the cold. The crippled tree that pressed against the side of the house was creeping surreptitiously into the sitting room on its fingertips of gnarled twigs. A few first snowflakes had softened the windowsill and drifted to the floor, sticking to the curtains and shining like beads of light.

They took off their coats and boots, stamping away the snow and squeezing their overclothes into the crowded closet, whose door was bursting open with loose arms of felt, wool and fur. As Rainey looked around her, she noticed that the women of the house were anonymous in a flurry of arms and pots and aprons, with fine layers of perspiration on their lips and hairlines, while the men were idle as usual, watching the football game on TV and arguing gloomily about fishing, guns and race relations over their cans of Schlitz and Old Milwaukee. Uncle Ervald played with the electric knife, pretending to cut off his arm, to the delighted screams of Rainey's dozens of cousins.

'Glad you could make it,' Ingebjorg said. 'Everyone's here already.' Then she caught herself. 'Except Harald and Eve, of course.'

'It's such a pity,' Mormor said, slowly shaking her head.

'Yes.'

'Shame.'

'Such a shame.' They all nodded sadly.

'And, Rainey, how's my little tiger?' Ingebjorg asked.

Rainey blushed happily. She loved Aunt Ingebjorg more than anyone else in the world, and secretly wished Ingebjorg would adopt her. Mormor's sister Ingebjorg was forty-seven years old, never married, tall and squarely built. She had short, pale hair pressed close to her head, and rosy cheeks that made her look like a kind of Mrs Claus. Rainey wanted to fall into the folds of her arms and be pressed against that solid neck, maybe even submit to a kiss on the cheek. She wanted to go back to Ojibwa Falls, where Ingebjorg taught third grade and led the local 4-H Club. 'I'm OK,' Rainey said, still blushing. 'Guess what? I got an A-plus-plus on my report about "Millard Fillmore – Our Unappreciated President".'

'*Utmerket!* That's fantastic. I'm glad to see you have repented for your evil ways,' Ingebjorg kidded. 'Perhaps Katrina and Karina will show you their new dolls.'

'I'm trying extra hard to be a good girl,' Rainey replied in a tone of voice that understood Ingebjorg's humour and still managed to mock Mormor's warning about her behaviour.

'Rainey's been told. If she isn't a good girl, Santa won't come this Christmas,' Mormor said evenly.

'I want an air rifle,' Rainey suddenly burst out. 'And I want a little brother, and a little sister, and a Tom Seaver rookie card, but most of all I want an air rifle.'

'For shame, Rainey! You'll get no such thing. Air rifles are not for little girls. You'll shoot your eye out,' Mormor warned. Ingebjorg laughed.

'Can I go upstairs now?' Rainey asked, suddenly tired of adult conversation and longing to re-discover the wonders of the attic.

'What do you say?' Mormor insisted.

'Can I please go upstairs?'

'Go on,' Ingebjorg said, patting Rainey's shoulder as she skipped towards the staircase. 'She sure has grown,' Ingebjorg said admiringly.

'That child is a nightmare sometimes,' Rainey heard Mormor answer. 'The Good Lord is punishing me, and she's my cross to bear.'

When Rainey clattered down the staircase two hours later, so engrossed in an old fur coat she had found that she hadn't heard Ingebjorg's first three attempts to call her to supper, she was immediately enveloped in the strange and serious silence of the dining room. Her steps slowed and quieted as she neared the landing, realising that she was somehow entering a room very different from the one she had left earlier. The football game was still on the television, but the volume had been turned down to a whisper, rising only slightly when someone scored a touchdown, and the frantic plates and pots and spoons had stopped their singing, and now waited on the table with an air of gracious expectation.

All the aunts and uncles and cousins stood stiffly behind their seats, even blind Farfar Jens, Mormor's uncle, who stared into the pale candle flame and clutched his hand-carved chairback which trembled slightly and tapped against the floor. Rainey walked self-consciously down the aisle of stern-eyed relatives who seemed to be rebuking her for keeping them waiting. She slid into her spot at the children's end of the table, next to Aunt Ingebjorg. 'How was the upper room?' Ingebjorg whispered, squeezing Rainey's hand and giving her a secret smile, as if she already knew the answer, and had been with her discovering the fractured ornaments, the coonskin cap, the yellowed wedding dress and the box of tarnished coins and beads.

'Oh, I found a—' she started, but she was cut off by Uncle Torgrim, who tapped his glass, calling everyone to attention.

'We would like to now give thanks for this bountiful meal which the good Lord has had the grace to set down before us, rude sinners that we are. We would like to thank Him for the blessings of this past year, and pray that He may grant us peace, happiness, and prosperity in the months to come. *I Jesu navn, går vi til bord, spise og drikke, på dit ord . . .*' Rainey listened to the rhythm of the Norwegian table prayer while she watched the people beside her, paying special heed to their creased eyelids, their down-turned mouths, their solid hands. They were farmers, farmers' wives, and sons and daughters of farmers who, even though they worked in offices in cities and towns, still had the soil worked deep into their skin. She watched the candlelight reflect off the polished silver that had been carried years ago in a wooden crate from Norway, and she studied the delicate needlework of the napkins, folded like wings above each plate. She felt a current of connection run through herself and these people. She was one of them, and yet completely separate. *I am myself, my self alone, my thoughts belong only to me.* And yet she was absolutely certain of the fact that she wasn't alone; she never had been and she never would be. She felt off-balance, as if lifted briefly and set down again in a deft gesture that no one else noticed, and she was nearly, but not exactly, in the spot where she had been before. The disturbance of the dust around her feet seemed to prove this, and she shivered with a secret sense of herself.

'. . . forever and ever, Amen,' Uncle Torgrim ended in English, and everyone ended with him, so that the shared 'Amen' echoed like a bell and rose above the table, drifting higher and higher until it melted into air. 'Amen,' Rainey whispered, and as she said it, the word became real. A chalice inside her tipped as she did give thanks. For what, she was not certain. *A God who thinks of me. Yes. Why not? Even me.*

She looked at the table with suddenly unfamiliar eyes, and was overwhelmed with the density of the meal. *There was so* much *of everything*, she thought, as she gazed at the vat of mashed potatoes glistening with puddles of butter, the steaming tureens of cream corn, the kettle of butternut squash soup balanced over the glowing Bunsen burner. She watched the slightly sweaty quiver of the jelly moulds with their flecks of pineapple, carrot, marshmallow and lime. Rainey closed her eyes and filled her head with the scent of the cooked birds, the cranberries, and the stuffing of raisin, walnut and rum, and the pies: pumpkin, pecan, cherry and apple, stacked on cooling racks with steam still escaping from their centres, and on either side of the pie plates, cups of frozen custard and small dishes of cinnamon-speckled rømmegrøt.

The food seemed unbelievably rich, too rich, too luxurious, too lavishly drenched with giblet gravy to belong to Rainey and her family. Only the lefse and lutefisk seemed to be theirs. This was their true food, these concoctions of codfish, potatoes and lye. But Rainey chose not to think of that, preferring to meditate on thankfulness, and the way it had suddenly become real.

And then, just as Uncle Arne was about to slice into the succulent turkey, giving it practised taps with the electric knife, there was a rush of noise outside – sleighbells and doors slamming and the dull mad stamping of snow-covered feet. The sun had struck the fields in such a way that to look through the back window was to be temporarily blinded, but as Rainey looked and looked and looked, the dim figure of a boy, about her own size and age, gradually emerged. He glided through the door silently, effortless in his snow-softened boots and stopped in the centre of the room. He was covered with a glittering layer of snow, which dusted his cap and scarf and buttons like fine powdered sugar, and as Rainey watched him blink and shiver, she felt a dazzling sweetness sting her lips and settle on her tongue.

The boy pulled off his cap and brushed the snow from his magnificent coat. This coat was like no coat she had ever seen in Milwaukee. This coat was double-breasted and made of dark blue felt with a broad folded collar and red-and-white ribbon worked into the trim. The cuffs and epaulets were also trimmed with shiny ribbon. The coat boasted four oversized pockets, and the pocket over the left breast had some kind of crest on it. The design on the crest appeared to be an intertwined figure of an anchor, a flag, a snake and a crown. This was no ordinary coat and, clearly, this was no ordinary boy. He would have to be a prince, a knight, some sort of junior duke. He was destined to inherit the kingdom and rule the whole world. Rainey decided, finally, that she was gazing on nothing less than the future king of Wisconsin. She bowed her head, but kept her eyes focused on the round softness of his face.

The boy was accompanied by an adult on either side, although it had taken her several long moments to notice them. These two, a man and a woman, were vaguely tall people with fair complexions, but they made virtually no impression beyond that. Parents probably, Rainey surmised, but how could such plain people give birth to this boy? Rainey was aware of the others at the table, and how their attention was directed to the strikingly blond child whose eyes were pale as oysters, almost white in their centres, but rimmed with iridescent blue ink. His skin had been burnished by the wind, and a blush of scarlet beat in his cheeks.

'Who is that?' Rainey asked Aunt Ingebjorg beside her. She trembled as she reached for Ingebjorg's hand.

'Why, that's your cousin Andy,' Ingebjorg whispered back. 'You two were babies in the cradle together, years ago.' She too seemed taken aback by his sudden appearance, and the way everyone seemed compelled to stare at him.

'There's a bunch of chairs out on the porch,' Torgrim said. 'Pull up a few and make yourself at home.'

'Andy, there's room for you at the kids' end of the table,' Tante Anna said, pointing to the empty seat beside Rainey.

None of the three figures stepped forward, and the room remained strangely still. The boy moved only enough to whisk off his long red scarf with a theatrical flourish, and before the many winding folds of silk had unfurled and settled against his chest, he had his hands placed firmly on his hips and an imperial and insolent look gleamed brightly in his eyes. 'My name,' he said, in a high-pitched and richly accented voice, '. . . is not Andy. My name is Ambrose Torsten Dienst.'

FOUR

Thanksgiving 1979
Owauskeum, Wisconsin

Ambrose Torsten Dienst was shown to his seat, and as soon as he sat down, Rainey knew that he was likely to do something magnificent. She was afraid to look straight at him, so instead she stole sideways glances out of the corner of her eye, each time isolating a different feature – his pink, chubby hands; his sharply pressed sleeve cuffs; his shiny shirt buttons; the round protrusion of his tummy. A plate of food was prepared for him by Tante Anna, generously heaped with stuffing, potatoes and gravy, and he nodded solemnly, just a brief flicker of his pale eyelids, as the plate was placed before him. Clearly, he was accustomed to being waited on by people less important than himself. He took up his napkin and shook it out over the floor, and with a grand gesture, tucked a corner into the tight collar of his shirt. He lifted his knife and fork and began cutting his slice of turkey into thin, careful strips.

'Do you like baseball?' Rainey whispered to him, and was surprised to hear the words come out of her mouth. She had intended to ask him something more serious and sophisticated.

'Baseball?' he asked dismissively. 'Vati says it's a game for peasants,' he pronounced through a mouthful of mashed potatoes.

'Who's Vati?' she asked.

'My father. Holger Olav Dienst,' he explained, clearly irritated that she didn't recognise the name.

'Well, he must be a real jerk if he thinks that,' she told him. 'Baseball is the best game in the world. My friend Gus says it's what the angels play in heaven.' Ambrose shrugged nonchalantly. She watched the way he ate, holding the fork in his left hand and the knife in his right, pushing the food on to the back of the fork and then lifting it to his mouth, still balancing the knife in his other hand. Rainey was fascinated, having never seen utensils used in this way. She immediately started to copy him, but couldn't quite master the art of balancing the turkey and stuffing on the side of the wobbly knife.

'What in hell's name do you think you're doing?' Mormor asked from across the table, stopping both Rainey and Ambrose midmouthful. Neither one said a word. 'That's no way to eat. Put down that knife and fork and eat right.'

'This is the way we eat at home,' Ambrose said, clearly not frightened by Mormor. He looked down the table towards his parents, but they were too far away from him to see or hear the conversation.

'Well, it's not the way we eat here,' Mormor said sternly. 'Don't shovel your food. It looks disgusting. Like you were brought up in a barn or something.'

'It's the Continental way,' Ambrose insisted.

'Then do it at the Continental. Just don't do it at my table,' Mormor said, and this time, Ambrose relented. He dropped the knife to the plate and began stabbing at his food with the fork. Rainey watched as a wave of colour purpled his face. His tiny white eyebrows knit together, and he pulled in his lips as if he were about to cry.

'That was really cool,' Rainey whispered to him. 'No one ever talks back to Mormor.' She thought she caught the shadow of a smile from him, but then he seemed to remember he was sulking, and again glared down at his plate. 'Where's the Continental?' she asked, imagining a grand, downtown hotel, like the Pfister in

Milwaukee, with its chandeliered lobby and doormen in top hats and boxy black coats.

'It's in Europe.'

'Where in Europe?'

'Everywhere. It is Europe. That's what some people call it. Instead of Europe, they call it the Continent. Because that's what it is, it's a continent.'

'Wow,' Rainey marvelled, suitably impressed. 'They got a different name for everything there, don't they?'

After the main meal was finished, the pies were served, along with the tray of fruit breads and the dishes of walnuts, filberts and cashews, followed by the strong coffee and tea. Everyone was dull-eyed from over-indulgence, leaning back in their chairs and waiting for the mugs of hot gløgg to be passed around the table. The children were excused from the meal, and Rainey took Ambrose to the upper room, excited by the prospect of having him all to herself for a while, and away from the criticising eye of Mormor. She attacked the stairs two at a time and was surprised to find him lagging behind her, red-cheeked and puffing, struggling to catch his breath.

'It's quite stuffy,' he said once they reached the top, pulling a handkerchief from his pocket and holding it to his nose.

'Yeah,' she agreed. 'There's lots of old stuff around. Once I found a dead mouse up here. You could see its skeleton and everything.'

Ambrose poked around the many boxes, brushing off the dust and watching it glitter as it drifted to the floor. 'I'm bored,' he pronounced. 'Bored, bored, bored. I want to go home.' He plopped down on an old crate and held out his squat, dimpled hands, inspecting each pale little fingernail.

'There's a couple of coonskin caps in here somewhere. If I can find them, we can play Davy Crockett and Daniel Boone.'

'Who are they?' he asked.

'Don't you know?'

'No,' he answered.

'They were pioneers in the Old West. Don't you ever play pioneers and Indians?' she asked.

'Sometimes,' he admitted. 'But I like it better when I get to play

Kingdom. I get to be the prince, and my nanny, Françoise, and the maid, Rosa, are my subjects. This is how I banish them.' He stood up straight and then slowly lowered himself to one knee, bringing down an imaginary sword over his shoulder. 'Ohhhh, ye are banish-ed, disloyal peasants,' he said severely.

'Cool,' she told him with admiration. She began to rummage through a pile of old sheets and towels, and some boxes that had never been unpacked and still had strange Norwegian words written on the side. 'How come you got three names?' she asked him suddenly.

'Because my father has three names and I take after him. He owns the Norregard Dienst Corporation. It's in Europe. We go there sometimes to visit my grandparents. Oma came from Germany and Bestefar came from Denmark, but he's dead now. Most of the time we live in New York City, because that's where Vati's office is. Some day, I'm going to own the company, and I'll get to have his office, which looks out over Central Park. You can see people roller-skating and they look so small, they could be ants.'

'I can roller-skate,' Rainey said, poking her head up from behind a rack of old clothes. 'But Mormor only lets me go to the end of the driveway and back.'

'I can't roller-skate. I'm not allowed,' he said quietly.

'Why not?'

'On account of my operation.' His voice was barely a whisper.

'What operation?' she asked, sidling up close to him.

'A hernia operation,' he explained.

'What's that?'

'It's a thing that comes out of your stomach, and if they don't put it back in, you can die.' His eyes looked suddenly dark and serious, the pupils widening to the edge of the iris.

'Can I see it?' she asked.

He squinted at her, balancing his chin in his hand as if weighing up the relative merits of revealing something so intimate. 'OK,' he said at last. 'But you mustn't tell anyone else about it. Not ever. I haven't told anyone. Except Françoise and Rosa.'

'I promise.'

'Swear,' he insisted.

She sighed. 'OK. Cross my heart, hope to die, stick a needle in my eye.' She crossed her chest.

He looked at her and nodded, satisfied by her vow. He stood, slowly took off his jacket and pulled up his shirt to reveal a pale, soft, flabby stomach divided in half by a thick, segmented scar that inched down his torso like a huge pink caterpillar. 'Oh yuk, that's so gross,' Rainey said. The scar started between his ribs and descended all the way to his navel. Rainey felt both fascinated and repelled. She had never seen skin broken and sewn back together again. She moved closer to him as if to touch it, but he ducked away from her.

'Did it hurt?' she asked, withdrawing her hand.

'I don't remember. But I know I got loads of presents afterwards.' His face brightened at the mention of the presents. 'The surgeons had to operate. Otherwise I couldn't take over Vati's company some day. I'm his son and heir.' Ambrose took great pains to tuck in his shirt, smoothing each wrinkle and refastening his sleeves.

'So is that what you want to be when you grow up – a sun-in-air?' she asked.

'No, of course not,' he scoffed. 'Don't be a silly goose. I'm going to be an actor. A star of stage and screen.' He leaned back on the wooden crate, crossing his legs and spreading out his hand behind him. He lifted his face towards the dim light, smiling slyly.

'How do you get to be that?' Rainey asked him.

'I'm not sure, but I know you have to memorise things.'

'What kind of things?'

'Oh all kinds of things – speeches and plays and things,' he answered.

'I memorise things,' Rainey told him.

'What have you memorised?'

'I know the Pledge of Allegiance and the Nicene Creed,' she said proudly.

'Then we could both be stars of stage and screen,' he said with confidence.

'I guess so.' Rainey had never considered that possibility. 'But I'm going to be the first girl baseball player. Either that or a spy. Probably I'll be a spy.'

'Girls can't be spies,' he insisted.

'Well then I'll be the first girl spy, and the first girl baseball player.'

'You could be my agent,' he told her. 'I'll need an agent when I'm famous.'

'You mean a secret agent, like a kind of spy?' she asked.

'No, a Hollywood agent. It's the person who gets the money for you if you're a star,' he explained.

'I'd rather be a secret agent kind of agent,' she told him.

'Suit yourself, but it won't be as much fun as being a star of stage and screen,' he said. He toed the floor and looked down sadly. 'I once had a puppy. His name was Dodger and he liked to play ball with me.' Ambrose bit his lip, which had begun to tremble. 'One time, I threw the ball too hard and Dodger ran out to get it.' Tears clotted the corners of his eyes. He sniffled bravely. Rainey dreaded what she knew was coming next. 'The driver didn't see him. Dodger didn't get out of the way. Not in time, he didn't.' The first tears tipped and dribbled down his cheeks.

'Did he . . .?' Rainey asked.

'He didn't make it,' Ambrose whispered, his cheeks red with pain.

'Oh.' Rainey felt hot and awkward. 'I'm sorry about your dog,' she offered.

Ambrose stopped toeing the floor and looked up at her. 'Really?' he asked.

'Of course really. What do you think, I would lie about being sorry?' she asked.

He smiled and wiped his face, whisking away the remaining tears with the back of his hand. 'I was only acting. I didn't actually have a dog,' he said triumphantly.

'What? That was mean. You shouldn't lie about stuff like that. It's not fair to other people,' she told him.

'I know. I'm sorry, Rainey. I just had to check if I could still do it,' he said.

'Do what?'

'Cry on cue. That's what child stars have to do. That's the way it is in Hollywood. If they want you to cry in a scene, they make you imagine that your dog is dead.'

'But you don't have a dog.'

'No,' he agreed, kicking his heels against the wooden crate. 'I once had a hamster named Muffin. But he had to go live on a hamster farm in Connecticut. At least that's what Mutti told me. Can you cry on cue?'

'No. I don't think so. I've never tried. Anyway, why would I want to? Crying is just for cry-baby girls,' she reasoned.

'Oh, but, Rainey, it is excellent!' His face shone. 'You can get as many presents as you want, if you just learn to cry at the right time. You wouldn't believe the stuff I've gotten because of it – a sword with a real metal handle, a book about the Crusades and my own puppet theatre, with real puppets!' He tapped his jacket pocket. 'Excuse me, but do you have a light?' he asked, squinting up at her.

'A what?'

'A light. For my cigarette, of course.' He reached into the pocket and took out a small packet of Lucky Stripe. Rainey's jaw dropped, until she realised they were only candy cigarettes. Ambrose slid one chalky stick out of the pack and held it to his mouth, balancing it delicately on his puffy bottom lip. Rainey watched the painted red end of the cigarette quiver as he breathed in and out.

'I bet you have lots of friends,' she said admiringly.

'No,' he answered, looking surprised. 'Do you?'

She thought about it for a moment. 'Matt Conroy was my best friend, but he moved to Denver. I don't have a best friend any more. Do you have a best friend?' she asked.

'Mutti is my best friend,' he said proudly. 'Vati goes away a lot and then Mutti plays games with me. We do puppet shows, but I have to make all the voices. Then we have a cocktail afterwards, because it helps us relax. Well, Mutti has a cocktail, and I have a Coke-tail.'

'What's a Coke-tail?'

He rolled his eyes at her, apparently amazed at her ignorance. 'It's Coke, in a martini glass, with an olive. Mutti makes them for me all the time. Let's go see if we can have one now.' He brushed the dust off his hands and arms.

'Aunt Ingebjorg might let us have some Coke,' she said. 'I'll go see.' She headed towards the stairs, then stopped abruptly. 'I know what would be fun. We could become blood brothers,' she said over her shoulder.

He lifted his cigarette off his lip and exhaled deeply. 'I don't know about that. What would I have to do?'

'Nothing. Just mix some spit and blood and then we shake on it. I'll get us a knife,' she said, not bothering to wait for his answer.

Rainey sneaked downstairs carefully, trying to avoid being seen by any of her uncles, who would quiz and cajole her about baseball and hunting, taking bets on when she'd bring down her first buck. When she was younger, she had loved the teasing and the attention, but recently she had begun to understand that they were, in fact, making fun of her. She could see now that the joking was rude and mean-spirited, and she no longer wanted to be any part of it.

Since the meal had ended, the family gathering had divided naturally into three distinct groups, each of whom kept to separate rooms. The first group was mostly made up of men and children. They were in the living room being entertained by Uncle Torbjørn, who, after half a bottle of blackberry brandy, had removed his false teeth and shoes and had taken off his shirt. The children were goading him on, singing 'On The Good Ship Lollipop', while he danced around the room rolling his shoulders and flexing his stomach muscles, making the ship tattooed on his midriff bounce up and down like a boat on choppy waters. In previous years, Rainey had been delighted by this display, but now she felt embarrassed and beyond such silliness.

As Rainey slipped past the den, she peeked in and saw the older generation, Jens and Johan and the others, who sat in semi-darkness around the fireplace, quietly reminiscing about the Old Country. '*Jada*, life was different then.'

'Mmmm, you didn't buy things from a freezer, serve them to your family and try to call it food, that's for sure.'

'We expected to work hard and weren't disappointed; we knew the value of a dollar then, didn't we?'

'Not like today. These young people – what can you do?'

They nodded, mumbling in their almost forgotten tongue. '*Det er sant, sann. Slik var det.*' They huddled under hand-knit sweaters and crocheted afghans, looking pale and small beneath the squares of garish colour. They blew sadly across their mugs of coffee and rocked slowly back and forth, agreeing that yes, everything was better in the past; the old places, the old ways, the old ideas were the best, and there was not much hope for the days to come.

At last Rainey came to the kitchen, which was, as always, filled with women. Mormor and her five sisters – Anna, Ingrid, Christina, Elsa and Ingebjorg; her nieces and some of the older girl cousins sat at the big Formica table. All the dishes, pots and pans were cleaned and stacked in drying racks, with the steam still rising from their shiny surfaces, clouding the opened window whose edge was frozen solid. The women were eating a leftover cherry kringle, carving it into thin slices and dipping it into their cups of tea, brushing away the crumbs that clung to their fingers and lips. Rainey approached slowly and could hear the heavy hush of serious conversation. The women were discussing Anja, Harald and Eve's daughter, who had killed herself five months ago, the night before her final exams. 'A bright, pretty girl, she always studied so hard,' they said. 'No one knew she had it in her to do something so drastic. She was always so quiet.'

'*Javisst, ja,* it's the quiet ones you have to watch out for,' Tante Christina was saying. The discussion ceased completely as Rainey entered the kitchen – this was the kind of grown-up talk she wasn't supposed to hear.

'Can me and Ambrose have some Coke?' she asked politely.

'Can Ambrose and I have some Coke,' Mormor corrected.

'Yeah, that's what I meant,' Rainey said.

'No,' Mormor answered. 'You've had enough to eat and drink. It'll sour your stomach.'

'Oh, go on, Sonja. Let them have some,' Ingebjorg said, nudging Mormor with her arm. 'It's Thanksgiving, after all. A little soda won't hurt, with everything they've had to eat. It might even do them some good; it might get their digestion going.'

'All right then,' Mormor said. 'But don't come crying to me if you get a bellyache in the middle of the night.'

'Thank you. I won't,' Rainey said, opening the refrigerator and taking out one small bottle of Coca-Cola. She reached up to the cupboard and took down two glass tumblers, and when she was sure no one was watching, she slid a steak knife out of the cutlery drawer. She concealed the knife flat in the palm of her hand as she left, carefully balancing the glasses and the Coke.

When she went back to the attic she found Ambrose standing in front of the old smoky mirror, wearing a cape he had improvised out of a green velvet curtain that had been bleached yellow in its centre from years in the sun. He had tied the drawstring around his neck, and the layers of fabric just brushed the floor, dipping and folding as he snapped his arm. At first she thought he looked silly, but in the next second, she was deeply impressed. No one she knew at Truman School had so much imagination.

He clicked his heels and bowed, his knee nearly touching the ground. 'I am the count of Copenhagen,' he said, lowering his squeaky voice. 'This cape is the colour of all the royals.' He bowed again and his face disappeared beneath his upraised arm.

'You're kinda weird,' she told him. 'But I like you more than the kids at my school. You know more stuff than they do. Come on over here,' she said, sitting cross-legged in an open spot on the wooden floor. 'I got us a knife. We can do the blood brothers ceremony.' She set down the tumblers and as she poured two small measures of Coke, she could hear the liquid whispering and escaping from the glass.

'All right, here goes,' she said. She held the steak knife carefully, grasping it in her right hand and testing the blade against the palm of her left. Ambrose took off the cape and sat down across from her, leaning close with rapt fascination.

'Have you disinfected it?' he whispered breathlessly.

'What?'

'Disinfected the knife. You have to disinfect it first.' He rolled his eyes at her again. 'They always do it in the movies, you know, when they have to operate on somebody out in the jungle. Otherwise you can get an infection. You have to put it over a flame or clean it in alcohol,' he explained.

She hadn't thought about that. Still, she wasn't going to cancel the procedure because of a small technicality. 'This'll be good enough,' she told him, grabbing the bottle of Coke and trickling a little over the serrated blade. Then she licked the palm of her hand, as an extra precaution against infection. She sat very still and took a deep breath. 'Ready,' she said. She gripped the knife handle and a queasy feeling bubbled up from her stomach. That was OK, she could still be strong. She closed her eyes and held tight, slowly drawing back the knife. She pushed forward quickly, down and in, and felt an even, liberating sting of pain. When she opened her eyes, she saw a clean line of bright red blood rising out of her palm, as perfectly curved as a smiling mouth. 'Did it,' she said triumphantly. Both hands began to quiver as she took a quick swig of Coke. She felt very happy. 'You're next,' she said, handing the knife to Ambrose.

'I don't think I can do it,' he said, shaking his head. His mouth was round and worried and his cheeks were flushed hot pink. 'You do it for me.' He squeezed closed his eyes and held out his hand to her, the palm facing up.

She took his hand in her wounded palm and she could feel him twitch and tremble. She pressed the blade into his skin, and a stronger feeling of sickness swelled inside her. His hand was ice cold and turning a mottled, bluish-pink colour. She looked up into his face. Small beads of perspiration stood out around his lip and his eyelashes quivered in little gold points. She could feel him breathing; a deep, desperate rattle like a small animal struggling to escape from his chest. In the silence, she thought she could hear his heart pounding. 'We don't have to do this,' she said. 'If you're scared we don't have to.'

'No, go ahead,' he said unsteadily. She lifted the knife a fraction of an inch away from his skin, ready to bring it back down. 'No, don't,' he blurted out.

Her own palm burned where the knife had sliced it, and a drop of blood quivered on her wrist, about to fall. She could hear the bubbles in the glass of Coke beside her; heard them rising, popping, then fizzling out. Ambrose breathed faster and faster; a high, light, swirling sound, as white splotches rose up and dotted his face. 'Maybe we just need the spit,' Rainey said quickly. 'Here, spit on my hand and let's shake.' She dropped his hand and held her hand up to his mouth. 'Then we'll be blood brothers. That will be good enough.' He spit weakly, and she grabbed his hand again, feeling the burn of the wound as they shook vigorously to seal their pact.

'Whew,' he said. At last he began to breathe normally. 'I'm glad that's over.'

'So am I.' She wiped her forehead with the back of her wrist.

'How long does it last? How long will we be blood brothers?'

'I don't know. I guess forever,' she said, lifting the glass, tipping her head, and gratefully swallowing down a mouthful of warm Coke.

It was nine thirty and they were well into playing Davy Crockett and Daniel Boone when Mormor called up the staircase to say that Ambrose's parents were ready to leave. 'I'm really glad you're my blood brother now,' Ambrose said as he stood and brushed the dust off his clothes. 'I never had a brother before.'

'Yeah. I'm glad too,' Rainey said. 'Brothers forever. Brothers for life. Hey, we need a secret handshake signal. Blood brothers always need a secret signal. Let's do this – point to the line in the middle of your palm, then lick it, then we shake.' Ambrose nodded. They both pointed to their palms, licked them, and shook. Rainey felt a sting as the wounded skin of her palm cracked open again. 'That's it. We're officially blood brothers now,' she explained. Ambrose grabbed her shoulders and leaned in, giving her two quick kisses, one on either cheek.

'What was that?' Rainey asked, touching her face in shock.

'It's just a custom,' Ambrose said solemnly. 'People do it in Europe all the time.'

Rainey decided not to follow Ambrose down to the foyer. Instead, she watched from the top of the staircase as Ambrose's parents put on their coats and boots and gloves. His mother was young, thin, blond and pretty, while his father was older: gruff and grey-haired, with square shoulders and a wide neck. Rainey watched them fussing over Ambrose, guiding his hands into his mittens, tying his red silk scarf, and squeezing the tight cap over his head. He struggled unconvincingly and pretended to paw at his cheek after his mother gave him a quick, surreptitious kiss. As they were walking out the door, Ambrose turned back and looked up at Rainey, doffing his cap and offering a slight bow. She waved down to him. 'Bye,' she said softly, too quiet for him to hear. The door blew shut, and she felt a chill down her back. But it wasn't the cold air that had touched her; it was the realisation that as soon as Ambrose was gone, she had started to miss him.

When Rainey came downstairs and into the kitchen, she had the impression that the celebration had ended, as it often did, just a little too late. Arne and Ervald were arguing, Torgrim's car wouldn't start, Sammy was crying and Stevie had thrown up on the carpet. If everyone had left at nine o'clock, it would have been bitter-sweet but pleasant, with full stomachs and clear heads, and the melancholy would have been genuine. The last people to leave would have been guardians of the silence, putting away the clean plates, folding the towels, squeezing dry the dishcloths and padding on stockinged feet to turn off the lights, put out the cats and bolt the doors.

But they had neglected to leave in that silver interlude. Everyone stayed a minute or two longer, to see the final play of the football game, to hear the punchline of the joke, and to finish the last of the lukewarm coffee. But even that was a minute too long, and the mood was subtly, but irrevocably, altered. The moment in which they didn't leave was the moment that the streets had turned treacherous; the soft lacing of snow had frozen over to deadly black ice, the temperature had dropped, and the drive home would be just that little bit further. The youngest children were tired and cranky, pulling the hem of the tablecloth, rubbing their eyes and begging to be held. They were bundled into their coats and boots and ski-pants, unsteady beneath all the weight. And so the relatives left, and shook hands and said good-bye before piling into their cold, damp cars and sliding out on to the frozen dirt-gravel road. And the silence that remained was a bored, tedious silence, not of grace and goodwill but of tight-lipped resentment. Mormor and Grandpa Garth were left to clean up, sweeping the floor and stacking the last glasses. Mormor's make-up had faded, and Grandpa Garth's hair had lost its careful side part. Rainey felt the tired, bored, worn-out silence of a day which was past being ready to end.

'I'm so stiff,' Grandpa Garth told Mormor as they struggled into the Oldsmobile and began the slow drive home. 'My back is aching and I can hardly turn my head.'

'Hmmm. I'm stiff too,' Mormor answered. 'Do you want me to bring out the Ben-Gay and Aspercreme?'

'Naw. I'll be OK,' Grandpa Garth said.

'It's right here in the glove compartment,' Mormor offered.

'No. Thanks.'

Rainey could hear them creaking, stretching and settling as they tried to quiet down their tough old bones.

'Kjell looked good,' Grandpa Garth said.

'He did,' Mormor agreed. 'You couldn't tell he'd had the,' she paused, 'o-p-e-r-a-t-i-o-n.'

'No. Not at all.' Grandpa Garth stroked his elegant moustache, glancing at his reflection in the rear-view mirror. 'Sissel sure seemed happy.'

'She should be! All that money. And now two months in Europe,' Mormor scoffed.

'Have you told Rainey yet?' Grandpa Garth asked.

'Told me what?' Rainey asked, yawning dully.

'Your cousin Ambrose will be coming to stay with us over Christmas,' Mormor said.

'Really?' Rainey asked, suddenly excited. 'Can he stay forever and ever?'

'God forbid,' Mormor answered.

'Sonja,' Grandpa Garth warned, clenching his jaw. 'Don't say things like that in front of her. Little girls have big ears, remember?'

Mormor sighed and folded her arms. 'Ambrose's parents have to go to Denmark to settle some business, and they thought he might like to stay with us. Won't that be nice?' she said dryly.

'Yes,' Rainey answered. 'It will be the best Christmas ever, in my whole entire life. You know what? I'm going to take him to meet Gus. Gus can tell Ambrose why it's good to like baseball.'

Mormor began to mutter under her breath. 'Sure, go off and have a European vacation, see if we mind. Just leave your son with us, leave him behind like he's an extra suitcase or something. That Sissel was always an irresponsible girl. Always. Never had half a brain, but she was crafty all right. Never even finished college, that one, but still she goes off to New York, gets a job in a big company, marries the boss, even though he's a foreigner, you marry the boss and go and live in Europe. That's how you do it, Sissel. Sure, act like you're better than us now, just because you got a little bit of money. Well, I'm not too proud to say my family are farmers. My family are farmers, and so are hers. I hope she remembers that, that Sissel. I hope she remembers that.'

Rainey lay back in the seat, closed her eyes and listened to Mormor's rambling speech. It had a strangely hypnotic effect, the rising and falling cadence of her voice seemed to blend in with the motions of the Oldsmobile, the lolling of the wheels and the purring of the engine. It was good to be a child and not have to watch the road. She knew there were deer hidden in the woods, deer that could jump out so fast and cause an accident, deer that were so quick all that could be seen before the crash was the red of its eyes and the white of its tail. But she would let Grandpa Garth watch the road tonight. Rainey wallowed in the warm stink of the backseat, surrounded by stale tobacco, rubber mats, and dirty newspapers. The floor was strewn with bent coathangers and a handful of abandoned coins, loose pennies and dimes that rolled and pinged beneath her feet.

'Selfish,' Rainey heard Mormor say. Rainey knew Mormor had left Sissel and had now moved on to Anja. 'What a selfish girl, to go and do that. Killing herself. How dare she do that to her parents? Poor Harald and Eve. Young people today take everything for granted. Everything. They have it too easy, that's the trouble. We had to work hard in the Old Country, we knew the value of life. Selfish, selfish girl.'

By the time the car stopped, Rainey was too tired to sit up. The door opened and the cold wind shot into her like an arrow. She pretended to be asleep, and all of Mormor and Grandpa Garth's nudging couldn't rouse her. 'We'll just have to leave her out here to freeze,' Mormor said rubbing her arms in the cold, but Rainey knew that Mormor didn't mean it. Rainey let her mouth slip open and she drew in a low, slow breath like a snore. Yes, she could be an actor too, as well as an agent and a spy. She and Ambrose could both be stars of stage and screen.

'Come on,' Grandpa Garth said, lifting her out of the seat and hefting her over his shoulder. His coat was warm against her cheek and smelled like Brylcreem and lashings of Old Spice. He brought her into the house, slipped off her boots and carried her up to her room. Her face brushed against his as he lay her down and she could hear him breathing heavily. She heard the bristly sound as he wiped his moustache with the back of his hand. She wanted something more from him, not a good-night kiss, nothing as dramatic as that, but something, a blanket tossed over her body or a hand gently pressed to her forehead. She thought for a moment that he might be watching her, the way she imagined real parents must, just for a moment watching her sleep, and thinking how she's changed, how she's grown and gotten older. She had grown; even Aunt Ingebjorg had noticed. Rainey thought Grandpa Garth might be standing over her thinking all these serious and grown-up things, but when she opened her eyes, he had gone, and she could hear him moving down the hallway towards the other bedroom. She climbed out of bed, took off her coat, dress, petticoat and tights, folding and stacking them neatly on the chair. She removed Little Joe and placed her gun and holster on top of her clothes. Then she slipped into her Speed Racer boys' pyjamas, which Mormor allowed her to have only after she had, for modesty's sake, sewn up the flies. The fabric was stiff and itchy against her skin, and a shiver inside her plucked at the tight strings of her chest. She looked down at Speed Racer's cartoon face emblazoned across her stomach and she thought about Ambrose's dramatic hernia scar. The fabric of her sleeves was covered with happy pictures: wheels, bikes and helmets, images which would fire her dreams and send her into peaceful sleep.

She bowed her head and said her nightly prayers. 'God bless Mormor and Grandpa Garth and my mommy, wherever she is, and Miss Sullivan and the whole third grade, and Aunt Ingebjorg and all the other aunts and uncles, and God bless Gretchen Stegner's fish because it's sick.' She began to stand up, but then sank back down to her knees. 'Oh and, God, please bless Ambrose; please bless my blood brother,' she added, before rising quickly and slipping into bed.

FIVE

Christmas 1979
Milwaukee, Wisconsin

Ambrose's impending visit changed everything. The gap between Thanksgiving and Christmas was usually the worst time of year for Rainey, and all she ever asked of Santa Claus and of God was to have the holidays end as quickly as possible. But this year was different – for the first time in Rainey's life, Christmas was something to look forward to. Ambrose was coming, he was coming, and she would finally have a brother for two whole months.

Mormor hated Christmas, and it was her unhappiness that sullied the season for everyone else. Not that she ever said she hated Christmas; no, she simply brushed aside all talk of holiday cheer, dismissing the festivities as a conspiracy of Catholics and a load of damn foolishness. 'We never made such a fuss in the Old Country,' she said. Still, Mormor did everything that was expected of a grandmother at Christmas time: she baked loaves of bread and fruit cakes and batches of kjeks and småkake, furiously stirring the batter, whipping the eggs into stiff white peaks and boiling the frosting until it was firm and shiny; she cleaned every nook and cranny of the living room, then decorated it with flags and candles;

she sent Christmas cards, and bought gifts for her nieces and nephews, all with the same tight-lipped determination. She often worked well into the early-morning hours, trimming the tree in silent, solitary labour. Rainey would creep to the top of the staircase and watch Mormor's shadow moving black and gnarled against the wall, in contrast to the picture window brimming with dazzling, untouched snow. Sometimes Mormor smoked a cigarette, her arms curled into her chest and her face turned away from the outside world of nativity scenes and plastic reindeer; closed off from the carols sung on street corners and the choruses of silver bells. Some mornings Rainey would find a crystal shot glass left by the side of the sink. She would lift the glass to her nose and smell the residue of akevitt, inhaling the ghost of that peppermint spirit.

Michael had died close to Christmas. Rainey knew about Michael, but she didn't know if Mormor knew that she knew about Michael. Rainey had only discovered her uncle by accident. While playing in the attic, one of her Matchbox cars had jumped its track and sailed behind the old armoire. When she moved the armoire to retrieve it, she found a battered green canvas duffel bag. Inside the bag was a collection of clothes, books and photographs, and a set of aluminium dog tags that had been stamped 'MCBRIDE MJ B716418 USA A PROT' in raised letters. She also found this letter:

Dear Mr and Mrs McBride,

As Platoon Leader, 2nd Platoon of J Company, I was with your son when he was fatally wounded on December 12, 1969, in the Republic of South Vietnam. I have always made it a point to relay to the families of the men who die while serving under my command as complete information as I can concerning the circumstances of their loved one's death. On December 12 we were operating near the village of An Khe when our company came under intense mortar and small arms fire. From the report I received your son Michael was struck by the initial first bursts and died instantly. He did not suffer from his wounds and his final moments were mercifully pain free. He served his country and upheld the finest traditions of the US Army. Please accept my condolences on your loss.

James P. Harper, US Army 2nd Lt.

Rainey wasn't sure what the letter meant; she only really under-stood the words 'died instantly'. *'Died instantly,'* she repeated again and again. *'Died instantly.'* The collection of bent, smeary photos showed a tall, slim, dark-haired teenager with a smile similar to Rainey's mother's. In one photo the boy was dressed in green combat fatigues, with his arm around another soldier and a small Vietnamese boy playing at his feet . On the back of the photo was scribbled 'April '69 – To Mamma and Pop – Check out my new friends! Love, Mike.' At the bottom of the bag, Rainey found a Christmas card with a drawing of a dove with a ribbon in its beak and a sprig of holly pinched in its claws. Inside the card was writ-ten 'To Mary Jane – Merry Christmas, 1969. Love, Bro.' The card had never been postmarked; it had been wrapped up in a T-shirt and stuffed among the rest of Michael's belongings.

Looking at the duffel bag and all its contents made Rainey realise it was possible to miss something she had never known existed and to long for something that had no structure, no name. She went to the bag often and consulting it became a kind of holy obligation. She was drawn by the sharp, antiseptic odour of the canvas; an odour in which she sensed blood, ammonia and rain. The mystery of life and death was hidden inside this bag and open-ing it never failed to give her a guilty thrill.

Rainey never heard Mormor say Michael's name, and she recalled Mormor acknowledging him only once. It was the Fourth of July in the Bicentennial year, when the whole world seemed on fire with banners of red, white and blue. Rainey had won first prize in a library contest for her painting of George Washington chop-ping down the cherry tree. As she, Mormor and Aunt Ingebjorg drove back home for an afternoon of picnics and fireworks, Rainey cradled her blue ribbon and her $10 cheque in her lap and didn't believe it was possible to feel more earthly pride and joy. As they reached the driveway, Aunt Ingebjorg looked up at the flagpole in the front yard. 'Sonja, you haven't raised the flag all the way,' she said, lifting her hand to her eyes. 'Look, there's still six or eight inches to the top.'

'Don't tell me how to fly the flag,' Mormor responded. 'I gave a son for this country.'

*

Worse than enduring Mormor's silences and surviving the Christmas season itself was having to attend the church's Luther League meetings three times a week. During the rest of the year, Luther League only met on Thursday afternoons, but during Advent attendance was expected on Mondays and Fridays as well, which meant three sessions a week of Religious Twister and Name That Bible Verse. Mormor had made Rainey a promise – 'Once you're confirmed, you never have to go to Church again.' But confirmation was still four years away, four years of dreary afternoons spent in the mouldy basement of Our Savior King of Kings Lutheran Church, Missouri Synod.

The basement was cold and damp and smelled of Elmer's glue, wet newspaper and the residue of endless potluck suppers where, thanks to Lutheran ingenuity, absolutely everyone brought tuna casserole, and no one ever ate the part that had been sprinkled with paprika, that suspicious and brightly coloured herb.

Pastor Jeff Wayland was the assistant minister at Our Savior King of Kings, and instructor of the Luther League. He had radically long hair, wore a silver bracelet and played the guitar. Rainey liked him a lot, but Mrs Tor Christiansen, the senior minister's wife, was Rainey's nemesis. She acknowledged, as most people did, that Rainey was intelligent. 'She's a bright girl, no doubt about it, but if only there were some way of legitimising the child,' she had said at one potluck supper.

Pastor Jeff sprang to Rainey's defence. 'Don't be so quick to condemn,' he warned Mrs Christiansen. 'She's been baptised the same as you and me. In God's eyes, she's no different than anyone else.'

Rainey also admired the deep mistrust that Pastor Jeff inspired in Mormor. 'Jeffrey Wayland,' Mormor would say. 'Just what kind of a name is that for a Lutheran minister? That doesn't sound like a good Lutheran name to me.' She decided he smiled too much to be holy, and suspected he harboured Methodist tendencies.

It was the second week of Advent when Rainey brought her end-of-semester project to Thursday's Luther League meeting. She was working on a report about the life of Martin Luther, presenting it in the form of the 95 Theses that Martin Luther had nailed to the castle church door in Wittenberg. She had cut out a rectangle of cardboard and painted it to look like wood. Then she had stapled sheets of lined paper to the front of the cardboard and on the top sheet of paper she had written, in very elaborate lettering, 'PART ONE – HIS VERY EARLY LIFE'. Beneath that she had written: 'Martin Luther was born in 1483. His parents were named Hans and Margaret.' That was as far as she had got, but she planned to show his complete life story.

'The next page will tell about his brothers and sisters, and where he went to school,' Rainey explained to her uninterested classmates.

'That's very creative, Rainey,' Pastor Jeff said, stroking his reddish-brown beard. His bright eyes shone like polished beads when he winked at her. 'You all might follow Rainey's lead in starting your projects well before the deadline.'

'Goody two-shoes, goody two-shoes,' Jill Moegenberger whispered. Timmy Schroeder kicked Rainey's leg beneath the table, but inside herself, Rainey began to glow.

Rainey was still feeling pleased with herself when Mrs Christiansen came downstairs with the class's afternoon snack. She carried a tray of stale windmill cookies and little Dixie cups half filled with cherry Kool-Aid, watered down to an anaemic shade of pink. Hungrily, Janna Jensen grabbed two cookies.

'One cookie each,' Mrs Christiansen said primly, pursing her lips and pulling the plate away from Janna's hand. 'Remember all those poor little children starving in China.' Janna, shamed, put both cookies back on the tray.

'I bet she eats the rest herself when she goes upstairs,' Rainey whispered to Gretchen Stegner sitting beside her. Gretchen smiled.

Mrs Christiansen stopped behind Rainey's chair, balancing the plate against her hip. 'I see someone's been busy. What have we here?' she asked, stretching over the table and breathing down Rainey's neck.

'It's my report on the life of Martin Luther,' Rainey answered, pleased that her work had been noticed. She ruffled the pages with her fingertips, lingering over the neatly printed letters.

'I see. You've certainly outdone yourself this time,' Mrs Christiansen said. 'I'm sure you've worked very hard. But don't be too proud, Rainey McBride. Don't go getting too full of yourself. Boys don't like girls who think they know everything. You especially have reason to be humble. Remember the circumstances of your birth.'

Rainey looked down at her report and noticed for the first time that some of the lines were crooked. Timmy Schroeder sneered and kicked her again, and this time the pain went deeper and lasted a little bit longer.

Rainey walked home from Luther League pondering the sin of pride, which she had been accused of more times than she could count. She tried not to be a show-off but she had so many ideas in her head, and sometimes they all just tumbled out of her mouth. She was often ordered to hold her tongue. 'Hold *kjeft*, Rainey, *hold kjeft*. Little girls are meant to be seen and not heard.' Or she was told, 'Rainey, go play outside, why don't you? No one here is interested in the opinions of a nine-year-old girl.' Always she would toe the ground and shuffle upstairs to converse with her toys. She couldn't help it if she loved to think; her mind was a thing with wings, a creature with arms and legs that longed to poke through the shell of her little world. Perched at her bedroom window she could look out and see the freeway overpass in the distance, and on sunny days it shone like the arch of a concrete rainbow; like a dazzling, enticing patch of light.

Rainey took the shortcut home, through the sports field between the schools. Mormor had forbidden her to go that way, but it was so much quicker, and she wasn't afraid of a pile of garbage, a few raccoons or the thin kids who crouched beneath the trees smoking clove cigarettes. As her feet crunched over the glazed surface of snow, she thought about Ambrose. Did he go to Catechism class? she wondered. Or did a holy man come to his house and bless him from a golden bowl? She supposed so. Why do Catholics put sugar on tomatoes? We put salt on ours. Did Martin Luther decide that too? The facts in her report danced together in her head as she challenged herself to remember everything she had learned. *Martin was born in Eisleben, East Germany.* East Germany is now a land of godless Communists. *Martin ate heartily. Martin married Katherina von Bora, a nun, and they had six children.* Grace, she thought. G.R.A.C.E. God's Riches At Christ's Expense. Justified by faith alone. The 95 Theses. No more selling indulgences. By

Christ alone. Nailed to the Church door in Wittenberg. A priest-hood of all believers. The Diet of Worms.

Yuk. Who would eat worms?

No, *voorms*, Pastor Jeff had explained. Voorms, not worms. It's a place.

Oh yes. A place.

Repeat the Nicene Creed. *God from God, Light from Light, True God from True God, Begotten not made, in one being with the Father . . .* The words followed the rhythm of her footsteps. As she reached the edge of the Truman Elementary School playground, where the street salt had burned yellow through to the pavement, several figures stepped out of the shadows and stopped her in her tracks.

'Brainey Rainey Do-Dainey,' a voice taunted.

'Carrot headed brain-iac,' said another. 'You think so much, your head caught fire.' At first she only heard the voices. Then, gradu-ally, four faces loomed into focus.

'What do you want?' she asked, hoping they couldn't hear the fear in her voice. She wasn't yet certain if it would be safer to run or to stay and try to hold her ground. 'Just leave me alone.'

'You think you're so smart on account of you get all A's,' a boy said. 'Miss Sullivan gives you good grades 'cuz you're her pet.' The others took up the chant of 'Pet, pet, pet.'

They began to circle her, moving in closer as the chant grew in volume and intensity. Rainey could see them clearly now – Jimmy Haepfner, Mark Kowalski, Kitty and Kolleen Kosciouszko. They were the four toughest kids in third grade. They all had bad skin and wore jeans and patched denim jackets to school. They came from Harrington Manors, close to the overpass and behind the Howard Johnson's, where the Puerto Rican maids and busboys all came outside at three o'clock to sit on the hill drinking Old Style and smoking Lucky Stripes. Although only six blocks away from the safety of Mormor's house on Sandstone Avenue, Harrington Manors was a world apart: dangerous, seedy, and mysterious. 'Pet, pet, pet,' the gang whispered maliciously, and the word seethed with evil.

'Shut up and leave me alone,' Rainey said. 'There's nothing wrong with being smart.'

'Give us your lunch money,' Kitty demanded. Her hands were

jammed into her pockets and her fringe of black hair fell heavily over her eyes.

'No way, José,' Rainey said firmly.

'Give it.'

'I used it for lunch. I don't have any more,' she insisted, her fear now turning to anger.

'Then find some, brain-iac,' Mark said, reaching out and punching her arm. It was a light punch but it told her what was coming if she didn't comply.

'You're just jealous because I'm smarter than you,' Rainey said, suddenly intoxicated by the cold fresh air, the fear in her stomach and the sharp stars sizzling over her head.

'You may be smart but we're gonna teach you a lesson,' Kolleen said.

'Go ahead, Pollack,' Rainey challenged.

That clinched it. She knew when she said the word that, as out-matched as she was, she'd have to fight her ground. She dropped her school bag and her lunchbox, pushed up her sleeves and spat in the snow to show she was ready. Before she had a chance to put up her fists, Jimmy clapped her on the back and pushed her face-down into the snow. Kitty and Kolleen were on her in the next instant, pulling Rainey's hair and digging their knees into her back and shoulders.

She looked up from the ground to see Mark grabbing her bag, the one with the big bright smiley-face sun on it, which Aunt Ingebjorg had brought back from her trip to Florida. 'In Florida, oranges grow on trees!' Ingebjorg had said with delight. 'It's just too magnificent to imagine. You can pluck an orange off the tree and eat it right then and there!' Rainey saw Mark plunge his arm deep into the plastic bag and pull out her Luther League project.

'Hey, what's this, brainy? It looks really dumb,' he said, waving it in the wind. The others laughed.

'It's supreme-o ugly. It looks like your face, brain-iac,' Kolleen said as Mark ruffled the pages.

'Don't touch that,' Rainey screamed, and she felt something rip inside her as he tore off the sheets of paper and dropped them one by one, and the black ink bled purple into the snow.

'Shut up!' Kitty ordered, pushing Rainey's head down to the

ground. She could feel the unyielding concrete beneath her, solid and merciless down to the centre of the earth. She twisted her head, searching for air.

'Face wash!' Mark ordered. Kitty pulled Rainey's head back up with a snap. She felt a brief, delicious flash of fresh air rushing through her nose and lungs. But then Jimmy smashed a snowball into her face, grinding it back and forth until her skin began to burn. 'Don't,' she pleaded. 'Stop it. Just stop.'

Jimmy stepped back and laughed. The cold wind ripped into Rainey's eyes, teasing out tears and slicing raw to the bone. 'Who's a smart girl now?' Jimmy said. He grabbed another handful of snow, packed it solid with his dark-mittened hand, and as Kitty and Kolleen held Rainey still, Jimmy lobbed it into her face, this time pushing the snow into her nose and mouth until she started to gag. She felt her eyelashes freeze shut and her teeth ached as the pain swelled behind her eyeballs. Suddenly she heard the sound of a car cruising through the empty lot. Jimmy stopped and stood upright. 'Let's go before we get busted,' he ordered. The girls dropped Rainey back to the ground and in a split second all four of them had darted away in separate directions, as swift and silent as frightened deer.

'You stupid Pollacks,' Rainey shouted after them. 'Big old Dufas. Go home and eat your mama's kielbasa.' She rolled over and felt a pain in her throat. Something hot quivered in her veins as she waited for her body to stop shaking. She brushed her damp lip and found her nose was bleeding. She reached down and scooped up a handful of snow. She held the snow to her nose and blew as hard as she could, feeling a squeezing pain deep inside her skull. The blood stained the snowball pink, so she grabbed another handful and pressed it firmly into her nose, holding it until the blood stopped flowing and her nose was numb.

She stood and picked up her scattered belongings – the plastic bag with one of its handles ripped; her hat, her mittens, her G.I. Joe lunchbox. Last of all she picked up what was left of the Wittenberg church door, torn and stained and ruined. She had done all that work for nothing. She wanted desperately to cry but refused to give in to the tightness behind her eyes. To cry would be to shame herself, to somehow give the Kowalski gang exactly what they had wanted.

She felt cold and shivery, even as the wind licked and singed her frozen cheeks. There was no comfort in the empty places around her; not in the dark, brick, windowless back of Truman Elementary School, or the neighbouring Rutherford B. Hayes High School's basketball court with the backboard and nets frozen solid, and in the distance, the expressway interchange buzzing with headlights. She could just make out the looming green signs with their illuminated arrows that pointed the way towards freedom, in Chicago, Madison or Green Bay.

Rainey touched her burning forehead and the tender tip of her nose. She knew she couldn't go home looking as if she'd been in a fight. Mormor would be furious that she had taken the shortcut home after she had been told not to. Mormor would slap her and send her to bed without any supper, saying it was her own fault and that she had gotten what she deserved for mixing with the wrong kind of kids.

Instead, Rainey cut across the schoolyard to Aloyisius Avenue, heading towards the bus depot, hoping to catch Gus before he went home for the evening. Gus the bus driver was a tall, lean, middle-aged man with one glass eye, a tanned face, and a bushy grey moustache which he called 'the cookie duster'. He wore a brown polyester uniform with red badges and lots of zippered pockets, and he punctuated his sentences with phrases like 'sure 'nuf' and 'mighty fine'. They had originally met when Rainey, then in first grade, had hit a softball through the depot's front window. Instead of being angry, Gus had been impressed. He said that Rainey showed signs of developing into a good power hitter, if only she could learn to lay off pitches high and away. After that they became fast friends. In summer they spent hours just chewing the fat, sitting on the stairs drinking grape Ne-Hi, whittling sticks and stringing soda can rings. In winter they sat in the depot's back room huddled over the space heater, listening to sports radio and discussing the Brewers, the Packers and the Bucks.

During the school year Gus drove the public school routes, and in summer he did runs to Will O' Wisp Day Camp in Menomonee Falls, a place where Catholic asthmatic kids learned to swim. Gus sometimes let Rainey ride along on these short journeys. She loved to sit high up in the front seat, listening to the Brewers game on the radio, cheering whenever someone hit a homer and leaning over to honk the horn. Mormor never approved. She didn't mind Gus, but she was concerned about the asthmatic Catholic kids. The 'Jesus Wheezers' she called them. 'Don't let them convert you to Popery. Run away if they try to baptise you in the river.'

Rainey opened the depot's front door. The depot was dark and empty, but she could hear the thin, muzzled noise of a radio coming from the back room. 'Hey, Gus, where are you, buddy?' she called loudly, peering over the warped Formica counter. Even on tiptoe she was barely tall enough to see the rows of radios lining the wooden peg-board wall.

'Back here, kid,' came the reply. Rainey stepped into the back room and was embraced by the warm winter scents of tobacco and boot leather.

'Jeez Louise, what happened to you?' Gus asked. He had been leaning back on two legs of his chair, his thumbs hooked into the loops of his belt. The chair tipped forward as he looked her up and down with his one good eye. 'All I can say, kid, is that I hope the other guy looks worse. What the hell happened?'

She dropped her bag and her lunchbox on the floor and pulled up the chair beside him. She warmed her numb hands over the small space heater on the floor. 'It was Mark Kowalski's gang.' She almost said 'that Pollack gang' but then remembered that Gus's wife Hilda was from Warsaw. 'They beat me up when I was walking home from Luther League. They wrecked my Christmas report.' Something sticky trickled down Rainey's lip and she was afraid she had started to cry, but then she realised the warm air had made her nose bleed again. Gus unzipped his top pocket, whipped out his handkerchief and handed it to her.

'Take this here snot vault,' he said. 'And help yourself to a dip of chaw.' From another pocket he produced a pack of Bazooka bubblegum and offered it to Rainey. Holding the handkerchief to her nose, she opened the gum with her free hand, popping a big pink wad into her mouth. She began to chew fiercely, and when Gus pointed to the spittoon with the stubbed toe of his industrial boot, she had a mouthful of saliva good and ready and she launched it into the small brass container with a thwack of her lips and tongue.

'Nice shot,' Gus said, leaning forward to peer into the spittoon.

'That one's a real doozie.' He took a round tin disk out of his top pocket and opened it, grabbing a pinch of tobacco and inserting it deep into his cheek. He replaced the cover and rolled the tin in the palm of his hand, letting it catch and reflect the overhead light. Rainey looked with reverence and longing at the shiny red Indian face glowing beneath a huge red feather headdress.

'Is it almost empty?' Rainey asked hopefully.

'Almost. Another few days, I'd say.'

'You promised me I could have the container when it's empty,' she reminded him.

'I know. Don't worry, I won't forget.' He smiled, a broad smile which carved creases into his cheeks and made the corners of his moustache lift up.

'When will you teach me to chew the real thing?' she asked eagerly.

He scowled in mock-seriousness. 'Not until you're twelve and a half. God forbid what your grandmother would do to me if she thought I was teaching you how to chew tobacco.'

'We don't have to tell her,' Rainey offered.

'Let's just wait until you're twelve, OK?'

'Deal,' she agreed.

'Say hey, d'ya hear Larry Hisle might need an operation on his rotator cuff?'

'No way!'

'It's true. Heard it on the radio about an hour ago.'

'Whee-oooow.' Rainey practised the long, slow, two-toned whistle that always accompanies baseball talk. 'That means he'll be out for the season.'

'He might be,' Gus agreed.

'What are they going to do? They can't expect Gorman to hit more than forty-five homers. And this is supposed to be our year to win a hundred games,' Rainey said in despair.

'Don't worry, kid,' Gus said, trying to soothe her. 'We've got Pauly, Sixto and Stormin' Gorman, not to mention Cecil Cooper, all of 'em ready to pick up the slack.'

'Mmm. Hope you're right,' she said severely.

They settled back into their chairs for an hour of easy banter. This was the time Rainey loved; it was a secret entrance into the grown-up world and a sanctuary away from Mormor; it was a blessed place where her opinions carried weight. She could expound on the things that really mattered to her, like the infield fly rule, and who would be the best Brewer's DH, and whether the team had any chance of finishing higher than third this year, behind those much-hated Baltimore Orioles.

Rainey glanced out the window and knew it was getting late. She could hear the wind picking up, and the eerie, crackling shiver-sound that occurs in the depths of winter, when the temperature drops from a steady zero to ten or twelve below. 'How's your better half?' Rainey asked politely. Always, the conversation had to end with Gus's wife.

'Super-duper.' His eyes glazed over. 'My Hilda's at home right now, bless her soul, making bobke and pieriogi. Gawd, that woman can cook. I'm a mighty lucky man, mighty lucky. She's still a looker too. A little wide in the bee-hind, but still a looker. I couldn't get much luckier.' Rainey nodded in agreement. She had never met Hilda, and she suspected she never would. Gus and Hilda lived only eight blocks from Mormor's house, but like the Kowalski gang, Hilda lived in a world apart. Hilda's friends were all Polish immigrants and they kept to themselves, many of them refusing to learn English. Instead of shopping at the corner grocery store, they took the city bus down to Mitchell Street and bought fresh food at the markets. They returned home laden with huge baskets of bread, bundles of onions, radishes and beets, and mysterious glass jars swimming with cloudy, pickled things. These women stayed in back rooms and wore flat shoes, and babushkas and scarves, even in summer.

'Guess what?' Rainey said to Gus as she wrapped herself up and prepared to leave.

'You've been offered a contract to play for the Brewers?' he asked.

'No,' she said impatiently. 'It's better than that even.'

'And just what could be better than that?'

'My cousin Ambrose is coming to stay with us for Christmas.'

'Ambrose? That kind of sounds like a cissy name to me,' Gus said carefully. 'I doubt he could ever play ball with a name like Ambrose.'

'He's not a cissy. He's Danish,' she explained patiently. 'He's super rich and he lives in a skyscraper in New York City, New York, where if you look out the window all the people look like ants. He's going to be a star of stage and screen and I'm going to be his secret agent when he goes to Hollywood, and while he's here I'm going to teach him how to whittle sticks and play Davy Crockett.'

'Well, you sure don't find his type in Milwaukee every day. Bring him by sometime, I'd love to meet him.'

'I will,' Rainey promised. She touched her face, which had cooled down considerably. 'Do I look like I got in a fight?'

'Naw,' Gus reassured her. 'None the worse for wear.' He patted her on the shoulder and sent her out into the wind. She turned back and waved, and headed for home.

The next morning when Rainey awoke, she knew right away that something bad had happened overnight. Her throat felt tight and scratchy and her head spun when she sat upright. At breakfast she couldn't finish her first Raspberry Pop-Tart and the sugary blue milk of her Captain Quisp cereal made her feel hot and queasy. She wanted nothing as much as she wanted to lie down, close her eyes and make the room stop spinning. As she struggled to get dressed, she felt herself break out in a cold sweat. 'Please God, don't let me be sick,' she whispered. She dreaded telling Mormor she wasn't feeling well. To Mormor's way of thinking, illness was a sin or a punishment for doing something wrong. An illness had to be endured, and the reward was being well enough to go back to work.

Rainey crept dizzily down the staircase and into the front room, where Mormor was ironing clothes, pressing back and forth with deep, shoulder-creasing strokes. She didn't notice Rainey until she looked up suddenly. 'What's wrong with you?' she snapped.

'I don't know, but I don't feel so good,' Rainey said softly.

Mormor's face darkened as she whisked the shirt off the ironing board. 'That's what you get for playing outside without a hat on. Serves you right. You'll probably end up with pneumonia. Just don't come crying to me when you're in an iron lung.'

'Sorry,' Rainey said feebly.

'Do you have a fever?' Mormor asked.

'No,' Rainey answered quickly, feeling drops of sweat condense in her hairline.

'Then you're not sick.'

'OK. I guess I'm not,' Rainey agreed. 'I'm just gonna lie down for a while.' She gripped the doorknob, trying to steady herself. Her stomach heaved.

'Come here, let me see if you've got a fever,' Mormor insisted.

'I don't,' Rainey said, as chills danced down her spine.

Mormor stepped over to her, grabbed Rainey's arm and pressed a hand to her forehead. 'Just as I suspected,' Mormor said. 'You're burning up. Let me get the thermometer.'

'No. You don't need to.' Rainey's chill turned to a hot sweat.

'Yes I do,' Mormor said.

Rainey tried to break away but Mormor grabbed her again and held on tightly. 'Listen here, young lady, I'm going to slap you if you don't settle down,' she warned. Her fingernails dug deep into the tender back of Rainey's arm. 'Now let me take your temperature. You know what to do. Wait here while I get the thermometer. Do you understand me?'

'Yes,' Rainey answered. There was no escape now. She pulled down her pants and trembled, dreading what came next. She knelt beside the sofa to prop herself up, her forehead pressed into the cushion. Her underpants were around her ankles, the carpet scratched her bare knees, and the air felt hot and dry on her bottom. She could hear sounds from the bathroom; the medicine cabinet's little glass door sliding open and closed, the clatter of the metal shelf as Mormor grabbed the big greasy jar of Vaseline. Rainey glanced over her shoulder and out the front window. She had a vision of the Kosciouszko twins looking in at her and laughing. They would go to school tomorrow and tell Miss Sullivan and the whole third grade about Mormor and the thermometer, and the sight of Rainey's big white bottom. The shame of it was worse than anything else; it was the shame that made her whole body turn red, red as the beets Hilda and her friends carried home from the market. Suddenly Rainey felt dizzy and dry, a blanched sensation and then a tingling in her throat as if she were about to vomit. Then, blissfully, everything went black.

*

At first, she dreams of Ambrose. Ambrose is ill, pale, pink, and coughing delicately, propped up in a big white canopy bed with flowery lace curtains. He is being attended to by several world-famous surgeons, who marvel at his scar, examine him from head to toe and consult one another gravely, their long fingers stroking their bearded chins. Then suddenly, seven smiling blond nurses in starched uniforms burst into the bedroom bearing frothy chocolate milkshakes in silver mugs and plates of grilled cheese sandwiches browned to perfection, held together with umbrella toothpicks and parsley garnish spilling over the side. Someone stands behind Ambrose and ties a silk bib around his chubby neck. He is about to cut into the sandwich with his engraved knife and fork when suddenly the dream switches to Mormor and Aunt Ingebjorg standing in Mormor's kitchen. Mormor is making lunch for Rainey, a dish of lumpy dumpling soup with a handful of dry oyster crackers and a piece of white bread with butter. 'Oh, Sonja, this soup is cold,' Ingebjorg is saying, taking a sip with a dull grey spoon. 'It doesn't matter. It's good enough. Good enough for her,' Mormor answers, kicking open the door and striding towards the table.

Rainey woke up briefly, a sort of half-awakening in which she could hear perfectly but couldn't quite see. Shapes moved darkly, as if trapped in liquid, drifting in and out of focus like active purple blobs. The doctor was hovering over her, touching her, but she couldn't feel his hands. 'How long have you had this rash on your chest?' he asked, and she wanted to answer him but she was too surprised by the fact that someone had taken off her shirt and she didn't know where it was. She thought she needed to find her shirt before she could answer his question.

'It's OK,' he said, patting her head. 'Just you rest for now. I'll be back later on.' Her body seemed to take that as a signal, for she fell asleep instantly and heavily, sinking down into the couch as if tied to lead weights and thrown into the water. She felt herself sinking deeper, slipping into a hole inside her mind where it was too dark to distinguish day from night. She could feel the world retracting, letting out its breath and squeezing down on itself, crushing her body inside its centre. Life was getting smaller and smaller and she had to fight for the space to breathe. She was alone in a dark, hot, airless room. Even a sparrow would suffocate in here. She imagined crows dropping from the curtains, and through the window she could see the sky clouding over, turning black with birds.

The world shuddered and something shook the bed. And then

the bed was all that was left of the world, and the side of the bed was the edge of existence. But when she closed her eyes, life shrank even further, reduced now to the two inches of cool soft pillow on either side of her head.

Finally she was left with only her own skin to live in. Her skin was the last edge of life, and she knew she could survive in a world this small, if only the pain would go away. But then her skin curdled and began to burn off, layer by layer. The fresh skin was cool and pale for a blissful instant. Then it ripened like fruit over a flame; the skin swelled and reddened and stretched thinner and thinner, growing tighter and shinier, until it split open and trickled cool liquid. And she could breathe again, at least in the few beautiful seconds before the next skin began to swell. 'Oh, Jesus, please come to me,' she prayed. 'You fasted in the desert forty days and forty nights, please give me strength.'

But as soon as she asked for Jesus, she was afraid He might come. She feared seeing Jesus, feared that He would be too thin and naked and foreign. She was scared of His glowing robe and suffering eyes and His naked bleeding ankles, trailing blood on Mormor's good clean carpet. 'No, Jesus, You better not come to me. You better not come to me.'

When she woke the next day her arms and legs were too swollen to move. Her mind was clearer but her head still ached and she could feel something, sunglasses, yes sunglasses, weighing heavily on the brow of her nose. Sweat trickled under the plastic frames, but she couldn't lift her hands to brush it away. She could hear Mormor and Grandpa Garth arguing in the kitchen.

'Burn everything,' Mormor was saying in a frantic, high-pitched voice Rainey had never heard before. 'Everything she touched. Burn it all: toys, sheets, clothes, everything. Do it now. There's some gasoline in the garage.'

'Sonja! Stop it!' Grandpa Garth said. 'It isn't that bad.'

'Scarlet fever!'

'I know,' he said patiently. 'But it's different these days. It's not like it used to be. They have penicillin now. She'll be OK.'

'Jens went blind and Astrid died. Jens went blind and Astrid died,' Mormor repeated.

'She won't go blind. Sonja, try to be reasonable.'

Mormor said something and then Grandpa Garth said something else but Rainey could no longer make out the words. She felt the big black sunglasses sliding down her nose. The sparrows and crows were curled up in the curtains; she could smell their dank odour and feel their beady bird eyes bearing down on her.

'We shouldn't have named her after Astrid; that was bad luck, I knew it,' Mormor said, suddenly loud again. 'All of Blue River Township – everyone's hair fell out and then their scalps burned. So many died or went blind. The healthy ones took care of the sick ones, until they got sick themselves and they just fell into the bed next to them. *Gud i himmelen!*'

Rainey must have fallen asleep again, because in what seemed like the very next moment Grandpa Garth was sitting beside the sofa, soothing her forehead with a cool, wet cloth. She opened her eyes and could barely make out his face; his worried grey eyes, his thin moustache. 'It's OK, Rainey,' he said quietly. 'You're gonna be all right.' He tried to smile. 'Are you hungry?'

'A drink,' she whispered.

He lifted the glass of water from the card table beside the sofa and held it to her lips, pinching the straw between his thin fingers. She took a sip but it was too painful to swallow. Instead she let the water run down her chin. It felt hot and sticky as it trickled on to her chest. 'Try to have a little chicken broth,' Grandpa Garth said. 'You need to eat.' He lifted a small mug of soup. The smell of the chicken made her gag. She shook her head no.

'Mormor,' she whispered.

'What?'

'I want Mormor.'

He seemed surprised. 'She's busy right now,' he said quickly. 'Do you want one of your toys?'

'Mormor's burning my toys,' Rainey told him.

'No she isn't. We won't let her do that,' he promised, covering her hand with his. 'Your toys are safe.'

'I want Mormor,' she insisted. She wouldn't rest until Mormor was at her side. The woman who had never in her lifetime showed Rainey so much as an ounce of love or affection, yet Mormor was who she wanted. Only Mormor was strong enough to fight off the crows and the blackbirds; Mormor would never let the light slip away forever under the door. No one else had that kind of strength. Grandpa Garth went away and came back a few seconds later. 'She's washing the dishes,' he told her. 'She says she'll come in when she's finished.'

Mormor pulled up the chair beside the sofa and slumped forward, her chapped, red hands balanced in her lap. 'Rainey,' she said, in a voice so weary it sounded like concern. 'I'm too old to put up with all this.' She smelled of ammonia and dish soap; the aromas of furious scrubbing.

'I'm sorry I got sick,' Rainey told her in a voice that strained to reach a whisper.

Mormor bit the edge of her lip. 'I know. It's just too much sometimes. I finished raising children years ago. I lost my son and my daughter left me. I never wanted to take care of another child, not in my old age. Diapers and high chairs; school, and sickness, and boyfriends at the back door . . . It's the last thing I wanted.' She sighed. 'But here you are. I guess it isn't your fault.'

'You're stuck with me,' Rainey offered.

'Yeah. And you're stuck with us. Sorry about that. It would be nice if you had a mom and dad and brothers and sisters, like most kids have. It would have been nice.' She glanced out at the snow drifted against the front window, and her tone of voice changed. 'But you know, a lot of kids are worse off than you.'

'I know. I know. Don't tell me that,' Rainey interrupted, not wanting to hear the lecture she had heard so many times before. 'Mormor, what's the Old Country like?'

Mormor looked startled. 'What a strange question. Why do you ask that?'

'Because you always talk about it but you never say what it was really like. What was the Old Country like?'

Mormor looked down and pulled a loose thread on the blanket, pursing her lips and shaking her head. Her face softened a little as the fringe of her grey hair fell forward. 'Oh, I hardly remember it now. That was so long ago. I remember apples from home. But there were apples here too, so I might be wrong. I was only six when we came over. Papa and his brothers came over first. They sent for us later, after they saved up enough money. Papa killed a man, that's why we left. He killed a man after an argument at the timber mill where we lived in Lyngdal. We went to hide with Mama's relatives in Kongsberg. Else was born there. Then we took the boat over and lived in Saskatchewan for a few years, and that's where Arne was born. Ingebjorg was the baby, the only one born in America. She was born after we settled down in Blue River Township.'

'Didn't you live in Owauskeum?' Rainey asked.

'No. Papa built the house in Owauskeum after I was out of high school. First we lived in Blue River Township, in Grant County, Wisconsin. That was a strange place. Nearly everyone in the town came from near Lyngdal. It was like the whole village had been picked up and moved to the New World. Everyone spoke Norwegian, even in church and in school and in the newspapers. I didn't speak a word of English until I was fourteen years old, and that was only because we had to learn English to get a high school diploma. There were towns on either side of Blue River; one German, one Lithuanian. All were Lutheran, but we never met them, we never mixed with their type. I never saw a black or a Catholic or a Jew until I was nineteen, when I went to work in Chicago. I got a job as a typist but I was very pretty then, tall and blond and big-boned, and they gave me a job modelling fur coats. Ten dollars a week! A fortune then, during the Depression. My hair was so long I could sit on the ends of it, and I had a big ba-zoom, so men were very friendly.' Rainey thought she saw Mormor blush. 'I once caught the eye of John Dillinger himself,' Mormor continued. 'He bought me a drink and asked me out to the pictures. I've often thought if I'd have said yes, I could have been the lady in red, I could have been there the night Hoover's G-Men shot him down.' Mormor smiled, a rare and bittersweet smile, behind which Rainey could see the ghostly shadow of Mormor's lost beauty.

'Did you ever want to go back there?' Rainey asked.

'To Chicago?'

'No,' Rainey explained. 'To the Old Country.'

Mormor shrugged. 'No. Not particularly. It's not our home any more. Scandinavia's changed – it's all Socialists and nude beaches nowadays, from what I read in the papers. Sex change operations!' She paused. 'Mama always talked about going back. She never wanted to come over here in the first place. But there was never enough money, and there was always Arne and Jens and Ingebjorg to take care of, and the farm, and then eventually the grandchildren, and Mama died without ever going home.'

Rainey suddenly felt sad. She had lost something, something that had mattered once. She thought about Hilda and Gus and the Kosciouszko twins, and the Puerto Rican waiters shivering in their thin coats behind the Howard Johnson's. Everyone dreamed of someplace else but no one ever went back to where they came from. 'Maybe I'll go to the Old Country someday,' Rainey said.

'You might. You just might,' Mormor agreed. 'But what could it mean to you? You're half-Irish. Well, a quarter Irish from Garth, and a quarter Norwegian from me. The other half could be anything. Who knows who your father was? I know for sure it wasn't the Spic she ran off with; she met him only a month or so before you were born. It had to have been someone else. You could be half-black or half-Catholic or half-Jap for all I know.'

'I don't think so,' Rainey told her. 'I know what I am.'

'And what's that?'

'I am Rainey McBride,' she said simply. Suddenly she felt the fever pulling her under again. 'How do you say ice cream in Norwegian?' she asked quickly.

'*Iskrem*,' Mormor said, rolling the 'r'.

'Snowman?'

'*Snømann*.'

'School?'

'*Skole*.'

'Sku-leh,' Rainey repeated. Suddenly she wanted to possess the language and be able to pronounce every word. She wanted it to glide easily off her tongue. Somewhere in the back of her mind, she must still know it. She could be a part of all the people who went before her, she could summon up those old ghosts, if only she could address them in their native language. 'Sku-leh,' she said, struggling to get the sounds right, the raised inflection on the second syllable.

'Rest now,' Mormor instructed, folding over the edge of the blanket. 'You just rest for now. Worry about learning Norwegian later on.'

'Iskrem. Snømann. Skole,' Rainey whispered, holding tight to the words.

Then came another wave of fever, and more pain and tightening in her throat. Grandpa Garth tried to cheer her up, brought her ten packs of Fleer and Donruss baseball cards, and he balanced a brand-new Louisville Slugger against the sofa, so she could reach over and feel it; she could caress the wood grain with her hand whenever the pain got bad. But still, the fever grew worse. She tried not to breathe. Breathing was too painful. Even the smallest breath was like a dragon breathing fire on the back of her throat. She began to cough, and with each cough her throat squeezed smaller. Then she felt something popping in her throat, and she spat out something thick and sticky which felt like grape skins. She realised to her horror that the blisters in her throat had broken open. She tasted the bitter liquid as it dripped down and hit the tight knot of her stomach, and as the room slipped a shade darker, she felt very afraid.

'Let go,' she told herself. 'You could just let go. You know it would be easy.' There was something she had never told anyone before, because it had been too frightening, and too important. She had been wrestling on the playground in second grade, when Carl Muller locked her in a full-Nelson and wrenched her head backwards, and for a second, she had stepped outside of time. She had stood beside her own life and seen black stars, huge and many-armed, dancing all around her, and for that moment she had known again the overwhelming goodness of God. The stars lasted only a few moments, and when they faded she felt lonelier than she ever had before, but she kept the memory of those stars smouldering inside her, refusing to let them die. Locked inside her head was the image of the sky torn in two and the real world visible beyond this one: tantalising, dazzling and blissfully free. *Someday, I'll let go. I'll let go of myself and fly to that place . . .*

Then she saw Gus in his uniform, moving towards the sofa. He smiled, and the edges of his moustache turned up. He held a chalice of grape Ne-Hi in his hands and Hilda, behind him dressed in a blue and white babushka, carried a tray of home-made bobke fresh from the oven, drenched in butter and glistening with raisins.

'Oh no, not me,' she pleaded. 'You aren't here for me.' They smiled and sat down beside her. Gus lifted Rainey's head and Hilda gave her a sip of the grape Ne-Hi and wiped her lips with her apron, which smelled of lemon zest and candied orange peel. Hilda spoke to her in a foreign tongue that sounded like the language of angels. '*Butchke, vasi-la mir, ekta, ekta, da.*' They cleaned her hands with a wet cloth and placed a clean, cold rag over her burning eyes. Then they tore the bobke into tiny pieces and fed them to her, while they gently stroked her stiff, swollen hands. She felt herself about to cry. She tried to pull back the tears, but the saltiness stung the sores in her throat.

'No no no,' they told her. 'It's all right, you should weep.'

'Go on,' Gus said heartily. 'The more you blubber, the less you'll pee.' And with their permission she did cry, until she felt cool and drained and completely empty.

The next time she awoke she still felt weak, but she knew she had turned the corner now and the worst was over. Her eyes burned mercilessly, as if she had been weeping acid tears that stained and scarred her eyelids, but something cool welled up from deep inside her. It took her a while to realise that Mormor was beside the sofa, telling her stories about Christmas in the Old Country or in Blue River Township, Rainey wasn't sure which one it was. 'For Christmas we got one orange and two pieces of licorice and horshound candy,' Mormor was saying. 'In a good year, the boys each got a nickel and the girls got a doll, which Mama made herself from Papa's old socks stuffed with cotton, a red stitched mouth, yarn for hair, and two button eyes. Of course we never complained, because poor folks got a lot less than that . . .' Her voice trailed away. Rainey wanted to weep again. She *was* high-minded and spoiled, she decided. The things people said about her were true. Her world was lush and opulent, and she wondered if she would ever suffer enough to be worthy of God's love.

She woke slowly from a peaceful dream to the sweet, close odour of maple syrup and lingonberry jam. 'Have I missed Christmas?' she asked weakly.

'Don't be a silly goose,' a high-pitched voice said beside her. 'It's today, and Tante Sonja says I can help you open your presents. I started with the G.I. Joe camper-ranger van. I hope you don't mind, only it was nearly open anyway, and the rest of the wrapping paper just came off by accident.'

Rainey sat forward, rubbed her crusty eyes and looked straight into the winsome, wintry rose face of Ambrose Torsten Dienst, and for the first few moments she didn't know if she was on earth or in heaven, and in the next few moments she realised she didn't care.

SIX

January 1980
Milwaukee, Wisconsin

Ambrose's visit provided the bliss Rainey had expected. She was still weak from the scarlet fever, so play time was limited to an hour or two a day, and even then she rarely wanted to do anything more energetic than spinning the wheels of her matchbox cars or making geometric designs on her Etch-A-Sketch. This lack of excitement suited Ambrose just fine. He loved to talk about himself and Rainey, in her semi-bedridden state, was more than happy to listen to Ambrose's stories of ski trips and cocktail parties, and meeting the president of General Motors. Ambrose sat perched in a chair beside the sofa, next to Rainey's head. He waved his wrist in a world-weary, well-informed manner, but his chin wiggled with excitement as he related his tales.

'At Oma's I have my own car,' he told her. 'I can't drive it on the road, but it's got a real motor. Smoke comes out of the back end and everything! Oma's house smells like medicine but my room smells like gingerbread. In winter we go skiing in Germany and last year we took Oma with us. I've got my own skis, except Mutti only lets me go on the little hill. Maybe when I'm eleven I can try the big hill, she says.'

Rainey lay stretched out on the sofa with her blanket in the crook of her arm and a cold rag draped over her forehead. Even though the fever phase of her illness had passed, Mormor insisted she lay still and keep cool. This disease had a mind of its own, she said, and just when you thought you were well, it could come back with a passion and steal your eyesight away. That thought scared Rainey, so while she slept, Ambrose kept watch, vigilant beside the sofa. He held his little rubber dagger in case the fever crept up on them unnoticed, although he usually fell asleep in the chair beside Rainey, his arms curled under his chin and his head against hers.

Rainey knew that Mormor, in her own way, was paying more attention to her than she ever had before. Mormor no longer let her stay up to watch Johnny Carson or to play chutes and ladders in the dark. She sometimes came into Rainey's room at night to check if she had kicked off all the blankets, and to leave a glass of orange juice by the side of Rainey's bed. For Rainey, life was good; being ill was not without some benefits, and best of all, she had the undivided attention of Ambrose Torsten Dienst.

'Last year, at the resort where we went skiing, the drama club put on a play, and I got to be in it. I was the queen's pageboy. I had to say, "Yes, your majesty", and then bow. They let me wear a little gold crown and the jewels fell off, but they told me it was OK because they weren't real jewels anyway. Whew! I was so glad about that.' He demonstrated how he doffed the crown and bowed, and as his knee touched the floor, a blush rose to his cheeks. His eyes glistened. 'And, Rainey, do you know what happened next? Do you know what? Everybody clapped.'

Rainey smiled. She knew if some of the kids at school met Ambrose, they might think he was a bragger, but she understood that he wasn't. He did talk a lot about his life, his travels, his little steamer trunk that went with him everywhere, but he described it all with so much enthusiasm and surprise, like a bystander plucked from obscurity to play a part in some grand drama.

Mormor came into the living room and opened the curtains, releasing a trail of fine dust that swirled and floated to the floor. 'OK, Ambrose, give Rainey an hour alone now. She needs to take a nap,' Mormor said.

'I prefer to stay here,' Ambrose insisted.

'No, you're going to help me make dinner,' Mormor told him. Dutiful as a royal pageboy, Ambrose lifted himself stiffly from his chubby knees and followed Mormor out of the room, turning to doff his imaginary crown and bow to Rainey as he passed beyond the door.

Rainey settled her shoulders into the sofa, curled her blanket around her neck, and tried not to fall asleep. That invisible blindness might be above her, stirring in the curtains. She listened to the silence and realised, with a sudden sting, that she missed Ambrose. She missed having him beside her; she missed the weight, the warmth and the softness of his head, even though she knew he was no further away than the kitchen. She thought maybe she could hear him talking to Mormor, standing on the little stepstool and helping her make supper. She tried to isolate the rising and falling arc of his voice. 'Someone in the kitchen makes all our meals for us,' she thought she heard him saying. 'Mutti likes peanut butter sandwiches, but cook only makes them when Vati is away.'

Rainey watched the soft snow falling and the world passing gently by outside the front window. She could see the day's shadows bend and lengthen, as the mailman did his rounds, followed by the salt trucks and the crossing guards, and, last of all, the paper boy who with a quick snap of his wrist could land the *Journal* squarely at the foot of the front door. The phases of the day moved like clockwork, building up to the din of early evening, when the wind took over, whipping and tearing through the tops of trees. She thought back to the first day of kindergarten, standing in the circle in the middle of Mrs Schiefle's room, clutching Mormor's hand. She remembered the circle breaking suddenly, the children arching backwards and falling out of alignment, and that sudden feeling of absolute unbending certainty: *I am myself, my self alone, my thoughts belong to me. I am Rainey McBride. I am Rainey, Rainey is me.* She closed her eyes and held her breath. Yes. It was still there. She was still Rainey.

She must have fallen asleep for a while, because the next thing she knew, Ambrose was leaning over her, breathing into her face with the sweet scent of cling peaches. 'Come on, Rainey, it's time to wake up now. We're having supper, and I was helping Tante Sonja stir the rice.' He grabbed her hand and pulled her forward, grunting with the struggle to lift her sleep-heavy limbs. 'Do you know, if we lived in China, we'd have to eat rice every day. I've never been to China but Vati has, and he told me it's true. Vati's the head of the Norregard Corporation, so he can't ever tell a lie.' She stood and waited for the dizzy, drowsy feeling to pass from the pit of her stomach before following him into the kitchen.

'Don't take another step with those dirty hands. Wash up before you eat,' Mormor instructed. She looked tired and hot; her fringe of grey hair was plastered to her forehead, and her hands were red and puckered.

'Where's Grandpa Garth?' Rainey asked.

'He's got a meeting at the Elks Lodge, and then bowling with the boys afterwards,' Mormor told her. 'Pete Johansson's got the flu, so your grandpa's the captain tonight.'

Rainey and Ambrose stood over the sink as Mormor dunked their hands in the steaming hot dishwater and scrubbed their faces with a sour-smelling cloth.

'Yuck. That smells like a dead rat,' Ambrose said, ducking away from Mormor.

'You'll wash up and you'll like it,' Mormor threatened, holding on to his arm. 'I won't have you coming to the table looking like little savages.' An enormous apple pie, bubbled and sugary, balanced on the windowsill, steaming the glass. Beside the pie was a tray of baked brown crusts, shaped like fists and knuckles. Rainey could taste them just by looking; a sweet reward for a dinner endured.

Rainey and Ambrose sat down. 'Rainey, go ahead – you say grace,' Mormor told her, bowing her head.

'*Signe maten, den er god . . .*' Rainey began. She watched as Ambrose mouthed the words with her, pulling faces and crossing his eyes. She kicked him under the table.

'Amen.'

'Amen.'

'Amen.' Mormor placed a bowl of oatmeal each in front of Ambrose and Rainey, to eat before the main meal of rice, sauerkraut and boiled ring bologna.

'I will not eat a bowl of oats,' Ambrose informed Mormor, tapping his spoon on the table. 'That's feed for horses.'

Rainey saw the flash in Mormor's eyes as she lifted her hand, but quickly brought it back down to her hip. 'I'll have you know, young man, your family and mine were all raised on oatmeal – sometimes we didn't even have that! You'll eat it and you'll thank me for it, by God. *Din fordømte snik!*' she yelled at him.

'*Sie sind eine grosse Esel,*' he answered her in German. This time she did slap him, swift and clean across the cheek.

'I won't have you using that language at my table,' Mormor yelled. 'Don't you know what those Krauts did to the Norwegian people?'

Ambrose's face changed colour quickly, from pale to pink to purple, as the outline of Mormor's fingers burned into his cheek. 'I'm going to call my father and tell him that you hit me,' he threatened, rubbing a vigorous fist around his eyes, blinking away the silvery tears.

Mormor snapped the towel against the side of the sink and went to the telephone, lifting it off its hook. 'Go ahead. I don't care. Maybe if they gave you a good crack once in a while, you wouldn't be such a spoiled brat.'

Ambrose looked shocked. His mouth fell open into a silent 'oh'.

'Well? Aren't you going to call?' she asked.

'Yes,' he said, very quietly.

'What are you waiting for? Here, I'll dial the number for you.' She began to dial, tapping her foot on the tile floor impatiently and twisting the phone cord around her long, thin finger. After a pause, she began to speak. 'Hello? Norregard Corporation? I'd like to speak to Holger Dienst, please. This is his wife's aunt, Sonja McBride. Yes, I need to speak to Mr Dienst about a very bad little boy.'

Ambrose was stunned. 'I don't want to talk to my father,' he said, waving his hand at Mormor. 'Tell them I don't want to talk to him right now.'

'OK then,' Mormor said, putting down the phone. 'But don't make me have to call him again.' Rainey reminded herself to explain later to Ambrose about this trick. Rainey had figured it out long ago, but she didn't want Mormor to know that she understood, because then Mormor would devise some new kind of punishment.

When Mormor threatened to phone someone important to report Rainey's bad behaviour, whether it be Santa Claus, the Easter Bunny, Principal Hollenbeck, Miss Sullivan or Pastor Jeff, she was in fact phoning the weather bureau hotline, which played a continuous loop of recorded weather information. Sometimes when Rainey listened carefully, she could hear the tape droning in the space beyond Mormor's ear. *The five pm temperature at General Billy Mitchell Field is twenty-three degrees and sunny, with a thirty per cent chance of snow later on. Winds are north by northeast at seventeen miles per hour, with a wind chill of minus eight . . .*

Rainey watched Ambrose still quivering in his chair, staring down at the dull grey dish of oatmeal. She tried to wink at him to let him know it was all right, but he was distant and inconsolable. She reminded herself also to warn him about the spelling. When Mormor and Grandpa Garth didn't want Rainey to understand their conversations, they would spell certain words; things like d-r-i-n-k, j-a-i-l, l-o-s-t-h-i-s-j-o-b, m-o-n-e-y. All but the most complex words Rainey easily understood, but she never let on, for fear they would find a new way to communicate which might really be beyond her comprehension. She held up her hand, palm facing Ambrose, and pointed to the fold in the middle, the signal for their secret handshake. He drew in a deep breath and smiled bravely.

Ambrose's visit opened Rainey's mind to new heights of imagination. While watching *Sgt Preston of the Yukon* on TV, they huddled beneath a blanket and pretended to be Arctic explorers shivering to death in the frozen north. When it was warm enough to play in the garage, the cars turned into cattle and the bicycles became horses, hers named Fury, his named Pal. The huge bags of road salt served as imitation snow banks, the tins of Mr Pibb were canteens of bison juice, and Rice Krispie bars were their rations from HQ, with occasional Slim Jims and strips of beef jerky thrown in for good measure.

It became clear to Rainey that Ambrose had no interest in any toys, games, sports or anything else which didn't involve dressing up or make-believe. She had always loved to play Cowboys and Indians or Davy Crockett and Daniel Boone, and sometimes, when she could round up enough neighbourhood kids, Land of the Lost Dinosaurs. But to Ambrose, this kind of playing meant something different. To him, it wasn't a game or a few hours of fun so much as a complete transformation, an entrance to a new and more compelling world.

Rainey liked to play make-believe but she never forgot who she was, she never lost her sense of self. She was always Rainey McBride; Rainey McBride in a coonskin cap pretending to be Davy Crockett shooting bears, or Rainey McBride with a toy gun behind the water heater; not really Daniel Boone on a cliff, staking out Indians. But when Ambrose was playing Adam Cartwright in a ten-gallon hat and spurs two sizes too big, his eyes blazed, his wrists were quick and his voice deepened as he told the outlaws they would never, ever steal his horse. To Ambrose, this make-believe horse was utterly and deeply real, a horse of flesh and bone. And when Rainey stood beside him, she was certain she could smell the horse's soft brown fur.

Ambrose cracked his whip and stepped closer. 'You'll never take Pal from me, not while I live and breathe,' he warned, pushing back his hat. 'This horse saved my life one time back in Frisco in '49. He pulled me to safety when I was hanging over the edge of a cliff. We won't ever be parted, as long as I walk this earth.'

'Ummm, I've got to take your horse, Mr Cartwright, sir, because we're bringing medicine to the sick children on the reservation,' Rainey said, struggling to remember the outline of the story as they planned it, and her role in it as the tender-footed Indian.

'No, that isn't right,' Ambrose snapped. 'That part comes later!' he cracked his plastic jump rope-whip dangerously close to her bare toes.

'OK, OK, sorry,' she mumbled. 'I forgot.' She looked up apologetically, but his face was hot with disappointment, white eyebrows arched in unhappiness. 'Start over again,' he said.

She wanted to pinch his arm and say, *'Hey look; it's me, Rainey. This is only a game. Snap out of it and just be Ambrose for a while.'*

'Let's take a break to water our horses,' she suggested instead. 'Maybe Hong Sue will fry us up some grub.'

'OK, but let's wait until we finish the next scene,' he said, wiping his forehead and puffing his cheeks. 'We just have to get through the part where you try to shoot my horse and I step in the path and take the bullet instead. You know how good I am at dying.'

In the middle of playing Ponderosa, just as Rainey was roping a wild steer and preparing to head off the sheriff's men and Ambrose, who had been held up and tied to a chair during a bank robbery, was busy extricating himself from the knots, Uncle Ervald came to visit. He announced his arrival with a sharp rap of his knuckles on the kitchen window. Rainey ran upstairs from the basement to let him in. She opened the heavy wooden door and the solid glass storm door, and a gust of bright cold light pushed Ervald inside. He was covered in ice crystals, from his frozen eyelashes and the tips of his hair, all the way down to the solid white cuffs of his coat, enclosing his wrists. He was surrounded by a smell of delicious freshness which entered the kitchen behind him, trailing like a cloud. 'Hey there, Tiger,' he said, lifting Rainey so high in his arms that her head nearly scraped the ceiling.

'Wheeee,' she called out in abandon. As he lowered her to the ground, Rainey could smell the outside world, which she had been denied for nearly a month now. She touched her tongue to the ice crystals on Ervald's shoulder, thinking they might taste of sugar.

'I was doing some work down on Capitol Drive and I thought I'd stop by,' he said, stamping his feet for warmth as his cheeks and broad forehead took on a healthy red glow. 'Any chance of some kringle up for grabs?'

'I bet we can find you something,' Rainey told him.

Ervald sat at the kitchen table and Mormor gave him a mug of hot, strong coffee and set out what was left of yesterday's blueberry kringle.

'How's Trina holding up?' Ervald asked her.

'Not so good, not so bad,' Mormor admitted, setting down a mug of coffee for herself. 'You know how it is. People talk, they say stupid things when they know someone is in p-r-i-s-o-n.'

'Yeah, sure. But at least she's got Tony at home. He must be helping her out,' Ervald said.

Mormor shook her head, lifting her fingers through her fringe of grey hair. 'Nope. Didn't you hear? Tony got e-x-p-e-l-l-e-d from school. That boy's hell on wheels, if you ask me.'

Ambrose looked confused, sitting with his elbows on the edge of the table, chin buried deep in his chubby hands. Rainey winked at him and he smiled. She loved listening to this little family drama, made more fascinating by its secretness, by the tantalising veil which kept it only slightly out of view.

Ervald dived into the kringle, forking the slices into his eager mouth. All the ice had melted off him but he was still covered with paint flecks which filled the white crescent moons beneath his fingernails, the creases around his eyes and the space beneath his bottom lip.

Rainey was enthralled. How much fun it must be to paint houses, she thought, to climb ladders all day, to carry huge buckets of paint and wear thick, bristly brushes in a loop on your trouser leg. She decided at that moment that she no longer wanted to be a spy, a baseball player or an agent, but a house-painter instead, which must be the most exciting job in the world.

'You well enough to Indian wrestle?' he asked Rainey as he wiped the crumbs from his face with the back of his burly hand, leaving a smudge of paint dust beneath his nose.

'You bet,' she said. Ambrose looked on in amazement as she rolled up her sleeves and squared her elbow on the table. Ervald spat on his palms, rubbed them on his white overalls and straddled the chair, balancing his arm on the table across from her.

They clasped each other by the hand and stared straight into each other's eyes. 'On your marks, get set, go!' Ervald said.

Rainey pushed one way and Ervald pushed the other. At first, both their hands shook, but neither one bent. Ervald strained and struggled until his face was purple and veins bulged out from his temple. The red of his scalp burned through his thicket of corn yellow hair but he would never let Rainey win, and she admired that about him, even as he forced her hand down hard on the tabletop. Her knuckles stung from the impact and she could hear rattling in the floor boards.

'You're not eating your Wheaties,' he said. 'You know what we do with children who don't eat their Wheaties.'

'Nooo,' she squealed, feeling the excitement rise inside her, building like the thrill of a carnival ride. Ervald got up and lifted her over his shoulder and carried her to the living room, opening the front door with one hand and pushing the storm door open with his foot.

'Don't you dare throw that child in the snowbank,' Mormor threatened, following them into the living room. 'You'll make her vomit.' But the door was already open and Ervald swung her back and forth, ready to launch. Rainey clung to his arms, laughing so hard that her stomach hurt. She had forgotten how delicious the cold air tasted and how much more brilliant the snow looked up close. It winked at her like diamonds and shattered glass, and left cartoon-like icicles, massive and gnarled, creeping heavily over the edge of every rooftop.

'*Ervald-stopp nå!* She's still getting over scarlet fever. The doctor will never forgive me if I tell him she's been thrown out the front door and only half dressed.'

'*Unnskyld*, Tante Sonja,' Ervald apologised. Rainey grasped Ervald's shoulders and he transported her across the room, tossing her down on to the sofa from a height that let her bounce several satisfying times. Each bounce took her so deep into the sofa that she could feel the springs coiled inside the cushions, creaking and pinging beneath her weight.

Ambrose hurried to her side. 'You looked scared,' he told her, placing his hand on her stomach as if to hold her in place.

'I wasn't,' she insisted, still reeling. 'You know me. I'm never scared.'

'You looked scared though. I was scared for you,' he confided, speaking to her from behind his hand.

Ervald smacked his palms together and rubbed them on his over-alls. His face was just returning to its normal colour. 'Hey, Dutch boy, how about a wrestle?' Ervald asked, turning to Ambrose.

'I'm not Dutch,' Ambrose sniffed. 'I'm half-Norwegian, a quarter Danish, one-eighth German and one-eighth Pomeranian. My father is descended from the royal house of Schleswig-Holstein.'

'Well, whatever you are, how about you take me on?'

'No, thank you,' Ambrose answered, quivering a little.

Ervald pushed up his rolled sleeves and squared his hips, swaggering towards Ambrose. 'Come on,' he said.

'Nuh-uh,' Ambrose answered, taking two steps back.

Ervald moved closer, with a playful gleam in his eye. 'I promise I won't hurt you,' he said.

'No!' Ambrose cried out. His hands flew up to cover his eyes and he turned away, hunching his shoulders. 'No. Don't.' Rainey could see every breath he took, each one a small tremor jabbing through his back.

'Hey, kid, I didn't mean to scare you,' Ervald said gently. 'Come on, it's just a game.' He took a step closer but then stopped. His hands looked large and awkward as he reached out to offer a pat on the shoulder. The room was quiet, except for the sound of Ambrose's breathing; a choppy, uneven noise, as if something were struggling to escape from his chest.

'Honestly! All that mothering has turned him into a cissy,' Mormor said. 'He needs to spend more time around men. If that niece of mine Sissel had any sense, she'd send him off to military school now, before it's too late.'

'Hey, don't be frightened. Rainey will tell you, I'm a softie at heart,' Ervald said mildly. 'My wrestling's never killed anyone yet. And I've been wrestling Rainey here since she was knee-high to a grasshopper's eye, haven't I?'

'Yeah, Uncle Ervald's OK,' she concurred. Ambrose dropped his hands and looked up. 'Go on,' Rainey encouraged him. 'It will be all right.'

Ambrose rubbed his face and tried to smooth down his clothes. 'I was just being silly,' he said. He tried to laugh but his face was still pale and his lip quivered.

'Here, give it a try,' Rainey said carefully, leading Ambrose to the kitchen table and sitting him down. Ervald sat down across from him, squaring his shoulders. They eyed one another carefully before grasping hands.

'On your marks, get set, go!' Rainey said. The match was over in a few seconds, after Ervald gave in to Ambrose's first meagre attempt to pin him down.

'Well, kid, you're sure a lot stronger than you look,' Ervald told him, clearly relieved the match was over. 'See, now that wasn't so bad.'

Ambrose's fear seemed to have been forgotten and a smile

brightened his face. 'Look, Rainey, I won. I won. That means I'm stronger than you.'

'Don't bet on it,' she said, folding her arms. 'He was just tired because he wrestled me first.'

That night they built a fortress in the basement, made of sticks and blankets and a few old plastic milk crates. Rainey wanted to make a conventional tent, but Ambrose insisted on creating something that could be converted into a stage at a moment's notice, in case he was struck with inspiration in the middle of the night. He was working on his masterpiece, a long play about a group of astronauts. So they compromised, folding up an old card table and resting it on its edge. They covered the table with an old curtain, and above that positioned a blanket, which, when its flaps were pulled back, could stand as a makeshift stage.

They sat inside the tent, enjoying the muffled quiet, the gentle dark. The rest of the world seemed far away. Rainey had found an old camping torch, which she pressed into the palm of her hand.

'Look, there are bones inside there. Just like in the skeletons you see on cartoons,' she told Ambrose. 'We could tell ghost stories and try to scare each other. We could say that whoever gets scared last gets to decide what we play tomorrow.'

'No, telling ghost stories is kid's stuff. Let's use this as a spotlight instead,' he said, grabbing the torch away from her and swinging it in loose circles, trailing patterns of light across the soft flannel ceiling created by the blanket. 'And now, ladies and gentleman, a command performance of "Ambrose the Happy Astronaut", starring that famous star of stage and screen Ambrose Torsten Dienst. Yay. Yay. Yay.' He whispered and rocked, his voice rising and falling in rifts of praise and applause.

'You really want to be an actor, don't you?' she asked him.

She felt the sudden heat of his breathing, intense and desperate. 'More than anything, Rainey. More than anything in the whole wide world. I just gotta do it.'

'Why?'

'Because. You can be totally free if you're on stage.' He grabbed her hand. 'Rainey, there's a place inside your head where you can go and no one can touch you. Go there and you'll find me. I'll wait for you, I promise.'

'I don't get it,' she said. She suddenly felt nervous, afraid of something which didn't have a name.

'If somebody told you not to tell something, what would you do?' he asked quickly, dropping her hand and bracing himself against the back of the tent. He held the torch beneath his chin and clicked it on.

'Depends.'

'On what?' he asked.

'Everything,' she answered. 'It depends on what it is and who told me not to tell.'

'But would it be wrong to tell? If you promised to keep a secret, if you swore on your life, cross your heart, hope to die, stick a needle in your eye, to keep a secret, would you tell it?' he asked urgently. The torch light illuminated his white hair, leaving his eye sockets two black hollows. The shadows of his eyelashes crept over the edges of his cheeks like tiny spiders.

'No. Not if it's that kind of secret.'

'That's what I thought you'd say,' he whispered, clicking out the light.

Playing in the basement one afternoon, they found an old leather jacket, with coloured flags the size of stamps sewn on to the sleeves. There was a stained fleece collar and a long, frayed tear where the waistband had separated from the body of the jacket. As soon as Rainey touched the jacket and the soft skin gave way beneath her fingers, she knew she was in love. The jacket seemed to hold so many secrets, secrets of a past life which Rainey could imagine but not quite enter.

'Let me try it on,' Ambrose said, once he saw her admiring the jacket in the crumpled old box.

'No.'

'Come on,' he pleaded. His eyes were wide, and as round as saucers.

'OK, but if you get it first, then I get to wear it for longer. It's only fair,' she reasoned.

She handed the box to him. He unrolled the sleeves but

stopped just as he was about to try on the jacket. 'No, you wear it,' he said, shaking his head and pushing the box back towards her.

'Why?' she asked, surprised. 'I thought you wanted it so bad.'

'No, you'd be a better fighter pilot than me,' he said, looking worried.

'Why d'you think that?'

He looked down and toed the floor. 'Because you're not afraid of anything.'

'OK, if you insist,' she said happily, grabbing the jacket and clutching it to her chest.

Rainey began a bombing campaign, raining toy soldiers from the top of the staircase on to the unsuspecting PlaySkool farm people beneath, while Ambrose, singing opera, led a group of nuns over the hills and into safety, a scenario somewhat inspired by his love of *The Sound of Music*.

'Look what I found,' Rainey told Mormor as she went upstairs. Mormor looked up absently from her knitting and her episode of *The Young & The Restless*, then glanced down and looked up again and, this time, her eyes sparked and narrowed.

'Where did you find that? Where did you get that from?' Mormor asked.

'It was down—'

'Take it off. Take it off right now,' Mormor said evenly. Streaks of red rose up her neck.

'I'll put it back where—'

'Take it off right now,' she said, in the voice that let Rainey know she had only moments to comply. Quickly, Rainey fought the jacket off her arms and let it slide to the floor. Mormor strode towards her, arm already lifted higher than her shoulder. Rainey ducked and cowered but the expected blow never came. She peeked through her tightly shut eyelids and watched as Mormor scooped up the jacket. Mormor cradled it in her arms, marvelling at its strangeness, its sudden appearance from the past. She pressed the jacket to her face, covering her nose and her mouth, letting the leather absorb her sobs. Rainey could see the tremors in Mormor's shoulders; her slim body bent at the waist.

Rainey stepped closer and reached out to touch Mormor's arm. 'Don't cry, Mormor,' she started to say, but Mormor looked up and slapped Rainey's hand away.

'Leave me alone, child,' she hissed. 'Get out of my sight.'

Rainey fled to the top of the basement stairwell and stopped, crouching on the top step. She wanted to go to her bedroom but she would have to pass Mormor to get there. So instead she waited and listened, sitting quietly with her knees hugged tight to her chest.

'Stupid, stupid boy,' Mormor was saying, in a soft voice that both scolded and soothed. '*Pokkers gutt. Nei, nei, nei.* That child had rocks in his head. Wanted to go off and play with guns. Where did he end up? Dead. Dead.'

Rainey listened to the strangely gentle refrain that reached her ears like smoke, creeping from room to room huddling close to the floor. 'Where did he end up? Dead. Dead in some jungle, killed by some Jap.'

Rainey knew at that moment she wanted nothing so much as she wanted to be punished. She wanted to be slapped hard, maybe even beaten, or thrashed with the yardstick. She wanted Mormor to hit her as hard as she ever had, hard enough for Rainey to feel an ache at the base of her neck, and see little shooting comets at the corners of her eyes. 'Please hit me,' she whispered to herself as she rocked back and forth, 'please hit me, Mormor', aware that the slap held back was the worst pain Mormor had ever inflicted. Rainey knew she had entered a serious place, too complicated for her child-mind. She wanted instead to feel the righteousness of being the wounded party, to cry in her own bedroom, to be free within her own simple world of ebbing and subsiding pains.

Ambrose came to the bottom of the staircase and began to creep up towards Rainey, step by step. 'What happened?' he whispered as he approached the top. He was breathing heavily; she could hear the air creaking and wheezing through his spongy lungs.

Rainey held her fingers to her lips, motioning for him to be quiet. 'Shhh,' she said. She patted the step and he plopped down beside her. They both sat quietly for a long time, listening to the silence. Mormor had stopped speaking, leaving only the rhythmic creaking of the chair in which she rocked slowly back and forth.

'I don't hate Mormor,' Rainey said at last, holding her fingers against her lips. 'Even though I sometimes don't like her. She had my mother, and my mother had me, so that must make it OK. Mormor wants to hate me but she doesn't. Not really, anyway. Even though she slaps me when I'm bad. Sometimes I think it would be better if Mormor did hate me. But she doesn't.' She shook her head. 'I guess we're both being punished.'

'It's OK, Rainey,' Ambrose said, clasping her hand. He pressed his cheek against hers, and she could feel the movement of the muscles in his jaw. 'No one could hate you, no way. Not me. Remember? Blood brothers for life.' She nodded, and then surprised herself by starting to cry. Ambrose cried too, a few loose tears that sprang from the sides of his eyes.

She reached up and touched one hot tear, crushing it beneath her finger. 'Are those real or are you just pretending?' she asked him, holding her breath.

'I don't know. I'm not sure why I'm crying.' He paused and swallowed hard. 'No, Rainey, these are real,' he told her.

'I'm so glad about that,' she said, relaxing. His soft, fat hands fumbled and caught the last tears that bottomed out and dropped from her chin.

Mormor locked herself in the bathroom that evening and Grandpa Garth couldn't coax her out.

'Sonja?' he called softly, rapping on the door. He stood perplexed, fists on his hips, speaking right into the wood. 'Sonja?'

'No,' she said softly, in a voice Rainey barely recognised.

'Sonja, what's wrong?' he asked.

'Leave me alone,' she pleaded. 'Just go away.'

Rainey, Ambrose and Grandpa Garth were left to eat butter and cold gravy sandwiches for supper, since Grandpa Garth couldn't cook. 'What happened to Mormor today?' he asked, piling his plate with slices of white bread. 'Do you have any idea why she's so upset?'

'I dunno,' Rainey said, feeling guilty as she peeled back the edge of her sandwich, and looked glumly at her tall glass of milk.

'Ambrose, do you know?' Grandpa Garth asked.

'Nuh-uhn,' Ambrose whispered in reply, shaking his head. 'I guess something must have happened but I sure don't know what.'

Later that night, after Mormor and Grandpa Garth had gone to bed, Rainey showed Ambrose the canvas duffel bag of Michael's things behind the armoire in the attic. Ambrose was fascinated. He rummaged through the items one by one, squinting at the photos, fondling the dog tags, holding the letters up to the light. 'Wow, pretty amazing,' Ambrose said, clearly impressed. 'He must have been a real hero to get all this.'

'Mmmm, I'm not sure about that,' she told him. 'I think all the soldiers had the same kinds of things. But look at this.' She pressed a letter into his hand.

My sweet little soldier boy, be careful. Vær forsiktig!! Kjæreste, elskede Michael, Jeg elsker deg så, Mamma.

'Wow. Did Tante Sonja write that?'

Rainey nodded.

'I think your uncle must have been really brave. Especially to get killed and all,' Ambrose reasoned.

'Yeah, maybe you're right,' Rainey admitted. 'I think he probably saved somebody else's life. Somebody who had a wife and baby at home.' She lay down on the floor and squinted at one of the photos. 'I bet this guy was Michael's best friend,' she said, pointing to another soldier, kneeling in the dirt beside a bicycle. 'This could be the one whose life he saved.' She was relieved to share these secret things with Ambrose and not have to carry Michael's ghost all alone any more.

'So he was your uncle?' Ambrose asked, lining up the photos side by side, in order of the dates pencilled on the backs. His stubby fingers were busy making all the edges straight.

'Yes. But I never met him.'

'How was he your uncle?'

'He was my mother's brother. He died when she was fifteen,' Rainey explained. 'And that was one year before I was born.'

'Where is your mother now?' he asked.

'I don't know. But I think she's going to come back for me some-day, I really do.' She liked how her voice sounded: clear and proud.

'And your father?' he asked.

'No idea.'

'Wow. I'd die if I didn't have Mutti and Vati to take care of me. You don't have anybody,' Ambrose said solemnly.

Rainey shrugged. 'I don't know. I've got Mormor and Grandpa Garth. I think they must love me. They got me that swing-set in the back yard, and I didn't even ask for it.'

'Yeah,' Ambrose agreed, nodding his head. 'They must love you. They could have just left you at an orphanage, like they do in the movies. Then you might have been raised by Cary Grant or some other famous person. And we wouldn't have met, or ever been blood brothers.' He smiled. 'Except we still might have met in Hollywood some day.' He opened his hand and pointed to the fold of his palm, the signal for their secret handshake. 'I'm glad they decided to keep you,' he said and smiled.

'Yeah. I guess I am too.'

The sign of the handshake lifted Rainey's spirit, but not enough to pull her out of the blood-stained squalor of Michael's lost life. She looked at his photos, his clothes, his damp, dog-eared books; the postcards tattooed with his urgent, desperate words. *Ambrose will always be my blood brother*, Rainey reminded herself, as she longed for something solid to hang on to. *Ambrose will always be my blood brother, but my uncle will always be dead. I'll never get to meet him, until maybe when I'm dead too.*

That night Rainey had a nightmare full of ghosts and blindness, dead uncles and dark birds. She couldn't sleep afterwards for fear of those ghosts sidling up beside her. She was sure she could hear them breathing, wheezing and creaking down the corridors like the old women they once might have been, giving off odours like onions and old clothes, damp leather and moss. Rainey sat straight up in bed, feeling the hairs tingling on her arms. These old ghosts were teasing her, trying to pinch her skin, whisper in her ear, walk their bony fingers up the nape of her goose-pimpled neck. 'Leave me alone,' she said meekly, swatting at them as if they were flies.

But they were so big, square-shouldered and faceless, and she felt so small and timid next to them.

She got up and padded down to Ambrose's room. 'It's only me,' she whispered, opening and closing the door carefully. She climbed into his bed.

He was telling himself a story, and his voice was full and expressive, rising above the darkness and dancing in the thin cool air above the sheets.

'And then Ambrose the Happy Astronaut jumped over the moon, and on earth everybody could see his footprints. "Look," they said. "That's where Ambrose walked. See, he must have been a brave boy to have walked across the moon." He was very, very brave, in the end.' Ambrose took a breath and swallowed. Rainey could hear him rustling candy wrappers between his fingers. 'His mother, her name was Sissel Svensen Dienst and she loved him very much. Once, when Vati was away, she bought him a pair of Buster Brown shoes that cost fifty dollars. Fifty dollars! But on the moon, you don't need money. You also don't need shoes . . .' Rainey elbowed him and he turned on his side, speaking softly into the blankets. His body was hot and solid, like a rock in the centre of the mattress.

He drifted to sleep mid-sentence and Rainey was lulled by the heavy, quiet hush of his breathing. She stayed awake, watching the movement of shadows on the ceiling as occasional cars drifted past the window. Rainey thought about her own mother, and wondered how much longer until she came back. *You've been gone a long time, Mommy*, she warned. *You could come home any day now and it would be OK.* Suddenly Ambrose turned over and stiffened. His eyes were open and he stared at the ceiling.

'Ambrose. Hey, Ambrose,' Rainey said. His mouth dropped open but his eyes remained fixed and expressionless. She put her palm above his mouth and felt nothing, not a stirring of air. She began to shake him violently. 'Ambrose! Ambrose!' she yelled in his ear.

Suddenly he sucked in a deep breath and his body began to quiver, first just a trembling in his limbs but this led to a convulsion that started in his stomach and moved through his body.

'Nooooo,' he moaned. 'No, please don't.' Rainey's hair stood up on the back of her neck. She recognised this sound; it was the same 'no' she had heard when Uncle Ervald first asked Ambrose to arm-wrestle. 'Stop it,' he whimpered, 'just stop it now please.'

'It's me, Ambrose. Wake up,' she said, rubbing his shoulder and hands. His breathing become more regular and he began to hiccup as he inhaled. Tears forced themselves out of the corners of his empty black eyes.

'Ambrose!' she said again. He blinked.

'Ambrose?' she asked softly. He blinked again and looked at her. His body stopped shaking and grew limp, his arms stretched out at his sides.

'Owww,' he whispered. 'Ouch.'

'Ambrose, it's OK. It's only me.'

'Oh,' he said, and suddenly became very quiet. She was sure he was holding his breath.

'Ambrose, what's wrong?' she asked.

'It's nothing,' he answered, twisting his face away from her and pulling the corner of the pillowcase between his teeth.

'Come on, tell me.'

'I can't.'

'Were you having a bad dream?' she asked softly.

'Kind of. Only sometimes it's not a dream.'

'What?'

'Sometimes it's real.'

She felt her heart start to beat quickly. 'Ambrose, I don't know what you mean.'

'It's him. I thought he was here.'

'Who?'

'I can't tell you.'

'Yes you can,' she insisted.

'No I can't. You said you thought it was wrong to tell if you've been promised to keep a secret.'

She felt herself losing patience. If he didn't explain, she would explode. 'I didn't mean from *me*, though. I meant you could tell me about it. Blood brothers, remember?'

'But, Rainey, if I tell you, then I'll die.' The words sliced her like a knife.

'You won't die,' she told him. 'How could you die from telling me something?'

He turned to face the wall. His back was to her as he dug his heels and his fists into the sheets. 'Uncle Billy takes me out to the shed at the summer house and touches me sometimes,' he said.

'What?'

'He touches me. I told him I had a pain and he said he'd take care of it. He does funny things to me. And he said if I told anyone about it, I would die.'

Rainey reached over. She wanted to see his face now. But she was afraid to touch him, afraid she might bruise him, might split his skin. Her own fingers seemed foreign to her, and capable of crime.

'Oh,' she said, unable to find any other words. 'Oh no.' A room inside her head was suddenly empty as the bottom dropped out of her heart.

'Rainey, promise me I won't have to go to the summer house ever again,' he asked her, his voice muffled, his mouth buried deep in the bed. 'Please. You can do it. You're not afraid of anything.' His feet kicked at the sheets as he pulled his knees up into his chest.

'I promise you don't have to go back,' she said.

'Really and truly?'

'Yes.'

'Swear it.'

'Cross my heart and hope to die, stick a needle in my eye,' she said. She crossed her chest quickly, feeling the ragged edges of her fingernails snag on the fabric of her Speed Racer pyjamas. 'I promise you won't ever have to go there again.'

He breathed a sigh of relief. 'Thanks, Rainey. I knew I could count on you. You're my best friend ever.'

When Rainey woke the next morning, Ambrose was gone. She went to look for him but he wasn't watching TV or in the kitchen eating breakfast. As she walked past the kitchen window, she saw him outside on the swing-set, wearing only his nightshirt and a pair of Grandpa Garth's boots. He was swinging so high that the hem of his shirt flapped in the breeze, revealing swaths of his soft, pale legs. She let the doors slam closed as she ran out to him.

'Ambrose, why aren't you wearing a coat?' she asked as she approached him. He stared straight ahead. The beads of sweat on his lip had frozen into a white line like rock salt. His cheeks were red and splotchy, and his chubby legs kicked swift, even strokes that lifted him higher and higher off the ground. Rainey knew that if it were summer the metal frame of the swing-set would be inching back and forth across its small cement base, dangerously close to overturning. But for now the frozen snow held the frame fast to the ground. She reached for the frame to balance herself and then tried to grab Ambrose's arm as he sailed back towards her.

'Rainey,' he called out in a voice that was edgy and wet. 'Look how high I am, look how high! I'm so high no one can stop me. Look, Rainey, just a little bit higher and my feet will hit the moon.'

'Don't, Ambrose, don't,' she warned him. 'Slow down now. Stop. Just stop.'

He took one more long riding arc, his legs carving the air in front and behind him. Then, when he reached the highest point of his flight, he held out his arms and leaped forward, soaring briefly and brightly, before landing face down in the snow.

'Ambrose!' she screamed, running over and kneeling down beside him. She was sure he was dead. She knew from watching *Emergency* that she had to turn him over and check if he was breathing. His body was rigid, the white of his nightshirt billowing over his back and sticking to his skin in damp pink patches. She tugged at his sleeves. He stirred slowly and lifted his face from its oval of snow. His eyes had a dazed expression and a thin line of blood dribbled from his nose.

'Did you see how high I was?' he asked breathlessly, smiling so broadly she could see all his teeth and the small circle of blood on his tongue.

'Come on inside, let me clean you up,' she said, grabbing him by the shoulder. He stood upright and swayed back and forth, trying to find his balance in the oversized boots. 'Come on, get inside before you freeze to death,' she berated him. 'You're lucky you didn't break your neck, you stupid fool.' In that second, she heard the echo of Mormor's voice inside her own, ringing in each syllable, coiled around each word.

She took him into the kitchen and tended him carefully, wiping the blood from his nose. He seemed impervious to the pain, but she flinched each time her fingers brushed his skin. He shivered from the cold but his face was bold and fiery, red from exhilaration. She wrapped a kitchen cloth around his shoulders and pressed a hot towel to the back of his neck.

'What does he look like?' she asked suddenly, surprising herself with the urgency of her question.

'Who?'

'You know who. Him.' She realised she had been thinking about it in the back of her mind since last night, and now she couldn't get Ambrose's words out of her head.

'I don't know.'

'You must know. He's your uncle.'

'He's not really my uncle. I mean he's not a relative. He's Vati's business partner, and I guess his best friend. That's why I have to call him Uncle Billy,' Ambrose explained.

'But what does he look like? Is he tall or short, old or young?'

'I don't know. I keep my eyes closed. Rainey, he's just a plain old man.'

'Hmmmm.' Rainey was quiet as she fashioned a compress for Ambrose's nose. She moved like a nurse, keeping her fingers quick and clinical, not lingering on his face too long. *Why didn't you just run away?* she thought, looking into his huge, excited eyes. *Why?* she thought again, but she didn't dare ask him.

Ambrose didn't tell her anything else about the summer house. But for Rainey the questions remained. Nothing made sense to her now. She longed for him to tell her more, to open the door to his private suffering, which grew in her mind each time she contemplated it. *'What did it feel like – how bad was it?'* she wanted to ask. *Touched. Pain. Did funny things.* Ambrose told her so little, if only he would say more, it would somehow, no matter how horrible, seem less.

She slept in his bedroom quite often after that, waiting for the bad dream to come again. She liked to believe she could make it better for him, that he might wake to see her beside him and not feel so alone. She had promised to take care of him, and now that responsibility weighed heavily on her like a sacred vow.

When the bad dream did happen again, it was the stillness of the terror which surprised Rainey the most. Ambrose never moved until it was too late, until he was captured, and by then it was futile to fight back. The sight of his eyes frightened her, open and fixed with huge black pupils and only a thin rim of blue – no shade, no colour, no light. She wished he would scream, or kick, or cry; do something, do anything, talk. The terror would be fathomable, controllable, even knowable, if only he could put it into words.

'Rainey,' he whispered to her one night after the bad dream had passed and he lay trembling in a pool of sweat, 'sometimes I pretend I'm a turtle, pulling into a shell. I pull in so far that Ambrose disappears and only a pebble is left. A little pebble which can't be hurt and can't feel anything.' He paused. 'Or I pretend that I'm dead. I close my eyes and hold my breath and try to imagine I'm a ghost, rising up and walking away from my body. Someday I *will* be dead, Rainey.'

'No, you won't,' she told him.

'Yes I will.'

'But then I won't have a blood brother any more,' she said.

'You can find another one,' he offered.

'No, I don't think I could,' she replied. 'How about if I help you? If I cure you of your bad dreams?'

'Oh, Rainey, that would be excellent,' he answered.

'OK then, I'll help you.' She rolled over on to her elbow and looked down into his eyes. 'But you have to trust me, no matter what.' He nodded. Something deep behind his face separated and revealed itself, dropping deep as the sea. For a second she could see into the pit of his fear, and she felt herself being dragged down to the depths with him.

'Well, sometimes I get a pain, right here,' he told her, pointing to his stomach. 'Especially when I think of the summer house. Then it really hurts.'

'Show me where it hurts,' she asked. He rolled over and turned on the reading light beside the bed.

'But I'm scared to show you,' he said. His lip was quivering.

'It's OK. You can trust me, you know you can. Ambrose, I can help you if you show me what's wrong. If I'm going to be your secret agent, you'll have to tell me everything.'

'OK,' he said warily. He rolled over and pushed the bedclothes beneath him until he lay flat on top of the sheet. His face was pale as he took a deep breath. The chill of the air gave him goosepimples, rows of tiny pinpricks up and down his arms. He pulled his nightshirt up to his neck and tucked the folds of fabric under his chin. Rainey saw the scar from his hernia operation, raised and puckered, slightly bluish from the cold and standing up from his ribs. He pushed down his underpants to his hips, leaving the white expanse of his stomach exposed.

'I don't see anything,' Rainey said warily.

'It hurts here,' he said, pointing to a spot above his navel, beneath his bottom rib.

Gingerly she poked the spot, letting her finger sink into the soft depth of his flesh. She moved around the area, gently prodding here and there, searching for something unusual. 'I still don't feel anything,' she said.

'But it's there,' he insisted.

'Let me listen to it.' She pressed her ear to his stomach and listened carefully. His skin smelled of oranges and cinnamon, she noted, and was as soft and downy as the bruise on an overripe peach. She could hear liquids gurgling inside him but nothing more than that.

She pressed her ear deeper and his skin pillowed around her head. 'I'm not sure . . .' she began to say, but before she could finish, there was the sound of footsteps and the bedroom door burst open.

Mormor stood in the grey-yellow light from the hallway, too shocked to speak. Like a cartoon character she stood with her hand clutching the doorknob and her jaw gaping, chin nearly to her chest. Rainey might have thought it funny if she hadn't been so scared. 'What the hell,' Mormor stammered, struggling to find words.

Rainey's ear was still on Ambrose's stomach. Like something exploding inside him, she could suddenly hear his heart. She began to tremble.

'What the hell . . .' Mormor whispered. Finally she could move. She dropped the glass of orange juice in her hand. Rainey heard the muffled splash and soft thud as it hit the carpeted floor, rolling under the bed. Mormor grabbed Rainey by the hair and pulled her off the bed, pushing her to the floor. Rainey's knee twisted beneath her and she cried out in pain. In the same movement Mormor lunged at Ambrose, first aiming for his exposed stomach, but instead slapping him hard across the face. Rainey's eyes were full of tears as she saw Ambrose's shocked reaction, saw the slap echo, quivering in his cheeks.

'Ond! Evil! Du er ond! Hva i Guds navn . . . what the hell do you think you're doing?' It sounded like she was spitting. 'Wait until I tell your mother and father, young man. They'll punish you and punish you good. And as for you, Rainey,' she paused, 'no TV for you, for, for, forever!' Mormor arched back and slapped Rainey hard, missing her face but catching her on the ear and the top of her shoulder. The sting of the slap splattered over her like boiling water. A lightness filled her head. 'No TV for you!' Mormor screamed. 'No TV for you,' she chopped out the words, wild with fury, battering Rainey's neck and hands as Rainey raised her arms, trying to cover her face.

Rainey wanted to laugh. Her whole body was full of laughter, laughter bubbled from every part of her. This was so silly, she knew, even as she began to shake with pain and her skin grew hot and tight where she'd been hit. No TV? What did that have to do with anything? *Mormor thinks we were doing something naughty.* Of course it looked like they were doing something naughty, he with his pants down, she with her face pressed to his naked body, but it was nothing. Surely Mormor would understand that, once the shock and anger had passed.

Mormor's arms shook so violently she had to hold them to her chest, but even then Rainey could see something quaking in Mormor's neck, the anger barely contained within her skin. Rainey could feel the dull numbness of where she had been hurt. She knew the real pain hadn't started yet, so she laughed inside herself, and held her mouth firm. Ambrose, still on the bed, had pulled the sheet over his body, up to his chin. He cowered like a wounded kitten, nibbling his swollen lip. Mormor's hair had escaped its loose braid and stood up like pencil squiggles around her head. This too seemed hilarious to Rainey. It was all she could do not to laugh.

Mormor rubbed her hands over her face, swiping across her

forehead and mouth. Her eyes were dark and glassy, but her neck was streaked, fiery red. Her fingers trembled as she touched her chin. 'That's it,' she said, struggling to gain her composure. 'I will not have such disgusting things going on in my house. Tomorrow I'll call your parents and have them take you home,' she said to Ambrose.

'They're on the Continent,' he whispered, clinging to the sheet.

'Damn it! Don't you dare talk back to me! They'll take you home or else you'll be out on the street, fending for yourself. See if I care, I never wanted you here in the first place.'

This time, Rainey did laugh, a small sputtering giggle that escaped unexpectedly from her lips.

'You think I'm kidding, young lady?' Mormor asked, turning on her heels. 'We'll see who's kidding here. How funny is this?' She grabbed Rainey's hand and twisted her arm high behind her back, until Rainey felt a tearing in her shoulder and a coldness down her wrist. The move knocked Rainey off balance, and as she fell, she hit her head on the bedside table. She was dazed for a moment and then she thought she felt sand pouring out of her ear. The side of her eye was wet and sticky as something slithered down her cheek. Ambrose wriggled over to the side of the bed and reached down to touch Rainey's head.

'Don't you dare touch her,' Mormor warned. 'You keep your filthy hands off my granddaughter.' Mormor grabbed Ambrose and pulled him from the bed. He still had the sheet between his legs, clinging to it for comfort. Mormor dragged him to the door. 'I'll deal with you, young man,' she said. 'Rainey, you stay here. Don't you dare leave this room until I tell you to or else I'll slap you again.'

'OK,' Rainey said, nodding, not finding anything funny any more. She balanced on her knees next to the bed. Her head was spinning and she pressed it against the side of the mattress to steady herself. Sand seemed to be pouring out of every part of her. Mormor closed the door and Ambrose was gone.

Rainey listened, expecting to hear the sound of the yardstick on Ambrose's back. But all she heard was Ambrose crying, 'Mutti. Mutti. Mutti, please help me. Please.'

A few minutes passed and there was still no sound from Mormor.

Rainey crept to the door and pressed her ear against it. She heard Ambrose's crying, heard it slowing and quieting as he swallowed and stifled his tears. Maybe Mormor had gone upstairs and left Ambrose alone in the living room. No, Mormor was probably still there, sitting in the darkened hallway, keeping watch outside that room. She too, like Rainey, would be listening to Ambrose's feeble cry, and that would be her punishment. Punishment enough.

'Ambrose the Happy Astronaut was dancing on the moon,' Rainey heard Ambrose say to himself in the other room. 'He *was* a brave boy in the end.' Rainey wrapped her hands around her elbows and lowered herself slowly to the floor. She could see the empty orange juice glass, lost deep beneath the bed.

The next morning, Aunt Ingebjorg drove down from Ojibwa Falls to pick up Ambrose and take him back to spend the rest of his holiday with her. Mormor gave Rainey her breakfast and let her return to her own bedroom, but she was forbidden to have any contact with Ambrose. As she sat on her bed, legs shaking, she tried to remember what Ambrose looked like. She wondered if he looked different today. Was he swollen and bruised or, like her, had his sores disappeared into her skin overnight, with no sign that he had been slapped? She panicked. She couldn't remember his face. She saw a sky full of faces, familiar faces, but no Ambrose anywhere among them. It was as if Mormor's slap had dislodged his image from her brain and her heart. Something inside her felt so mixed-up. Ambrose's words filled her head. *Hurt. Pain. Did funny things*. She stumbled. Where was God now?

Rainey listened to the noises downstairs, doors opening and closing, whispers and silences, the swinging and scratching of cupboards and chairs. At last, she heard footsteps coming towards her room. Maybe Mormor had relented and decided to let her see Ambrose one last time. Rainey braced herself, fingers clasped in prayer, back pressed to the wall. The door opened and Aunt Ingebjorg peeked into Rainey's bedroom.

'Where's my little tiger?' she asked. Rainey wanted so badly to be strong, but at the sight of Ingebjorg's round pink face and tufts of excited white hair, she ran over to her, disappearing into her chest, into the bends of her arms and fleshy elbows.

'Shh, it's OK, honey, it's OK,' Ingebjorg said, stroking Rainey's hair, letting her fingers rest gently on the back of her neck.

'Mormor hates me,' Rainey mumbled into Ingebjorg's porous, absorbing body. 'She hates me now.'

'No she doesn't.' Ingebjorg squeezed Rainey's shoulders. 'Rainey,' she said, 'let me put it to you this way. Your grandmother can be difficult, I know. She means well but she's not really the best person to be raising a child at this time in her life. I'm sure she's over-reacting, but God help the man who tries to tell her so. Kids will be kids. But Sonja doesn't understand that. Whatever happened here between you and your cousin, I'll always know you didn't do anything wrong.'

'Thanks, Ingebjorg,' Rainey said, rubbing her face with the back of her hand.

'I know that's not much comfort, is it?' Ingebjorg said sadly, stroking Rainey's hair.

Suddenly Rainey had had her fill of comfort. 'No. But it's enough,' she answered, turning away from Ingebjorg. 'It's enough.' She stood up straight, drew in her breath and held something in her throat which was as bitter as burned chocolate and tougher than tears. 'It's OK. I'm going to be fine now,' she said. 'I'm sure I'll be fine.'

Rainey stayed in her bedroom while Ambrose and Ingebjorg prepared to leave. She heard voices swearing and complaining as the grown-ups stumbled down the staircase with Ambrose's luggage. Rainey heard the door close and she ran to the window and watched them pack up the car. Rainey pressed her palms against the glass, in hopes that Ambrose would catch the secret handshake signal. But Ambrose, looking the wrong way, didn't see.

After a few minutes the car started, and Rainey watched Ingebjorg's yellow station wagon shift and slide down the gravel driveway and on to Sandstone Avenue, carrying Ambrose and his little steamer trunk far out of her life, away from her forever.

Rainey went to the basement and dismantled their fortress-stage. She found a secret store of damp and sticky candy wrappers, the camping torch and Ambrose's little rubber dagger. When she moved the milk crates and the blankets fell down around her shoulders, she could see the dim silhouette of Ambrose's face and hear the echo of his urgent voice. *'Yay. Yay,'* the voice whispered. *'More than anything, Rainey. More than anything. And do you know what happened after that? Do you know what? Everybody clapped.'*

The spring of 1980 was a dull wet season of despair and disappointment. Scatterings of grey snow continued to fall, falling duller and greyer than usual. Although the snow built up along the roads and in the empty car parks, it was too thin, too watery to build igloos or make snow angels. Freezing rains followed on the days it didn't snow, pelting down like bullets that stung the eyes and iced the sidewalks, making everything dangerous, and deceptively slippery.

In the middle of this freezing season, Rainey began to practise a kind of silence. She closed her face, diverted her gaze and let herself go numb around the mouth. She didn't look especially sad or troubled, and there was nothing in this new look that would provoke attention. It was an expression of solidness, of passivity and firm endurance. When she looked in the mirror she liked what looked back at her – a pale, serious face dusted with freckles, short red hair, cut like a boy's, and blue eyes that betrayed no sorrow, revealed no secrets. Only in the middle of the night did she sometimes wake up and think about Ambrose.

'What's wrong with you?' Mormor asked Rainey one night at supper.

'Nothing,' Rainey answered.

'If nothing's wrong with you, why are you stewing so much? Are you constipated?' Mormor said.

Rainey poked at the slice of pork roast marooned in a pool of gravy on her plate. 'No,' she answered.

'Well then, snap out of it. You look just like your cousin Lina when you do that. And you know what happened to her. She married a Catholic and had seven children.' Mormor swallowed noisily. 'That's what she gets for moving to Toledo. If only she would have stayed in school, she could have been a dental hygienist.'

'Maybe Rainey's got a boyfriend,' Grandpa Garth said with a twinkle in his eye, balancing his overloaded fork inches from his mouth. 'She's about that age when boys and girls start to mix. I remember when I was in the third grade, I had a crush on Melissa

Gunnarson and I used to follow her home from school every day. Had to go two and a half miles out of my way, but it was worth it.'

'Oh God forbid,' Mormor said, shaking her head. 'Don't encourage her, Pa. There's plenty of time for that. With our luck she'll grow up to be a little hussy, just like her mother.'

There were two brief, bright spots in the otherwise listless early April. A new kid from Des Moines named Jerry Lipke came to Miss Sullivan's class and was given the desk next to Rainey. This new boy was tall and well spoken, and had a reputation for worldly sophistication – not only were his parents divorced, which was rare enough, but he lived in a nice house with his father and his younger brother. Rainey was positively thrilled by the thought of a family with no girls in it at all, and she made several desperate attempts to become Jerry's friend. By the time she gave, not lent but gave, Jerry one of her Matchbox cars, she was well on the way to achieving her goal, but then Jerry turned out to be a disappointment. He had a hairy brown wart on his wrist which he sometimes scratched with his tooth, and when Miss Sullivan turned her back to the class, Jerry would pick his nose and hide the findings inside his desk.

The other brief brightness of the season was the air rifle given to Rainey by Uncle Ervald. It wasn't new – it had belonged to her cousin Ted who was now attending welding school in Illinois. The rifle was battered and slightly bent, but at least it worked, giving an excellent high-pitched whistle when fired.

'Thank you. Oh thank you, Uncle Ervald. Thank you so so much!' she told him, caressing it gently, rocking the rifle in her arms.

Mormor stood with her arms folded on her chest, pursing her lips in disapproval. 'And just what kind of gift is that for a little girl?' she asked.

Ervald shrugged. 'It's what she wanted. Let's face it, she'll never be one for Barbie dolls and playing house. If you ask me, she'll bring down her first buck before she's twelve,' he said.

'Well don't come crying to me when you shoot your eye out,' Mormor told Rainey. 'You'll get no sympathy from me.'

'I won't,' Rainey promised.

'And if you do shoot your eye out, you'll be driving yourself to the hospital,' Mormor warned.

'OK. I will,' Rainey said, deciding that sounded like a fair deal.

The first few nights Rainey slept with the rifle beside her in bed. It was still too cold to go outside and shoot. But she got bored with only being able to look at the rifle, to load and unload it, rubbing its barrel with an old oilskin rag. So she sneaked outside in the middle of a Tuesday afternoon and arranged five soup tins on the back alley fence and shot them out, one two three four five, so fast and accurate that the second shot was still ringing when the fifth shot hit its mark. Her thumb stung and the gun's recoil echoed through her body, making her elbows and knees wobble.

She hiked the gun to her shoulder and shot again, aiming for the middle of the fence. Bulls-eye! The board rattled and split in two pieces, leaving the top half to flap loosely in the wind. 'Oh yes she scores!' she bellowed. But the sound of her voice crackling in the cold air made her suddenly feel empty. She wanted Ambrose to practise his shooting too. *'There's a place inside your head,'* he had told her, *'where you can go and no one can touch you. Go there and you'll find me. I'll wait for you, I promise.'*

Where was he now? she wondered. On the Continent, most likely. She could imagine him skiing down a hill and drinking cocoa in a little Swiss chalet. His mother, slim and blond and pretty, would drink cocktails and wear enormous jewellery, stroking the head of her darling Ambrose perched at her feet in front of a fireplace. She would tell everyone how talented her son was, and he, blushing only a little, wearing a red knit cap and a boiled wool jacket, would recite some poetry, and glow at the subsequent applause. But she could not see him that way without having to imagine him hours later, wearing the white nightshirt that left his knees cold and naked. He was waking in a quiet, pine-scented room to a minute of paralysed stillness and then a thousand fingers poking him, teasing his skin. She could hear his silent scream, unheard by his parents, who would be drunk and dull and heavy in their bedroom.

Ambrose's broken nights began to haunt her broken nights; she could not close her eyes without seeing what she saw then – his body stiff and breathless, his eyes startled, his mouth a tiny, gaping black hole. The terror would pass over him like a ghost, she knew that. The boy would snap out of it, shake violently for a while and then begin to breathe again, burrowing his fists and his face deep into the sheets. That part of it was fleeting, true, but it was the horror of the knowing that would never pass away completely.

Rainey went to show Gus her air rifle, knowing he would be impressed by its size and weight. She hadn't seen Gus much since the operation to remove his gall bladder, which he kept in a glass jar on a shelf at the back of the depot, among the containers of nails and screws. Just after Gus's operation, his wife Hilda had had a stroke. The older Polish women all worked together to help take care of her. One brought food every evening, one did all the housework, another came to change the sheets and wash the clothes. 'The Good Lord never sends us more than we can handle,' Gus told Rainey when she asked how Hilda was doing. He looked tired when he said it. 'He never gives us more than we can bear.'

Rainey hoisted the rifle over her shoulder and walked to the bus depot. The gun was cold and heavy, and seemed to wear right through her gloves and leave a dent in the bone of her shoulder. Still, she liked how it looked when she saw her reflection in the passing windows. She paused, pretending to aim and shoot a wandering Injun who crouched, nearly invisible, in the hill of cardboard boxes behind the Stop-N-Go. 'None of Mark Kowalski's gang would dare mess with me now,' she said. 'And if by chance I passed a deer, a twelve-point buck, I could, like Uncle Ervald said, shoot it right between the eyes.'

When she got to the depot and opened the door, the front room was dark and smelled heavily of diesel fuel and axle grease. She could hear the tinny radio in the back room as she stepped over the piles of oily rags, stained newspapers, and empty Ne-Hi bottles, glued to the floor in bright purple rings. Gus had always kept the depot clean as a whistle, but lately it had become cramped and messy.

'Gus?' she called out. 'Gus?' The door to the back room was locked but the frosted glass windowpane felt warm when she touched it. She pressed her face against the glass and could just make out the oblong of glowing orange light where the space heater sat on the floor. She squinted and could barely distinguish the shadowy outlines of the crates, shelves and file cabinets that filled the little room. She thought there was someone inside but she wasn't sure. Then her eye caught a movement in the shadows. 'Gus?' she called out. 'Gus, you in there?' She pressed closer. Her chest touched the window and she felt her heart tapping against the glass. Yes, there *was* someone inside. She was sure about that now. Gus was sitting in the chair, listening to the radio. He was hunched forward with his face in his hands, his elbows dug into his knees. She rapped against the square of glass once more but the figure didn't move, and this time she knew for certain there would be no answer.

On the last day of classes before the Easter break, Miss Sullivan asked Rainey to stay behind while the rest of the students were excused for the lunch hour. Everyone seemed so excited, not just because they were three hours away from two weeks of holiday, but because there was a luncheon special on the menu today – hot ham and cabbage sandwiches with cream corn, blue Kool-Aid to drink and angelfood cake with pink frosting for dessert.

Rainey watched as Mark Kowalski, who was now more popular and more powerful than ever, thanks to his having shockingly begun to grow a moustache at the age of ten, led his troops out of the door and down the corridor. Suzi McRaney and Theresa O'Hanlon, in their pigtails and matching plaid skirts, were last out the door. They turned back to giggle at Rainey and point at her over their shoulders. Rainey gazed at the sea of empty desks surrounding her and felt shipwrecked, a lone boat in a dark pool of loneliness. She had never sat in the classroom when it was empty – that was only for naughty kids who didn't do their homework or threw spit balls or cheated in social studies by writing the names of the state capitols on their hands. Rainey was surprised how big the classroom seemed now, as the dying voices ricocheted down the hallway, moving out of earshot.

Miss Sullivan sat down carefully and beckoned Rainey to the small chair beside her desk. Miss Sullivan looked worried and serious, the way she looked when she taught about the sins of former President Nixon or life without bread under Communism. Her eyebrows were knit together and her lips pursed in such a way that a small dimple delved into her chin. She built up a little stack of papers in the centre of her desk and folded her hands on top of the pile. 'Rainey,' she began carefully, 'is something wrong?'

'No,' Rainey answered.

'Maybe something at home?'

'Nuh-uhn.'

Miss Sullivan touched the knotted sweater sleeves tied around her neck and allowed herself a brief, tight smile. 'I see. How can I say this? I know you don't live with your mom and dad—' she said slowly.

'My grandparents take good care of me,' Rainey said, not waiting for her to finish the sentence.

'Oh I'm sure they do,' Miss Sullivan answered. A light blush touched the tops of her cheeks. 'No, I just mean that . . . well maybe it's harder to talk to them. Because they're a little bit older than most parents, of course. Not that they aren't wonderful parental figures, I'm sure they are. But maybe you find it more difficult to talk to them. Could that be the case?'

'No, it isn't.'

'I see. All right. Well, then maybe there's something else. Are you having problems with any of your friends here at school? Has somebody been giving you a hard time? Because if anyone is bothering you, you know you can talk to me about it. Right?'

Rainey nodded her head emphatically, and was surprised to find tears conspiring behind her eyes. *Please don't be nice to me, Miss Sullivan,'* she wanted to say. *'That's the one thing that's bound to make me cry.'*

'Rainey, you are the brightest student in this class. One of the brightest students I've ever had,' Miss Sullivan said. 'Your grades are excellent, as always. Your report on magnets and their many uses around the house was wonderful, and your theme paper on famous Scandinavian-Americans was impressive, to say the least. I never knew that Walter Cronkite was part Norwegian! I've got no complaints about any of the work you've done.' She paused, looking down at the stack of papers. 'This may sound strange, but it seems to me that you don't smile as much as you used to. That may not be much of a criticism, and it's not something I would write on your report card, but I miss that sunny little girl who used to sit in the front row; the girl who always had two answers for every one question. When will that old Rainey come back and join our class?'

Rainey shrugged her shoulders and looked down at the floor. 'I don't know,' she said softly. 'I guess maybe never.'

– PART II –

1 9 8 3

SEVEN

Summer 1983
Milwaukee, Wisconsin

On 20 October, 1982, the Milwaukee Brewers lost the World
Series four games to three to the Cardinals in St Louis, and Rainey
learned what it meant to suffer from a broken heart. As a 3–1 lead
in the sixth inning dissolved into a 6–3 loss, Rainey started to cry.
'They can't lose,' she pleaded to the TV set. 'They can't. I've waited
my whole life for this moment.'

Grandpa Garth too seemed stunned. 'Vuckovich didn't have his
best stuff,' he said, fingering his glass of brandy. 'Plain and simple.
Our boys choked.'

Mormor remained unmoved. *'Åh, tåpelig . . . Dumt.* Foolish. It's
only a game. Why cry about that? There're people starving to
death in this world, you don't cry for them.'

'They didn't lose the World Series in the final game,' Rainey
replied.

'Uff da! – you're too big to cry about baseball,' Mormor insisted.

That night before she went to bed, Rainey took a good long,
hard look at herself in the mirror. *I'm almost thirteen,* she thought,
squinting her eyes and scrunching up her nose. *Maybe Mormor's right.*

*

At about the same time as the Brewers lost the World Series, Rainey began to notice the boys at school. She began to pay a lot of attention to them, especially to their slim hips, their sullen mouths, their mysterious eyes. She sometimes dreamed about kissing Bobby Pflueger, the tall, sexily dishevelled boy who sat behind her in geometry class, and she developed a secret crush on Daniel J. Travanti, the actor who played Captain Furillo on *Hill Street Blues*. *He has such great dimples,* she would think and then feel a little tickle inside her. She would imagine meeting him in Hollywood, having a drink at a bar, then going for a swim in a moonlit pool.

But the more Rainey noticed boys, the more she noticed that they didn't notice her. She wasn't sure what was wrong but she sometimes worried about what Mrs Tor Christiansen had told her years ago in Luther League – '*Boys don't like girls who think they know everything.*' She also remembered Mormor telling her once, after Rainey had brought home yet another perfect report card, 'It's a good thing you're so smart. It makes up for not being pretty. Even if you don't find a husband, you'll always be able to support yourself.'

Rainey was proud, maybe too proud, she thought, about her academic achievements. In June 1983 she graduated first in her class of 217 students at Coolidge Middle School and won the Governor's Prize for public speaking. At the state finals in Wausau she did a recitation of The Gettysburg Address and a dramatic interpretation of excerpts from 'The Song of Hiawatha'. People were said to get chills when she recited the section:

> '. . . Showed the Death-Dance of the spirits,
> Warriors with their plumes and war-clubs,
> Flaring far away to northward,
> In the frosty nights of Winter;
> Showed the broad white road in heaven,
> Pathway of the ghosts, the shadows,
> Running straight across the heavens,
> Crowded with the ghosts, the shadows.'

But what good would success be if she were doomed to a life of solitude? She would gaze out her bedroom window sometimes and watch the cars on the overpass in the distance, the overpass which would someday serve as her bright concrete bridge to freedom. 'I don't think I belong here,' she'd tell herself. 'There are great things waiting for me somewhere in the world. I'm not like other people; I'm not going to get married, have kids and live in Milwaukee for the rest of my life.' She had already chosen her future career – she was going to be a foreign correspondent for NBC News. She could see herself standing in a war zone, with bombs exploding all around her and gunfire crackling over her head. *This is Rainey McBride, from three miles behind enemy lines, reporting for NBC News. Tom Brokaw, back to you in the studio.'* And she could imagine Mormor and Grandpa Garth, very old and feeble, sitting at home watching that very newscast, hunched beneath their crocheted blankets, shaking their heads soberly and saying, 'It's amazing. Our granddaughter's done so good.'

Rainey's best friend now was probably Pastor Jeff. As much as she was interested in boys, and interested in Daniel J. Travanti, she came to realise that Pastor Jeff was the true love of her life, and had been since the age of seven. 'I'm not going to get married,' she told herself. 'But if I did, I would marry him.' She practised writing his name and hers on all her notebooks and in the margins of her history text. *'Rainey McBride Wayland. Rainey Wayland. Reverend and Mrs Jeffrey Wayland. This is Rainey McBride Wayland, reporting for NBC News, from Leningrad.'*

Rainey once confided in Pastor Jeff her desire to have a boyfriend, and her fears that it might not happen, that no one would ever fall in love with her. 'Rainey, God made you in His image, and you are beautiful to Him,' Pastor Jeff explained patiently. 'Our outward appearances are like the clothes we wear – they don't mean anything. It's inner beauty that counts. What it means to be beautiful is to have a beautiful heart, a beautiful soul.' Rainey said nothing, but took this as proof that she was indeed, as she suspected, terribly ugly.

The summer of 1983 was a milestone for Mormor and Grandpa Garth as they celebrated their fortieth wedding anniversary. Grandpa Garth and Rainey spent hours huddled together in the basement, supposedly working on a jigsaw puzzle of The Statue

Of Liberty but in fact conspiring over the Sears Catalogue and debating about what to give Mormor as a surprise gift.

Grandpa Garth wanted to buy her a new living-room set, complete with a leatherette ottoman, a three-section wooden magazine rack and a Lay-Z Boy recliner. 'Look, Rainey, it converts into four completely different positions,' he said enthusiastically. 'It's so cosy you could just about use it as a bed.'

'It looks nice,' Rainey offered, trying to be diplomatic. She suspected this gift was intended more for himself than for Mormor.

'Or we could go for the Zenith twenty-seven-inch television set, complete with video cassette recorder and cable hook-up,' he said, pointing to the glossy photo of a giant, blank television screen with three fascinated children perched in front of it.

'Mormor doesn't watch much TV,' Rainey reminded him, 'except *The Young & The Restless*, and you don't need cable hook-up for that.' Rainey took the hefty catalogue and flipped to the back section. 'I think you should get her a diamond ring,' she said, pointing to a simple yet elegant diamond solitaire ring, which she had circled in red marker pen. 'That would be *so* romantic.' Rainey knew this was a good suggestion because it was what she would want Pastor Jeff to give her on their future fortieth anniversary.

'No, I don't think so,' Grandpa Garth said, shaking his head. 'It's a beautiful ring but I'm not sure she'd like that. Your grandmother doesn't approve of jewellery. She says it's vanity to wear gaudy things just to call attention to yourself.' That was true; Rainey had never seen Mormor wear any jewellery at all, other than the small silver confirmation cross around her neck. It was hard to imagine a diamond ring, slipped over her ragged fingernails and coming to rest just below her chapped red knuckles.

'How about a trip to Hawaii?' Rainey suggested.

Grandpa Garth stroked his moustache. 'Hey, that's an idea.' His grey eyes brightened. 'We've never taken a trip. But we don't have passports – how can I get her a passport without her knowing?'

'You don't need a passport to go to Hawaii,' Rainey explained. 'It's one of the fifty states, it's just like going to Iowa or Minnesota.'

'Only hopefully it'll be a little bit warmer! I'll have to check into that,' Grandpa Garth said.

'When did you first fall in love with Mormor?' Rainey asked

as she leaned forward, balancing her elbows on the flimsy card table.

'The twelfth of February, 1942. At two o'clock in the afternoon,' he answered.

'You remember the exact time?' she asked in amazement.

'Of course.' He sat back in his chair and folded his hands over his stomach, the way he usually did when he intended to tell a story. 'I remember that moment she walked into the malt shop, the old Joe O'Brien's, on Wacker Avenue in Chicago. She was so beautiful, I thought my heart stopped. She was so tall, with such broad shoulders and hair so long and golden she could sit on the ends of it! I knew right away that she wasn't like other girls. She was more like a woman; she knew who she was, where she was from, and where she was going. I asked her out on a date that very evening,' he said proudly.

'And?' Rainey asked excitedly.

He raised his bushy white eyebrows and winked. 'Well of course she turned me down. She looked at me as if I wasn't worth the time of day.'

'So what happened after that?'

Grandpa Garth smiled slyly. 'One of her friends gave me the address of the girls' rooming house where she was living. I was, shall we say, persistent. Eventually I wore down her resolve. I think she went out with me just so I would stop pestering her!'

'So then you fell in love and got married?'

'No!' He laughed. 'If only it had been that easy. I remember the first time she took me back to meet her family in Owauskeum. I thought Uncle Jens and Sonja's brothers were going to run me out of town. Her father had only recently died, so Uncle Jens and the brothers were very protective. They hated me. Well, I wasn't Norwegian, so I couldn't ever measure up.' He shook his head. 'I never understood their sort – why did they come to America if they wanted only to be with other Norwegians? Why not stay in Norway, I wonder.' He sighed. 'Mormor's mother hated me as well. To her dying day she was convinced I was a closet Catholic and had plans to convert the entire family once she was out of the way. Whenever Mor Svensen came to visit us in Milwaukee, she would peek behind the bookcase and the picture frames to check if we had pictures of the Pope hidden anywhere.' He chuckled to himself. 'But it was worth it – I was in love with your grandmother and wild horses couldn't have driven me away.'

'I wish I had known Mormor then,' Rainey told him, trying hard to imagine the beautiful young woman Mormor had been all those years ago.

He nodded. 'Yeah. I wish you had too. She was so . . .' His voice trailed away as he searched for the words. 'Well, all she ever wanted was to be a mother and have lots of children. We wanted five or six, but it didn't work out that way. So we were happy with the two we had. Then when we lost our boy, and your mama ran away. . . . Well, things like that take a lot out of a woman. You couldn't expect a person not to change after all that. You just couldn't . . . But those days are past now,' he said with quiet finality. He picked up the catalogue and began to leaf through it quickly. 'Hawaii. Well. I think I'm starting to like this idea.'

'Grandpa Garth, do you still love Mormor?' Rainey whispered earnestly.

'Yes,' he answered. 'I do.'

Grandpa Garth began to collect brochures and leaflets from travel agents, and after some intense negotiations, he and Rainey decided on a six-week cruise from Long Beach, California to Honolulu and back again, including stops on the islands of Oahu, Hawaii and Maui. Two weeks before the anniversary, Grandpa Garth let Rainey slip the tickets under Mormor's plate while Rainey set the table for supper. Mormor was halfway through her beef stroganoff before she noticed the envelope. 'What's this?' she asked, sliding it out.

'It's your anniversary present, Sonja,' Grandpa Garth said, his eyes twinkling as he winked at Rainey. 'Break out the suntan lotion, because we're on our way from Milwaukee to Maui.'

'Oh – really? Oh dear.' Mormor opened the envelope and shook her head slowly, pressing her hand against her forehead. 'We don't need to go on any cruises,' she said, holding the tickets limply. 'Especially this summer, when the roof needs fixing.'

'But I thought we should do something nice,' Grandpa Garth said, his face deflating slowly, like an old balloon. 'This year is special and all.'

'Well, if we could afford it, maybe. But we can't.'

'Fine. If you want me to take the tickets back, I'll take them back,' he said quietly, stabbing his fork into a sliced mushroom.

'No, I didn't mean that,' she said quickly. 'I just mean we should use the money for something more practical, that's all.'

'Of course, I don't think I can get a refund this late; it'll just be money down the drain. But if you want me to take the tickets back, I'll take them back,' he said edgily.

Rainey looked down at her plate and realised, with a twinge, that she had lost her appetite.

'No. Now that you've bought the tickets, we might as well go,' Mormor reasoned. 'But what about Rainey? We can't just leave her here, you know. She's too young to be on her own that long.'

He sighed. 'We've already talked to Ingebjorg about it and she said Rainey could stay with her. She's got Torgrim's kids, and Margaret and Tom's kids all staying with her this summer. She said she'd love to have Rainey there too,' Grandpa Garth said glumly, his eyes sinking down towards his moustache.

'Oh. I see. Looks like you've thought of everything then,' Mormor said evenly. 'It's a nice idea. Thanks.' Her voice dropped. 'Nothing left to do but pack, I guess. Well, just think, Hawaii. That's so far away.' She slid the tickets back under her plate, picked up her knife and fork and began to eat.

'I could—' Grandpa Garth started to say.

'No, don't,' Mormor cut him off. 'I said it's OK.'

The kitchen was so quiet, with only the noise of knives and forks and everyone trying not to swallow too loudly. Rainey searched for a glimmer of pleasure in Mormor's impassive face but found none, just a firm line of resolution etched around her mouth. By this time in Mormor's life, all the years of frowning had left their mark, so that even when Mormor smiled, which wasn't often, the ghost of her disapproval was still visible, written into her skin.

After two weeks of silence and sulking, Mormor and Grandpa Garth were ready for Hawaii. Mormor agreed to let Rainey help her pack. Rainey was as excited as if she were going herself. She jumped on and off the bed, tipped the top of the suitcase to judge its weight, played with the latch and key.

'It's going to be soooo romantic,' Rainey swooned. 'All those palm trees and sandy beaches, midnight strolls watching the sun set.'

'We'll probably get seasick,' Mormor said, folding her flannel nightgown into a neat little square and smoothing out the wrinkles with her hands. 'I better bring some Dramamine. And some Kaopectate, you never know what kind of food they'll be serving. We'll probably get poisoned swordfish or some fool thing. I'll bring a box of Ritz crackers, in case there's nothing to eat. Write that on my list.'

Dutifully Rainey scribbled 'Ritz crackers' at the bottom of a list that included 'Woolite', 'Q-tips', 'Ear plugs', 'Emery boards', 'Metamucil', 'Dramamine' and 'Kaopectate'.

Mormor pulled out a drawer from her bureau and dumped the contents over the bed. She began rummaging through the tangled pairs of tan nylon stockings. 'These are all too old. They've got runs in them, I should have thrown them out,' she said, holding up the reinforced toes. 'Add that to the list and I'll see if I have time to get another pair before we go.'

'Mormor, don't you want to go to Hawaii?' Rainey asked her carefully. 'Don't you like your anniversary present?'

'Of course I want to go,' Mormor said. 'This just isn't a good time, that's all. I'll miss my bridge tournament at the end of the month. Ethel will never forgive me.'

'I bet she will. I bet she wishes she was going to Hawaii,' Rainey said. 'I bet everyone around here wishes they could go to Hawaii. I don't know anyone who's ever gone farther than Florida, and that isn't half as far away as Hawaii.'

'I know,' Mormor said with a sigh. 'It's a nice idea, but we're too old for Hawaii. Hawaii's for young people; people on their honeymoons, people who can wear bikinis. One look at Pa and me and they'll be laughing behind our backs.'

'I don't think they'll be laughing,' Rainey said. 'They'll think it's romantic, being married so many years and all. Someday I'm going to go to Hawaii. Maybe there'll be a volcano eruption there someday and I'll have to cover it for NBC News. "This is Rainey McBride, reporting from what used to be WaiHeLeLeLe."' She held her pencil up to her mouth and pretended it was a microphone. She looked at herself in the mirror and imagined streams of molten lava flowing down the hill behind her. 'Where did you go for your honeymoon?' she asked suddenly.

Mormor pressed closed the suitcase and sat down beside it on the bed, leaning against it for support. 'Your grandfather and I never had a honeymoon. We were supposed to drive to the Great Smoky Mountains, but then Garth got called up into service. It was 1943, remember. We had to sell our old truck in order to have enough money to buy him a decent suitcase and a new pair of shoes. And I used the little money that was left over to go stay with my sister in Red Wing. Poor Else, she was pregnant with Kjell at the time, and Lars had just been killed.' Mormor pushed her fringe of hair off her forehead and took a deep breath. 'Rainey, your generation will never know what it was like in those days, how hard times were. I had been married for only five days and I had to say good-bye to my husband, right there at the bus stop, thinking I might never see him again. But did I cry? No. Not so much as a single, solitary tear. Nope, if I never saw my husband again, I didn't want him to remember me blubbering like a fool. I wanted him to remember me being strong. I wanted him to be proud of the woman he had married.' Her voice trailed away, but then came back again with renewed vigour. 'As I was walking from the bus station to Else's house along that old dirt road, so many houses I passed on the way had a red star in the window. That meant the family had lost somebody in the war. I remember thinking, "I'll have one of those soon. Garth will get himself killed and that will be my window next, one with a red star."' Mormor looked out at the wisps of smoke from the pork sausage factory, wafting up and curling towards the clouds. In the distance, an airplane caught the reflection of the sun and glinted down, dazzling the freeway interchange signs. 'Poor Else. All those years without a husband, raising those children all alone. She never had forty years of marriage, she never had a trip to Hawaii.' Mormor sighed and rested her chin in the palm of her hand. 'It just isn't right. We shouldn't be going, especially when the roof needs re-doing before winter. There're so many better ways we could have spent the money.'

Rainey, in her mind, was re-writing this story, casting herself as Mormor and Pastor Jeff as Grandpa Garth. She saw how romantic and tragic the scene could be. She was clenching a damp handkerchief in her hand and Jeff's reddish-brown eyes were moist with tears as their lips quivered and touched. Her fingers stroked the stubble where he had just shaved off his auburn beard.

'Darling, remember me forever,' she was saying, dabbing her dewy, black mascara-ed eyes.

'Yes,' he said manfully. 'We'll always have that night we spent at the Young Lutheran Leadership Camp in Schwano.'

Rainey felt a brief rain shower of religious guilt, but she succeeded in nudging it away. 'It's not like he's married,' she told herself. 'And he's allowed to get married if he wanted to, so he wouldn't be breaking a vow or anything. It's OK to have impure thoughts about Pastor Jeff,' she decided, as the Greyhound bus in her mind's eye arched and pulled away, carrying her brave lover, thin-armed and misty-eyed, to his almost certain death.

The next day Rainey waved good-bye to Mormor and Grandpa Garth as they set off for their vacation, still arguing about whether they were expected to bring their own beach towels or not, and whether Ethel Gurtz could be trusted to water the plants and take in the mail. As their copper-coloured Oldsmobile pulled out of the driveway, Rainey was struck by the sight of their white hair and their grim faces perched above their flowery shirts. *I might never see them again*, she thought wildly. She often felt this way when they left, even when they ventured no further than a Sons of Norway dinner at the Elks Lodge, and returned home by ten pm. Even under such safe circumstances, she felt a vague anxiety, a worry that they might get robbed, fall over, get hurt.

This growing tenderness surprised her, especially when she remembered back to the times when she really wished they would die. As a child she had wanted so badly to be a real orphan so she could be raised by Aunt Ingebjorg, or anyone else who was kind and indulgent. Perhaps this rough-edged worry was her punishment for all those years of despairing, for the days of wanting them dead.

Rainey didn't have many friends, and she felt so different from the other kids at school. They, at age thirteen, were beginning to break away from their parents, to turn against their values and beliefs. They challenged their authority, defied them openly, smoked cigarettes out on the street and didn't come home until eleven pm. For Rainey it was so different. Sometimes she woke up in the middle of the night for no reason other than to remember how old Mormor and Grandpa Garth were. As she counted out the numbers in her head, she considered the Bible verse about a man's years being three score and ten. 'Three score and ten, three score and ten,' she would say to herself, and then she would start to panic, wondering if she should go to their room and check if they were all right. They were sixty-three years old and she could not believe they would still be alive in ten years' time. 'They'll definitely be dead before then,' she would tell herself, 'definitely by then,' as if by practising the words, by saying them over and over, she could somehow keep that fear at bay.

Rainey's friends' parents were forty or forty-three at the oldest, and some were still younger than thirty-five. They had lifetimes to spend together, to redefine their relationships, to give them grand-children; but for Rainey, that kind of life seemed an unbelievable luxury.

Mormor and Garth were her only true family, for she had given up on ever seeing her mother again. She no longer remembered her in her nightly prayers and she no longer expected Mary Jane to one day stroll through the front door with her husband Carlos and Rainey's six dark-haired half-siblings, all in hand. Rainey did still occasionally read the newspaper article about her birth, but now when she opened that envelope, she felt only a bruising uncer-tainty. She no longer recognised the face of her mother; lost was the memory of her touch, the smell of peaches and incense, and the sound of her heart.

Mormor and Grandpa Garth would be gone someday, and then she would be completely alone. As much as she resented them at times, and she did sometimes dislike them with a pointed bitterness, she desperately didn't want them to be old, didn't want them to get older; she didn't want them to die. She felt such sadness for their thinning bones and their fading colour, their daily defeats and resignations. Mormor's hands were too stiff for her to knit any more and Grandpa Garth no longer dared climb a ladder. It was painful for Rainey to watch them leave for Hawaii, seeing those two solid grey faces, driving away from her and into dangers unknown. She could picture them on their cruise ship, huddled small and cold against the salty waves, shamed by the vast and glorious sunset.

Rainey had the house all to herself until that evening, when Uncle Ervald would arrive to spend the night and then drive Rainey to Aunt Ingebjorg's in Ojibwa Falls the next morning. As Rainey stood in the living room and listened to the silence of the empty house, she knew for certain that she was getting older. This was the truth about growing up – there was no one home to yell at her and yet she felt no desire to jump on the beds, or to peek in Mormor's drawers, or to leave the refrigerator door open while she made herself a Braunschweiger and mayonnaise sandwich.

Rainey went to church that evening, hoping to run into Pastor Jeff one more time before she left for Ojibwa Falls. Rainey had been confirmed at Easter, having stood before the entire congregation of Our Savior King of Kings and declared the articles of her faith. After three years of catechism classes and three years of confirmation classes, she was now a full-fledged member of the church, which gave her such heady powers as voting on the church council, helping to decide both where to hold the summer picnic and whether to send part of the weekly collection to the Lutheran nuns of Namibia. True to her word, Mormor told Rainey she had kept the promise of her baptism and now never needed to go to church again. Displaying a rare sense of humour, Mormor even baked Rainey a cake with a little picture of a steepled church in frosting, and beneath it, wrote in pink letters 'Rainey is free'.

But even after her confirmation, Rainey continued to go to church most Sundays, which surprised everyone, especially Mrs Tor Christiansen, who said, 'There's hope for that girl yet. Enough good works and she may someday redeem the circumstances of her birth.'

Rainey became the assistant leader of the third grade's Luther League class. Mostly this was for the sake of being close to Pastor Jeff, but if she were honest, she would have to admit there was more to it than that. She needed to feel the cool quiet of the narthex, a sanctuary where in silence and in solitude she remembered she was Rainey, and with that, she remembered she was loved.

Rainey sat in the front pew of Our Savior King of Kings, not exactly praying but hoping in a way that felt like prayer, waiting for Pastor Jeff to come and catch her being penitent. She thought if he saw her there, he might be moved by her devotion and her piety, which in turn might inspire him to love. She folded her hands and placed them in her lap. *'Please learn to love me, Pastor Jeff. Try to love me, just a little bit.'* Halfway through her prayers, her mind began to wander. *How do I look in this position? Do I have a double chin when I tilt my face down? Will Pastor Jeff notice the golden rim of my eyelashes; and with my shoulders straight and upright, can he see the movement of my chest? Do I mean anything to him?* she wondered. *Does he think of me as a young woman, or am I still the little girl who made the Wittenberg church door and wrote the report about Martin Luther? What would he look like without his shirt?* she thought suddenly, then cursed herself for thinking of Martin Luther and Pastor Jeff's naked chest both in the same breath.

Rainey looked around and tried to think more serious things. True to the spirit of Lutheranism, there were no paintings of Jesus, no crucifixes, no graven images anywhere in this building. The emphasis was on simplicity, on plainness to the point of being barren. The walls were whitewashed plankboard, the carpet a deep beige shag and the cross at the altar two unadorned beams of bleached maple wood. Here there was no place for flowers, stained glass or figures in marble and stone.

Rainey took the first hymnal out of the wooden shelf in front of her. No one ever sat in the front pew because it was considered bad manners to be on such close terms with God; the assumption being that anyone who sat there thought themselves more holy than everyone else. Rainey turned to the back pages, where between verses of 'A Mighty Fortress Is Our God' she had placed a postcard. On the postcard was a photograph of a sculpture, cool and white, of a woman holding a dying saint. Rainey could see every tiny detail of the sculpture – the break in the ankle, the rivulets of blood, the bent nails, the shrivelled ribs. She thought the picture was so sad and beautiful. She was overwhelmed by how much she wanted to touch that statue, wanted her fingers to trace those sinews and feel the curves of muscle and bone. She believed the figure would come to life beneath her steady, loving, patient touch. She knew this was sacrilege; it was sacrilege to think these things and that made the thoughts more exciting. It was wrong to love God that way. But that was the way that felt right, that was the way she was ready to love, to love someone or something. She was embarrassed, and yet somehow liberated, by her desire to touch and hold and comfort, to feel blood move beneath her hand.

She heard the whistles from the ball-bearing factory next door wheeze and peal, signalling four thirty, the end of the first shift. Church softball was scheduled for five, so that meant there would be no sign of Pastor Jeff until after she got back from Ojibwa Falls. 'Forgive me, God, for wanting more,' she whispered, hot breath over bent knuckles. 'For wanting more than this.'

Uncle Ervald arrived that evening, pulling up to the house in his battered old pick-up truck. Rainey opened the kitchen door to find him stamping his feet on the welcome mat. He looked tired, grey-faced and overweight. 'Hiya, Rainey,' he said. As he smiled, his blue eyes disappeared into the slits of his puffy eyelids. Ervald was known to be drinking a lot these days. He was turning into a b-o-o-z-e-r, according to Mormor, who still preferred to spell unpleasant things. Ervald had been drinking heavily ever since his wife ran off to Acapulco with her dentist, and his son Ted, who was married and had four children, never came to visit.

'Come on in,' she told him.

'Whew, the skeeters are really biting tonight,' he said. 'I must have gotten ten bites between the truck and the front door.'

She wasn't sure how to answer him. 'Hmmmm,' she responded.

He came inside and went to the sink. Rainey noticed how his fingers shook as he washed and dried his hands. She brought out the tuna casserole that Mormor had left in the Tupperware containers in the fridge and they sat down to eat. Rainey knew that Ervald felt awkward around her now; he was afraid to look her in the eye, and he was nervous about noticing her breasts. He tried not to stand too close to her or to say anything that might have an undiscovered double meaning.

'The food OK?' she asked at last, when she couldn't tolerate the silence a moment longer.

'Sure. Fine,' he answered.

'More coffee?'

A weak smile. 'Please.'

'The weather's not bad,' she said as she filled the coffee cup.

'No. It's not. Not for this time of year, anyway.'

'Uh-huh,' she answered.

She remembered the first time Uncle Ervald came to visit and didn't call her Tiger, didn't pick her up and lift her towards the sky. She had stood with her arms wide open and waiting as he brushed past her, pretending not to see.

'I'm going out to get my pipe,' he told her when the meal was finished, motioning over his shoulder towards the door. 'I must have forgot it when I came in before.'

'OK,' she said, clearing away the dishes. 'Take your time.' She knew he was going out to take a swig of bourbon from the bottle he kept in his pick-up truck, hidden beneath the passenger seat.

The five-hour drive to Ojibwa Falls was a slow, hot, tedious affair, but once they arrived, Rainey's first sight of Aunt Ingebjorg put everything right. Ingebjorg never changed from year to year; she was still big and bold and had bright pink cheeks. She seemed to be everywhere at once – her hands were busy kneading bread dough, swatting at flies and scolding her old collie dog, and then a second later, she was wrapping Rainey in those same arms and kissing her on the chin. 'Oh, you look so pretty! And so tall! What a young lady you're becoming,' she said. 'Come tell me,' she added conspiratorially, 'have you begun your monthlies yet?'

After she unpacked her suitcase, Rainey walked down to the lakefront, following the narrow gravel path that ran through the blueberry patch behind Ingebjorg's house. Once she reached the lake, something about the open water both excited and frightened her, making her feel dizzy. The sun glinted off the water in knife points out past the end of the pier. She could hear many voices, mostly children, and see a flotilla of bobbing heads and glistening bodies; inner tubes and old tyres, babies in yellow water wings. The sand was damp and sticky and she couldn't find her footing, nearly stepping on a broken bottle by mistake. She cupped her hand to her eyebrow and made her way towards the cool shade of the boathouse.

When she pulled open the warped wooden door, she was hit by the odour of seaweed and old fish. The interior of the boathouse appeared pitch black after the blazing yellow-white of the sun on the sand and it was several seconds before she could see a thing. But even before her eyesight came back, she could smell burning tobacco and was aware of the presence of someone else inside the boathouse. She could feel quiet breathing and sense a shadow huddled in the darkness, a pair of thin arms curled around black-clad legs. 'Who's there?' she asked. 'Show me who you are.'

Her eyes found the lightness of the hair first, set apart from the darkness. The blond head rolled upwards and the eyes looked straight through her, the huge black pupils set in circles of iridescent blue.

'Ambrose,' she said. His name slipped out of her mouth. Her hand flew to her lips and covered them, held them closed as if she had just said something horrible or had just remembered something terrible she had done.

'Yes,' he said. He was smoking a cigarette. Not a candy cigarette; this time, it was real.

'What are you doing here?' she blurted out.

'I could ask you the same question,' he said nonchalantly, stubbing out his cigarette on the damp wooden bench and then taking another cigarette from the packet at his side.

'Mormor and Grandpa Garth went to Hawaii for their anniversary. They sent me here to stay with Aunt Ingebjorg,' she told him.

'I guess they didn't know I was going to be here too,' he said, curling his lip.

'Oh, Ambrose, that was so long ago,' she answered. 'I barely remember what happened back then.' She realised she was lying. 'Why are you here?'

He shrugged. 'Same reason as you, more or less. My grandmother died last month. Mutti and Vati are in Germany for the summer. I've got to go back to school in August, so they thought it would be better for me to stay here for a few weeks instead of travelling back with them.'

'Oh,' she said. 'I'm sorry to hear—'

'It's too crowded in here now. I need some air,' he said suddenly, cutting her off. He stood up and moved towards the door.

Instinctively, she followed him out of the boathouse. He stood on the narrow concrete stoop and stretched, bracing his hands on his hips and pulling up his neck and chest.

Ambrose had changed a lot in three years. He wasn't very tall, in fact he was probably two inches shorter than Rainey, but he was much thinner than he had been the last time she saw him. Through his T-shirt she could see the curve of his shoulders and the bones of his spine. He had a very European face – his cheeks were high and arched, and his chin angled to a point. His chest was small and narrow and he had a slight paunch, just a roll of skin poking over the waistband of his jeans, which was the only remaining sign of his childhood chubbiness. His legs ended in narrow, bare feet that turned inwards, slipping one under the other like guilty prisoners.

So many grown-up phrases passed through her head but none of them seemed appropriate. 'How's life?' she asked, then immediately thought how stupid that sounded.

He pursed his lips and gave her a studied shrug. 'All right. Could be better, I guess. Could be worse.'

'What have you been doing?'

He made a show of slowly lighting his cigarette and taking a slow, deep drag off it. 'You mean for the past half-hour or the past four years?'

She frowned. 'Whatever.'

'I go to Essex Academy now. It's a prep school out East.'

'I know what Essex is. I'm not that stupid.'

'Maybe not. But you're still a hick,' he said, squinting into the sunlight. He dropped his cigarette and strode away. She watched the tossed cigarette smoulder, stuck in a crevice between two smooth rocks.

Rainey avoided Ambrose for her first few days in Ojibwa Falls. There were other kids her age in town, not to mention half a dozen of her cousins, all staying at Ingebjorg's house. There was a bicycle path that cut through the forest, past the haunted spot where a small plane had once crashed, and even twenty years later all the trees were black on one side and the highest branches were still torn and stunted. Even so, Rainey spent most of her time indoors. She found a store of old scrapbooks and magazines that Ingebjorg had collected as a teenager. Ingebjorg had had crushes on both Dean Martin and Joe DiMaggio, and the flimsy construction paper scrapbooks were filled with photos cut from magazines and hand-written captions covered with hearts and stars that said things like 'Here's Dean with Frank Sinatra at the Hollywood premiere of *From Here To Eternity*', 'Here's Joe in his uniform; here he is hitting a home run.'

Even though Rainey didn't talk to Ambrose, she kept a close watch on him from a distance. He spent most of his time sulking or brooding, but something about his mood was too studied, too self-conscious to be completely believable. He may have been able to fool everyone else, but Rainey knew he was still an actor, he was still planning to be a star of stage and screen. He wore dark sun-glasses and faded blue jeans and always a T-shirt, either black, off-white or occasionally pale yellow. He constantly carried a book, under his arm or peeking out of the back pocket of his jeans. Rainey squinted and could just make out the titles of these books – Kahlil Gibran, *The Prophet*, Rilke's *The Notebooks of Malte Laurids Brigge*, *The Penguin Guide to Metaphysical Poets* or Konstantin Stanislavski's *An Actor Prepares*.

Ambrose liked to sit on the end of the pier dangling his feet over the edge or to slouch against the overturned rowboats, round-shouldered and absorbed in his reading. He tried to look completely engrossed in his book but Rainey noticed that once in a while his face emerged to search for an audience among the seagulls, the stray dogs and the children fishing off the end of the pier.

Rainey could not keep her eyes off him. She wanted to study him from every angle, in every possible light. Her own red hair had dulled and darkened with time, how had his fair hair stayed so magnificently white? At the dinner table she made note of every-thing about him – how his hair curled behind his ears and at the nape of his neck; the delicate thinness of his nose, which flared at the tip; his full upper lip that tensed and arched as he talked, on the rare occasion when he had something public to say. His arms were thin and tanned and covered with fine white hairs, and his hands were very expressive; smooth and animated when he used them to illustrate his words. The brightness of his childhood was still on him, Rainey decided, but more and more she thought the centre had burned out. It was as if the eerie beauty of his skin hid a gaping black hole inside him. He became for her a kind of malevolent angel, a stained altar boy. She began to worry that the change in Ambrose was her fault. He was her blood brother; she had sworn her soul to taking care of him, and had promised that he would never have to go back to the summer house. Maybe he hadn't forgiven her for breaking that vow.

After a week of shadowing Ambrose, ducking in and out behind him and marking his every step, Rainey realised she was angry with him. Each time she saw him, she began to seethe. At first she assumed her anger came from his rebuff of her, but gradually she came to see that that wasn't the reason at all. She was angry because Ambrose reminded her of her own loneliness. When she looked back at her life, that month she had spent with Ambrose over Christmas was the happiest time she had ever known. That wonderful month stood out in high relief from the rest of her life; a brief, bright dazzling light that cast in darkness all that had gone before it, and all that had come after.

It was a tradition in the town of Ojibwa Falls to celebrate their Founder's Day over the last weekend in June. They always celebrated by staging an entertainment evening at the old Sammi's Supper Club at the end of Lake Ojibwa's biggest pier. Sammi's Supper Club, although in a state of disrepair, had been famous once, and it still bore the marks of its lost grandeur. During Prohibition, Al Capone and his cronies had often stopped there on their way from Chicago to Wisconsin's Great North Woods, where illicit liquor stills were easily hidden in the deep evergreen forests, where miles of nothing separated the quiet little towns. The front door of Sammi's had two bullet holes in its wooden frame, which were said to have been the result of an FBI raid on some bootleggers and their subsequent gunfire. But other people said the bullet holes were, in fact, the result of a shotgun wedding that had gone awry.

Sammi's Supper Club was no longer used as a restaurant but now served as Ojibwa Falls' unofficial town hall. It had a swampy, musty odour that never went away, and was filled with the most elaborate insect life, from the delicate daddy long-legs suspended high in every corner to the swarms of huge bluebottle flies nested in the men's room. The kitchen was full of battered old dishes donated by the townsfolk. Nothing matched; all the pans were scorched and dented, and all the table linen mended in the middle. There was a huge refrigerator from the 1940s which still worked, stocked with Coke and Ne-Hi, and a pantry always full of eggs and home-made butter. On the back porch stood a vending machine that dispensed dried bait but the machine only accepted old quarters, from before 1971.

The town of Ojibwa Falls had not been blessed with an enormous amount of raw theatrical talent, Rainey realised as the entertainment evening began and she, Aunt Ingebjorg and the cousins sat through several displays of fat girls tap dancing, Tabitha and Tania Thorstad playing 'Lady of Spain' on their duelling violins, and the sixth-grade 4-H Club interpreting selected scenes from *The King And I*. The high point of the first half of the programme was Mrs Irene Rasmussen's rousing rendition of 'God Bless America'. The widowed Mrs Rasmussen was the vice-principal at Ojibwa Falls Middle School. She was a tall, rotund woman, with a cap of thick brown hair and a gruff, no-nonsense manner. No one had ever heard her sing before, and there was a note of trepidation in the air as she sturdily strode towards the stage, sheet music in hand. She took her place, nodded to the pianist, and began to sing in a lusty, forceful voice that rang all the way up to the rafters:

'God bless America, land that I love. Stand beside her, and guide her, through the night with the light from above.
From the mountains, to the prairie, to the ocean, white with foam, God bless America, my home sweet home. God bless America, my home sweet home.'

As she finished singing, the applause was thunderous but Mrs Rasmussen didn't smile, didn't loosen her shoulders, she simply nodded to the pianist, grabbed the sheet music, and walked off-stage.

There was a twenty-minute interval, during which refreshments were served; Pabst Blue Ribbon and Hamm's Beer for the grown-ups, orange Kool-Aid for the kids, and to eat, cream puffs and cherry kringle from Ole Olsen's Bakery, along with some surplus cheese and curds from the factory in Doeville. During the interval, Aunt Ingebjorg coaxed Rainey to get up and perform some of her speeches during the second half. 'Go on,' Ingebjorg said. 'Do something. You won a prize for it, after all.'

'But I can't,' Rainey told her, cringing with embarrassment.

'Oh, go on. Do us all proud. There's never been any talent in this family before, you know. Well I guess your cousin Lina was a pretty good baton twirler but I don't know if that counts. Shame she married that man in Toledo. She could have been a dental hygienist.'

'But I don't want to do anything,' Rainey protested, folding her arms and remaining determinedly in her seat.

'Åh, jaså, you're too modest, that's your problem.' Ingebjorg fanned her red face and leaned over to Mrs Wilson. 'She's at that age, you know. Doesn't want to be embarrassed in front of the fellas. You know how it is; oh the tyranny! – when you've got to look good for the boys.'

The second half was just underway, in fact a lot of people hadn't yet returned to their seats, when the Master of Ceremonies, Clem Henderson, strode on to the stage. 'Ladies and Gentlemen, for our first performance of the second half, I'd like to introduce a young man who comes to us all the way from New York City, New York. His name is Ambrose Torsten Dienst and he's Ingebjorg Svensen's nephew. He's going to entertain us with the dramatic reading of a poem.' Clem bowed and the audience clapped politely.

The curtain shuddered and Ambrose stepped out into the spotlight. Rainey felt a flutter of nerves in her throat – the people of Ojibwa Falls tended not to be too impressed by poetry and she worried how Ambrose would be received. She watched him blinking softly in the light, his eyelids flickering like an insect, but his body was still and smooth, as firm and graceful as a dancer's. 'This is a poem by a man called George Herbert,' Ambrose said. 'I bet none of you has ever heard of him.' He cleared his throat and began to recite:

'I struck the board and cried, no more, I will abroad.
What? Shall I ever sigh and pine?
My lines and life are free; free as the road,
loose as the wind, as large as store.
Shall I be still in suit? Have I no harvest but a thorn,
to let me blood and not restore what I have lost with
    cordial fruit?. . .'

Some of the men in the back rows began to mutter. Rainey
could feel the derision sifting through the room. She was sure she
heard someone say the word 'cissy'.

Ambrose blinked; his voice caught, but he continued:

'. . . Not so my heart; but there is fruit.
And thou hast hands.
Away; take heed: I will abroad.
Call in thy deaths head there: tie up thy fears.'

A rift of laughter sifted upwards from the last row of folding
chairs. Ambrose faltered for a moment, then continued bravely to
the end:

'. . . But as I raved and grew more fierce and wild at every
    word,
Me thought I heard one calling, "Child!" And I replied,
    "My Lord."'

As Ambrose finished and bowed his head, there was one
moment of horrible, unbearable silence; a white silence which
seemed to swallow everything in the room, everything but the
soft sound of water lapping like a dog's tongue underneath the
floorboards of the Supper Club. Suddenly, Rainey jumped to her
feet and began to clap loudly. 'Wonderful,' she called out. 'That
was great!' A few other people slowly stood up and began to clap,
not as loudly or as enthusiastically as Rainey but it was enough to
stifle the silence. 'Bravo!' Rainey called out, and the clapping
began to grow louder, until it reached a respectable level, at least
equal to the response given to most of the performances in the

first half of the evening. Ambrose lifted his head, fixing his gaze far at the back of the Supper Club, and nodded. Then he bowed severely, and strode off the stage. He disappeared into the crowd of townspeople, swallowed up in a sea of anonymity. Rainey searched and searched but could not pick out the sight of his white-blond head.

Several more performances followed, mostly singing and occasional tap-dancing but Rainey hardly paid attention. She worried about Ambrose and she wondered where he had gone. She knew again what she had known at the age of eight – he had the power to enter her imagination in a way no one else could. She was moved by his performance – despite the crowd's uncertain reaction, he had spoken beautifully. Something of the rhythm of that poem echoed in her ear, reverberating slowly, with each beat lighter than the one before it.

The final performance of the night came from old Farfar Jens, who was led to the stage by either arm. He sat down and began to play his fiddle, his face tensed and scowling, and his sightless eyes gleaming like polished mother-of-pearl. He played all the old favourites – 'Yankee Doodle Dandy', 'Oh My Darling Clementine', 'On Wisconsin' and 'Greensleeves' – before settling into some old Norwegian folk tunes, sad mountain music that filled the room with melancholic longing. All the old people loved it, even the ones who weren't Norwegian. Rainey imagined that everyone was homesick for somewhere, and even those who weren't homesick secretly wished to have another country, dear and distant, that they could miss.

The audience hung on Farfar Jens' every note, trying to stretch the sound through their necks, to feel it move through their bodies and play itself out in their hands. The men swivelled their bottles of Hamm's and Pabst Blue Ribbon, looking out the big window and across the water towards Saginaukee, seemingly fascinated by the pattern of waves. Rainey realised that everyone was weeping in their secret heart but no one dared be the first to break that silence. No one wanted to be responsible for unleashing that torrent of grief inside themselves, blocked and dammed and reduced, over the years, to a trickle. Rainey felt her own private sorrow, keening and rocking, growing stronger inside her. *Ambrose.* He was here; so close at hand, and yet for all his distance, he might have been a thousand miles away.

The night of the fish boil two weeks later, on 12 July, was a magical midsummer's night, cool and breezy, with a much-needed respite from the oppressive humidity. Local men dressed up as Vikings in helmets and decorated breastplates and ran along the lakeshore to the incessant rhythm of distant drumming, a gathering war cry of violence. They grabbed their women by the waists and hiked them skyward, then jumped into wooden boats carved to look like dragons' heads and raced each other to the far side of the lake and back. Their shouts and wallops echoed in the cry of the owls and the call of the loons.

All up and down the lakeshore at quarter-mile intervals were huge black-bottomed kettles, hung from enormous chains over blazing fires. The pots were boiling over, hissing and spitting with slices of perch and grouper, skinned potatoes, onions and salt. The rows of picnic tables, set slightly apart and covered with blue and white cloths, were spread with breads, black rye and caraway seed, coleslaw and pickled herring, flatbread crackers and little pots of mustard and horseradish. The children were excited and noisy, running up to the fires to roast their marshmallows on cleanly whittled sticks. Out over the water, Roman candles exploded and the Viking ships sliced quietly through the water, parting the glassy surface with strokes so smooth they didn't make a wave, as the looming dragon faces bore down towards the shore.

Rainey walked along the sheltered ridge where the trees ended and the rough, rocky sand began. She could see the kettles blazing and feel the heat against her face even from here, but her back to the forest was cold and took the brunt of the evening chill. She liked to inhabit this distance, where she was close enough to see everything that happened but was separate from it, set apart. The sound of children laughing was not as loud as the crackling of the twigs and branches beneath her feet or the hooting of the owls hidden high in the trees above her head. Her own thoughts were prominent, filling the centre of her mind.

Maybe I should have done something for the talent show, she thought to herself. *Maybe Aunt Ingebjorg was right. After all, I'll have to get used to talking in front of a lot of people when I'm working for NBC News, especially if I want to be an anchorwoman someday.* She cleared her throat. 'Good evening, everyone, this is Rainey McBride. The White House announced today . . .' No. Something about her voice didn't sound right. She began to recite The Gettysburg Address, using the tones which had captured the Governor's Prize in Wausau. '"Four score and seven years ago, our fathers brought forth on this continent, a new nation, conceived in liberty . . ."'

Ambrose stepped out of the woods in front of her, blocking her way. She stopped suddenly. 'Shit,' she said. 'You scared me.' She started to walk away from him.

'Sorry.' He fell into step beside her, keeping pace as her stride quickened. 'Look, I want to talk to you about something,' he said. 'It's about the entertainment evening two weeks ago.'

'Yeah, what about it?' she asked, stopping in her tracks and turning to face him. Her back felt the heat of the fires behind her but over his shoulder she saw nothing but the forest's blank darkness.

'I didn't need you to stand up for me like that.' His face looked bewildered and cruel.

'What do you mean?' she asked, genuinely not understanding him.

'I mean, you didn't have to stand up and clap like that. You didn't have to protect me from the audience. If they didn't like it, it wouldn't have been any big deal.'

'Is that what you think – that I was protecting you from the audience?' she asked. She heard the drumming grow louder as the first boats began to reach the shore. The smoke of the fires grew denser and the air was filled with the smell of molten metal as the black-bottomed kettles began to singe and burn. Rainey felt the gritty dust of ashes, sticking to her tongue and to the corners of her eyes.

'Yeah. That's exactly what you were doing.'

She started to laugh. 'Did it ever occur to you that maybe I just thought you were good?'

His face went blank. 'Did you?' he asked.

'Yeah. I did. You were brilliant, I thought. Of course, if you didn't think you deserved applause, that's your opinion. But I thought it was really, really good.'

'Oh,' he said, very quietly. He looked down and began to tease the dirt with his foot. 'I guess I never thought of it like that.'

'So how do you like being at Essex?' she asked.

He seemed surprised by her question. 'It's OK. I like it.'

'Do you have a lot of friends there?'

'No. Not really. A few of the guys are nice but I'm mostly on my own.' He paused, still smoothing the ground with his shoe. 'How's your school?' he asked.

'Good,' she told him, plunging her hands into her pockets and rocking back on her heels. 'I like it a lot.'

'Friends?'

'Not too many,' she admitted.

'I guess we belong together,' he said.

'Yeah, we must. No one else likes us much.' She started to smile, but then a chill breeze caught her cheeks and a shiver darted up her spine.

'Are you cold?' he asked, moving closer.

'Yeah. A little,' she replied, crossing her arms over her chest.

'Here.' He slipped off his leather jacket and draped it around her shoulders. As his hand brushed the back of her neck, her skin began to prickle and burn. She leaned close to his chin and smelled expensive aftershave. She searched, but found no sign of razor stubble.

'Let's walk,' she suggested, striding towards the lake. He kept pace, staying close to her side.

'Why didn't you ever write to me?' he asked suddenly, in an urgent voice that crept over her shoulder and into her ear.

'I didn't have your address.' She walked more quickly, trying to stay a few steps ahead of him, trying to avoid the soft seduction of his voice.

'You could have gotten the address from Aunt Ingebjorg.'

'Yeah, I guess I could have,' Rainey answered. 'But then again, you could have written to me.'

'I couldn't. I was too scared,' he admitted. He stopped and knelt down, grabbing a handful of dirt and squeezing it tightly in his fist.

'Scared of what?' She turned on her heels to face him.

'Scared that you hated me, after that night.' He tossed down the dirt and watched it scatter, pinging and rolling over tiny stones.

'What do you mean?' she asked, pulling his jacket tightly around her arms.

'When Tante Sonja came in and found us like that . . . I thought maybe you blamed me,' he said softly.

'No. Never,' she said. 'We weren't doing anything wrong.'

'I know. But I thought Tante Sonja hit you again or something.' He paused, shaking his head. 'I couldn't stand to think of her hurting you that way.'

Rainey sighed, inhaling the cool, smoky air. 'Mormor didn't hit me. She just ignored me for a long time. I actually think that hurt worse.'

'I know,' he said and nodded. 'It always does.'

'Let's go into the woods,' she suggested, looking deep into the tightly woven mesh of trees, an enticing canopy of darkness and glowing shadows beckoning just over Ambrose's shoulder.

'I'd rather not.'

'Why's that?'

'I'm scared of dark places,' he answered, his hoarse voice nearly a whisper. 'I still get bad dreams.'

'I'm sorry,' she told him. 'That's OK. We can just walk along the ridge instead.' She pointed to the rocky ledge that divided the dense woods from the open, sandy beach.

'All right.' He stood up and brushed the dirt from his hands, rubbing them against his black denim jeans. 'I'm glad you're not mad at me,' he said.

'I was never mad at you,' she insisted. 'Blood brothers forever, remember? Blood brothers for life.'

He nodded sadly. 'Rainey – I have to ask you – did you ever miss me? Even a little?'

'No,' she said firmly. 'Much more than that.'

'Good. In a way, I'm glad. Then I haven't been totally alone all these years.' He held out his hand to her and she took it, memorising its texture, its shape and warmth. Something, long hidden, came to life again inside her. She smiled, and felt a fullness in her throat which she recognised as happiness, but a happiness honed and tempered by sadness over the time they had lost.

Rainey visited Ambrose's room that evening. He was sleeping in the attic at the top of the staircase; a hot, airless little cell that none of the other visiting cousins had wanted. Rainey sneaked up the staircase confident that no one would know where she was going, least of all Aunt Ingebjorg, who was snoring deeply in her bedroom, mask over her eyes and TV blaring loudly. Rainey heard the whispers and noises from the other bedrooms along the way. Her other cousins were sleeping three or four to a room, engaging in pillow fights and games of Truth Or Dare, and ghost stories that ended in ineffectual screams. Rainey felt so much more grown up than they were; she understood things they couldn't possibly imagine.

Rainey knocked on the door. 'Ambrose?' she called softly. She could feel the sound of his name, the curving of the word in her breath against the wood. She heard him moving furniture and fiddling with a series of locks. He opened the door and she stepped inside, nearly tripping over the stack of books that had been balanced against a chair.

She looked at the top of the dresser where a wooden-handled bread knife lay. She could see the dull smudges where the blade had been frequently and nervously fondled. 'What's that for?' she asked.

'Nothing.'

'Come on, you don't have a knife in your bedroom for nothing,' she insisted.

'I was making myself a sandwich and I forgot to take it back downstairs,' he said.

She moved towards the bed as Ambrose pushed the dresser back against the door. The single lamp on the bedside table offered little light; only a narrow, luminous triangle that spread from the bed to the wall.

She felt awkward for a moment, not knowing what to say. 'So this is your room. It's nice,' she offered. She paused, admiring the photos he had taped to the wall; autographed 8 × 10-inch glossies of Robert DeNiro and Dustin Hoffman, and someone she had never seen before. 'Who's Derek Jacobi?' she asked, reading the caption beneath the photo of a slightly built blond man in doublet and tights.

'A famous British actor. We watched a movie of him doing *Hamlet* in our Shakespeare class. He was amazing! That's exactly how I want to be when I'm older.' Ambrose drew a deep breath, squared his hips, and lifted an imaginary sword above his head. He began to speak in a deep, sonorous, mock-Shakespearean voice. '"'Swounds, I should take it: for it cannot be but I am pigeon-liver'd, and lack gall to make oppression bitter, or ere this I should have fatted all the region kites with this slave's offal: bloody, bawdy villain, remorseless, treacherous, lecherous, kindless villain! O, vengeance!"' He brought the sword down over his head, and dropped cleanly to his knee, bowing close to the floor. Rainey didn't understand all the words, but the giddy passion in Ambrose's voice gave her chills.

'Wow. That was amazing. So I guess you still want to be an actor,' she said, sitting on the edge of the bed and letting her leg inch towards the centre of the flimsy mattress.

'Oh yes. More than anything,' he answered, sitting down beside her. 'More than anything in the whole wide world. I'm in the drama club at Essex, and last semester I was one of the sons in *Death of a Salesman*. Most of the cast were upper-class men. I was the only eighth-grader in the play,' he said proudly. 'It was the most exciting and terrifying thing I've ever done.' Rainey watched his pale eyes sparkling in the dusky light. 'If I can't be an actor when I grow up, I don't know what I'll do. I'll just die. Die, die, die.' He drew out the last 'die' so it rolled off his tongue and dissipated slowly to the corners of the room. Rainey realised he was completely serious. 'So what about you?' he asked, grabbing an understuffed pillow and punching it between his arms. 'Have you decided yet between being a baseball player or a spy?'

She laughed. 'No. I've given up on both of those. Now I want to be on TV. I want to work for NBC News as an anchorwoman or a foreign correspondent.'

'Wow – that sounds really exciting. I bet you'd be good at something like that.' He squinted and held his hands to his face, making a small box with his thumbs and index fingers, looking at her intently through the narrow gap. 'Yep. I can see it. Rainey McBride, doing the six o'clock news.' He dropped his hands suddenly and looked down at the bed. 'Rainey, has your mother ever come back?'

'No. She hasn't.'

'Do you think she ever will?' he asked quietly.

She shook her head. 'No. Don't think so.'

Ambrose pulled the blanket up to his neck and burrowed into the bed, shivering as if suddenly struck cold, even in the stuffiness of the windowless attic room. 'I'm sorry about that. I've thought about you lots. About you not having any parents, I mean. I think it must be so lonely.'

'Sometimes it is. But at least I've got Mormor and Grandpa Garth,' she said.

'Gosh, they must be really old by now!' he said in amazement, and they both burst into giggles.

'Yeah, they are. They're the same as ever, only older! They won't ever change.' She smiled. 'So what about your parents, how are they?' she asked.

'Oh, they're all right.' His pale eyelids flickered as he straightened his shoulders beneath the blanket. 'I hardly ever see them, actually. Mutti still has a lot of cocktails and Vati spends a lot of time away. Nothing's changed, really.'

'Hmmm. I'm sorry about that.' She paused. 'Ambrose, can I ask you something?'

'Sure,' he answered.

'You'll think it's stupid,' she warned.

'No I won't.'

'Promise?'

He sighed. 'Cross my heart and hope to die, stick a needle in my eye.' She watched his fingers dance across the front of his shirt as he swore the vow.

'All right, here goes.' She took a deep breath to steady herself. 'Do you still have the scar from your hernia operation?'

'Well . . .' He started to blush, a light rush of red rising up his neck. 'Yeah. I still have it,' he said softly. 'But it's not as big as it used to be. The doctor says someday it might disappear completely.'

'Oh yeah?' She tried not to sound too interested.

'Do you want to see it again?' he asked shyly.

'OK,' she replied. 'If you don't mind.'

'I don't mind.' He dropped the pillow and blanket and sat forward. He grabbed the back of his yellow T-shirt and lifted it slowly, sliding it over his arms and dropping it carefully in front of him, into the cleft of sheets where his feet were crossed. He perched further forward, and the folds of skin over his chest hid any remainder of a scar.

'I can't see it,' Rainey told him, stretching closer. 'Maybe it really did disappear.'

'No. Here, I'll lie down so you can see it better.' He tossed the T-shirt to the floor and leaned back, sliding down the bed, while propping up his head and shoulders on the pillows. He lay flat and still, turned slightly towards the triangle of light. His pale fingers moved up and down the length of his torso, indicating an invisible line below his ribs, extending all the way to the edge of his thin leather belt. 'See, it's still here,' he said quietly.

Rainey rolled onto her knees and leaned over him, peering closely while squinting her eyes. 'Oh yes, I see it,' she said, watching the pink, puckered ridge of skin moving up and down as he breathed. His breathing was rapid and shallow as tiny white bumps began to pepper his pale, naked flesh. 'Ambrose, the scar's almost gone,' she whispered. 'It was so big when you were younger and now it's really small.'

She felt how close she was to him; only inches from his stomach, his arms and naked chest, and yet she didn't dare move any closer. She could feel him trembling. A slight flutter moved through his body, the fear whispering out of his skin. 'Your uncle – is he still doing it?' she asked quickly.

'No,' he answered, closing his eyes and fiercely shaking his head.

'That's good. When did it stop?'

'He's dead.'

'What? How did he die?'

'Vati killed him.'

'You're kidding. How? Did you tell your father what happened?' she asked anxiously.

He sat up and grabbed his T-shirt, clutching it against his body. 'I told Mutti. She didn't believe me. She told Vati and he didn't believe me either. He whipped me for saying it. Mutti said I would go to hell for telling lies about . . . about someone. Rainey, I can't even say his name.'

'That's OK. I know who it is. You told me last time. So what happened after you told your mother?'

He took a deep breath. She could see a tiny muscle twitching in his cheek. 'About a month later,' he began, 'Vati saw me crying and then he saw him coming out of the wood shed. He must have looked guilty or something, because after that Vati believed me.'

'And then he killed him?' she asked breathlessly.

Ambrose shook his head. 'No, not right away. But Vati punched him. He beat him up and knocked him so hard he fell and hit his head. That didn't kill him. But that night he ran away. Before the police came,' Ambrose said softly.

'What did the police do?' she asked.

'They made me tell them everything. But I can't explain it, I can't talk about that part,' he said. His face was pale and his breathing heavy.

Rainey didn't want to push him into revealing more than he was ready to say. 'It's OK,' she said, trying to soothe him. 'Just tell me what you can for now.'

Ambrose sighed. 'So he ran away before the police came. No one's seen him since but I know he's dead. Vati won't say anything but I know he went out with his pistol that night and shot him dead.'

'But if they never found a body . . .'

'Rainey, I know he's dead.'

'How can you be sure?'

'Because I felt his hands on me; his body, his breath, his smell . . . I would know if he's alive or dead. He's dead.' Ambrose shuddered, releasing a small tremor inside him that couldn't be stilled, even as he squared his narrow shoulders and balled his hands into tight white fists.

'But that's good. If you know for sure that he's dead, then it's all over with. You're safe now and he'll never be able to hurt you again,' she offered hopefully. 'Don't you realise – you're free!'

'Yeah,' he laughed feebly. 'Free.'

'Well, aren't you?' she asked.

'Yeah,' he said. 'I guess so.' She reached over to touch his shoulder, but he pulled away. 'Sorry,' she said quickly, withdrawing her hand. 'Sorry, sorry, sorry.'

'It's just that . . .' he started to explain, but then suddenly a loud bang shook the room. Ambrose jumped up, landing beside the bed, still clutching the edge of the blanket. 'What the hell was that?' he asked in a hoarse whisper.

'A firecracker, probably,' Rainey answered quickly, grabbing the other edge of the blanket and pulling him back towards the bed. 'Kids are always playing with them this time of year.' She motioned for him to sit down. 'It's so stupid. Don't they know how dangerous those things are? Stupid, stupid kids.'

He sat down next to her and she put her arms around his shoulders. She could feel him shaking, could feel his heart pounding, surging up through his neck. She pressed her cheek against his, trying to hold him still. Her lips caught the briefest taste of his skin. 'It's OK,' she whispered. 'It's OK now.' She pressed her head against his and felt the heat of his forehead. 'I'm so sorry, Ambrose. This is all my fault.'

'How is it your fault?' Ambrose asked, pulling back in surprise.

'Because I promised that you'd never have to go back to the summer house. I didn't keep my promise. And now it's all my fault.'

'It's not your fault. It's his fault. He's the one who did it to me,' Ambrose insisted softly, relaxing against Rainey's side.

'I know. But I want to make it better.'

'You can.'

'How?' she asked, surprised.

'Just stay with me. Just keep being my friend.'

'OK. It's a deal,' she replied, folding him into her arms. She took a deep breath and imagined she was pressing him into a tight, silent corner deep inside her chest, a secret hiding place where she could clasp him like a locket, never to be dislodged.

Rainey and Ambrose met every day from then on, either at the boathouse or in the blueberry patch behind Ingebjorg's house, where they could sit and talk, or lie down close to the ground, enjoying the warm sunshine but away from the noise and commotion of the children and dogs and abandoned ice-cream cones which littered the lakefront.

'Do you think you'll ever get married?' Ambrose asked her one afternoon.

'No, I don't think so. I don't think I'm supposed to, somehow.' She wrapped a vine around her little finger and pulled it tight.

'But how do you know that?' he asked urgently.

She shrugged. 'I don't know. I'm just guessing. I suppose I might get married some day. Anyway, I'm only thirteen, so it doesn't really matter now,' she said.

'I bet I'll never get married,' he said glumly. He lay belly-down in the dirt, balancing his chin on the backs of his hands.

'Why do you say that?' she asked.

'Because. No girl will ever love me,' he said softly, blowing at the dusty layer of top soil.

'Of course one will. Lots will, probably,' she said.

He shook his head sadly. 'No, Rainey. Because when I think about kissing a girl, I get this queasy feeling in my stomach. I could never *want* to do that to anyone. Once I was on a bus and a man and woman in front of me started kissing. She leaned over and kissed his cheek, and her tongue came out and touched his skin. When she moved away, I could see the spit on his face. I could smell it. It smelled like her mouth, like what she had eaten. I got off the bus and threw up in the bushes.'

Rainey thought for a moment. 'Well if you don't want to kiss anybody, you don't have to. No one can make you do that now,' she said.

'Maybe you're right.' He sighed. 'But doesn't that mean I'll never have a girlfriend?' He turned over and lay on his back, lacing his hands behind his head. 'I like girls, I really do. I just don't want to kiss them. Or do anything disgusting with them. I know I'm not like other boys. They can do things to make girls happy. I can't.'

'Well, if a girl really loves you, she'll understand,' Rainey insisted. 'She'll love you just the way you are. That's what love is, accepting someone, good or bad, for better or worse.'

'I don't know . . .'

'Ambrose, believe me. It would be easy to love you that way.' She leaned over and kissed him quickly. She found his face surprised and his body light and limber as he started to sit up. She slid her arms around him, cradled his back and gently pressed him to the ground. She liked that she was taller than he was; her body covered the whole length of him and her feet were still two inches beyond his. She was amazed at how easy kissing was, how natural it seemed. His mouth was hard the first time she kissed it but then she pulled back, and when she kissed him again, he relaxed. His lips were dry but he was trying. She tried to hold her legs firm so she wouldn't hurt him, so her knees wouldn't bruise the soft parts of his body. Just as she was about to kiss him again, a sudden, unwelcome voice entered her head. *A hussy. Just like her mother. What do you expect? She's just like her mother; she's her mother's child through and through.* Rainey rolled off Ambrose and grabbed a handful of blueberry vines. She felt herself starting to shake. *So this is what it was like,* she thought. *This is what my mother was.* Rainey's conception, her birth suddenly became real events for her. She understood that she was the result of sin.

'Rainey, we shouldn't do this,' Ambrose said, sitting up and leaning close to her. His fingertips were small and busy, tracing nervous circles on her back.

'Was it bad?' she asked breathlessly.

'No. It was nice. Really nice. Nicer than it would be with anyone else. But we can't because we're cousins.'

'Second cousins,' she reminded him.

'Yes, but that's still blood.'

'I know,' she said, shifting away from him with a sudden wave of cold, hard self-disgust. 'You're right.'

'I know – let's just be like angels to each other,' Ambrose suggested lightly. 'Above that kind of stuff.'

'Angels?' she asked.

'Sure.' He cleared his throat. '"For spirits when they please, can either sex assume, or both; so oft and uncompounded is their essence pure."' He quoted in a sweet voice, his hand pressed solemnly against his chest.

'That's really pretty,' she said. 'Did you make that up yourself?'

He laughed. 'No. It's from *Paradise Lost*. We studied it in English Lit. last semester.'

'We did *Gulliver's Travels*,' she said and sighed, relieved that the awkwardness of her kiss had passed. 'I wish I could go to your school.'

'I wish you could too,' he told her. 'Then I'd always have at least one friend. But we can go to college together.'

'College?'

'Sure.'

'But that's five years away,' she said.

'So? We'll keep in touch. Promise we'll go to college together.' His eyes were wide and excited.

'OK. Deal.' She kissed him stiffly, once on either cheek. He sat back on his knees, looking surprised. 'It's a custom. People do it in Europe all the time,' she explained. 'And I understand it's OK, even for second cousins.'

'I'm sure you're right,' he said. He smiled, and lay back softly in the warm dark earth.

The amount of time that Rainey and Ambrose spent together did not escape the notice of Aunt Ingebjorg. 'Oh, it's not good to spend so much time at the boathouse,' Ingebjorg warned Rainey as they baked bread together in the kitchen. 'It's no good. You should spend more time with the girls in town. Go to the picture show, meet some nice boys. A summer romance at your age is always a good thing. No heavy petting though, eh? You're too young for that. We don't need any more tramps in this family.' She slapped the bread dough so hard it made the whole table quiver.

'Yes, Aunt Ingebjorg,' Rainey said dutifully. She looked down at her palms, which had been stained purple by blueberry juice. She rubbed her hands on her trousers but the stain wouldn't come off.

'Now your cousin Ambrose, I suppose he's handsome,' Ingebjorg said carefully, dusting the table with flour. 'I bet you think he's good looking. I've never known a girl who could resist pouty lips.'

'Of course not. He's my cousin. That's disgusting,' Rainey said, feeling the hair rise up on the back of her neck.

'I'm just saying, don't spend too much time with a blood cousin, even if he is only a second cousin. OK? Mingle a little bit more, you won't be sorry.'

Rainey poked her finger into the soft lump of dough and watched as the indentation filled in quickly. 'Ingebjorg . . .' she said, stretching out the name as long as she could, '. . . what was my mother like? What was she like when she was my age; I mean, could you tell then that she was going to run away someday?'

Ingebjorg stopped kneading the dough and faced Rainey, fists on her ample hips. 'You know not to ask me about that,' she warned.

'I know, but if . . .'

Ingebjorg shook her head. 'No. I'm sorry, Rainey, but your grandmother doesn't want us to talk about your mother. I've promised Sonja not to talk about Mary Jane and so I won't,' she said sternly.

'But I won't tell Mormor anything you tell me, I promise. It could just be a secret between—'

'No. Sorry. I know it sounds hard and unfair but look at it this way. Your grandmother took you in, she raised you, she provided for you, and she's done a good job, most of the time. You're a fine young lady and she has reason to be proud. When your mother ran away, my sisters and I said we'd do whatever we could to help Sonja raising you. Just about the only thing she's ever asked of us was that we not talk about Mary Jane. Sonja will tell you what she wants you to know, and in her own good time. I don't necessarily agree with my sister about this but I've made her a promise and I'm bound to stick by it.'

'Yeah, I know,' Rainey said sadly. 'I just wondered, that's all.' She looked down at the pale and sticky lump of dough. 'Ingebjorg, did you ever love someone? You know, a man?'

Ingebjorg puffed out her cheeks and started slapping the dough again, harder than before. 'Oh yeah. Who didn't? But I was a silly girl back then.'

'Well, who was he?' Rainey asked, desperate to hear more.

'His name was Jeremiah Mecklenburg and he sold paper supplies. Oh, he was so handsome! A young man but he had a streak of white right through the front of his jet-black hair.'

'So what happened?' Rainey asked.

Ingebjorg rubbed her chin and looked out the window. 'He went to Chicago, to make his fame and fortune. I wanted to get married right away but he said no, not until he could give me everything. I told him I didn't want everything; I only wanted him. He said he would send for me, once he was settled and earning good money. Three months later I got a letter from him saying he had glandular fever and it would be best if we postponed the wedding.'

Rainey stepped back and let the information sink in. 'Wow. Did you ever hear from him again?'

'Nope,' Ingebjorg said simply.

'Maybe he died,' Rainey said sadly. 'Maybe he died because he didn't have your love.'

'He didn't die,' Ingebjorg said matter of factly. 'Someone from town saw him in Kenosha, selling typewriter ribbons. Turns out he had another woman there, all along.'

The words touched Rainey deeply. She felt the ancient betrayal of Jeremiah Mecklenburg echoing down the years and stopping to take up residence in the deep recesses of her mind. 'Oh, that's awful,' she said. 'You must have been so sad.'

Ingebjorg shrugged, grabbing a dish rag from the pocket of her apron and using it to mop her damp and florid face. 'I don't know. That's how things work out, sometimes. That's life, I guess. Better to find out something like that before you're married, instead of after.'

'Yeah. I guess so.' Rainey leaned back and looked at Ingebjorg, seeing her as somehow different from the aunt she had known all her life. This was so romantic, Rainey decided. For all these years, Ingebjorg had been carrying the ghostly memory of her secret love, locked up inside her and never to be spoken of to anyone. 'That will be me someday,' Rainey told herself. 'I'm sure it's my destiny to have a tragic love.'

At the end of July, Mrs Irene Rasmussen's eighteen-year-old son David was killed in a car crash. The accident happened in California, where David was going to college. For the first day after the news came through, the whole town of Ojibwa Falls was waiting to see what the tragedy would mean to them, both as a town and individually. Rainey, for her part, became fascinated. She had never known anyone who died. She couldn't believe how normal everyone was acting; kids still rode their bikes over the railroad tracks, everyone continued to water the lawn at six in the evening. But Rainey felt an intense desire to see the grief of David's death somehow made visible. She tried to remember David Rasmussen. She hadn't seen him since two years earlier and her memory was hazy. She got him mixed up with his brother Darren, who was two years younger. Or was Darren two years older?

Rainey thought about Mrs Rasmussen, remembering her deeply felt rendition of 'God Bless America' at the talent night. Her voice had been so solid; so confident and unwavering, and her gaze had been so steady, as if she had been seeing something far beyond the tattered flag hanging at the back of the Supper Club. Did she suspect that her son was about to die? Could she see the shadows creeping up on her even then?

The neighbours, being sensible and sympathetic people, all brought casseroles and covered dishes; a parade of cookware was making its way to Mrs Rasmussen's front door. Rainey knew that was what people did following a death. There was nothing else to do but bring food. *But why?* Rainey wondered. *What good is food when someone you love is dead?* She tried to imagine Mrs Rasmussen opening her refrigerator in the middle of the night and finding comfort in a mouthful of cold noodles, as if she could fill the empty ache inside her with a lump of spicy tuna. Mr Barnes, who worked at the soft drink bottling plant in Oshkosh, would be delivering a crate of root beer to Mrs Rasmussen's front door. He would ring the doorbell, take off his cap, and when Mrs Rasmussen answered, he would say hello, offer his condolences and then apologise for the root beer not being cold. 'Sorry it's room temperature,' he would say, 'but this batch is fresh off the assembly line. Hasn't been chilled yet.'

'Oh, that's all right,' Mrs Rasmussen would tell him. 'Thank you anyway.' And then she would accept the wooden crate, drag it into the kitchen, take out the top bottles and place them in her refrigerator, whose door could barely close for all the containers of paprika chicken and Spanish rice casseroles.

Rainey thought about the death of David Rasmussen without relief. How could everyone act so normal? How could anyone eat, in a house full of grief? Hunger itself would be a betrayal of David; there was a dull insensitivity in the inevitable continuity of life. How could Mrs Rasmussen feel hunger or thirst in a world without her son? The world is two places, two rooms, Rainey decided. One room is filled by those who know grief, and the other by those who wait quietly behind that door. 'One day I will enter that other room,' Rainey told herself. 'There is a place already waiting for me, a place at that table . . .'

A week after the funeral of David Rasmussen, the traffic had picked up speed down Main Street, and children were again laughing and swimming and scaring their parents by doing swan-dives into the lake. The 7-11 had taken down the 'Remember David' lettering on its sign and had replaced it with 'Charcoal Briskets, 10lb bags $3.87'.

'Do you ever think about dying?' Rainey asked Ambrose as they lay side by side in the sweltering attic, barefoot and sweating on the thin, ragged mattress.

'Yes. All the time,' he answered, turning on his back to stare at the ceiling, lacing his hands behind his head.

'What is it like?' she asked, lifting a length of hair off her neck and twisting it into a loose, scratchy knot. 'Do you think we go to God and live in heaven in a state of everlasting peace and happiness? Do we get to meet Elvis and President Kennedy and eat lunch with all our ancestors?'

'No,' he said with the certainty of someone who had thought about it many times before. 'No, it's nothing like that. I think death is a cold dark room where we lay down alone; a place where we wait to be empty and free. We won't have a body to tie us down, we won't have to worry about eating and sleeping and breathing. We won't know that things are moving inside us, even when we sleep. I think it will be blissful nothingness; no longing, no desire, no pain. Just a field of freedom; a plain that stretches out in every direction, and goes on forever and ever in silence.'

'But Jesus is there,' Rainey answered quickly. 'I'm sure He's there.' She felt herself start to shake; the thought was so immense, and so frightening. 'I think Jesus takes us in His arms and loves us a little bit first, before we step through that doorway. He loves us a little bit first, just to show us what we've been missing here on earth. Ambrose, I've never told anyone this before, but sometimes I want to die. I don't want to kill myself, I just want to know everything about death. I want to feel myself being held in God's arms, I want Him to rock me back and forth; I want to feel that kind of happy.'

'I know,' Ambrose said, closing his eyes. 'I know I know I know. So do I.'

EIGHT

August 1983
Ojibwa Falls, Wisconsin

On 2 August, Rainey left Ojibwa Falls to return to Milwaukee. After a great deal of coaxing, Rainey convinced Ingebjorg to let her take the bus back by herself, arguing that there was not much opportunity to get into trouble on a direct, five-hour journey that passed through nowhere more interesting than Wausau, Tomahawk or Stevens Point. Aunt Ingebjorg and several of the cousins walked Rainey to the Greyhound station at the end of the street, past Ole Olsen's Bakery, the Ben Franklin five-and-dime and the head-quarters of the Northern Wisconsin Republican Party. Ambrose was nowhere in sight during this leave-taking; he and Rainey had said good-bye that morning, in the attic, alone.

'I'm going to miss you a lot,' she had told Ambrose as they sat side by side under their makeshift tent, enjoying the muffled quiet; the gentle, midday dark.

'Yeah, I'll miss you too. I almost wish we hadn't met again, because then I wouldn't know how much I'll miss you when you leave,' he said sadly. 'I wish I could take you back to New York with me, and we could hear a play on Broadway. "Hear" a play, not see a play. That's what they said in Shakespeare's time, "we'll hear a play". The words were more important than anything. We could go to a matinee, and still have time for dinner at the Russian Tea Room, and some shopping at FAO Schwartz.' His pale eyes glowed with excitement.

'And maybe a Mets game?' she asked hopefully. 'Or better yet, a Yankees game; Yankees against the Brewers.'

'OK. We'll see about a baseball game too,' he said mildly. 'But only if there's time. Oh, before I forget,' he said, shifting to his knees and reaching into his pocket. 'This is for you.' He handed her an envelope torn into two parts, on which he had scribbled 'Angie Danvers' and an address at Essex Academy, Warmouth, Massachusetts. She looked up at him, confused.

'It's me,' he explained. 'At least we can pretend it's me. That's the name I'll use when I write to you, so your grandparents don't get suspicious.'

She nodded. 'All right. Let's make a solemn vow – no more than two weeks between letters or phone calls.'

'OK. It's a deal,' he answered.

'Rainey, come on! It's time to go,' Ingebjorg called from down-stairs. 'If you don't hurry up, you'll miss the bus.'

Rainey and Ambrose looked at each other and nodded, then slid out from under the tent. Ambrose grabbed the blanket and was about to pull it down, destroying the tent forever. 'Wait a second, our ghosts are still inside there,' Rainey said suddenly, rising from her knees and standing beside the bed. 'The memory of our breath, mixed together. That little space holds a part of us – let it live a little longer.'

'Wow. That's intense,' Ambrose marvelled. 'What made you think of that?'

Rainey shrugged. 'I don't know. When I'm with you, I'm not afraid to think about grown-up things. With you, I feel like I can be my real self.' She grabbed her duffel bag off the bed and hefted it over her shoulder. 'Ambrose,' she said carefully, 'before I go, I have to tell you one last thing. I'm glad it's finished. I mean, I'm glad your uncle . . . I'm glad he's dead. I'm glad it's over with.'

'It's not over with,' he said softly. The light shimmered and died behind his eyes.

'What do you mean?' she asked. 'You told me he was dead.'

'Oh, he's dead all right. But now it's like he's a spirit or something.' Ambrose looked down at his hands, folding them tightly at his waist. 'I think he wanted to die so he could come back and hurt me and never get caught. Rainey, he's with me all the time now, he can touch me whenever he wants. Sometimes I have to talk to myself all night to keep him away. He won't ever leave me alone. Until I'm dead too, I guess.'

'No, Ambrose, don't say that,' she pleaded. 'It's finished now. He's gone, and you're still alive. He's nothing, and you're going to be a great actor one day.'

'Maybe. Hopefully,' he whispered, his eyes filling with tears.

'Rainey! Get your derrière down these here stairs,' Ingebjorg called up angrily, rattling the old wooden banister and pounding on the bottom step.

'Please, Ambrose,' Rainey said, reaching out to touch his face, wanting to stop the first tear before it touched his chin.

'Go on,' he whispered, gently pushing her towards the door. 'It's better if you just leave.' She nodded and turned away from him, moving quickly down the stairs.

'What the heck took you so long?' Ingebjorg asked, tossing Rainey her jacket.

'Nothing,' Rainey said softly. 'It was nothing at all.'

The last image of Ambrose's pale mouth and watery eyes remained in Rainey's mind, even as she stood watching her luggage being loaded into the bus and her red, white and blue ticket was studied and stamped by the driver.

'Good-bye, Rainey, good-bye, have a safe trip,' her cousins all said and waved dutifully but without much emotion. Rainey realised she had hardly spoken to any one of them during her six weeks in Ojibwa Falls. 'Well,' she told herself, 'too late to do much about that now.'

The engine started revving and the driver adjusted his cap. 'I better go,' Rainey told Ingebjorg.

'OK, kiddo,' Ingebjorg said, giving her a pretend punch on the arm. Ingebjorg was trembling, lips and eyelids set to a slight flutter. 'I've made you three ham salad sandwiches with extra relish and I've put them in your bag,' she said. 'And there're some cookies in there, and some olives too. I know how much you love olives. I'm so proud of you, Rainey; you're the best of us,' Ingebjorg told her solemnly as she hugged Rainey good-bye. 'You've done us all proud. You'll be the one to succeed, mark my word. I've known that since you were born.' Rainey felt smothered by Ingebjorg's hot, heavy, sweaty body and the swollen hands pressed against her back. She wriggled out of the embrace and stepped aside.

'This bus goes all the way to Peoria,' Ingebjorg said, checking the sign above the driver's window. 'Remember to get off in Milwaukee, OK?'

'I will,' Rainey promised.

Ingebjorg climbed up the first two steps into the bus. 'Make sure she gets off in Milwaukee,' she whispered to the driver. 'You might not have guessed it, but she's only thirteen years old.'

As the bus pulled away and down the street towards the county trunk highway, Rainey watched Ojibwa Falls slip out of her sight. In a matter of minutes it was gone; a town of 6,500 could disappear just like that, leaving a dense forest of poplar and birch trees, and thin streaming creeks that ribboned over glossy rocks. Even inside the bus, the air smelled clean and fresh. Rainey opened the bag of sandwiches. At the bottom of the bag was a $20 bill stained with pickle relish. Folded over the bill was a note from Ingebjorg – 'Buy yourself something nice', it said, and was signed with a big heart and a smiley-face.

Rainey wanted to cry. 'I shouldn't have pushed away from Aunt Ingebjorg,' she scolded herself. 'Who knows when I'll see her again. I should have at least let her spoil me a little bit. I'm better off with my grandparents; they give me so little and it's exactly what I deserve.'

Rainey watched the landscape change as the bus headed south; the forests disappeared and were replaced with cornfields and cow pastures; a flat, yellow band of farmland that stretched like a golden belt across the broad belly of the state. She thought about Mormor's family coming over to this country and settling in Wisconsin all those years ago. How brave they were, spending so many weeks at sea, knowing they would never go back, they would never see their home and family and friends again. Rainey tried to picture herself as an immigrant girl – how would she live with no *Hill Street Blues*, no Johnny Carson, no *Tiger Beat* magazine; no baseball, no Twinkies, no Hostess pies? She knew she would never be able to survive that. *We can never live up to what they did for us; we'll never be worthy of their sacrifice.*

Rainey remembered what Mormor had told her when she had had scarlet fever: 'Papa killed a man at the timber mill, so we had to leave Lyngdal. We had to escape before Papa went to jail.' *My great-grandfather's burst of anger sent us in exile,* Rainey thought. *Maybe that's why we all like to be unhappy. There is murder in our blood. But, one day, I'll make it right. When I work for NBC News, I'll get myself sent to Norway and I'll go to Lyngdal and see where we came from. I'll find my distant cousins who still live there and the break will be healed after all these years. Then I'll go back home and tell Mormor and Ingebjorg and everyone else all about it.*

Rainey grabbed a pencil and a scrap of paper and began her first letter to Ambrose. 'Dear Angie,' she wrote, in case Mormor found the note. 'I'm so glad we met each other in Ojibwa Falls . . .'

Rainey reached Milwaukee's Greyhound Bus depot at Sixth Street and Wisconsin Avenue early in the evening, and used the $20 to take a taxi back to Sandstone Avenue. Mormor and Grandpa Garth must have arrived home only a few minutes before Rainey did – they were still busy opening the windows and unpacking the car as the taxi dropped her off.

'I'm back,' she announced happily. They both glanced up and nodded, looking worn and tired.

'Help us bring in the big suitcase,' Mormor told her. Rainey grabbed the large case and hefted it through the back door. Mormor opened the curtains and turned on the lights. She surveyed the kitchen and den with her fists on her hips, seeming satisfied that all the houseplants had died. 'See? What did I tell you? I knew Ethel wouldn't come in and water them every day. I knew it. She's just a little too busy watching *Days Of Our Lives.* I bet she only came over once or twice.'

'So how was Hawaii?' Rainey asked.

'Magnificent,' Grandpa Garth said, beaming. His face creased where he had been sunburned around his eyes and a red patch of skin was peeling off the top of his nose. 'We've already decided to go back again next year.'

'It was really nice,' Mormor added. 'Just like the brochures – palm trees and coconuts and white sandy beaches. It rains a little bit in the morning and then it's sunny all the rest of the day. It's beautiful. Too beautiful, really. Just think, some people get to wake up and see that place every single day. I'm glad I'm not them. That would be too brutal. It's too much.'

When they sat down to unpack, there was a newness, a formality in the air. They had the politeness of strangers, behaving as if they hadn't all lived together for thirteen years. In those thirteen years, this was the longest they had ever been apart, or been away from home. 'Let's order out for some Italian food,' Grandpa Garth suggested. 'I'm so hungry I could eat a horse.'

'Oh yes, yes please,' Rainey said.

'I don't know about that dago-food,' Mormor muttered, shaking her head. 'It gives me heartburn, all those spices. What's wrong with pork roast and potatoes? We don't have to cover our food with all that seasoning. We like to be able to taste what we eat.' But Mormor was too tired to cook and the fridge and pantry were empty anyway, since no one had time to do any shopping.

So they ordered Badalamente's pizza and spaghetti and ate it out of the cardboard boxes, which was also something they never, ever did. 'It's sinful not to eat off a plate, with knives and forks,' Mormor said. 'We may have come from farm folk but we're not farmers now.' Rainey and Grandpa Garth both ignored her. The food was good and hot and spicy, full of pepperoni and onions, and warm bread and rich sauces that left stains on the napkins and the makeshift plates. It was only when she had finished eating that Rainey realised how hot and dry and hungry she had been from the travelling, and how surprisingly happy she was to be back home.

After supper, Mormor and Grandpa Garth gave Rainey her gifts. First she opened a box containing a multicoloured T-shirt, which, as she tried it on, was tight in the sleeves and too small across the chest. Then she opened a long pukka shell necklace and matching pukka earrings. 'Thank you, these are great,' she said, trying not to look disappointed. But she was sure Mormor and Grandpa Garth could tell how she felt. These weren't bad gifts, they just didn't suit her. Either Mormor and Grandpa Garth, while they were away, had imagined Rainey as being younger than she actually was or else she had grown up more than a summer's worth during her time in Ojibwa Falls. It bothered Rainey that she didn't know which was true.

'Did you have a good time in Ojibwa Falls?' Mormor asked her, settling down with her cup of coffee.

'Yes. It was excellent,' Rainey answered.

'Did you meet any nice boys?' Grandpa Garth asked.

Rainey shook her head. 'No. I mostly hung out with the girls from town,' she told them, biting her lip. She wanted so badly to tell them everything about Ambrose, how he'd grown and changed, become taller and thinner. He was a young actor now, serious and solemn and utterly devoted to his dreams. And yet that kernel of friendship which she had planted years ago was still inside him, growing like a greenstalk, like a tough and tender shoot. *Don't you understand, he is my brother. The brother God wanted me to have, because I was never meant to be an only child, I know that now. This is your fault – my mother left before she could give me a brother, so circumstances gave me Ambrose instead.*

'So what did you do with the girls in town?' Mormor asked. 'Did you go to the picture show?'

Rainey could think of nothing to tell them that was true. 'No, but I met one girl named Angie Danvers. We went swimming and shopping and stuff. She's from Boston and I'm going to write to her there. We promised to keep in touch.' She was ashamed to have to lie but she accepted her shame as a kind of punishment. Sometimes that felt right; it was better to feel bad.

Suddenly the phone rang. Mormor and Grandpa Garth looked at each other, both too tired to move. 'I'll get it,' Rainey offered, standing up.

'Hello?' she said.

'Hi, Rainey?' It was Aunt Ingebjorg. 'I'm not checking up on you or anything but did you make it home OK?' She paused. 'I guess you must have, 'cause I'm talking to you now.'

As Rainey got ready for bed, she was glad to hear her grandparents' familiar steps through the bedroom and hallway. Rainey waited patiently for them to finish in the bathroom so she'd be free to begin the twenty-minute ritual designed to arrest the growth of the few small pimples that had developed between her freckles. She loved spreading the sulphur-smelling ointment on her chin and forehead – it made her seem like a real teenager at last – and she felt excited and scared every time she shaved her legs and under-arms of their peach-coloured fuzz.

Hearing their bedroom door close, Rainey smiled to herself. All those terrible fates she had imagined for them had come to nothing; they were home, and they were fine. But still she did not admit, even to herself, how tired they looked, and how much older than she remembered. Rather than refreshing them, the trip had worn them down. She doubted they would travel ever again. Even as Grandpa Garth talked about another trip next year, she had a feeling this was more of an end than a beginning for them.

The bedroom door opened and footsteps moved towards the bathroom. Then came a sharp rap on the door. 'Rainey, did you forget to take out the garbage?' Mormor asked.

'Yes,' Rainey said slowly, seeing herself wince in the mirror.

'That dago-food is going to stink up the whole house. Just because we've all been on vacation, that doesn't mean you can stop doing your chores,' Mormor said sternly.

'I know. I'm sorry I forgot. I'll go do it now.' Rainey reached towards the doorknob.

'No, don't bother,' Mormor said wearily. 'It's late. Get up early and do it tomorrow morning instead.'

'It's OK, I can go and do it now,' she insisted.

'No, Rainey. Just go to bed. Good night.' There was an unfamiliar softness in Mormor's voice.

'G'night,' Rainey replied, surprised.

– PART III –

1 9 8 8

NINE

January 1988
Milwaukee, Wisconsin

Rainey McBride was seventeen years old and six months away from high school graduation when, for the first time in years, she climbed up to the attic and grabbed the envelope containing the newspaper article reporting her birth. She carried the envelope down to her bedroom and sat on her bed, hands shaking as she slipped the envelope open and stared at the brittle, fading photograph of her mother. Rainey studied her mother's long dark hair, her dazzling smile, her triumphant green eyes. *There is nothing of Mary Jane in me,* Rainey thought sadly. *She left before she could give me anything solid or lasting. Every year that I get older, I remember her less and less. Now it's as if I never had a mother at all.*

Rainey looked up and studied her reflection in the mirror. She had a slim figure, and had reached her adult height of five foot six. Her thick red hair was shoulder length and flecked with gold. Even so, she despaired about her stubby nose, her determined little chin, the dusting of freckles, which hadn't faded as much as she had hoped. She worried that her own face lacked her mother's warmth, and she had inherited Mormor's pale, watery, ice-blue eyes.

Rainey looked down at the picture of her mother more tenderly, tracing the line where Mary Jane's feverish face was pressed
against her own baby scalp. Rainey felt a flutter of nerves down her
neck as she tried to remember that touch. She ached for that close-
ness; the caress, and the whisper of breath against her head. 'You
were so young then,' Rainey said to the photo. 'Sixteen. A year
younger than I am now.' Rainey touched her flat stomach; her
small, firm breasts. She couldn't imagine carrying a baby in the
thin, depressed pocket of flesh between her ribs and hips. At the
age of seventeen, Rainey had never even French-kissed with
anyone. 'You were scared, lonely, still grieving for your brother,'
Rainey said to the photo of her mother. 'It's easy to forgive you for
running away.' She paused and took a deep breath. 'What's harder
to understand is why you never came back.'

Rainey looked around her bedroom, still full of plush stuffed
animals and dog-eared baseball cards wedged into the wooden
frame around the mirror. Nearly every inch of space on the walls
was taken up by an award or certificate of some kind – National
Honor Society, Young Lutheran of the Year 1987, Rutherford B.
Hayes High School Honor Roll, The Presidential Council on
Academic Excellence. Rainey was proud of how hard she'd studied, but nothing could erase the nagging emptiness she felt inside;
a hanging, hidden shadow falling just beneath her heart. Ambrose
always said that she hadn't found her 'passion', but once she did,
she would embrace it with all her being, and that would fill up
every emptiness.

'But what does this passion feel like?' she had asked him
anxiously. 'Maybe I've had it all along and I've just never noticed.'

'No, you'll know when it hits you,' he explained patiently. 'It will
touch your soul and tickle your skin; it will be the thing that creeps
up behind you and whispers in your ear, saying, "I'm right, I'm
right, I'm right."'

Rainey sighed and slipped the newspaper clipping back into the
brittle yellow envelope. It was too painful to think about her
mother right now. 'I am myself, my self alone, my thoughts belong
only to me,' she said softly, closing her eyes and slowly rocking
back and forth. 'I am Rainey, Rainey is me.'

'Rainey! Get down here – it's time to go,' Mormor bellowed up the staircase in a firm voice that broke Rainey's concentration, bringing her back to the reality of this snowy Friday morning.

'Coming,' Rainey called down, slipping the secret envelope into a hiding place beneath her bed. She stood, straightened her simple skirt and blouse and tried to smile. 'This is it,' she said to herself. 'In a few hours, I'll see Ambrose again.' She felt a tremble of excitement, along with the sweet, weighty guilt of their long-term secret friendship.

Rainey opened her bedroom door to find Mormor and Grandpa Garth standing impatiently at the bottom of the staircase. Mormor was drying her hands in a frayed dish towel, and Grandpa Garth, beaming beneath his grey fedora, was pulling anxiously on the ends of his bulky scarf. Rainey rushed down the staircase towards them, taking the steps two or three at a time. She hurried not because they were waiting for her, but because she liked the sweep of feeling when she took them in this way; moving quickly, all at once. *Mormor and Grandpa Garth are so old*, she thought tenderly, *old old old*. They had started to resemble the ancient photos on the wall, assuming the grim, lined features of their immigrant ancestors.

'You look pretty as a movie star,' Grandpa Garth said to Rainey as she reached the bottom of the stairs and grabbed her coat. He tied his scarf tightly and tossed the tattered end over his arthritic shoulder. 'Rhonda Fleming, that's who you look like.' *Rhonda Fleming?* Rainey knew Grandpa Garth hadn't been to the cinema since before 1964. 'Doesn't she look pretty, Sonja?'

Mormor tucked a corner of the dish towel over the waistband of her apron and held out her arms, surveying Rainey carefully through squinted eyes. 'She looks fine,' Mormor said evenly. 'But I still don't approve of all that make-up! We don't want those fast-living college boys to think our girl is easy.' Mormor moistened her thumb and began to rub the blush off of Rainey's cheeks. Mormor's hands smelled like cabbage, sour apples and ammonia; odours so intense they brought tears to Rainey's eyes.

'Mormor, don't,' Rainey said, ducking away.

'Don't what?'

'Don't fuss.' Rainey reached up and clasped Mormor's fingers, gently holding the swollen joints.

'*Uff da!* Just remember to behave yourself down there in Illinois, or they won't ask you back in September,' Mormor said sternly.

'It's an orientation weekend for prospective students,' Rainey reminded her. 'If they accept me, it will be mostly based on grades.'

'If? If they accept you?' Grandpa Garth protested. 'How could they not? You're first in your class, you're in the top one per cent of the SATs. Of course they'll take you, and more than that, they'll be lucky to have you.'

'Pa, go easy on her,' Mormor warned. 'We don't want her getting too big-headed. Now go on, you two, before you're late.' She ushered them towards the door, then stopped suddenly. 'Oh! Before you leave . . .' Mormor grabbed a brown paper bag off the hall table and jammed it into Rainey's duffel bag, forcing the zipper open and closed. 'I know they have food in Illinois, but I made you a snack in case you get hungry on the way.'

'A snack?' Rainey asked.

Mormor nodded. 'Just a little something. A handful of olives, a few chocolate chip cookies and two sandwiches – braunschweiger and mayonnaise on white bread with mustard.' Mormor held Rainey hard by the wrist and looked her sternly in the eye. 'Rainey, before you go, there's something I've been meaning to tell you.'

'OK,' Rainey said. She straightened her shoulders, waiting to receive something serious and significant.

'Make sure you don't eat any shellfish at the university,' Mormor warned, waving a finger at her. 'I read about some school out west where a bunch of kids caught hepatitis from the cafeteria.'

During the ride to Evanston in the decrepit, copper-coloured Oldsmobile, Grandpa Garth lectured Rainey about repelling the advances of junior and senior boys, and not studying too hard, and not feeling inferior to people with more money or a better education. 'You come from good, honest, hard-working people, Rainey, and don't ever forget it,' he told her. 'Some people, they want to make folks feel bad on account of their not having the best car or the best clothes or the best anything. But don't let them get to you. You hold your head high and tell them proudly, "I am Rainey McBride."'

Rainey sighed, sweating profusely in the artificial heat of the car's front seat. Grandpa Garth was driving so slowly that other cars crept up close behind them, tailed anxiously and then burst forward, honking and gesturing as they sped down the snow-covered expressway. 'Grandpa Garth, college doesn't start for nine months. Why are you telling me all this stuff now?' she asked.

He chuckled. 'Because. You'll probably stop listening to me long before September. I gotta get all my advice in now, while I still can.'

Rainey knew he was only kidding, but still, she felt hurt. 'Do you really think I'll stop listening to you? Haven't I always followed your advice?' she asked.

'Yes, up to now you always have,' he admitted. 'Rainey, I'm just saying. We're always betrayed by the ones we love best.'

Once they reached Evanston, Grandpa Garth pulled the Oldsmobile over to the side of the road, about a block away from the entrance to the Northwestern University campus. 'I'll let you out here,' he said carefully, his eyes scanning the road. 'Otherwise I'll have to park, and I'll never get home before nightfall. Are you sure you have enough money?'

'Yes, I'm sure,' she replied. 'I've got one hundred and fifty dollars.' She patted the roll of bills inside her purse.

'Clean handkerchief?'

'Yep.'

'Gum?'

'Uh-huh. Four packs,' she answered patiently.

'Good. Now, remember to keep a quarter in your shoe, in case you need to call us,' he said.

'I think I've got everything I need,' she replied.

Grandpa Garth cleared his throat, fiddling with the grooves in the steering wheel. 'Rainey, your grandmother – she doesn't like to talk about her feelings, but you know . . . she *is* proud of you. Real, real proud.'

'I know,' Rainey said, looking away. 'I know she is.' Rainey grabbed the door handle, ready to spring out of the car. Grandpa Garth reached over and took her hand.

'And if your mother were here,' he said carefully, 'well I'm sure she'd . . .'

'I know. But I gotta go,' Rainey said quickly, feeling herself near tears. 'See you Sunday night.' She leaned close to kiss him good-bye, but her heavy coat got in the way of his chunky scarf and she couldn't quite reach his face. Instead she grabbed her duffel bag and sprang out of the front seat, rushing across the open, snowy field without looking back.

After filling out her registration forms and attending two 'Meet the Professors' sessions, Rainey walked around the campus, revel-ling in the dark wintry beauty of the university. She tried to picture herself attending classes in September. *I'll have my English class over there, science will be in that building, and history will be here on Thursday afternoons.* She was inventing the whole scenario, but the fantasy felt right. She knew she would fit in well among the ivy and icicle-covered buildings, the tall stained-glass windows, the quiet courtyards scooped out and softened by snow. She sensed that here was a place where learning was taken seriously, a place where she would never have to apologise for wanting to think. Each day would bring a new feast of ideas – Aristotle, economics, Jane Austen; and she pictured herself, about to sit down to a place at that table with Ambrose, clear-eyed and smiling, always at her side.

Rainey skipped the four o'clock seminar on 'Affording College: Financial Aid and You', and went instead to meet Ambrose at the Barrington Hotel in the centre of Evanston, just beyond the edge of the campus. She felt like a secret agent or a spy, pulling up the collar of her heavy coat, burying her chin deep into Mormor's hand-knit scarf. She couldn't believe she and Ambrose had kept in touch for four and a half years, and Mormor and Grandpa Garth didn't seem to suspect a thing.

She walked into the hotel through the revolving glass doors, past the queue of silver limousines, the top-hatted doorman and the red-capped valets. The lobby was packed with well-dressed women in bright gold jewellery and designer shopping bags. In the middle of all the commotion, at the reception desk, stood Ambrose Torsten Dienst. He was slim and straight-shouldered; magnificently blond, and dressed all in black.

She came up quietly behind him. 'Hi there. My name's McBride, and I'm your secret agent,' she said, tugging on his sleeve. He turned around quickly, then stepped back in surprise.

'Rainey!' For a second he seemed not to know if he should touch her or not. He ducked towards her face and then leaned back on his heels, before hugging her stiffly, bestowing a quick kiss on either cheek. 'You look great,' he said, smiling. 'You look so much more grown-up than I imagined. The photos you sent don't do you justice.'

'Thanks. You look great too. You look really . . . artistic,' she offered, unable to think of a better word. She was impressed by the tall, handsome young man standing before her, even as she felt the absence of the chubby little boy Ambrose had been. She found herself searching for the ghost of that lost child, hiding somewhere over his shoulder, or clinging to the tall Ambrose's elbow.

'Artistic. Hmm, I think I could get used to that,' Ambrose said. He blushed, then turned around in a wide, sweeping circle. 'Très chic, no? I know black is such an actor-ly colour. But I love it!' The man behind the reception desk handed Ambrose a flimsy piece of paper and his American Express platinum credit card. Ambrose glanced at the receipt, furrowed his brow, and signed his name in a wide, looping signature at the bottom of the slip. 'Now you're certain my room has been prepared with synthetic pillows and allergy-free sheets?' he asked the receptionist. 'And a copy of the *Chicago Tribune* along with my breakfast tomorrow morning?'

'Yes, Mr Dienst. Everything you've asked for has been taken care of,' the man said mildly.

'Very good,' Ambrose responded. He flipped open his billfold and slid the credit card back inside, where it nestled snugly among the nine or ten others. 'Let's go have a drink,' he said to Rainey, pointing to the row of small glass tables arranged on the landing just above the lobby.

'No,' she said, shaking her head. 'Let's go upstairs. To your room.' He looked slightly puzzled. 'We can talk more up there,' she explained. She didn't want to share Ambrose, not even with the dozens of uninterested guests, all milling about the hotel's glass-lined lobby.

They took the gilded lift upstairs, and Ambrose opened the

door into a plush, luminous room, with two double beds, a mini-bar and long sashed curtains tied back with golden ropes.

'This is amazing,' Rainey said, running in and plopping down on one of the beds. She felt the firm mattress crease and sing beneath her body. 'This place must cost a fortune.'

'It's not too bad. Besides, Vati's paying for everything.' Ambrose took off his long black coat and draped it carefully over a chair, then began to inspect the closets and drawers.

Rainey lay back and let her head sink into one of the deeply stuffed pillows. 'Thanks for sending me the reviews of *Romeo and Juliet*,' she said. 'It sounds like you were terrific.'

'Well, I was lucky. It was a good production,' he answered. 'I don't think Mercutio is a part I was exactly born to play.' He paced the room nervously, opened and closed the closets, positioned and re-positioned the TV. He opened his designer suitcase and took out several bottles of pills, arranging them neatly on the bedside table.

'What are those for?' Rainey asked.

'Oh, it's just sleeping pills and some vitamins,' he said nonchalantly. 'My nerves have been acting up lately. Say, have you looked around the campus yet?'

'Yes, a little,' she replied. 'It's breathtaking. It looks very Ivy League, all the old brick buildings and tree-lined paths. Everybody looks so smart. I bet the classes are really hard.'

'Rainey, you'll do fine here, don't worry about it,' he said, sounding slightly exasperated as he moved over to the full-length mirror and inspected his pale forehead, squinting his eyes. 'Are you hungry? Do you want something to eat?'

'I don't know,' she answered. 'I guess so.' She thought about the sandwiches in her duffel bag, but decided Ambrose might not appreciate Mormor's braunschweiger and mayonnaise. 'There's a Burger King around the corner from here,' she offered.

He shook his head. 'No. It's too cold to go outside again. Let's order room service.' He grabbed a small cardboard menu and glanced at it with furrowed brow. 'Any preferences?' he asked.

'No, you go ahead.'

'OK.' He grabbed the telephone beside the bed and punched a few numbers. 'Yes, this is Mr Dienst, room five thirty-seven. I'd like to place an order. One Caesar salad, one Waldorf salad, one Club sandwich deluxe, one smoked salmon platter and two pieces of Irish Whisky cheesecake. Oh, and two regular Cokes. Uh-huh. That's correct. Thank you.' He put down the phone and smiled sadly. He kicked off his shoes and began to rub his feet on the carpet. 'Hope you're hungry,' he said. 'I've got that weird feeling where I'm not sure if I'm hungry or not.'

'Ambrose, is something wrong?' she asked carefully. 'Are you OK?'

'I'm fine. Just a little tired,' he said, rubbing his feet more quickly, leaving two depressions in the thick burgundy carpet. 'Final exams before Christmas were really tough.'

'Don't tell me you've changed your mind about Northwestern,' she pleaded, sitting up in the bed. 'Not after all we've been through. Please don't say you'd rather go to Yale.'

'No, it's not that. This seems like a great place. An amazing place.' He leaned forward and ran his fingers through his long feathered fringe of white-blond hair, which brushed his eyebrows and rested just behind his ears. 'Rainey, this place is everything we've ever dreamed of.'

'Then what's wrong?'

'I didn't want to tell you right away, but I am a little . . . distracted.' He took a deep breath. 'Before I left school, Vati called to say he wants to take me to Europe this summer as a graduation present.'

'That does sound awful,' Rainey replied. 'I'll be lucky to get a trip to Ojibwa Falls.'

Ambrose sighed. 'We're supposed to fly to Rome, then rent a car and drive north, covering the whole length of the Continent, all the way up to Løgumgårde in Denmark. I'll finally get to see those places Vati talks about so much – the beach at Bådsbøl, the sand dunes at Ballum, and the tomb of the Niehlesen-Diensts, the gravestones of the lost princes of Schleswig-Holstein.'

Rainey shook her head. 'Sorry, but I still don't see what's so bad about that.'

Ambrose rocked back and forth, balancing his chin in his hands. 'Oh, I know it sounds good. But I just wish I could talk to my father. *Really* talk to him,' Ambrose said in anguish. 'About everything. I love Vati so much; he's an amazing man, the way he built up his company from nothing, how he came to this country as a little boy and had to go to school not knowing a single word of English. He's sent me to the best schools, made sure I've got the best education; first Essex, now Northwestern . . . I just don't want to disappoint him.'

'Ambrose, he could never be disappointed with you,' Rainey told him. 'No one could.'

'But I want to ask him what really happened that night. When he found out about Uncle Billy. Until I ask him . . . it's like there will always be this gigantic wall between us. Like I'll never really be his son.'

Rainey rolled over and rose to her elbows. 'You *are* his son. And you always will be, no matter what. Try not to focus so much on the past. Think about the future instead, and how great it will be when we're both here at Northwestern, how many great parts you'll get to play on stage. Did you see the theatre? It's huge, and right next to the lake.'

'Yeah. You're right,' he said, not sounding convinced. 'I'm sorry for bringing you down, especially when this is supposed to be our special secret weekend together. We've been waiting for this for four and a half years. It must be my Scandinavian heritage – I always get morose at the worst possible moments.'

'There's more to this, isn't there?' she asked carefully. 'Something else you haven't told me.'

He took a deep breath and she could see the tight muscles struggling in his neck. 'Yes,' he said at last. 'I still think about the summer house sometimes, and when I do, I get that pain, right here in my stomach. That's what those pills are for – they think I might have an ulcer.' He clenched a fist over his abdomen and his face split into tiny lines of pain. 'You're the only person I can tell this to, but it happens most often when I'm happy, when everything is exactly right. I was Petruchio in *Taming of the Shrew* last semester, and just before I was supposed to go on stage opening night, I heard his voice.'

'Whose voice?'

'His. His,' Ambrose insisted. 'I haven't heard his voice in years, but I heard it that night saying, "You think you're somebody, boy. You can convince people you are this character on stage, but I'll always know the truth. You might fool the audience, but you'll never fool me." Then I got a cramp in my stomach so bad I couldn't go on stage. I ended up in the emergency room. It took days for the pain to go away.'

'Ambrose, I'm so sorry. Show me where it hurts. Maybe I can help.'

'It's here,' he said, pointing to the space beneath his ribs. 'It starts here, and then it moves all over, all the way up into my neck.'

'Let me see it,' she said softly, crawling to the edge of the bed. 'I'll try to make it better.' She beckoned him to the bed and he approached nervously, sitting down stiffly beside her. She placed her hand on his shoulder. 'You've never let anyone touch you, have you?' she asked softly. 'I mean in a good way.'

'No. But of course I don't meet many girls at a boys' boarding school.' He tried to laugh, but his laughter sounded hollow and painful. 'What about you? You must have a boyfriend,' he said, slowly lying down, stretching his legs the full length of the bed.

'No.' She shook her head. 'I've gone out on a few dates, but never anything serious.'

'Are you lonely?' he asked, looking up at her.

'Yes,' she said slowly, and the word sounded like steam escaping from a trapped place in her throat. 'Yes, I am.' She was leaning over him now, her fingers hovering just above his skin. She stopped for a second, scared of hurting him. She knew she was the only person who had ever touched him with love, and she felt the full weight of that responsibility. She remembered what his fear and despair had felt like; how it quickened, like another heart, beneath her hand.

'It's OK,' she soothed him, stroking his hair. 'You know you can trust me.' He lifted his black jumper and she began to examine his stomach, which was outlined by muscles, without an ounce of fat. She poured over the tiny, faded scar high up between his ribs. As she ran her fingers over the long thin length of it, she felt him shudder, felt the mass of coiled energy tightening just beneath his skin. 'I don't see anything unusual,' she told him, leaning close to his chest. 'The damage must be too deep to see.'

'I know,' he said sadly. 'I was afraid you'd say that.' He held her hand against his chest, and she felt the small movements beneath his skin. His eyes were fully opened, the pupils growing round and dark. 'But at least you are willing to look. Rainey, when you look at me, I see hope; I see generosity in your eyes. I sometimes feel like everybody else in the world thinks I'm so, so ugly. My body is disgusting, even to me.'

'No, no, no,' she told him. 'You are beautiful in every possible way.' She rested her head against his stomach and felt him tense beneath her, drawing in a breath. She started to lift her head, but he pressed it down gently, laying his firm, soft hands against her ear.

'Shh,' he told her. 'It's OK. Just stay there. I like it.' He relaxed, reclining back into the bed. They were quiet for a moment, and he began to stroke her hair. He caressed it from root to tip, grabbing it in loose handfuls and brushing the blunted ends against his wrist and the palm of his hand. She closed her eyes and let her mind drift a little; first she was back with him in the attic at Aunt Ingebjorg's, then they were together at that long-ago Owauskeum Thanksgiving. The images shifted quickly, like a dream, although she wasn't asleep: now she was holding his hand in hers and preparing to slice it open with the steak knife, then a moment later she was kissing him in the blueberry patch behind Aunt Ingebjorg's. She was saying good-bye to him on the staircase in Owauskeum, and turning around to greet him in the hotel lobby only a few minutes ago.

Rainey held her breath and listened hard. She could hear his heartbeat, but it made a muffled, distant noise, and she was sad to think that even so close to him, even pressed against his skin, such a vital part of him was elusive, still out of her reach. She turned her face and kissed him, brushed her lips against the tail end of the ghostly scar. Her hand moved up his leg and felt the swelling, which at first took her by surprise, but then felt right.

'No,' Ambrose said softly. 'Don't. Not that.'

'Why?' she asked. 'Why not?'

'Because I want you up here. Near my face.'

'Near your face?' she asked.

'Yes. So I can see you.' He reached down and took her shoulders, using his substantial strength to pull her close to him at the head of the bed. His arm was around her, pressing her to his chest. 'You don't belong down there. You're too good for that. We don't need those base, unholy things. Those gross desires. It's better if we stay eye to eye, face to face, and heart to heart.'

There was a brisk knock at the door and Ambrose shot forward, hurriedly pulling down the hem of his jumper. His hands were frantic, dancing over the bedspread. 'It's just room service,' Rainey reminded him. 'They're delivering the food.'

'Of course,' Ambrose said, blushing darkly and hopping off the bed. He slipped into his shoes and went to the door as Rainey sat forward, straightening her clothes and her hair. She was shaking, embarrassed and slightly exposed. *It was nothing*, she comforted herself. *It's not like we were doing anything wrong.*

Ambrose opened the door and two sober, dark-suited men stepped inside, carrying enormous silver trays laden with white china plates and mounds of delicately displayed, brightly garnished food. Ambrose grabbed his billfold and opened it, peeling away several large notes from the wad of cash inside. The men's faces showed no reaction as Ambrose slipped the money into their hands.

'Thanks again,' Ambrose said, ushering them quickly back into the corridor and shutting the door behind them. 'Well, this looks like quite a feast,' he said, turning back to Rainey. 'I didn't realise there would be so much food.'

They sat down awkwardly and Ambrose began to divide up the servings, filling each plate with generous amounts of smoked salmon, salads and sandwich quarters held together with frilly plastic toothpicks. They ate quickly and quietly; the room tense with nervous silence. Rainey was aware of her throat as she swallowed, and the sound of the liquids gurgling noisily in her chest and stomach. It suddenly seemed strange to her, how her whole body was full of squeaks and pulses, strange functions she knew nothing of. *Ambrose is right*, she thought, looking across at him, eating with depth and relish. *We'll be fine, if we stay away from base desires. That way, we'll always be safe.*

As evening fell, Ambrose walked Rainey back to the residence hall where she was spending the night, sleeping on the floor in a student's room. 'I bet it's not very comfortable in there,' Ambrose offered, looking up at the rows of grim little windows lining the side of North Alison Hall. 'If you'd prefer, you could stay with me, in the hotel.'

'No, I don't think that's a good idea,' she said quickly. 'Besides, the room here isn't too bad, and it is a good way to see what dorm life is like. Most of the prospective students are staying here. Didn't you want to?'

'I thought about it. But, you know . . .' His voice trailed away and he buried his hands in the deep pockets of his coat. The day's last few flakes of snow began to quiver in the clouds and slowly fall. 'I didn't want to sleep in a room with a bunch of strangers. Sometimes I still get those bad dreams,' he said softly.

'Oh,' she said. 'I didn't know. I'm so sorry.' She reached up and touched his cheek, which felt cold and solid beneath her fingertips.

He took her hand and held it for a second, pressing it against his skin. 'It's OK,' he told her. 'I'm learning to deal with it. It's really OK.'

'Why didn't you tell me?' she asked.

'I don't know.' He shook his head. 'I guess I was trying to wish it away. Schmidt's dead. It's only dreams now, and dreams don't mean anything.'

'I would do anything to be able to take those bad dreams away,' she told him.

'Oh, Rainey,' he said sadly, 'if only you could. That would be excellent.' Suddenly a group of girls burst through the dormitory's back door and darted into the snow-covered streets, jumping and laughing, pulling at each other's jackets. Ambrose pulled away slightly, stepping back in response to the noise.

'It's OK,' Rainey told him, reaching up to whisper in his ear. 'It's only a bunch of girls. Have a good night, and I'll see you tomorrow morning.' He nodded, and she walked the few steps towards the building. She opened the door and stepped into the damp, dark stairwell, which smelled of stale pizza and cheap, watery beer. She could hear drunken singing and laughter like shrill little bells echoing through the floors above her. She stood for a second, imagining Ambrose, still outside, standing on the other side of the heavy, steel-plated door. He would be pulling up the collar of his coat and just now turning to walk back to the hotel. Rainey closed her eyes and thought about her bedroom at home, remembering the secret store box at the back of the bookcase, filled over the years with trinkets sent by Ambrose – photographs, reviews, drawings and poems. *I'm right, I'm right, I'm right.* The words rang through her head. She realised for the first time something she had known for years – Ambrose's passion may have been for acting, but her passion was only for him.

On Sunday afternoon, Rainey walked Ambrose to the 'L' station to catch his train to O'Hare Airport, and the flight back to Boston.

'Remember to request a room at 1835 Hinman Avenue,' she told him as they climbed the stairs to the creaky wooden platform that bucked and teetered in the wind. 'From the research I've done, that's the dorm closest to where our classes will be. And someone told me their cafeteria has the best food,' she said, struggling to catch her breath in the thinly bitter air.

'OK, as long as I can get a single room. I don't think I'd be able to handle a roommate.'

'But you have a roommate at Essex,' she reminded him.

'True. But I've known Gary since I was ten. We . . . understand each other,' Ambrose explained.

'Hey, I almost forgot. I've got something for you,' she said, slipping her hand into her pocket. She pulled out a Robin Yount baseball card and gave it to him. He turned it over and over, inspecting it closely.

'"Height, six foot. Weight, one-sixty-five. Bats right, throws right. Born 9/16/55, Danville, Illinois",' Ambrose said, reading through the statistics on the back. 'This is really cool.'

'I know you're not way into baseball or anything, but Robin Yount is a great player, and that's his rookie card. It might be worth a lot of money some day.'

'It's beautiful,' he said, brushing it with his thumb. 'I know how much this must mean to you. Thanks.' He began to fumble in his pockets.

'It's OK, I wasn't expecting anything from you,' she said carefully, aware of his distress as he patted the thick layers of his clothes.

'As a matter of fact, I do have something for you.' He reached into his attaché case and pulled out a small, fabric-bound book which he slipped into her hands.

'Paradise Lost,' she said, reading the title engraved in gold letters on the padded fabric cover. 'I can't believe you remembered.'

'Of course. "For spirits, when they please, can either sex assume, or both; so oft and uncompounded is their essence pure",' he quoted, closing his eyes.

'But I can't take this,' she said, quickly handing the book back to him. 'You didn't plan on giving this to me; you weren't expecting the Robin Yount card.'

'Is that so?' he asked. 'Check inside.'

She opened the book to the first page, where he had written in broad, loopy letters, 'To Rainey, my best friend and blood brother. Love forever and ever, Ambrose.'

'It's amazing. We must be able to read each other's minds,' she said, laughing.

'If so, then you'll know that right now I'm thinking of the number two hundred and thirty-seven,' Ambrose said and winked.

'Why that number?' she asked, turning her face as the wind brought tears to her eyes.

'I counted it this morning, and we've got two hundred and thirty-seven days until we come back here for our first day of classes on September 18, 1988. Remember that day.' The 'L' train appeared in the distance, rattling down the tracks and pulling up in front of them.

'Two hundred and thirty-seven days. I'll start counting down,' she promised him. She kissed him quickly on the cheek and turned him towards the train. He grabbed his suitcase and attaché case, tossed his garment bag over his shoulder, then climbed on board. The automatic doors hissed shut, and as the train pulled away, he turned to face her. He pointed to his palm and then pressed it flat against the glass window, looking out at her with anguished eyes.

'Wait, come back. Let me look at you again,' she whispered. She tossed her scarf over her shoulder and looked up at the dark grey sky, which suddenly seemed heavy with a veiled sense of sorrow. The train steamed away down the tracks, leaving in its wake a wave of sharp, cold air. She took a deep breath, struggling to fill the empty hollows of her lungs. 'Ambrose,' she said, clutching the small padded book. 'Two hundred and thirty-seven days.'

When Rainey returned to Rutherford B. Hayes High School on Monday morning, she was taken aback by how dull and dreary high school seemed after the excitement of a university. Before her first class, Rainey met with Mrs Mitchell, her guidance counsellor, to hand in the form excusing her from classes the previous Friday. Rainey couldn't stand Mrs Mitchell, and the feelings seemed to be mutual. Mrs Mitchell had never really forgiven Rainey for being first in her class three years running and preventing Martha McCluskey, the perennial second, from ever sharing in the glory.

'Did you like it down in Evanston?' Mrs Mitchell asked Rainey, glancing over the form. Mrs Mitchell stuck a pencil into her pile of tightly permed hair and began to scratch her scalp.

'It was OK,' Rainey answered, not wanting to show her true enthusiasm.

'I hear the campus is real pretty.' Mrs Mitchell paused. 'Real, real pretty.'

'It is.' Rainey folded her hands in front of her and tried to look modest.

Mrs Mitchell clicked her tongue against her teeth and shook her head. 'For what you pay to go there, it oughta be. You know, you could still go to Madison. It would cost only a quarter of what you'll pay at Northwestern and it is one of the best schools in the country.'

'I know,' Rainey answered. 'But I don't want to go to Madison. I want to go to Northwestern. I think I'll feel more at home there.'

'Uh-huh. I guess you just think you're that much better than the rest of us,' Mrs Mitchell said.

'I don't think that,' Rainey replied.

'Look at me – I went to Madison. I didn't need to go to some snobby Chicago school.' Mrs Mitchell stretched out her hands and motioned to her desk; the stacks of papers, the scissors and rulers, the photos of her sons, Pete and Chip.

'But, Mrs Mitchell, I don't want to be a guidance counsellor,' Rainey pleaded.

'I see. I suppose you're too good for a career that involves helping people. But you'll get your come-uppance. You'll see – there'll be a lot of smart girls at NU and they'll know more than you.' Mrs Mitchell signed and stamped the form and flattened it on the top of a pile. 'You can go now, Rainey. We don't want you to miss any more of your classes.'

That night, Rainey grabbed a piece of paper and began a letter to Ambrose, telling him how frustrated she was, and how her daily life was filled with small-minded, idiotic people. 'Just think, only 236 days,' she wrote at the end of the letter. 'That's not much longer at all.'

When Rainey came home from school on 3 February she found Mormor talking softly on the telephone, nodding her head and whispering in a quiet, chiding voice. Rainey stood behind her, steeling herself for bad news. Her first thoughts were of Grandpa Garth – where was he? Was he OK? She had lived so long in the expectation of grief, what if this was it, here and now? She remembered how pale he had looked at breakfast that morning and how he said he hadn't slept very well. 'God, please let him be OK,' Rainey whispered to herself.

'Yeah. Uh-huh. OK. Well, let me know. Bye.' Mormor put down the phone, turned around and looked at Rainey. 'Oh, I didn't see you come in,' she said absently. Mormor's chin was trembling but her hands were still.

'Well, what is it? What's wrong?' Rainey asked breathlessly.

'That was Anna. It seems that Sissel's husband died last night.' Mormor's eyes looked grey and twitchy.

'What?' Rainey asked, not sure what she was saying.

'Your Uncle Holger is dead, Rainey.'

It took her a few more seconds to understand the words. 'You mean Ambrose's father . . .' she began.

'That's right.'

'What happened?'

Mormor shook her head. 'They aren't sure. Some kind of stomach haemorrhage or something, that's what it sounds like.'

'When's the funeral?' Rainey asked, her mind still racing.

'I don't know. Anna didn't say. I suppose they have to wait until after they do the tests to find out why he died.'

'Oh,' Rainey said. 'I suppose they will.' Her own voice sounded foreign to her, and the syllables seemed to rattle in her skull.

Mormor shook her head again and wiped her hands on her apron. Then she turned back to her work in the kitchen. 'Poor Sissel. She never should have married someone so much older. What did she expect? I bet she's sorry now.'

'Yes,' Rainey said, grabbing her schoolbag and running upstairs. She felt desperate and panicky. She needed to be alone. She couldn't concentrate, couldn't connect Ambrose to anything that Mormor had told her. Where was Ambrose right now; what was he thinking and feeling? *But his father can't be dead. He can't be. They were going to go to Europe this summer. Now they'll have to cancel the trip.*

She looked at her calendar on the wall – 229 days until Northwestern. The red Xs jumped out at her, suddenly resembling scars. 'Ambrose, where are you?' she asked. 'Why didn't you call?' Ambrose seemed so far away as she tried to place him somewhere in the world; somewhere, quietly sheltered, within the house of grief. She tried to imagine what he would look like right now. But all she could see in her mind's eye was Ambrose on the 'L' train in Evanston, standing near the window with his stern, sad face and his hands pressed flat against the glass. Rainey thought that maybe he had sensed then that his father was about to die, but he could not tell her. He had seen that passing shadow inching towards him, but was forbidden to speak. 'Oh no, you should have told me,' she whispered. 'I would have understood.' That night Rainey took the copy of *Paradise Lost* and slept with it in her arms, the shiny fabric cover resting cool and smooth against her skin.

For a long and agonising week, Rainey heard nothing from Ambrose. Anna had phoned to tell Mormor that the funeral would be in Denmark and Sissel wasn't expecting anyone to fly over for it – it would just be Holger's immediate family; Sissel and Ambrose, and Holger's relations still living abroad.

Rainey knew it would be useless to phone Ambrose at Essex Academy; wherever he was, he wouldn't be there. Holger Dienst's death meant nothing to Rainey, because she couldn't find a place for it inside herself. *Poor Ambrose,* she told herself over and over, but the words rang hollow and untrue.

Then on Tuesday after school the phone rang and Rainey answered. 'It's me. Are they home?' Ambrose asked.

He sounded so old and weary that it took Rainey a second to recognise his voice. 'Yes. Are you at Essex?' she said quickly.

'I am.'

'OK. Stay right there. I'll go down to the Stop-N-Go and call you back,' she said.

'OK.'

'OK,' she whispered, putting down the phone. She grabbed her coat and ran downstairs. 'I'm going out, I'll be back in half an hour,' she yelled to Mormor.

'Bring me back a gallon of milk,' Mormor called after her.

Rainey ran down the slushy, muddy grey street and into the phone booth, letting the door slam behind her. Her fingers shook as she dialled the number. 'Ambrose?' she asked, as he picked up the phone.

'Rainey.'

'Ambrose, I don't know what to do. Please help me. Tell me what I should say.' There was a heavy silence on the line. 'Say something, please.' Her breath began to cloud the damp glass sides of the phone booth.

'My Vati is dead.' His voice was vacant; light and dry.

'I know. I'm sorry. What happened?'

'I'm still not sure. It's all been like a weird dream. I expect to wake up and find out he's still alive.'

'Tell me everything – how did it start?' she asked carefully, trying to slow down her racing brain.

There was a silence and then Ambrose took a deep breath. 'He was in New York when it happened,' he started softly. 'He was having stomach cramps for several days and on the third day the pain was so bad that he went to the hospital. They thought it might be appendicitis, then they said a bleeding ulcer. They did some tests and gave him drugs for the pain. He was stable at that point. Mutti called me at school. She told me Vati was sick but that it wasn't life-threatening and he would be OK. I wanted to fly to New York that night, but she told me not to. "You've got exams now," she said, "and you can't afford to miss them." Then later that night, after Mutti left, something happened. Vati had a blood clot, or a haemorrhage. Something in his stomach escaped, and he died. Just like that, he died.'

'I don't know what to say,' Rainey told him. 'Ambrose, I'm so sorry. I can't believe this has happened to you. I wish I could do something to help.'

He sighed. 'I flew to New York the next day. So I missed my exams anyway. And then the next day, at least I think it was the next day, I've lost all track of time . . . then Mutti and I flew to Denmark. They buried my Vati in the village churchyard in Løgumgårde. Next to his father, his grandfather, all our ancestors. The tomb of the Niehlesen-Diensts. You should have seen it, Rainey! I thought we were princes, but we weren't. So much for the royal house of Schleswig-Holstein. Really, they were pig farmers.' He was silent for a long and painful moment. 'It was snowing on the day of the funeral, and it was so, so cold. Mutti and I didn't understand anything the pastor was saying. We don't know that much Danish, we never spoke any Danish after Bestefar died . . . I think Vati should have been buried in America. He shouldn't be that far away from me and Mutti. We'll never be able to visit him now, all the way over there.' He sighed. 'But it's what he wanted – he asked in his will to be buried in Denmark. My father never became an American citizen – I didn't know that until now. Imagine, not even knowing that about your own father.'

'What happens next?' Rainey asked. She looked up and saw the sky above the phone booth begin to darken. It was four thirty, and starting to snow.

'Nothing.' Ambrose paused. 'He's dead, and there is no more. No more of Holger Olav Dienst. Rainey?'

'Yes,' she said, watching a little boy in a snowsuit chase a ball into the street. She held her breath, praying that no car was about to turn the corner.

'I haven't been able to cry yet. It's like I don't even remember who he is, what he looked like or anything. There's just a big blank, a black hole, where my father's image should be.'

'You're still in shock, I'm sure—'

'Oh shit, it's almost five,' Ambrose said quickly. 'I've got to get back to the dining hall before the second bell. But, Rainey, there's one more thing I have to tell you.'

She swallowed hard. 'What is it?' she asked.

'He was there.'

'Who?'

'Him.'

'Who?'

'You know. The one who . . . My uncle. From the summer house.'

'My God,' she said, caught completely off-guard. 'He was at the funeral?'

'Yes. He still owns a share in the company, apparently. That's what Vati's lawyer told me. He might try to take over the company, according to the lawyer.'

'But I thought he was dead,' Rainey said.

'So did I. But he's not. Rainey, he was there, and he was laughing at me. He looked me straight in the eye and then he laughed.' Ambrose's voice trailed away and he slammed down the phone.

'Ambrose?' she asked. 'Ambrose?' She waited, but there was only silence, and a static crackling sound from far away. Rainey put down the phone and stepped out of the booth.

The world around her seemed suddenly cold and harsh and cruel. The falling snow stuck to her eyelids, making it difficult to see. The noise of traffic was so loud, so metallic. Rainey was too shaken to go home, so instead she walked around the old playground for a while, trying to clear her head.

She couldn't understand what had happened, what had changed. It was something monumental, and yet everything around her seemed exactly the same. 'My uncle has passed out of the world.' She spoke the words aloud, to herself. But she had only known Holger Olav Dienst as Ambrose's father, not as a person in his own right. And now she would never know him; he had disappeared forever. *There isn't enough in this earth to hang on to,* she thought. *Names and faces mean nothing, people pass away quietly. They slip off in the middle of the night and leave you with nothing but a cold, snowy graveyard and strange people standing next to you, speaking in a language you once knew but have now forgotten. I've never seen my own father. I don't know where my mother is. She could be dead, too. I was once a part of her body and now I don't even know if she is alive or not. Ambrose has no father. Just like me. We are more alike now; we are both orphans. No,* she decided, changing her mind, *we are less alike now — Ambrose has passed through that door which is always in front of me; he has entered that other room.*

Rainey circled back to the Stop-N-Go and went inside to warm up. Three truck drivers in parkas and fur hats stood huddled over the counter, sipping cups of coffee, holding them so close to their faces that the steam rose up and melted their icy eyelashes. Rainey grabbed a handful of junk food off the rack – two Little Debbies, a Hostess pie, a Sno-Ball and a bag of Cheetos.

'An attack of the munchies?' the girl behind the counter asked her.

'Um, yeah,' Rainey said quickly. She looked at the brightly coloured metallic wrappers and realised she had lost her appetite.

Rainey felt tired and heavy as she returned home. Her back ached and her hands hurt as she bent to unlace her boots. She dreaded the thought of supper, of having to sit over a dish of liver and dumplings and talk about school, pretending nothing was wrong. It occurred to her that this might be her punishment; this silence might be the price she had to pay for her relationship with Ambrose.

'Are you all right, Rainey?' Mormor called from the kitchen.

'Yeah,' she answered.

'Did you remember to pick me up some milk?'

That night Rainey crossed another number off her list – only 222 days left until Northwestern. She climbed into her bed and thought about praying. 'I should pray for Ambrose. For Ambrose and his father,' she told herself. 'Yes, that's what I need to do.' She got out of bed and knelt beside it, clasping her hands over the layers of blankets. 'Dear God . . .' she started. 'Dear God . . .' She couldn't continue; she couldn't find the right words. Death was present, looming all around her, but there was nothing real or concrete about it.

She got back into bed and when at last she fell asleep she dreamed of something from a long time ago, something that had been buried deep in her memory for many years. She dreamed about Grandpa Garth's brother, Rory. Rory had been the black sheep of the McBride family, and by the time he died, when Rainey was ten, Garth and Rory hadn't spoken for nearly twenty years. Rory had died in his sleep at a sleazy roadside motel in Reno, Nevada after a hard day of drinking and gambling. It was a prostitute who found his body.

Because Rory had no other family, it fell to Grandpa Garth to have Rory's body brought back to Milwaukee and buried. Pastor Jeff offered to perform the funeral service, which didn't please Mormor at all. 'Rory wasn't baptised a Lutheran,' she insisted. 'He should be laid to rest among his own people. He belongs with his own kind.' Garth's family were all Irish Protestants, a fact which Mormor often seemed to forget, since Garth himself had never bothered to become a Lutheran, either.

Normally in Mormor's family, children were not allowed to attend funerals. But when Rory died, Mormor decided Rainey and her cousins should take part. Mormor said it would be all right this time, perhaps because no one really loved Rory, or perhaps Mormor meant it as a warning – if you left the family, this was the way you were bound to return.

Rainey, Grandpa Garth, Uncle Ervald and Ervald's son Stevie, along with two men from the funeral home, went to meet the body coming off the train at the Amtrak station.

'Did they give Rory a ticket?' Stevie whispered to Rainey standing beside him.

'No, I don't think so,' Rainey answered. 'I think dead people get to go for free.'

'Wow. That isn't fair – you could just pretend to be dead.'

'Shut up, stupid, no you couldn't,' Rainey insisted.

'Is his body in a seat?'

Rainey thought about it for a moment. 'No, 'course not. I bet they wrapped him up and stuck him in with the luggage. That's why he doesn't need a ticket,' she explained.

With a loud whistle and a gush of wind, the Hiawatha Special pulled into the station and blazed to a stop. Dozens of people poured out of the train and on to the platform, at first in a thick, steady mass, and then more slowly, in fits and starts.

'He isn't there,' Rainey had started to say, when suddenly two men came down the platform from the far end of the train, wheeling a cart with a large wooden box on top of it. Rainey was awe-struck by the solemn ceremony of the long brown box being wheeled towards her on a set of graceful, well-oiled wheels. The attendants turned the cart over to the funeral home men, who wheeled it out of the station and on to St Paul Avenue. Grandpa

Garth nodded severely as the two tall men, with their sharply parted hair and neat lapels, loaded the coffin into the dark belly of the waiting hearse. Rainey and Stevie peeked into the frosted windows of that mysterious, jet-black station wagon with its ruffled, cream-coloured curtains and the words 'Torgesen Brothers Funeral Home' painted in gold letters on the tailgate. The men slammed shut the tailgate, and that noise seemed to echo above them, hanging in the air just a moment too long.

Stevie poked Rainey in the ribs and whispered, 'Hey, just think, there's a body in there. There's a body inside there.' As he said it, she felt the dead arms and hands and knees thudding against the sides of the wooden box, and she imagined the dead face rolling towards her, pale and expressionless. The horror of death bit into her stomach and she felt suddenly, violently, alive.

The next day at the funeral parlour, there were black cars everywhere and a bitter, cold, scathing rain which pock-marked everything it fell upon. More people attended the service than anyone had expected. Rainey had never seen so much black – black hats, black coats and shiny black shoes, black as June bugs and beetles. She felt excited by the organ music, the bright fluorescent lights and the veiled, mysterious women who smelled like whisky and cigarettes and all claimed to be old friends of Rory's. Rainey gazed up into their veiled faces and their darkened eyes, and although she felt afraid and overwhelmed, she loved every bit of it; she lived on the terror, the utter despair that filled the muted parlour.

After the service, they all drove in a long, slow cortege to the memorial park on the south side of town, a stream of dark cars with a tiny black flag fluttering on the bonnet of every one. For the first time in her life, Rainey saw Grandpa Garth weep. He had tears in his eyes and his cheeks looked raw and moist as he blinked them away. A bunched-up handkerchief covered his moustache and mouth. 'I may not have seen him for twenty years,' Rainey heard him say, 'but damn it, he was my brother.' Garth's sister Molly held on to his arm, as her long, faded red hair draped across her shadowy face. Rainey's head spun as she tried to breathe in the atmosphere, hoping she'd be able to hold that funeral air in her lungs and sample it later, to taste it again when she was alone. She longed to chew and swallow grief, and to give sorrow another life inside her. She felt herself start to shake. She loved the quivering torment of being so close to tears, and yet, as always, she was able to step back from that part of herself.

Pastor Jeff in his long black coat and his stiff white collar stood in front of the mourners, speaking the words of the service – 'Ashes to ashes, dust to dust . . .' His face was pale and serious as the cold wind whipped and parted his hair. Rainey inched towards the front of the mourners and stood peering over the edge of the freshly dug grave. She looked down into the hole, which shone with ice crystals frozen deep beneath the surface. She heard the scrape of the shovels, and that sound quivered up her spine. She watched the black dirt falling, slowly filling the hole. She imagined she could taste that soil, could taste its deep, rich darkness.

Rainey woke suddenly and sat forward in her bed. She pulled the blankets around her shoulders, curling them under her chin. 'I'm sorry, Ambrose, I'm so sorry,' she said to the dark. 'I feel so ashamed, now that it's you who's suffering.' She touched her face and only then did she realise she was crying.

TEN

May 1988

That bitter winter ended, and the spring of 1988 began. The long, dark months of snow, ice and freezing rain gave way to daffodils and wood violets; red-breasted robins plucking up worms from bright green lawns. A new season of Brewers baseball began with high hopes for a pennant, and Rainey passed all her mid-semester exams with perfect marks. But in Rainey's inner world, the wintry gloom never lifted, as Ambrose Torsten Dienst sank deeper and deeper into grief. He refused to write or speak a word about his father's death, and so stubborn silence grew like a deep and bitter weed between them. She spent many hours locked in the quiet solitude of her bedroom, or perched at the attic window, staring out at the concrete highway overpass, whose shiny brightness seemed further and further away.

In the middle of May, Rainey was named valedictorian of the senior class, the highest possible academic honour. She would graduate first among all the students, and give the ceremony's commencement address. Rather than being pleased, Rainey felt selfish and shallow. Yes, she had worked hard, but what did her success matter if she couldn't help Ambrose? All her talent and dedication could do nothing to pierce his silent veil of grief. Mormor, however, was thrilled about Rainey's achievement, and began planning a party to follow the graduation ceremony in June.

'We'll invite all your aunts, uncles and cousins,' Mormor said, hunched at the kitchen table, peering over the rim of her bifocals and writing out a list on a large pad of yellow legal paper. 'Of course Christina won't come, since her gout's been acting up, but I know Else and Ingebjorg will be here.' Mormor ran the pencil along the edge of her lower lip. 'We'll have cake and punch, but no beer. Remember what Tony did at Tor and Sally's wedding! I'm amazed that boy is still willing to show his face in public. Should we have steak or shrimp?'

'Steak,' Rainey said dully, staring out the window and kicking her feet against the legs of the chair.

Mormor shook her head. 'No, too expensive. What are we, made of money? Maybe meatballs and herring instead, and a big fruit salad. This is going to cost a fortune, of course.' She looked up suddenly and called into the living room, where Grandpa Garth was busy with the crossword puzzle. 'Pa, can we afford this? Can we afford shrimp?'

'We can afford a party,' Grandpa Garth called back mildly. 'We can't afford shrimp.'

'Åh, jaså, I'll get shrimp anyway,' Mormor said cheerfully, scribbling on the pad. 'It'll show Margaret that her Barry isn't the only smarty pants in this family. Look at Rainey – valedictorian! First in her class.' Mormor smiled, a rare little smile which revealed her row of narrow teeth and cleft soft wrinkles around her powdery eyes. Suddenly Mormor frowned. 'Stand up, child,' she ordered, motioning with the pencil. 'Turn around, let me get a good look at you.' Rainey stood and turned dutifully. 'That's it. That's the way.' Mormor took off her glasses and began to wipe them briskly on the loose hem of her faded denim shirt. 'You were such a terror when you were younger,' she said, shaking her head, allowing the small smile to return. 'But who would believe that to look at you now?'

*

Rainey hadn't heard a word from Ambrose for nearly a month, and the last message from him had been a brief note saying, 'I'm not auditioning for the spring play. Molière isn't my favourite, and I think I need a break from acting for a while.' It was now the end of May, two weeks before graduation. Rainey was pretending to be studying in her bedroom while glancing through some photos of Ambrose, age fourteen, in costume for an Essex Academy production of *A Connecticut Yankee in King Arthur's Court*. He had played a prince, complete with a rhinestone-studded crown and purple tights, which gathered in dark rings around his knobby knees. His soft white hair glistened in the spotlight, and there was a look of such fire in his pale, round eyes. On the back of the photo he had scribbled, 'Mutti and Vati sat in the third row. There was so much clapping, it almost hurt my ears. If only you were there too, Rainey. But you <u>were</u> there, in my heart.'

Rainey was so engrossed in the photo she didn't at first notice Grandpa Garth standing in her doorway, wearing a defeated smile and bandages on both wrists. 'Mind if I come in?' he asked.

'No, go ahead,' she answered, quickly shoving the photographs under her biology textbook. The warm breeze through her window ruffled the stack of tattered notebooks, and she was suddenly aware of the smell of honeysuckle and lilac, borne heavily on the night wind. She wondered what time it was, and how long she had spent staring at the photo.

'Sorry to bother you when you're studying,' Grandpa Garth said.

'It's OK, I wasn't doing much,' Rainey answered guiltily.

Rainey's graduation gown hung over the edge of the door, the silky gold sash pinned flat to the V-neck front. As valedictorian, Rainey's sash was gold; everyone else's would be white. Grandpa Garth looked at the long black gown, brushing it softly with the back of his bandaged hand.

'Mormor wants me to hang it in the bathroom while I'm taking a shower to steam the wrinkles out,' Rainey said and smiled. 'I think that Mormor has a solution for everything.'

Grandpa Garth lifted the gown's draped sleeves and held them up, creating a shape like a thin black angel. 'Your mother never graduated from high school,' he said, staring straight into the shiny fabric. 'But Michael did. He was so tall and skinny at eighteen. And handsome. The mortar board was too big for him, and it kept sliding down over his eyes.' Grandpa Garth let the sleeves fall to the side. 'I remember the first thing Michael did after he got the diploma was show it to me. He pointed to his name. "Michael Johann McBride", as if I wouldn't believe it was really his.' Grandpa Garth rubbed his moustache. His grey eyes were small and shadowy, looking deep into the past, seemingly amazed that he could be touched by something from so long ago.

'Was he a good student?' Rainey asked. This was the first time she had ever directly asked anything about her uncle.

'No, no, no,' Grandpa Garth said quickly, shaking his head. 'Not like you are. Michael was very bright, but he wasn't the academic type. I think he graduated ninety-seventh, in a class of just over two hundred. But he kept a strong C average and never failed a class, so we were happy with that. Michael always wanted to be a cop. He loved guns. I think he would have been a good cop too, if the Army hadn't gotten him first.'

Rainey wanted to hear more about Michael, but she could see on her grandfather's face that he had finished; he would say nothing more. Instead he came to the bed and sat down stiffly, tugging at the loosely knotted ends of the gauzy bandages.

'How are your hands?' Rainey asked.

'Oh, not so bad; not so bad.' He lifted his arms and shook them gently. 'The old joints were a little stiff, so Sonja rubbed on some Aspercreme, and now they're good as new. Well, almost good as new.'

'I'm glad to hear it,' Rainey said.

'You know, Audie Howatchek gave me his tickets to the Brewers game tomorrow night. I wondered if you wanted to go.'

'Oh sure,' Rainey said, surprised by the invitation. 'That would be fun.' She could hear the note of uncertainty in her voice.

'If you've got too much homework to do, that's OK,' Grandpa Garth said quickly, glancing at the haphazard pile of books stacked atop the bed. 'We can go some other time.'

'No. Tomorrow's fine,' she replied. 'Just fine. A baseball game. That should help take my mind off . . . everything.'

That evening, Rainey overheard Mormor and Grandpa Garth

talking in the kitchen. They were both losing their hearing; she could hear their conversations from every room in the house. Unknown to themselves, they had no secrets from Rainey now.

'Sonja, I think something's wrong. She's so quiet,' Grandpa Garth said. 'It's not normal for a high school girl.'

'*Uff da!* It's good that she's quiet,' Mormor countered. 'Think what a terror she could be at this age – car dates, prom, college boys at the back door. Have you forgotten what her mother put us through? No, we should thank our lucky stars our girl is . . .' Mormor paused. 'Well, she's quiet that one, but she's deep. Quiet but deep.'

'But she didn't want to go to the ballgame,' he protested. 'That's not like her at all.'

'Come on, Pa.' Mormor's voice sounded chiding and brittle.

'What?'

'Do I have to spell it out?'

'What?' he asked impatiently.

'She's eighteen. Do you really think she wants her friends to see her going to a baseball game with her grandfather? Think how embarrassing that must be.'

The kitchen was completely quiet for a moment; so quiet Rainey could hear the crickets humming outside the screen door. 'Hmmm. You're right, Sonja,' Grandpa Garth said at last. 'I hadn't thought about that. I'm sure you're right.'

On her way home from school the next day, Rainey was pleased that she'd have the house all to herself for a few hours while Mormor made her weekly appearance at Ethel Gurtz's sewing circle and Grandpa Garth was bowling with Ralph Schlicter and the team. In her solitude she had found freedom; she didn't have to try so hard to act like nothing was wrong. Unlocking the front door, Rainey grabbed the mail from the table in the front hallway and quickly leafed through the envelopes and fliers. Suddenly a small, stiff envelope stuck out of the bunch, and her eyes were drawn to the familiar return address of 'Angie Danvers, Warmouth, Massachusetts'. Rainey's hands were shaking as she tore open the envelope and unfolded the flimsy piece of notebook paper.

Dear Rainey,

By the time you get this, I'll be gone. I'm leaving Essex at the end of the week. I've recently learned some shocking news – my father didn't die of natural causes; Uncle Billy killed him. So now it's my solemn duty to find my uncle and make him answer for his crimes. Don't try to contact me, and don't expect to hear from me again. I do love you. Your brother in blood for all eternity,

Ambrose Torsten Dienst.

Rainey shook the envelope and out fell the Robin Yount rookie card she had given Ambrose in Evanston, which now looked bent and badly worn at the edges. 'Oh my God,' she said to herself, as something hard and heavy punched her in the stomach, forcing all the air out of her lungs. 'No, no, no,' she whispered, struggling to catch her breath. She couldn't think straight; her mind was racing, and ideas emerged half formed. Mostly she was aware of the fear; an overwhelming, all-consuming fear, but also a strength beyond anything she had ever felt before.

Rainey went to her grandparents' bedroom and took her $647 scholarship money out of Grandpa Garth's sock drawer. The cash had been there for weeks, after Grandpa Garth's bowling buddies had raised it for her in a bowl-a-thon, and Grandpa Garth, after showing her where he was keeping it in case he forgot, had never gotten around to depositing it in the bank. Rainey grabbed the soft wad of threadbare bills, mostly tens and faded twenties, and clutched it in her hand. She squeezed the roll so tightly that an inky odour rose to her face and the pale green colour seemed to rub off on her skin.

She packed quickly, not even thinking about what she was doing. In the bedroom her graduation gown still hung over the door, sleek and freshly pressed. But now it resembled a slack black ghost; a dark and hollow shroud. The gown seemed like a sign of something dead, while within her raged the will to save Ambrose's fragile life.

As Rainey passed through the kitchen on her way out the back door, her eye was caught briefly by the hastily scribbled note stuck to the refrigerator. 'Remember the Brewers game tonight,' Grandpa Garth had written. 'Don't spoil your dinner – I'll treat you to a brat with special sauce. If you promise not to tell your grandmother, I'll even let you have a little beer.'

Rainey took the bus downtown to the Amtrak station and, using the alias 'Astrid Svensen', bought a ticket for the first train to Chicago. She needed to get out of Milwaukee as soon as possible; then once she got to Chicago, she could catch the first train heading northeast. She was in a state of full-blown anxiety; every face looked familiar, ready to capture her and turn her in. Every middle-aged man could be her biology teacher, every old woman looked exactly like Ethel Gurtz. Rainey was frantic with fear, but behind the terror she could hear the resounding echo of that voice Ambrose had promised her long ago, *I'm right, I'm right, I'm right.* The certainty of what she was doing radiated through every inch of her body.

At the Amtrak station, she grabbed a postcard and stamp and scribbled a quick note:

Dear Mormor and Grandpa Garth,
    Don't worry. I'm fine, I'm safe and I haven't run away. I've gone to help a friend who really needs me. I'll be home as soon as possible. I've borrowed my scholarship money, but I promise to pay it back. Please don't be angry, I love you both very much,
                                                                    Rainey.

She pressed her lips to the postcard before depositing it in the big blue mailbox.

As the train pulled away from the station, Rainey sat back in her seat. *Now I am like my mother, now I am her child through and through*, she thought suddenly. *I have found a part of Mary Jane in me. Now I know what she felt when she jumped into that car with Carlos and drove away, leaving me far behind. I understand her passion, her longing, her need to be free. I belong to her again.* Rainey sat back, surprised at the happiness that accompanied such an unexpected blessing.

Rainey watched the slow progress of the lazy brown Menomonee River and smelled diesel, chocolate and Red Star yeast. Everything looked and smelled of corruption; living in the suburbs she had forgotten how old and skeletal the inner city really was. All her senses were heightened by panic and excitement. For the first time in her life she felt both achingly alive and completely powerful – she would rescue Ambrose; she would save him from himself.

The train, building up speed, passed burned-out warehouses and disused rail tracks; mahogany-toned bricks and rusty metal works. Milwaukee was incredibly ugly, Rainey decided, and yet she loved it desperately now that she was leaving. She longed to grab hold of the low-lying valley, the carbon and steel heart of the city, with the three clogged rivers that billowed into the lake. She leaned forward and watched as the train broke free of the city and delved deep into farmland, like a bright bullet heading towards Sturtevant and places unknown.

By early evening she had changed trains in Chicago, and darkness began to fall across the vast prairie of Indiana, throwing into shadow the tiny, one-stoplight towns, where men got out of their cars at the crossing and waved to the train passing by. Rainey felt so anonymous. 'I am Astrid Svensen,' she said, looking at her ticket. 'Astrid Svensen is me.' But she was beginning to tire. The panic and excitement were wearing away, and creeping into her consciousness was the reality of what she was doing; and what she had already done. 'It will be OK,' she told herself. 'Ambrose is probably just upset about his dad. I'll talk some sense into him, and everything will be OK. I'm sure it will work out fine in the end.'

Rainey was asleep when the train pulled into Boston. It was three o'clock in the morning and she nearly jumped out of her seat when the ticket collector touched her on the shoulder. 'Sorry, miss, but we're in Boston. You have to get off the train now,' he told her. She nodded, and struggled to collect herself.

'Are you gonna be OK, miss?' the ticket collector asked. 'Do you have someone waiting for you here? Boston can be pretty scary if you're on your own.'

'I'm all right,' she told him. 'I'll be fine. Thanks.' She rubbed her face and nodded, grabbing her backpack and slinging it over her shoulder.

She followed the other passengers off the train and stood in the middle of the station, wondering what to do next. Three o'clock in the morning was too early to head to Essex. She got a Pepsi from the soda machine, and a little packet of crackers with cheese. She made a note in her notebook, keeping track of the money she'd spent so far. 'I'll be home by the beginning of next week,' she promised herself. 'I won't spend more than a couple hundred dollars. I can pay that back over the summer.'

She found a reasonably clean seat in the waiting lounge and sat down. Rainey's only companions were an old woman, with all her earthly possessions in a supermarket shopping cart, and a yellowy drunk in a shabby coat, who leered at Rainey and winked at her over the upturned bottom of his bottle. Another man fiddled nervously with the pockets of his flak jacket, then slid out an enormous carving knife and began nonchalantly filing his fingernails. Rainey rested her head on her backpack and covered herself with her coat, closing her eyes. She started to recite the Nicene Creed: '"God from God, Light from Light, True God from True God, Begotten, Not Made . . ."'

At last seven am arrived, and after cleaning up in the restroom, Rainey steadied herself for the next step of her journey. She took a taxi from the train station to the suburb of Warmouth, twelve miles away. She had the driver drop her off at the entrance to the well-manicured campus of Essex Academy, which, according to the sign on the lawn, had been established in 1828. The whole place looked like money, old brick buildings and deep green grass. *So this is out east*, she thought, stopping for a second to survey the place. *It doesn't look that different from the rich neighbourhoods at home.* She realised how disappointing it would be to discover that all of the United States looked exactly like suburban Milwaukee. 'I'll get to see lots of America when I work for NBC News,' she told herself. 'I'll be travelling out east all the time, going to Washington and New York and places like that.' But even as she said it, she had doubts. 'Final exams are in two weeks. If I miss them, I won't graduate on time. And that means I won't be able to start college.'

Rainey strode quickly across the large, leafy campus to Codec Hall, Ambrose's dormitory, and went up to the third floor. She knocked on the door to his room and was greeted by Gary, Ambrose's tall, dark-haired roommate, whom she recognised from photos Ambrose had sent her years ago.

'Can I help you?' he asked, looking puzzled.

'Yes. My name is Rainey McBride and I'm looking for my cousin, Ambrose Torsten Dienst. Has he left yet?' she asked frantically, pushing her way into the room.

'You're Rainey?' Gary asked.

'Yes.'

'*The* Rainey?'

'I'm the only Rainey I know,' she said impatiently.

'So this is you?' he asked, grabbing her sleeve and pulling her towards a small oak desk in the corner of the room. It was Ambrose's desk, and above it was a collection of things she had sent him over the years – photos of her in a girl-scout uniform, a ticket stub from a Brewers–Blue Jays game, a picture of her handprint in gooey yellow paint, through which she had drawn a thin red line – a reference to the secret handshake. She was touched by the almost shrine-like quality of the display, and the way the images were laid carefully one atop the other, indicating the passage of time.

'Yes, this is me. I sent him all these things,' she said. 'I got a letter from Ambrose yesterday and it really upset me. I came to see if he's OK.' She paused. '*Is* he OK?'

'I don't know. I haven't seen him for days,' Gary said mildly.

'Where and when did he go?' Rainey asked, her panic rising.

'I have no idea. Ambrose flipped out a few months ago. I don't see him much; he's hardly ever around. But all his stuff is still here, so I doubt he's gone very far.'

'Where do you think he might be?' Rainey asked.

'Try the shed,' Gary offered.

'The shed?'

'Yes. He spends the night there sometimes.'

'And where is this shed?'

'It's just over that way.' He pointed out the window to a small workman's shed, its corrugated metal roof visible just beyond the soccer field and the pool house.

'OK, thanks,' she said. She rushed out the door but then stopped in the hallway and turned back to Gary. 'Do you care at all?' she asked slowly. 'About Ambrose, I mean. Aren't you worried about the way he's behaving?'

Gary shrugged. 'Ambrose and me, we go way back. I care about him. But he's eighteen years old. I can't tell him what to do.' Gary paused. 'When did you last see him?'

'January,' she replied. 'About six months ago.'

'I better warn you,' Gary said, shaking his head. 'He's changed. He's probably not the Ambrose you remember.'

Rainey set off across the bright green field, passing two teams of strong-legged boys playing flag football, and a group of sweaty young men, jogging in pairs. She was irritated by the prettiness assaulting her from every angle: the manicured bushes, the gleaming tennis courts, the artificial lake complete with swans.

Rainey approached the shed slowly and knocked on the door. At first there was no response, but suddenly she heard an urgent rustling noise inside. 'Ambrose?' she called softly. 'Ambrose? It's me, Rainey. Open up.'

The door inched open, allowing a thin shaft of light to leak into the dark interior. Ambrose peered around the corner of the door and stood shivering in an undershirt and shorts, with a loose sock fallen down around one ankle. He opened the door an inch further, and stood in the shadows, rubbing his stained and puffy face.

'What the hell . . . Rainey. How did you get here?' he mumbled sleepily.

'There's no time to explain,' she said, pushing past him into the dim light of the shed, which was cluttered with wheelbarrows and rusty tools, and smelled of stale beer and sweat. 'I was so worried that you had already left. Look, you can't go . . .' She stopped suddenly when she saw a man lying on a threadbare mattress in the middle of the room. He was on his back, with one arm draped to the floor. His mouth hung open and he was snoring loudly. 'Who's that?' she asked.

'That's Mr Barron,' Ambrose answered matter of factly, kicking away an old yellow newspaper that slid across the floor.

'What's he doing here?' she asked.

'He lives here. Sort of. He's the groundskeeper. It's his shed.' Ambrose scratched his head and yawned dully, curling his arms over his chest as if to keep himself warm, even though the shed was hot and unbearably stuffy.

'Then what are you doing here?' she asked.

'I'm keeping him company,' he answered simply.

She looked at Ambrose more closely as he stood before her, head hanging, shoulders slumped into his chest. His hair was close to shoulder length now and filthy, matted nearly grey with grease. There were dark circles under his eyes, and a pale and patchy beard stood out on his pimpled chin. *This can't be Ambrose. It just can't be.* She looked down at the man on the mattress, then looked up at Ambrose, trying to understand what connected the two of them.

'Let's just say we're old friends,' Ambrose said, noticing her confusion and nodding down towards the man. 'I don't expect I'll be taking him to the senior's cotillion this year. But he'll do.' Ambrose's voice was raspy, hard and dry from a combination of beer and cigarettes.

'Ambrose,' she said, feeling like her head was about to burst. 'What's happened to you?'

He shrugged. 'Nothing. I've just been lucky enough over the past few months to find out what a disgusting human being I am, and now that I know that fact, I intend to celebrate.' He flashed a sad, defeated grin.

'Ambrose, are you going to look for your uncle?' she asked.

'Yes. I am.'

'You can't. I won't let you.'

Ambrose let out a deep breath and stumbled towards the bed. He kicked the mattress, and when Mr Barron didn't move, Ambrose grabbed the man's leg and shook it hard. Finally Mr Barron woke up, licking and smacking his lips. He stood and stretched, seeming undisturbed by the arrival of Rainey. His eyes, sealed with a sticky layer of sleep, never fully opened. He rubbed his dark, oily face and smiled, then leaned over to kiss Ambrose. Rainey watched as Ambrose stiffened and held back. 'Get out of here,' Ambrose told him. 'Don't come back until tomorrow morning.' The grey-haired man nodded, scratched himself and shuffled out of the shed.

'What made you come here?' Ambrose asked Rainey, closing the warped tin door behind Mr Barron.

'Your letter. I was so scared. I thought you were going to do something drastic.'

He motioned for her to sit down on the mattress, which she did, delicately, afraid of the greasy surface and the horrible smell.

'Who knows you're here?' he asked, standing in front of her, holding his cheeks as if they were tender and painful.

'No one,' she answered.

'Good. Then go back to Milwaukee now, while you still can,' he insisted, staring right through her with his hollow, red-rimmed eyes.

'No,' she said firmly. 'Not until I know you're OK.'

'I will be OK. Once I find Schmidt.'

'Then let me help you. That's why I came.'

Ambrose sat down on the mattress next to her and held his knees, cradling them close to his chest. He took a deep breath and held it a long time, then slowly let go. 'I never wanted you to get in trouble because of this,' he said edgily, almost in tears.

'I know. But it's too late, because I am here now.' She reached over and gently touched his back, feeling the tight muscles twitch and pull beneath his dirty white T-shirt. 'I want to help you,' she said softly.

He held his face in his hands, and she touched him again, this time letting her fingers stroke and caress his shoulder blades. 'You're the only person who's ever cared about me, Rain. The only one,' he whispered and then started to cry. As he lifted his hand to brush away the tears, she saw the bruises on the inside of his arm.

'What is this?' she asked, grabbing his arm and holding it up to the grimy yellow light. She traced the rows of brown-black bruises, the size and shape of pennies. 'Are you taking drugs?'

'No,' he said drawing back quickly. 'It's not drugs. See? No needle marks.' He pressed a finger into the skin near his elbow and lifted it away, watching the blood flow back into the hollow white dent.

'It was that man,' she said suddenly. 'That man who was here. Ambrose, you let him hurt you like this? Why? I don't understand.'

'No, you don't understand it,' Ambrose told her bitterly, flashing with anger. 'We have a relationship, Mr Barron and me. I guess that's what you'd call it. I let him do things to me. I pretend to enjoy it, although I suspect he knows the truth. He does whatever he wants, and then afterwards, he hits me and slaps me, and if I cry, he burns me with matches and hot wax.'

'But why?'

Ambrose shrugged, forcing a wan, hollow smile. 'It's better than nothing, I suppose. It beats being alone.'

'Let me love you instead,' she said passionately, grabbing his hands and holding them in her lap. 'I wouldn't ever hurt you, I won't do anything bad, I promise.'

He pulled away and looked at her with something like hatred burning behind his eyes. 'I *want* it to be bad. I want to know the awfulness of it. Rainey, you are too good. Too kind. Too full of love. That makes me feel suffocated. And guilty. I don't deserve the good part of yourself that you give me; you give it to me over and over, and I feel like I want to die. You're strong and generous and good; you're so damn good it makes me sick. You deserve the Young Lutheran of the Year award. You deserve every award they could ever give you! I'm not like you. I need to see the bad in things. Stop loving me so much. Just stop it! Being with Mr Barron feels better. It's horrible and disgusting and dirty; he's dirty, he smells so bad, and he hits me and burns me until I cry, until I know I'm wallowing in the most sad, depraved and disgusting part of myself. When I get down there, I'm like a rodent, and I stop being human. That's when I start to feel something like comfort. That's the only time I can look up and see the sky above me.'

Rainey pressed her hands to her lips to hold back the horror. Her eyes filled with tears. 'How long have you felt this way?'

'A long time,' he admitted. 'I wanted to tell you but you always seemed so . . . happy.' He paused. 'It's gotten worse since my father died.' He looked up, searching for shapes in the hot dusty darkness of the shed. 'Vati protected me, even when he wasn't here. Knowing he would beat up anyone who touched me, then I could manage. But not any more.'

'How do you handle it?' she asked, wiping her face. 'How do you live?'

He shrugged, scratching his pimply forehead with a long broken thumbnail. 'I black out sometimes, I guess that's the best way to describe it. My imagination sets me free. You remember when I told you about that place inside my head where I can go and no one can touch me? Well, in the worst moments, I imagine myself in the blueberry patch behind Ingebjorg's house. I see that blood-purple colour and all the little blossoms weaving through the wire fence. I can smell the sunshine and hear our feet crunching over the vines. We'd steal so many berries, me and you, and pop them in our mouths and keep eating until our lips and tongues turned black, our hands turned purple and the sky a bright hot blue. We could eat in that field forever and never finish; if we stayed there, we would never, ever be hungry. As long as I see that field, Schmidt can never reach me.' Ambrose looked up at her, his eyes shining with a hard, dead sheen. 'It's pathetic, I know. I'm so pathetic.'

'No. You're not pathetic. Not to me. You're going to be OK,' she told him. 'I'm here to help you. You're not alone.'

'God, you don't know how much I want to believe that,' he said, leaning against her shoulder. 'Rainey, you are an angel here on earth.'

As much as she wanted to believe it, something dark and feathery sprang to life inside her, rising up her spine. 'I'm not an angel,' she insisted. 'I'm only Rainey. Rainey McBride.' She was silent for a long time, matching her breath to his. 'Where are you going, and how are you planning to get there?' she asked quietly.

It took Ambrose a second to understand her. 'From what I've found out, it sounds like he's in Baltimore,' he said. 'I bought myself a used car two days ago. I've parked it about half a mile from here, in the woods on the road to Dorset.'

'OK,' she said with quiet certainty. 'Then I'm going with you. You're not going alone.'

That night they packed the car full of things he had stolen from Mr Barron, and she with her scholarship money, which felt greasy, in her pocket and against her fingertips. The night was very dark; no stars looked down on them and there was no moon to witness their deed. It was cold and misty, and she could hear bull frogs and crickets croaking and singing in the distance. She felt a twinge of excitement inside her, as if an adventure were about to begin, even in the midst of so much shame and horror. She looked at Ambrose in the darkness and he offered her a sad smile, which reminded her of his face from a long time ago. 'Thanks for doing this,' he said softly. 'I'll make it up to you somehow, Rain, I promise. It will all be over sooner than you think.' He turned the key and the motor buckled and droned, struggling to turn over. Finally the engine started and he began to inch the car through the thick trees, the noise muffled by the soft bed of pine needles beneath the wheels.

'Where's your mother?' Rainey asked him suddenly as she leaned forward, searching for deer hidden deep among the trees.

'In Colorado.'

'What's she doing there?'

'She has a boyfriend. She's living with him, I think,' Ambrose answered.

'That was quick,' Rainey said.

'They've been together for years,' he said dryly.

'Oh. I'm sorry.'

'So am I.' Ambrose sighed. 'So am I.'

'Ambrose, what did your letter mean? What makes you think your uncle killed Vati?'

'Because the death certificate said "death caused by chemical substance or substances unknown",' Ambrose explained.

'But that could mean anything,' Rainey argued. 'That doesn't show he was murdered.'

'Of course it does. Who else would want him dead? And what better way to do it than poison him? Uncle Billy worked as a chemical engineer before he and Vati went into business. He knew how to kill him and still cover his tracks.' Ambrose sighed. 'Poor Vati – his wife was cheating on him, and his best friend caused his death. But it's OK, Vati, because I'm going to set it right. I'm going to set it right, all right.' Ambrose scratched a scab on his arm, first just flicking at it with his fingernail but then scraping off the skin.

'Don't do that,' Rainey asked him, seeing a few drops of blood rising to the surface of his arm. 'Please.'

He stopped scratching. 'You know these marks on my arm,' he said carefully. 'Well, Mr Barron isn't responsible for all of them.'

'What do you mean?' she asked.

'Some I did myself. I cut myself sometimes too, to take my mind off the pain. The pain of everything else. Look here, this really hurt a few days ago,' he said, pointing to a long, thin scar on his wrist. 'And now I can touch it and feel nothing. Isn't it amazing, how fast pain goes away? It's like it never even hurt at all.'

ELEVEN

June 1988
Chicago, Illinois

The vibrant bright energy of late-night Chicago was lost on Rainey and Ambrose, silent in the dark Chevy, with Ambrose edgy behind the wheel. Baltimore had not yielded up the elusive William Schmidt, and neither had Akron or Indianapolis. After two and a half weeks of searching, the latest information placed Schmidt on Chicago's near North Side, staying with an old Army buddy named Washington Taylor. Ambrose managed to track down Taylor's address, and so he and Rainey left Indianapolis and headed northwest on Interstate 65.

They entered Chicago from the south, drifting through the grim, arid, industrial despair of Gary, Hammond and East Chicago. They sailed past water towers with painted roses and occasional trains that charged the barren concrete and steel landscape with brief glimpses of light. After so many days, and so many miles, of Centerburgs and Westervilles, Chicago, even from its edges, seemed an oasis; a massive, spiralling city, right in the middle of everything and still, surrounded by nothing. The billboards and the stripmalls and the street lights disturbed Rainey, nudging her out of her road-induced stupor, and for the first time in days, something more than just quiet dread stirred inside her. She had always liked Chicago's toughness – the way it muscled away from Lake Michigan and elbowed itself on to the prairie, gobbling up farmland and corn fields and still asking for second helpings, but now the city's strength seemed to her shallow and menacing.

'One hundred and one,' Rainey said to Ambrose.

He fiddled with the empty pack of cigarettes and drummed his long fingernails against the steering wheel. 'What's that supposed to mean?'

'One hundred and one days. That's how long until our classes start at Northwestern,' she said.

'Look, you didn't have to come along with me, you know. You could hop on a bus and be back in Milwaukee in less than two hours,' he said.

'I know. Don't tell me that – it only makes me feel worse.'

'I remember, I was about five the first time I went to Chicago,' Ambrose said, his voice lightening. 'Vati was giving a lecture at Loyola and then leading a seminar at DePaul.'

Rainey didn't respond, and Ambrose was silent for a few moments too. 'I remember Mutti took me shopping at Field's and bought me a ton of presents, and when Vati came back to the hotel, he was mad. He said spending so much money was shameful, so we took the presents to a hospital and gave them to sick kids.'

'Where are you going?' she asked suddenly, as the car sped past the Eisenhower Expressway and headed east towards the gritty glitter of the Loop.

'Twenty-five seventeen North Sheffield,' he answered.

'I know that. I mean why didn't you take the Kennedy and get off on Fullerton?'

'Because. I'm going downtown.'

'You don't need to,' she said.

'Well this is the way I've decided to go,' he answered. 'I'm taking Clybourn.'

Rainey picked up the map off the floor, tearing it out of a puddle of dried root beer. 'It would be quicker if we took the Kennedy,' she said evenly. 'There's no point in going downtown.' She traced the red vein of the route with her fingernail.

Ambrose sighed, wiping the sweat from his forehead and pressing on the accelerator. Rainey felt the car pitch and hum as it picked up speed. 'One of those kids, I think he had leukaemia, he got this big teddy bear and he was so excited! You should've seen his face! The nurse took a picture of him and Vati, and Vati kept it on the desk in his office.' Ambrose licked his lips and his voice took on a soft, dreamy quality. 'We're going to find him soon, Rain, I know it . . . I think the boy died. He died after Christmas. Vati kept the picture on his desk . . . Vati died after Christmas.'

Please don't start this again, she wanted to say, but she held her tongue. She sat back in her seat, crushing a Styrofoam cup in the small of her spine. She turned and retrieved it, tossing it into the back seat. The car was littered with debris – shrivelled orange rinds and darkened apple cores, torn T-shirts and frayed cleaning rags, hamburger wrappers translucent with grease, and a stack of muddy towels they had stolen from a Budgetel.

Ambrose fiddled with the broken air conditioner, and getting no response from it, began to play with the ruined tape player, twisting and pulling the coiled loops of tape that spilled out over the dashboard. 'We're gonna find him,' he whispered. She could feel his body begin to tremble. 'I bet we find him here, Rain. That fat, stinking pig. I can't wait to see him sweat. William Schmidt. Mr William Schmidt. I've come for the sake of Holger Olav Dienst. No one gets away with murder. Not the murder of Holger Olav Dienst. That fat pig, I'll drop his body in the lake. Bang. Bang. Plop. Body in the lake. Bang. Bang. Plop.' She squinted out of the corner of her eye. Ambrose held his thumb and forefinger in the shape of a gun and pressed against the windscreen until his fingertips turned white. 'Pow. Plop. Pow. Plop,' he whispered, puffing his thin, pale, trembling lips. Rainey leaned back and closed her eyes, searching for words to fill her silent prayers.

They found the apartment building at the intersection of Sheffield and Altgeld, underneath the 'L' tracks, between a currency exchange, a 24-hour laundromat and a Gold Coast Kosher Dogs. They pulled open the wrought-iron front door and stepped into the darkened lobby, which stank of ammonia and mould. An indistinguishable liquid dripped from the ceiling and huge bluebottle flies buzzed around the one bare light bulb. The lobby was empty except for a broken-backed chair and a stack of wet newspapers rotting in the corner. 'We should come back tomorrow,' Rainey said. 'It would be safer here in daylight.'

'Don't be such a girl,' Ambrose scoffed. 'We're here now, we might as well see if we can find Taylor. If we find him, it's just one short step to finding Schmidt.' They looked at the wall of mail slots and followed it down to 'Apt 3C'. A yellowed strip of paper that read 'McGuigan' in faded pencil script was taped above the slot.

'This isn't it. It isn't his place,' Rainey said.

'You don't know that. Taylor might live here. It's worth a try.'

The lift was broken, so they walked around to the alley behind the building and found a circular steel staircase which twisted up to the roof. Rainey heard the rough rattle in the distance as an 'L' train approached. The sound built to a bone-shaking blast as the train bolted over their heads, passing within inches of the building. 'Come on, we don't want to wait here all night,' Ambrose said.

They soft-shoed it up the staircase, past the blackened, broken windows and the pools of slime and urine, and she felt her shoe treads catch on the rusty stairs. Rainey kept her eye on Ambrose's back, the shoulder muscles visible beneath his T-shirt, and the tight curve of his belt.

They stopped on the third floor, both breathing hard. The door with the crooked letter 'C' hanging by one nail looked as if it had been hacked through with an axe. The door knob was separated from the door jamb, and slashes of black duct tape held the split wood together like the bandage on an ugly wound.

'I don't know about this,' Rainey whispered. Her heart was still pounding and her ribs felt bruised.

Ambrose knocked confidently. 'Vati would be so proud of me,' he whispered, and his words sliced into the tenderness of her chest.

Ambrose knocked again, louder this time.

'I don't think this is it,' Rainey said.

'There's only one way to find out.' He went to the window and began to slide it open, jimmying it back and forth out of its plastic track. When it was open five or six inches, he stuck one leg through.

Rainey heard a shuffling on the other side of the door and the metallic ting of the door knob twisting in its broken holder. 'Ambrose! Watch out!' she whispered, expecting to see the end of a gun as the door rattled and opened. Instead a small, frail man, hunched at the shoulders, stepped on to the landing, rubbing his eyes and blinking in the dimness. He was barefoot, dressed in tight blue jeans and an old leather vest with no shirt beneath. His arms were thin and gnarled, with knotted veins visible around his elbows.

'Yeah? What is it? What do y'all want?' the man asked vaguely. Ambrose jumped back as the window slammed closed.

'Sorry to bother you. We're looking for Mr Washington Taylor. We got this address from a friend of his in Indianapolis – do you know where we might find him?' Ambrose asked politely.

'Hmmmm.' The man flicked out a thin wrist and began to stroke his narrow, darkly stubbled chin. 'C'mon in a sec,' he said, nodding towards the shadowy interior of his apartment. Rainey hesitated, but Ambrose was quick to step inside, leaving her no choice but to follow.

The man was younger than he first appeared – maybe forty-five or fifty, with a drawn, sallow face, sharp features and a full head of kinky dark brown hair. His eyes were pale blue and cloudy, seemingly without a pupil. Rainey thought he might be blind, but then he caught her eye and winked, flashing a grin with his row of spindly teeth. 'Let's see. Taylor. Yeah. I think that's the guy who lived here before me. Tall, black, heavy-set fella. Nice guy. Helped me move my furniture.'

'Do you know where he is now?'

'Yeah. Think he moved to Minnesota.'

'Did he leave an address or phone number?'

'I can't remember. I s'pose he did, but I'd have to search for it somewhere in this mess.'

'Damn.' Ambrose spat out the word like a piece of spoiled food. Rainey was ready to leave but Ambrose was determined to find out more. 'Look, I wouldn't ask you to look for it if it wasn't really important,' Ambrose pleaded, 'but we've been on the road for a while and we got to find him before we run out of money.'

'Friend, I can see you're troubled,' the man said. 'All right, I'll try.

But it's too dark to find anything now and my eyes aren't so good. Why don't you crash here tonight and I promise I'll look for it first thing in the morning.'

'Really?' Ambrose asked, his voice light and surprised.

'Sure. I got a couch in the den and an extra bed in the spare room. It's a Christian duty to help a stranger in need. "For I hungered, and you did give me meat, I was thirsty and you gave me drink, I was a stranger, and you took me in",' the man said.

'Great. That's fantastic, man. Can't thank you enough. I'll go down and get our stuff. Is there somewhere safe to park around here?' Ambrose asked, thrilled by the prospect of a bed for the night.

'Pull in the alleyway between Seminary and Lill. The cops won't check back there until eleven o'clock tomorrow morning,' the man said. Ambrose hurried out the door and Rainey was left awkwardly facing the stranger. He bowed and motioned for her to step deeper into the apartment.

She smiled weakly, trying to be friendly. 'Sorry to put you out like this, so late and all,' she said to the man, getting a better look at the shabby apartment, which was cluttered with dirty dishes and laundry strewn over the sofa. A close, sweaty odour emanated from the kitchen, a mixture of fried onions, bacon and chicken noodle soup, and there were other odours too, incense or dope, and something pungent and sweet, which seemed to come from the man himself. A huge poster took up most of the living-room wall. It was a picture of a giant cross with two smaller crosses on either side. Beneath the crosses was the inscription: 'Come unto me, all ye that labor and are heavy laden, and I will give you rest.' Matt 10:28.

The man saw her looking at the poster and he nodded towards it. 'I like to be able to gaze on The Good News from every corner of the room,' he said. Alone with him now, she realised the strangeness of his voice – high-pitched and nasal, but compelling – a voice that needed to be heard. Out of the shadows came an old yellowish dog, some sort of Bulldog/Bassett Hound mix, wheezing asthmatically. The dog waddled up to the man's leg and dropped his chin on to the man's bare foot.

'There's my boy,' the man said, squatting down and stroking the dog's quivering head. The dog shook happily and his tongue unfurled to the floor. 'Oh, who's been a good boy? That's right. You've been a good boy. This here's Damascus,' the man said, looking up at Rainey and pointing down to the dog by means of introduction.

She smiled and noticed another poster on the other wall. This one was smaller, about the size of a theatre playbill, with a photo of a curly-haired man in a cap, playing a harmonica. Beneath the photo it said: 'Live In Concert. Sixties Folk Legend Woody Stern. Tuesdays in August at Billy Simmon's.'

She looked at the photo, looked at the man and made the inevitable connection. 'Wow. So you're Woody Stern! A real-life folk legend.' She felt herself blush.

'So you've heard of me?' the man asked, intrigued.

'No,' she answered honestly. 'Sorry about that.'

The man shook his head. 'It's all right. You're a little young to remember me anyway,' he said. 'I come from before your time.'

'Well, maybe I would recognise some of your songs,' she offered hopefully. 'Were you ever on Johnny Carson?'

He smiled with genuine pleasure. 'As a matter of fact, I was on Johnny once. I was on the same night as Buddy Hackett and the lady from the San Diego Zoo. But that's a long time ago now.' He paused. 'So you know who I am but I still don't know who you are.'

'My name is Rainey McBride,' she said, shaking his hand, which was thin and cool and tiny, not like a man's hand at all. 'And he's my . . .' she stumbled. 'And the guy I'm with is my friend, Ambrose. Ambrose Torsten Dienst.'

Seemingly at the mention of his name, Ambrose returned to the apartment. 'Ambrose – guess what? This is Woody Stern!' Rainey said, pointing to the man beside her as if he were an inanimate object; a statue, or a sign along the road.

'Who?' Ambrose asked, nonchalantly.

'Woody Stern. Sixties folk legend.'

'Never heard of him,' Ambrose said.

'He was once on Johnny Carson and everything,' Rainey told him.

'Great,' Ambrose said, showing no interest.

'He was never too big on watching television,' Rainey said to Woody, trying to apologise for Ambrose's lack of excitement.

'You've been friends a long time then, hey?' Woody asked, scratching his forehead.

Rainey realised she'd been caught. 'Yeah,' she answered quickly. 'We grew up next door to each other. We've been friends forever.'

Woody showed them to the spare room, which Ambrose immediately took for himself. Rainey dropped her bag on the living-room sofa, and Woody brought her a threadbare afghan. 'Do you want something to eat?' he asked. 'I don't have much; some eggs, a few bagels, some chorizo and beer, but whatever I got is yours. If you're starving, I could run to the 7-11 across the street and buy some more. Except they only got bear claws and nachos left this time of night.' He smiled. Rainey felt dry and dizzy with hunger but the door to the spare room was closed, and Ambrose wouldn't emerge again until daylight. The sight of Woody standing before her, painfully thin with his narrow arms folded in front of his chest, made her feel unbearably sad.

'No, that's OK,' she told him. 'We've been on the road all day and I think we're probably too tired to eat.'

'Well go ahead and help yourself if you feel hungry in the night,' Woody offered. He rubbed the top of one foot with the toes of the other, and as he ran his hand through his mass of curly hair, Rainey noticed a large shiny scar cleft into his forehead.

'What happened there?' she asked, stepping close to him and inhaling the rank, sweet odour that rose from his body. She realised she was taller than he was, as she bent to touch his forehead, but she stopped just before her fingers found the wound. Only after she said the words did she consider how rude her question sounded, but he just smiled again and didn't seem to mind. He yanked up a handful of his hair and tilted his face towards the dim light so Rainey could get a better view of the oval, concave scar, which scooped out a segment of his hairline and dipped down towards his thick, wiry brown eyebrow.

'What happened?' she asked.

'This was done to me by my fellow man. I was working in the soup kitchen down in Lawndale, when some guy hit me over the head with a fry pan and stole my wallet,' he explained.

'I'm sorry. That sounds awful,' she said. This time she touched his forehead, pressing her fingertip into the dent. She could feel a ridge of bone where the skull had been broken beneath the skin.

'Hurt like hell, but I forgave him. I haven't written a decent piece of music since. It's like he broke my head and all the songs spilled out.'

'Wow,' Rainey said, both horrified and strangely impressed. 'You must really hate him for doing that to you.'

Woody shook his head energetically. 'No, not at all. Do you know what I told him when it happened? I said, "Please, take more. Take everything I have. It's not right that I have a home and you don't. It's not right that I have food and clothes and money. You deserve to have some of mine." Did I forgive him for hitting me with a frying pan? Seventy times seven. You bet I did. Seventy times seven.'

Rainey suddenly wanted to confess all her sins to this person. He seemed to be a completely generous being, a wise older man who had seen and done everything, and nothing she could tell him about herself or Ambrose would shock or disturb him.

'Good night now,' he said softly. 'I better let you get some sleep.'

'Yeah. Good night. Thanks again,' she said. She could hear the slap of his bare feet on the floor as he went towards his bedroom. She lay down on the stained and threadbare couch and pulled the knitted afghan over her head. It smelled of hairspray, cigarettes and sweat, and the yarn tassels scratched her face. She pushed it away and sank into the cushions. She lay very still, listening to the clock tick in the kitchen. 'I'm so hungry,' she said to herself. She felt a tickle as something skirted over her feet. Mites, she guessed. She just hoped it wasn't lice. Outside the city seethed, catching its breath between the frantic night and the roaring day, but still in this hour of darkness it was noisy – an argument in Spanish next door, cars and horns and city crickets, the ring of bottles tossed into the street.

'I'll never be able to sleep,' she told herself, but she must have fallen asleep, at least for a moment, because in the next instant, she was awake and knew that she had been dreaming of love. But it was a grown-up love she longed for now; these were not the same feelings she had at thirteen, when she toyed with images of Pastor Jeff's naked chest. She wanted something baser than the kiss of angels, darker than the touch of their feathery wings. She wanted a sweaty, oily certainty. She remembered suddenly that Woody had yellow teeth. He was very old, she decided. But if she kissed him, while their lips touched, he might be young again.

The roar of another 'L' train shook her completely awake. She had to see Ambrose, just to make sure he was all right. He hadn't been out of her sight for this long since they left Essex Academy. She went to the spare bedroom and pushed open the door. 'It's just me,' she whispered.

Ambrose lay on the bed with the edge of the blanket wedged between his knees, wearing only a pair of white boxer shorts. She could tell he wasn't asleep, but he was very still, curled and hard as an insect. She stepped closer and watched his body tighten on the bed until he was as solid as stone. She remembered what he had told her once, about how he had endured it. By pretending to be dead. By closing his eyes and holding his breath and withdrawing, pulling in further and further, until the boy disappeared and only a hard little pebble was left.

She wanted to unfold him limb by limb, open him up and crawl inside his pain. *Ambrose, what's it like? Tell me, what's it like?* she wanted to ask. If only he would tell her about the pain, she could hold it, swallow it, neutralise it. She could make it go away. He had tried, during their long hours on the road, to tell her what he felt: *'It's like falling into a black hole. You can see the sky above your head, you know it's there but you can't crawl out. The world loses its flavour — food, drink, music, love, everything is sawdust. Every colour turns grey. To walk ten feet seems impossible and overwhelming; each step you take pulls you down deeper, each step drags you towards the centre of the earth.'*

'Ambrose, are you OK?' she asked carefully, sitting down in the chair beside the window.

'I'm tired,' he said, breathing into the mattress. 'So, so tired.'

'What happens if Woody can't find Taylor's address? Are we just going to keep chasing rumours and phantom leads forever?'

'We will find him. I know we will,' Ambrose insisted. 'Either we find him or we die trying.'

'But I don't want to die,' she said softly. 'I want to go home.'

'Then go,' he said simply. 'Just go.' He pulled his knees up into his chest and dug his fists into the pillow.

'I wouldn't leave you,' she said. 'Not the way you are now. Ambrose, you're sick. You need a doctor. You have to go to someone who can make you better.'

'I don't like doctors,' he said softly. 'I don't trust them. They get their kicks by touching people. It's disgusting.'

'I know you think that, and I'm sorry. But it's the only way. You do realise that you're sick, don't you?'

He sighed. 'The past few months have been difficult, but if I can just find Schmidt, everything will be all right. Rainey, let's not talk about it right now, OK? Let's talk about it tomorrow. When I'm not so tired.'

'OK. But we will talk about it tomorrow.' She stood up and pushed the chair back against the window. 'I'm going to bed,' she said, frustrated. 'I'm tired too.'

'Rainey,' he whispered urgently. His voice still had the power to raise every hair on the back of her neck. 'Rainey — stay a little longer,' he pleaded. 'Until I fall asleep. I don't want to be alone. I feel a bad dream coming on.'

'OK,' she replied. 'For a while.' She sat down again beside the bed. She was surprised to find that after a few minutes, her anger and irritation evaporated and she began to relax. This room had the only breeze in the apartment, and it felt light and cool compared to the sitting room, and the smell was better, like talcum and lavender. She watched Ambrose motionless on the bed, so quiet that he seemed not to be breathing. There was enough light for her to count the bones in his back, the ridges of his spine poking up beneath the skin. She thought about how round and chubby he had been as a little boy. Before she had time to stop herself, she was imagining what it would feel like to touch him, to touch him more intimately than she had ever touched him before. She had been having these thoughts, these ideas, since Akron, or earlier, maybe even Baltimore; and with each passing night they seemed to grow in their detail and their intensity. She had never loved anyone other than Ambrose, and she knew she never would. Like Aunt Ingebjorg's paper supply man, he had become Rainey's tragic love.

But there was no harm in imagining. So she let herself imagine that she was stroking Ambrose's fine cool hair, which was clean now, and cut short again. She traced the contour of his face; the eyebrow bone, the high-bridged nose, the hollow cheek. She followed the clean, firm lines, and searched for the wound that no one else could see, the crack in the surface that let in the pain. Her fingertips brushed the stubble of his pale, patchy beard, and her hand ran down his long, sinewy neck, stopping at the small tuft of hair at the base of his throat, which suggested the spread of fair hair across his chest; curling around his nipples and over the puckered, pale pink scar from the hernia operation, so small it was barely visible any more. She imagined the many dazzling colours and textures of his hair, from the ripe corn-silk white of his head, to the pale yellow of his arms, to the darkest hair between his legs, still only as dark as burned butter.

Her hands began to tremble and her throat ached. *This is not love. This is lust, pure and simple.* The words stabbed into her head. *A hussy, just like her mother.*

Rainey stood and went quickly to the kitchen, filling herself with what little food she could find – a glass of sour orange juice, a shrivelled gherkin, and a piece of Wonder Bread, airy and tasteless. She tore off a corner of bread, squeezed it into a gummy ball and placed it on her tongue. She stood by the kitchen window and looked down, imagining the streets beneath her full of silent crime. She could see dark acts as they happened; behind the iron grating of the locked and bolted storefronts, beneath the burned-out lamp-post, in the blackened alleyways where only rats and pigeons watched. Silent crimes were taking place in the sewers flooded with piss and beer and bloated candy wrappers, and in the passageways where the wind gave a lonely moan as it passed between high-rise apartments.

She heard Woody get up in the next room, stumbling in the dark and cursing as he stubbed his toe. His feet slapped the floor as he went towards the bathroom. Her skin prickled. 'Oh, please let him come to me, please, let him find me here like this,' she prayed. After a minute she heard the toilet flush and the clatter of pills being shaken out of a bottle, and then the creak of the door opening and closing. A few footsteps, then heavy, portentous silence.

'Tough time sleeping?' he asked softly, in his gentle whine of a voice, which made her throat ache.

'Yeah,' she said, fingering the greasy latch on the window. He moved closer. She felt him watching her, felt the heat of his weakened eyes and his sly, thin-lipped smile. She could feel him outlining the clingy ribknit of her undershirt stretched across her breasts, and the hem of her boxer shorts, with the seam curled behind her thigh and no chance to surreptitiously pull it out now. She was aware of a gap of a good two inches between the edge of her undershirt and the waistband of her shorts.

'I know how it is. I'm sometimes up eight or ten times a night.' His face was creased and swollen. His eyes were pale and constricted, even in the darkness, and his matted curls were pressed to his head, tied beneath a red bandana. He smelled of apricots and Aqua-Velva.

'It's hard sometimes, sleeping in a strange place,' she said, glancing out the window, watching the neon sign above the 7-11 across the street, with its insistent orange letters: OPEN, OPEN, OPEN. A cold rhinestone of sweat inched between her breasts as the 'L' thundered over the tracks and the tremor echoed up her legs.

'You're a sad girl, I can tell,' he said, reaching out his hand. 'There's a darkness in your soul.'

She lifted her eyes away from the window, but she didn't dare touch him. 'Yes,' she said. 'I guess you could say that.'

'Do you want to tell me about it?' he asked carefully.

'I don't know. I can't.' She desperately wanted to confess to him, to list her many sins, from the time she and Ambrose became blood brothers, up until they set out on this desperate search for William Schmidt.

'You can tell me,' he reassured her. 'Whatever has happened, the Lord forgives.'

'Not this.' Something solid settled at the bottom of her stomach.

'Yes. Anything.' His face was firm and certain. 'As long as you repent, the Lord will forgive you. If you are truly sorry—'

She interrupted him. 'And what if I'm not sorry? What if I would do the same thing all over again?'

His eyelids flickered, but his stance remained firm. 'The Lord still forgives.'

'God,' she said, 'you don't know how much I want to believe that.' She looked back out the window, and as she started to cry, he came to her and wrapped his arms around her, holding her close to his chest.

'Hush,' he told her. 'Hush now, hush.' His words rose like a prayer. She wanted to speak; she thought this might be the time to tell everything, to tell it once and then let the truth dissolve forever, but her throat was swelling, pressing closed over the words. 'Hush, darling, it's OK, it's OK.' His kindness wore away her resolve and she felt herself start to soften. As she sank further into Woody's chest, she was struck by how thin and frail and old he seemed, how the arms encircling her body felt as light as the wings of a sparrow.

'I'm so scared,' she whispered against Woody's sweet-smelling skin. 'Scared out of my mind. Scared for Ambrose, but also scared for myself.'

'It's OK to be scared,' Woody told her, his long, thin fingers stroking her hair. 'Even Our Saviour was afraid, that night the soldiers came to take him in the garden of Gethsemene.'

Rainey wanted to sink deeper into Woody's arms and stay there forever, stay until everything else disappeared, but instead she lifted her head and pushed herself away from him. 'I can't do this,' she said. 'I can't. It's not right.' She turned and went back to the sofa in the sitting room. She lay down and pulled the quilt up to her chin. Her whole body was shaking, racked by a chill even in the sticky late-night heat. But she knew this was for the best – she couldn't accept Woody's kindness towards her; not while Ambrose lay curled up alone in the other bedroom, as cold as a stone and beyond the loving touch of anyone.

TWELVE

June 1988
Chicago, Illinois

Rainey awoke from the tail end of a beautiful dream, a Christmas in Owauskeum surrounded by Mormor and Grandpa Garth, Aunt Ingebjorg and all the cousins. The air was filled with the aroma of apple spice and cinnamon, and bristly fir trees standing high in every room, strewn with candles and red ribbon. Rainey was showing everyone her air rifle, not a hand-me-down from Uncle Ervald, but a brand-new air rifle, fresh out of a brightly wrapped box. 'Don't you dare aim that gun in the house,' Mormor said sternly. 'Or else you'll be having Christmas dinner all by yourself.'

'OK, Mormor, it's a deal,' Rainey said, mumbling in her sleep. *Mormor?* Rainey sat forward suddenly, blinking in the dusty morning light. Her mind slowly surfaced from the depths, reminding her where she was. Chicago. And a long way from Christmas. She rubbed her face, taking a deep breath and filling her lungs with the pungent odour of incense and chicken fat. She was surprised she had slept so heavily – even at six am the air was stifling hot and the noise of traffic boomed through the open window. She crawled off the couch and wandered into Woody's bedroom, where Ambrose was sitting cross-legged on the floor.

'Where's Woody?' she asked sleepily.

'He left already, to go work in that soup kitchen. I've been busy for hours,' Ambrose said. 'I woke up at three o'clock and I couldn't sleep any more. I dreamed that I would find Taylor's address today.' Four large boxes took up most of the room, and the floor was strewn with mounds of shabby junk – old clothes, blankets, record albums. Ambrose rifled through one of the boxes, separating the contents into two wobbly piles on either side of him.

'You shouldn't be doing that,' Rainey said. 'Those are Woody's private things.'

Ambrose shrugged. 'It's all right. Woody said I could look through his stuff. Saves him having to do it. Give me a hand, why don't you? That box looks promising.' He motioned to the large cardboard box behind him.

'I don't think we should be doing this,' Rainey said, sitting cross-legged behind him. But she had to admit she was intrigued by what Ambrose had uncovered – the collected ephemera of Woody's mysterious middle-aged life. She picked up a large sketchbook and flipped it open. Inside was a collection of lyrics and music for an album in progress titled 'Notes From My Exile'. She glanced through the haphazard scribblings. She couldn't read the music but she found the lyrics fascinating.

'I'm three times an exile, an exile from the promised land . . .'

'The Midwest, neither east nor west, neither here nor there. The middle of nowhere is the middle of everywhere, and I am lost in it, lost in the middle of you, baby, lost in the middle of you.'

'Division Street: ride the rich seam of the mighty Mississippi, America's dividing line . . .'

'Hey, listen to this, Rain,' Ambrose said, grabbing a cassette tape from the table. He popped the tape into the tape player and pressed 'play'. The tape began with a simple guitar solo of three basic chords, and a wailing harmonica accompaniment. Then came Woody's voice, breaking into song: 'I'm three times an exile, an exile from the promised land . . .' His voice was thin and scratchy, and only occasionally hit the right note.

'Man, does he suck or what?' Ambrose said and laughed madly. 'I hope he doesn't give up his job at the soup kitchen.'

'He was once on Johnny Carson,' Rainey offered in defence. 'They must have thought he was all right.'

'Yeah, but that was the Seventies. You didn't have to be able to carry a tune in those days.' Ambrose reached over to turn off the tape, but Rainey held his arm back.

'No,' she told him. 'Leave it on. I like it.'

Ambrose shook his head. 'You must be crazy. Or deaf.'

Rainey listened intently to the rising rhythm of the music. She knew Woody's voice was not beautiful, not in any traditional sense, but it moved her with its simplicity and honest emotion. The more she listened, the deeper the music seemed to touch her, peeling off layers of her skin and reaching a softer place inside.

She leaned over and picked up another cassette, which was cracked into two pieces. 'I wonder what happened to this one,' Rainey said, holding it up to the light. She read the label, which said in shaky lettering: 'Hymn of The Forgotten Man, Jan. '88, tape II'.

'Oh, I did that. I kneeled on it by mistake and it broke,' Ambrose said nonchalantly, ripping through another box.

'Ambrose, it won't play now, it's cracked in two. How are you going to explain this to Woody?' she asked.

He leaned back on his knees and looked at her over his shoulder. 'Would you just relax?' he said. 'Take a chill pill. I'm looking for Taylor's address, and all I care about right now is finding it, OK?'

'But you broke his tape.'

Ambrose nodded towards the cassette player, still playing Woody's song. 'The way I figure it, I'm doing the guy a favour. If I had any sense at all, I'd go ahead and break the rest.'

Ambrose spent the day searching through Woody's belongings, while Rainey watched the Cubs game and drank iced tea. When Woody returned that evening, Rainey was surprised at how glad she was to see him. Her heart lifted at the sight of his slight body struggling through the front door, bent beneath the weight of three heavy plastic bags filled with surplus from the soup kitchen.

'The Cubs took two,' she told him, running to help. She lifted the heaviest bags out of his arms and placed them on the table. 'Five-three in the first, seven-one in the second, over St Louis.'

He smiled slyly. 'Oh yeah, my boys,' he said proudly, nodding his head. 'They're heartbreakers, those Cubs.'

Rainey helped him unload the groceries into the pantry and refrigerator while he boiled a pan of water on the stove. Beneath the bags of groceries, Rainey found a stack of religious pamphlets: 'The Parable of the Mustard Seed', 'More Sinned Against Than Sinning', 'Jesus and You', and a battered old Bible with Post-It notes sticking out of the pages. Rainey looked at the Bible, then reached down and touched it, fingering the stained cover and the broken spine.

'You can borrow it if you want,' Woody offered, looking over at her. 'I don't need it 'til tomorrow night. Bible Study at St Adalbert's.'

'No, thanks. That's OK.' She drew her hand away and started to blush.

'Not a believer?' he asked casually.

'Actually, I am,' she replied. 'I'm Lutheran, baptised and confirmed. I'm even the assistant leader for our church's Luther League. I just haven't thought about it too much lately, I guess.'

'Well, the Lord is ready and waiting, whenever you are,' he said mildly.

'Yeah. I know He is.' She began to chop up the withered carrots and toss them into the pan of boiling water. The heat from the stovetop made her forehead sweat.

'So why is your friend so desperate to find Washington Taylor?' Woody asked, kneeling in front of the fridge, swinging the door back and forth. 'I mean, he seems more than just desperate. It's like he's possessed.'

'Ambrose is an intense person. That's just the way he is,' she answered evasively. 'He and Taylor have some business to settle, stuff from way back. It doesn't have anything to do with me.'

'Except . . .' Woody said slowly.

'What?'

'Last night you were scared. For Ambrose, and for yourself. Seems to me, that has a lot to do with you.'

Her skin started to prickle, and a chill ran up her spine. 'I want to tell you, but I can't,' she whispered softly, feeling a brutal coldness creep across her back. 'Not right now. He might come in and hear us. Look, let me tell you later on.'

Woody nodded. 'OK. Tell me later,' he said softly, mouthing the words.

That night, after Ambrose had gone to bed and Rainey settled down on the sofa, she thought about what she had promised Woody. She tried to plan out what she would say, how she would find the right words, but it was impossible to ignore the rising argument down the corridor, the drunken men shouting in the streets, and the lingering scent of stew that hung heavily above her head.

She found him in the kitchen, sitting at the table. Damascus lay at Woody's feet, resting his heavy chin against Woody's ankle. At first she thought Woody was reading quietly to himself. His shoulders were hunched forward, his head steady. As she came closer, she saw his eyes were closed and his hands were spread out flat on the table, palms down. 'Are you praying?' she asked him softly.

'Yes,' he said, opening his eyes and looking up at her. His gaze surveyed his cramped and modest little kitchen, and he smiled serenely. 'This is a good place to pray. My bedroom, now that has too many memories of my wife. I think that Jesus hears me better in here.' He pulled out the chair beside him with his foot and motioned for her to sit down.

'But aren't you Jewish?' she asked. She was suddenly embarrassed by her question.

Woody shrugged. 'It all depends on how you look at it, I guess. My father was a Russian Jew but my mother was Irish Catholic. My real name isn't Woody – that's only my stage name. My real name is Francis Xavier Leopold Stern. I'm a typical American, you could say. I was born on April 15, 1940, and born again on April 15, 1979. I don't feel any conflict. This is the life I lead now.'

Rainey thought back to Our Savior King of Kings and her postcard of the statue of the dying saint. She wished she could go back there right now and find the postcard still hidden inside the hymnal. Home seemed so far away; it was so long since she had known grace, had felt the certainty of goodness; and the hand of God above her head.

'What happened to your wife?' she asked Woody.

His eyes sparked and narrowed. She was suddenly sorry she had asked him. 'Emelita died. A long time ago. At least it seems like a long time ago now,' he said, shaking his head.

'Did you have any kids?' she asked, even though she somehow knew that he didn't.

'Nope. No kids. It was just us three; Emelita, me and Damascus here,' he answered, nudging the dog with his foot. Damascus responded with a loud, windy howl, before settling back to sleep.

'So you must get kinda lonely sometimes,' she offered.

He looked up at the bare light bulb over his head and ran his fingers along the edge of his thin, pale lip. He shrugged. 'Oh, it's not so bad. I keep busy with my music, singing at clubs whenever I can. And working at St Adalbert's soup kitchen during the week. The way I figure, I've got a pretty nice life. I'm like the lily of the field – the Lord gives me everything I need. I want nothing more than what I have right now.'

'What about love?' she asked, surprising herself with the urgency of the question.

'What about it?' he replied. 'My heart is always open. But I was blessed once in my life, I don't dare ask for it to happen twice.' He tipped the chair, leaning back on two legs and lacing his hands behind his head. 'So what about you – where's your family?' he asked.

She hesitated before she answered. 'My family is . . . around. I live with my grandparents. My mother abandoned me and I never knew my father.'

'And Ambrose?'

'Yes. Ambrose,' she said carefully, letting out her breath.

'How does he fit into the picture?' Woody's eyelids flickered slightly, and he drew his lips firm. 'Last night you were about to tell me all the ways you think you've betrayed him.'

She glanced towards Ambrose's closed bedroom door, and then she pulled her chair close to Woody, so close her breath brushed against his skin. 'Ambrose is my cousin,' she whispered quickly, her heart tapping frantically against her ribs. 'My second cousin, really. We're looking for his father's business partner, William Schmidt, who abused Ambrose ten years ago. Ambrose's father died in February. Ambrose thinks Schmidt killed him and he's out to avenge his father's death. Ambrose was so desperate, I thought he might hurt himself. I ran away from home to help him.' She stopped speaking and a deep pain jolted through her throat.

'And have you helped him?' Woody asked pointedly.

'No. I don't think so.' She took another deep breath, and her arms started to shake. 'He's worse now than he's ever been.'

He reached over to touch her face, but stopped halfway and smiled. 'I have not seen such faith,' he told her with admiration.

'What does that mean?' she asked.

'It's what Jesus said to the Roman centurion when he healed the man's servant. "I have not seen such faith; no, not in Israel."' He paused. 'Your cousin is ill; he's got a deep sickness in his heart and soul. You need to confront him, tell him honestly what he's been doing to himself, doing to you. You've got to make him understand that he needs help.'

'He won't listen to me,' Rainey interrupted quickly. 'I'm sure he won't.'

'I'll help you,' Woody promised. 'Don't start thinking you're alone in this. How about tomorrow night, you and me, we'll sit him down and talk some sense into him. That's the first step. Depending on how he reacts, we'll decide what to do after that.'

'You're willing to help me?' Rainey asked, surprised.

'Why not? You two seem like decent kids. I would hate to see this end badly.' He reached over and cradled her hand with a gentleness that made her want to weep. 'Hey, come on,' he said, his voice both chiding and soothing at the same time. 'Chin up, hon. It'll be OK. Go on now, get some sleep.' He smiled softly, and his pale eyes rose towards the ceiling. 'I've still got an appointment with the man upstairs. And He hates it when I'm late.'

She drew her hand back and pushed the hair off her sweaty forehead. 'OK. Sorry to bother you,' she said. 'Good night.'

'It's no bother. None at all. Good night,' he said, bowing his head.

Rainey went back to her spot on the sofa and lay down, watching the shadowy dance of reflected headlights drifting across the crumbling ceiling. She heard the energetic lovemaking of the Puerto Rican couple next door, and the rustle of the wind through the streets and treetops, signalling the beginning of a squally summer storm. Rainey stayed awake a long time, rubbing her elbows and watching out the window, trying to empty her mind. 'It will be OK,' she told herself hopefully. 'Woody will help me, and Ambrose will get well.' She sighed and turned over, burying her face in the pillow. She slipped into sleep thinking about home, thinking about Ambrose, but always trying, without success, to think about nothing at all.

Rainey was woken the next morning by Ambrose's harsh cry from the other room, stabbing the silence of her deep and dreamless sleep. 'Rainey! Rainey!' he bellowed. 'You'll never believe this!' She sat forward suddenly and struggled to catch her breath. He ran into the sitting room and jumped onto the sofa beside her, pushing a small leather notebook into her hand. 'I've found it! It's Taylor's address.' Rainey rubbed her eyes with shaky fists and looked down at a note scribbled in scratchy handwriting: 'Wash Taylor, 2676 N. 118th Street, Mankato, Minne.'

Rainey looked up at Ambrose and he was beaming. 'Can you believe I found it?' Ambrose's eyes glistened with excitement. 'Isn't this the best news ever?'

'Yeah, I guess so,' she said quietly, as the hope of last night twisted and died inside her. 'Yeah, it's great.'

'It's a sign from Vati. He's telling me we're about to find Schmidt. Come on, pack your bags. We've got to go,' he said, jumping off the sofa and heading towards the bedroom.

'Hang on, what do you mean?' she asked.

'We could be on the road in half an hour, if you get your butt in gear. It will only take me ten minutes to pack, so I'll get the car ready while you organise your stuff,' he said. 'Make some sandwiches – we'll need something to eat on the way.'

'But we can't just leave,' she said, starting to panic.

'Why not?'

'Because. We have to tell Woody,' she insisted.

'Leave him a note. Say, "Thanks for the leftovers." He won't care if we go or not,' Ambrose said, sitting down briefly on the arm-rest of a chair. His cheeks shone brightly, and Rainey could see the quick pulse darting beneath the tight skin of his neck.

'Why don't we leave tomorrow? That makes a lot more sense,' she said, trying to bargain for time. 'Let's get ready today, and then leave first thing in the morning.'

Ambrose shook his head. 'No, we're leaving now. Every minute that Schmidt has his freedom is a minute too long.' He jumped up and began grabbing things from around the room: an ashtray, some magazines, the blanket on the back of the sofa.

'What are you doing?' she asked.

'Stocking up. You never know what we'll need on the way to Mankato.'

'You mean you're stealing all this stuff?' she asked in disbelief.

'No, just borrowing it. Come on, you don't really think he needs all this junk,' he said, shaking his head.

She climbed off the sofa and followed him into Woody's bed-room. He began to rummage through the dresser drawers, tossing out armfuls of clothes. He grabbed Woody's pillow and threw it to the floor. Beneath the pillow was a carefully folded, faded flannel nightgown with a pattern of little blue roses. Ambrose picked up the nightgown, unfolded it and held it to his chest. 'Look at this old rag,' he said, laughing.

'Stop it! That was his wife's – leave it alone,' Rainey yelled at him.

He dropped the nightgown and pushed everything off the top of the dresser with the back of his arm. 'Fuck this,' he said.

She picked up the nightgown and examined it closely. Her hands moved over the fabric, and she found a corner where Woody's fingers had worn away the pattern of roses. Rainey put the nightgown to her face and breathed in its essence; its secret, lost perfume of lavender and vanilla.

Rainey dressed quickly and sat at the kitchen table, squeezing a yellow Post-It note in her fist. True to his word, Ambrose had everything packed within fifteen minutes. He came upstairs from loading the last of his luggage and approached Rainey slowly. He was sweating profusely, and winded from the exertion, and yet there was something bright and hopeful shining in his eyes, something Rainey hadn't seen in him for several weeks.

'The car's ready. I'm set to go,' he said carefully. When Rainey didn't respond, Ambrose knelt down in front of her and peered deep into her eyes, taking her hand in his. 'Rainey, come on, don't look so sad,' he said, stroking her fingers and wrist. 'You don't really want to stay here, do you?'

'Look at this,' she said, pushing the note into Ambrose's hand. He read it aloud:

'"Hey, Rainey and Ambrose – I've got a gig tonight at Billy Simmon's, down on 35th and Wallace. It would be great if you two would stop by. We can have a drink, and a good long talk afterwards. Call me at St Adalbert's this afternoon if you need directions. Woody."'

Ambrose looked up at her. 'And?' he asked.

'Woody's been so kind to us,' she said sadly, shaking her head. 'We can't just leave without saying thank you and good-bye.'

'Rainey, we can,' he insisted, shifting closer to her. 'If you knew how strong I feel right now, you'd never ask me to stay. Here, touch this,' he said, pressing her hand against his chest, letting her feel the frantic galloping of his heart. 'That's how sure I am that it's time for us to leave. We can call Woody from Mankato and thank him for everything. I know only one thing in the world right now, and that is that I absolutely have to do this; I have to find Taylor, and through him, Schmidt. But I can't do it without your help. Are you with me on this?'

'I guess so,' she said with a slow, deep sigh. 'Blood brothers forever, right? Blood brothers for life.'

'I still don't think we should be doing this,' she said as she settled into the car. 'It's bad enough leaving, but why steal his stuff?' She knew Ambrose wasn't listening. His head was reeling, and she could feel it. Everything about him was spinning and turning: his mind, his heart, his tongue, all working double time.

'Mankato is about five hundred miles from Chicago, so I figure if we can make Dubuque by, by what do you think? Eleven o'clock tonight? That's reasonable, isn't it? Anyway, the way I feel now, we won't need to stop. You can sleep in the car, because this way we'll be in Mankato by Thursday morning . . .' His voice trailed away as she stopped listening.

She had a duty to watch over Ambrose, but she allowed Woody to inhabit her imagination. As she and Ambrose drove away, she thought about calling Billy Simmon's and leaving a message, apologising to Woody for not saying good-bye. Ambrose would stop if she said she had to go to the bathroom, and while he waited in the car, banging the steering wheel and tapping the dashboard, she could sneak away and use the phone. 'Yes, it would be that easy,' she decided.

She began to quiver with her secret deception as her eyes searched for a place to stop. But mile by mile, Chicago's steely structure dissolved into gas stations and root beer stands, and ancient farm implements that stood watch in the fields. Her mind dulled, and she lost the will to act.

She tried to imagine what might happen at Billy Simmon's that night. Woody would stand on stage and sing his songs of exile and longing. The club would be less than half-full, with only a few old hippies, some college students, and a middle-aged suburban couple. When Woody's set is almost finished a band tunes up behind him, practising the first riff of 'Sunshine of Your Love'. Woody tries to pick out Rainey's face among the crowd; he believes he sees her as he squints into the light. His raspy voice scrapes the sides of his sandpaper throat. Rainey imagines a spotlight catching the amber crescent of liquid in the glass in Woody's hand. He sips the last of the Budweiser, licks the tip of his cigarette, and waits patiently; for he has not seen such faith. He will think he sees her in the haze and smile to himself, knowing that she moves somewhere beyond his vision, confident that she is just out of sight.

THIRTEEN

18 June, 1988

Harper's Ferry, Iowa

By late afternoon, Rainey and Ambrose had left Illinois and crossed the border into Wisconsin. They were surrounded by some of the richest farmland in the world, and yet Rainey felt strangely desolate, staring out at the deep green fields and the towering rows of golden corn. She remembered Pastor Jeff once telling the Luther League that the southern quarter of Wisconsin had been covered by glaciers for thousands of years, and when the glaciers retreated, they deposited minerals into the soil, minerals not found in such abundance anywhere else on the planet. This rich soil could produce enough grain to feed every person on earth. *'God doesn't cause famine; politics cause famine,'* Pastor Jeff had said. Lost in the middle of this landscape, Rainey was shamed by its richness and beauty; shamed by the thought that God had chosen to put it here.

The journey to Mankato passed through Blue River Township, where Mormor and her family had originally settled after leaving Norway. Rainey and Ambrose approached from the south, and Blue River Township seemed to be at first just an ordinary

Wisconsin town, with a single main street, imaginatively named Main Street; clean-paved and ramrod straight. There was a bank, a grocery store, a Ben Franklin; rows of clapboard houses, sturdy wooden mailboxes, and toys in every driveway. The porches had wooden swings and screen doors, and stout women in housecoats, hanging fresh laundry on the line.

'Let's turn back and get something to eat,' Rainey said suddenly, reaching over to Ambrose and touching his arm, feeling the familiar twitch of muscle over bone.

'What?'

'Let's go back to Blue River Township. I'm hungry. I'm sure I saw a little diner in the middle of town,' she told him.

'Why? You ate lunch,' he said, gripping the steering wheel.

'I know. But that was hours ago,' she insisted. 'This might be our last chance to get something tonight.'

Ambrose shook his head. 'No. We can't stop. We gotta keep going, until we get to Iowa, at least.'

She sat back and folded her arms. 'If Taylor is there, he's there. One more day isn't going to make much of a difference,' she argued.

'Fine,' he said, easing off the gas pedal. 'If you really want to, we'll go back.' Ambrose slowed down to look for a break in the corn fields, or a driveway to a farmhouse where he could turn off the road.

They doubled back to Tryggve Larsen's, an old-fashioned diner in the middle of Main Street. The diner's interior looked as if it hadn't changed in thirty years – the metallic countertop and red vinyl stools, the cosy booths, the photographs of shakes and hamburgers taped inside the windows and faded beige by the sun. A poster advertised the church social dance and the Grant County Fair – 'Last chance to see Elsie, our prize-winning Holstein, last year's best of show.'

They sat down and Rainey ordered a slice of sour cream raisin pie, while Ambrose ordered a root beer float. 'Coming right up,' the waitress said. The waitress, Gretta, reminded Rainey of Aunt Ingebjorg. She had grey-blond hair tucked up under a black hairnet and a burnished, worn-out, floury face. She wore a white apron stained with cherry and meringue, pulled tight under her arms and around her generous neck.

'I don't know why we're here. This is stupid, stopping for no reason when we've still got so far to go,' Ambrose said, slouching against the vinyl seat.

'Because I'm hungry,' Rainey replied. 'Since we left Essex, we've done everything your way. It's my turn to decide.'

The waitress returned with the root beer float and an enormous piece of pie, which she set down in front of Rainey.

'Go on now, eat up,' Gretta said, nudging Rainey's shoulder. 'Skinny little thing like you, gotta get some meat on those bones.'

Rainey blushed. 'It's delicious,' she told Gretta, taking a bite of the pie.

Gretta smiled widely. 'Freshly made less than an hour ago. People have been known to drive here all the way from Dubuque and Waterloo, just for a slice of sour cream raisin. Of course, cream cheese cherry is our specialty, but we only make that on Wednesdays.'

'We'll just have to come back,' Rainey told her.

'So how's the float?' Gretta asked, nodding towards Ambrose.

'It's OK,' he said dully. 'I've had better, especially in New York.'

The disappointment registered deep in Gretta's face. 'Well, we may not be all fancy-schmancy here in Blue River Township but we try our best.' She turned slowly and lumbered back to the other customers.

'What'd you go and do that for?' Rainey whispered angrily.

He shrugged, curling his top lip over the straw. 'She asked me a question and I gave her an honest answer. Since when is that against the law?'

'It's not. I'm just saying.' Rainey sat back in her seat and continued eating the pie. She thought about Gretta, the waitress. Gretta's husband would be named Hank or Irv, and her kids would be Sally, Mark and Dale. They went to Blue River Township Community School, and it would be their toys she saw in the driveways as they rode past. *This is where my family started in this country. This is the first place they looked at and said, Yes, we belong here,* Rainey thought. But as she thought it, she felt sure that something inside her was irreparably damaged; part of her interior was ravaged and lost. She wanted to stop at Blue River Township's Lutheran cemetery behind St Olaf's Church, which they had passed along the way. Rainey wanted to walk among the rows of broken headstones nestled in the yellowy grass and gaze at the simple stone crosses whose inscriptions had worn away. She wanted to find her namesake, Mormor's sister Astrid, who had died at seven in the scarlet fever epidemic of 1933. Astrid Svensen, one of the many Svensens whose bones were settling beneath that ground, working and turning the dirt, becoming part of that dark, rich soil.

Rainey looked up at Ambrose sitting across from her. The sun poured through the window, illuminating the top of his bright, white head and shining through the thin pink skin of his ears. She looked at him steadily and tried to find kindness inside herself, tried to track down the elusive source and proof of her love. *Tell me again who you are.* She remembered him talking about the tomb of the Niehlesen-Diensts, the lost princes of Schleswig-Holstein, buried in the village churchyard in Løgumgårde. *Your ancestors are buried there. And also here, right beside mine. We could uncover the thread in this rich soil, we could find the thin stream of blood that ties us together. This is the place, in this very ground, where the dust of the Old World turns into the roots of the New.*

Rainey looked at Ambrose again, then looked away. He was tapping his feet, drumming his fingers against the shiny metal tabletop, nervously slurping his root beer through the bendy plastic straw. *He would never take me to a graveyard, not now,* she thought. *He is going somewhere, someplace far away. I am sitting ten inches across from him. And yet we have never been further apart.*

Rainey convinced Ambrose to stop for the night in Harper's Ferry, Iowa, where they took a room in an old boarding-house hotel on the western bank of the Mississippi River. The hotel was hot and humid, and stank of the sulphur and sewage coming off the river. The only room left had one double bed, so for the first time in several days, Rainey and Ambrose slept side by side.

Rainey climbed into bed exhausted, her tightly knotted muscles crying for sleep, but Ambrose was nervous and jumpy, hot as a live wire as he kicked and twisted beneath the grimy sheets.

'Ambrose, come on. I want to sleep,' she pleaded, turning to face the wall. 'Why can't you just be quiet?'

'I'm trying. But Mankato! Mankato. We're gonna find him in Mankato,' Ambrose whispered urgently, clutching the sheet in his fists. 'Maybe I should go out to the car and check those maps again. I want to be ready to leave first thing in the morning. I'm too excited to sleep. Mankato, that's the place. First we find Taylor, and then Schmidt. Hey, maybe Schmidt's in Mankato too. That would be great, save us another trip.'

Rainey turned to face Ambrose and rose to her elbow, looking down at his bright, sweaty face. 'What's wrong with you?' she asked, exasperated.

'I don't know,' he answered. 'I can't calm down.'

She pressed her palm against his forehead. 'You're feverish,' she said, her fingers recoiling at the heat. She had been angry with him, but as soon as she felt that warmth, she was overwhelmed with tenderness, with the urge to hold and soothe him, to rock his fever away. 'You're burning up. No wonder you can't settle.'

'I try to relax, but I feel so buzzed,' he admitted, bolting forward to scratch his leg. 'Especially at night, when I think about Schmidt. I'm just about to fall asleep, when I get this rush. My head spins, my heart pounds, and I see crazy things; colours and shapes and weird designs. It takes hours to calm down.'

'I know,' Rainey said, lying back on the pillow and crossing her arms over her chest. 'I know it's not your fault, you can't help the way you are.'

He was quiet for a moment, rubbing his chin. 'I've been a bastard, haven't I?' he asked. 'Especially the past few days.'

'Yes,' she said simply. 'You have.' Suddenly she thought she might cry, and fought to keep the tears away, blinking quickly and swallowing hard.

'You didn't want to leave Chicago, did you,' Ambrose said softly. 'You liked Woody. You're sad that we left.'

'I didn't like him in "that" way,' she answered quickly, rubbing her eyes. 'But I liked him. He was nice. There aren't a whole lot of good people in the world. You have to appreciate them when you can.'

'Yeah, you're right.' He sighed and flopped back into the mattress. 'Maybe we'll go back there after we find Schmidt and all this is finished. We could go see him perform at that club,' Ambrose said brightly.

'We can't,' Rainey insisted. 'We can't go back now. You stole all that stuff from him, remember? It would look pretty stupid if we went back.'

'Oh, you're right. Sorry. I forgot about that.' Ambrose turned over and spoke softly, his voice nearly lost in the pillow. 'Thanks, Rain, for coming with me. For staying with me, no matter what. I couldn't have done this without you.'

'It's OK,' she said, staring up at the ceiling. 'I wouldn't have let you go alone.'

'You're my guardian angel,' he said. 'You know why? Because you protect me from myself.'

'Yes,' Rainey replied, covering her mouth with the pillow as the first tears slipped from her eyes.

Despite his nervous energy, Ambrose fell asleep surprisingly quickly, leaving Rainey to wallow for hours in the humid, stinking heat. She watched the curtains turn pink as a floating casino slipped past the window, before plunging the room into semi-darkness again. She stared hard at the water-stained ceiling and listened to the ferries and houseboats chugging up and down the river, just beyond the door. Everything smelled, from the stale cigarette smoke trapped in the curtains, to the oily odour of her own greasy hair. She wondered if this was the lowest point of her life, or if there were worst things still to happen, things so bad she hadn't yet imagined them. She allowed herself to think about her future, something she hadn't done for weeks. What hope could there be for anything good to come out of this now? She listened to Ambrose breathing beside her, and she watched the dark hump of his slumbering body, moving slowly up and down. She ached with a desolate love; it was her supreme punishment to lie this close to him, and still not be able to touch. Suddenly Ambrose rolled over onto his back and drew a deep, gasping breath.

'Ambrose, what is it? What's wrong?' Rainey asked, sitting up beside him. His eyes were fixed and vacant, the pupils two huge black holes, while his pale lips were drawn back in silent horror.

'Ambrose, wake up,' she yelled, shaking his shoulder. His arms and legs began to quiver, and a strangled cough emerged from his throat.

'Ambrose, it's OK, it's OK,' she said, stroking his head, holding him still through the worst of the tremors. After a few moments he blinked and swallowed, and the light slowly crept back into his eyes.

'Rainey, that was a bad dream,' he whispered, regaining his breath. 'So bad, I thought I might die.'

'You're OK. I'm here with you now,' she promised. 'You won't die as long as I'm here. I'll always take care of you.'

He was quiet for a long time, sighing occasionally and quivering in her arms. 'Do you think there's something wrong with me?' he asked gently. 'Really wrong?'

She was surprised how quickly her eyes filled with tears. 'Yes,' she whispered. 'Yes.'

'Hey, it's OK,' he said, trying to comfort her. 'I didn't mean to upset you. Rainey, don't cry. I'll be OK.' He had forgotten himself for the moment and sat forward, wiping her face with the sheet.

'No, you won't. Ambrose, you're sick, and I'm afraid you won't ever get better.'

'I will get better, once we catch Schmidt. Then I'll be fine. You'll see. C'mon, you worry too much.' He stroked her hair, his fingers fumbling in the dark to separate the tiny, tangled knots. She tried to stop crying, squeezing her lips to block the tears.

'It's no use. Just kiss me,' she said quickly. 'Please. Do it now.'

He brushed his lips dryly against her forehead.

'That's not what I mean.'

He drew back to the far side of the bed. 'Rainey, what are you saying?' he asked.

'You once told me that we are like angels, above those base, unholy desires. How does that quote go?' she asked urgently.

He cleared his throat nervously. '"For spirits, when they please, can either sex assume, or both; so oft and uncompounded is their essence pure. Not tied or manacled with joint or limb, nor founded on the brittle strength of bones, like cumbrous flesh, but in what shape they choose, dilated or condensed, bright or obscure, can execute their airy purposes, and works of love or enmity fulfill",' he quoted.

'Ambrose, that's beautiful. But it has nothing to do with us,' she insisted, as her tears stopped and her voice grew stronger. 'My essence is not pure.' Ambrose said nothing, but she could feel his shocked silence permeating the dark. 'We've done the worst of everything already, why not go all the way?'

'We can't,' he said, resigned.

'Do you know what day it is?' she asked.

'The middle of June, sometime,' he offered. 'I've lost track of time. Why?'

'Today is the eighteenth of June.' She paused. 'Graduation. Valedictorian. First in my class.'

'Oh, Rainey, I'm sorry,' he said in anguish, burying his face in his hands. 'I completely forgot about that.'

'I know you did. And it's OK. I chose to be with you because I love you so much. And if we love each other, then it was worth giving up everything else.' She swallowed hard. 'I don't know how else to say this, so I'll just say it. I love you. I want you. At night sometimes, I ache to touch you, to be close to you, to feel a part of you inside me.'

'Rainey...' he said, lost for words.

'I know you're my blood cousin. I know every rule on earth says this is wrong, and I'm not trying to change that; I'm not saying it's right. But what we've been doing all along is a lie, based on the lie that we are angels; we are heavenly creatures with no earthly desires. I have those desires and I can't ignore them any longer. We aren't those little kids in the attic now. You are a man and I am a woman. I can't hide the way I feel.'

She waited. He was so quiet he didn't seem to be breathing, perched forward, wide-eyed and motionless in the dark.

'Rainey, I have those feelings too,' he said at last. His voice sounded different now; soft and low. 'I hoped I'd never have to tell you. You are beautiful. I'll never look at another woman and not see your face. That's my cross to bear. I have been in love with you always. Since I was eight.' He sighed. 'This is totally hopeless.'

'No it isn't. Just once,' she promised, 'one time only, so we know what it's like. I've been lonely for so long, and I know you have too. Those things you did with Mr Barron – it doesn't have to be like that. I can take that pain away. I can show you something different – something better. I can show you love.'

'What if we can't stop after the first time?' he asked.

'We will,' she insisted, feeling a sharp ache rise inside her. She was ready, now was the time, as the pressure built beneath her skin.

'OK,' he said heavily. 'Just once.'

'With the lights on, so we can see each other,' she insisted. 'Don't let this be something sick and tawdry that happens in the dark. I want you here, near my face.' She grabbed his arm and drew him closer. 'Eye to eye, mouth to mouth and heart to heart.' She could feel the nervousness in his tightly coiled muscles, the straining in his arms and neck. 'It's OK,' she said, stroking his face. 'We'll figure out how to do it. It's not like we're stupid.' An unexpected smile rose to his lips.

It felt good, even in the heat and humidity, to touch his damp, smooth skin. She rubbed his forehead, drawing her fingers through his fine, soft hair. He lifted her arm and kissed it, running his chin from her wrist to her elbow. She kissed his mouth and he relaxed, clasping her fingers and stretching his legs, locking them around her waist.

She looked at him, *really* looked at him – his soft hair stuck in points to his forehead, the huge dark pupils of his eyes, his plush little mouth. This was the way she wanted to see him, this was how she wanted his face always to appear to her; his image burned into her heart. She kissed him again, and ran her fingers down his neck. With each stroke she moved closer to his chest. Her fingertips were searching for the ghost of the old scar, which she found, thin and rippled, just between his ribs. She felt him quiver. His hands slid up the back of her T-shirt and lifted it over her head in one swift move that left her breasts exposed, full and loose and brushing down close to him. He grabbed a handful of her hair and held it, stroking the tips against his chin.

'Oh, your hair has always been so pretty, so thick and soft,' he whispered.

She felt the muscles of his thighs, well defined from years of fencing and dancing classes. She grabbed the waistband of his shorts, which lay against his stomach. She slid the shorts to his knees, and he kicked them off his ankles, losing them in the depths of the bed.

'You've always been so much better looking than me,' she said. 'I used to feel so dull and colourless compared to you.'

'No,' he said huskily, 'that isn't true. You were always beautiful when I was just a fat and ugly little boy.'

She stopped kissing him for a moment, surprised and hurt by what he had said. 'You weren't ugly. I never thought so.'

'Then you were the only one,' he said. 'You see things in me that no one else sees. You make me more than what I am.'

They kissed more deeply and pressed into each other, and she felt her skin disappearing as if her body were melting into his. All the tension and irritation of being on the road dissolved as he steadily worked into her. Suddenly they were together, clasping and unclasping in a way that she had never felt before, and yet seemed completely natural. Her body took over while her mind was lost someplace else, drifting in a world without thought. She felt so close to Ambrose now, and through his body, he made her feel close to everyone else on earth. It was as if he had pulled a string deep inside her, unravelling years of loneliness. The movement inside her body made her feel liberated and warm with love, like a stream of hot liquid washing away the pain of old wounds and letting her true blood run free. She began to see tiny stars at the corner of her vision, crowding out the dusky light. These bright little stars shivered in a field of indigo darkness, dancing in the air above her head.

'Do you love me?' he asked suddenly, desperately, as if it were a matter of life and death.

'Yes, I do,' she answered, the words rushing out of her with their need to be told. 'You know I do.'

'Good. I love you too,' he said. 'We'll never be able to love anyone else.'

She held on to his shoulders and felt him shaking. 'Don't let go,' he told her. 'Hold on tight.' He closed his eyes and she looked at him, but his face was creased and serious, intently lined with light and shadow, and she closed her eyes too, feeling she couldn't impose on his private silence. The spasm worked through him and the black sky rattled and shook. She felt herself taking it, and the pleasure was so dark and sensual, like licorice, like vodka or akevitt, so intense she couldn't stand it a second longer. She heard herself cry out as the stars behind her eyes broke open, fizzled, and immediately began to disappear, even as she sought to hold on to their light. She and Ambrose collapsed against each other, falling deep into the pit of the springy mattress, where the sharp little coils sprang up and surrounded them like thorns.

'OK?' he whispered, exhausted and tender.

'Yes,' she said, catching her breath. 'Yes, I think I am.'

'OK. Good.' He leaned back and she rested her head against his chest, listening to the slowing of his heart. She had started to cry, but she couldn't tell where the tears came from – they seemed to be springing up from a secret, hidden passage somewhere behind her brain. She wondered if this was what happiness felt like, and how she had survived without it for so long. She turned and kissed his chest. She tasted the saltiness of his skin, and her tongue felt his ribs, and the taut tissue between them. Her hand moved over his stomach and around his back, reaching up to grasp his shoulder blades which arched back like solid, pointed wings. She cradled the full width of him in her arms, revelling in the warmth and softness of his skin.

'Rain?' he asked gently, lips against her forehead, nuzzling her hair.

'Yes,' she answered, even though she didn't want to speak.

'We can't ever do this again, you know.'

'I know.'

'It was so beautiful. But tomorrow, we'll have to be sorry,' he said. 'There's no other way.'

'Yes,' she agreed, burying her chin in his body, sinking it deep into his sweet, sweet flesh. She knew the sunrise would bring shame and sin and regret, a lifetime of being sorry. But until then, she was determined to lay back and let herself wallow in love.

Rainey slept a few restful hours, and woke up in the bleary half-light of five am. She reached over and searched for Ambrose's arms and legs beside her. She needed to touch him again, she needed to feel his body and indulge in that warmth. She wanted to fill herself with memories to carry her through her future loneliness, a loneliness that she knew would equal and exceed all the loneliness she had felt before. She understood that there were depths of sadness not yet fathomed, fields of sorrow still to be explored.

Her hands searched for Ambrose, but he was not beside her, and she had the familiar, breathless sense of missing him. She went to the bathroom and found him kneeling over the bathtub, shaking with tremors.

'Ambrose, what's wrong?' she asked quickly. 'What happened?' She bent over and lifted his head. His eyelids flickered, allowing a little light into the tiny pupils.

'I'm sorry, Rainey, I had to do it. I love you and I want you to be free. You'll never be free as long as I'm in your life,' he whispered, then sank to the floor.

She saw the handful of pills scattered on the tile beneath the sink. 'How many did you take?' she asked, panicking.

'I don't know. A few,' he whispered.

'Oh no,' she said. 'No. You idiot. Why didn't you ask me? This isn't right.' She wrapped her arms around him, feeling the spasms in his stomach and chest. 'Try to throw up,' she told him. 'Try it now.' She helped him to kneel back over the tub, resting him on his elbows and holding his head.

'Stay with me, Rain,' he whispered.

'Don't worry. I'll be right back.' She ran into the bedroom, picked up the telephone and dialled 911. 'Help me, I need an ambulance,' she said, voice quivering. 'I'm at the Coachlight Inn, on Highway twenty-six, along the river. Room two-seventeen. My cousin took an overdose of drugs.'

'What kind of drugs and how much?' the dispatcher asked.

'Sleeping pills, I think. I'm not sure how many.' Her legs started to sag beneath her as she sat down on the bed.

'Is he breathing?'

'Yes, he's breathing. He's conscious but drowsy, and he's shaking a lot,' Rainey said. The room started spinning and she could barely speak.

'OK, ma'am, you just sit tight. We'll have the paramedics there as quick as possible,' the woman reassured her.

'That's the Coachlight Inn, Highway twenty-six, Room two-seventeen,' Rainey repeated, suddenly wondering if she had got the numbers all wrong.

'OK, they're on their way.'

Rainey put down the phone and ran back to the bathroom. Ambrose was as she had left him, shaking less and trying to catch his breath. She knelt down beside him, cradling his head. She could feel his breathing, quick and jerky against her skin. She grabbed a bath towel and covered him, draping it over his shoulders. She didn't want anyone to see his pale, naked chest, his broad back, his tapered waist. He belonged to her now; it was obscene to think of him being touched by anyone else.

'You can't die, Ambrose,' she whispered in his ear. 'Because if you die, I'll be totally alone.' She began to kiss him, consuming him as greedily as she could. Her lips brushed his forehead, his temple, the edge of his eyebrow. 'I'll never be able to hold you like this again,' she said, and the pain she felt was absolute; a clear and crushing loss.

The ambulance sirens sped closer and closer, then stopped all of a sudden, the sirens cut off mid-wail. She listened to the rough rattle and crash as the paramedics pounded several times and broke through the door.

Two strong, confident-looking men stormed into the bathroom and pulled Ambrose away from her, lying him flat on the cold tile floor. 'Are you OK?' one of the paramedics asked Rainey, as he felt her wrist and pried open her eyes. 'Have you taken any pills at all? Have you taken any pills?' She was surprised to find herself treated with such kindness, didn't they know what she had done?

'What's your name, honey?' the man asked, rubbing her hands and turning her face away from Ambrose, who lay pale and motionless beneath the other man's busy hands. 'Come on, darlin', can you tell me your name?'

'Rainey,' she said softly. 'My name is Rainey McBride.'

– PART IV –

FOURTEEN

15 September, 1988
Lake Forest, Illinois

Sisters of Mercy Psychiatric Hospital was set on top of a rare Illinois hill, fifteen miles north of Chicago in the leafy suburb of Lake Forest, which was glowing in its mid-autumn glory. Fourteen weeks into his treatment, Ambrose had sent Rainey an urgent letter, asking her to come to the hospital immediately. After a surprisingly easy time convincing Mormor and Grandpa Garth that she was ready to be trusted on her own again, Rainey found herself standing outside the imposing entrance to Sisters of Mercy. She let the taxi pull away before she began the short but terrifying walk to the hospital's front door. Her hands shook and her stomach quivered. She had missed Ambrose desperately, and yet she wasn't sure if she ever wanted to see him again. Life without him had returned to something approaching normal, what if now they had nothing to say?

Rainey entered the lobby, which was brightly lit and almost supernaturally clean. 'I'm here to visit my cousin Ambrose Dienst,' she said to the receptionist. The woman looked down at an appointment book and wrinkled her forehead. 'I received a letter from my cousin,' Rainey said quickly. 'Dr Ramirez signed it and said it was OK for me to visit today.' Rainey braced her knee against the desk to steady herself, afraid she might faint.

'What did you say your name was?' the receptionist asked, tracing down a long column in the book.

'Rainey McBride.'

'OK, Miss McBride, have a seat. Someone will come for you in a moment.'

Rainey went to the waiting area and sat down. She looked at the stack of magazines fanned out on the glass table, and she glanced at the handful of other people waiting around her. She read Ambrose's letter for the hundredth time:

> Rainey, please come to see me on 18 September. I'm well enough to have visitors, and the doctor said it's all right. There's so much I have to tell you, so much I have to say.

Rainey folded up the note and slipped it into her pocket, where it rested against the Robin Yount rookie card, which she planned to give back to Ambrose, a peace offering to put all this pain behind them.

After what seemed like hours, but was in fact only twelve minutes, a tall young man came into the waiting room and called out her name. 'Here,' Rainey answered meekly, standing up and crossing the lobby.

'Right this way, Miss McBride,' the attendant said, holding open the door for her as he guided her down the corridor. After a short walk, he stopped in front of a heavy door with a small glass window just above eye level. The man opened the door and motioned for her to step inside. 'Thanks,' she said briskly.

Rainey moved past the attendant into the small, brightly lit room and was surprised to find Ambrose slouched comfortably in an overstuffed chair, his legs crossed and his gaze intent on the magazine in his lap.

'Ambrose?' she asked in disbelief. She had been prepared for a cartoon lunatic, a crazed madman with shaking head and lolling tongue, but instead she found Ambrose, her Ambrose, with no sign of the illness he had endured. His face looked incandescent, as if his soul had burned through his skin and was shining all around him, clear and bright. He had been soaked and scrubbed, his fingernails filed; his white hair neatly parted and clipped short at the neck.

'I'll just take your handbag and coat, please,' the attendant said. 'The rules forbid bringing anything into the visiting room. Don't worry, it will be perfectly safe.' She handed the man her handbag without looking away from Ambrose. 'You have twenty minutes to visit. I'll be back when the time's up,' the man said. With a swift nod of his head, he left and closed the door, which shook with a sharp, wavering echo.

'Go ahead, sit down,' Ambrose said, motioning to the chair across from his.

She sat down quickly, sinking deep into the cushioned seat. They looked at each other for a moment, neither knowing what to say. 'How's the food?' she asked awkwardly.

'OK. Good.'

'How do you feel?'

'All right,' he replied.

'You look good,' she offered.

He gave a shy smile. 'Really? Thanks. It's not like the asylums on TV. No strait-jacket and chains, no nurses holding me down while injecting me with enormous needles.'

'I guess that's what I expected,' she mumbled apologetically.

'It's OK. So did I. Until I got here, anyway.'

'And your treatment?' she asked politely.

'Oh, it's fine. Drugs and psychoanalysis. Some behaviour modification therapy. I'm still very tired, but they say that's from the medication. Once my blood levels normalise, I'll get my energy back.'

'Tante Anna says your mother misses you a lot,' Rainey offered carefully.

'Yeah. I miss her too,' he replied.

'So when can you go home?' She leaned closer to his chair.

His face suddenly darkened. 'I don't want to go home. Home is here now.'

'Yes, but when you're well . . .'

'I'm not ready yet.' He shook his head severely. 'Here they take care of me. Out there . . .' His eyes flickered and moved upwards towards the light. 'That's still scary. I won't be ready to handle that for a while.'

'But when you're better, you'll go home, right?' she asked.

'Oh yes of course,' he said quickly. 'When the time is right. But I've still got a lot of treatment ahead of me.'

'I see.' She looked around the little room, taking stock of the walls, the carpet, the small glass plate in the metal door. 'So what's it like?' she whispered conspiratorially, leaning closer. 'What happens when the sun goes down and visiting hours are over?'

'It's wonderful,' he said, his face awash with relief.

'Wonderful? Really?' she asked.

'Yes. I used to feel so alone, but now I see how many people are exactly like me. I used to be afraid to tell people what had happened, not because it seemed so big, but because it seemed so . . . small. What happened to me used to seem seedy, dark and secret. I was afraid to think about it or talk about it, because it had such power, and I didn't want to let that power escape. I thought I'd go insane just by saying the words, by giving it a name, by giving that man his name. But the treatment is like . . . daylight. Like somebody just threw a whole lot of daylight on my sad and tawdry life, and all the sick little weeds have curled up and died. You see, the words had no power, they could not survive the light.'

She nodded, noticing the details she had missed at first. This room had been designed to give it a feeling of comfort and informality. But she now saw that the table and chairs were bolted to the floor. The chairs' cushions were sewn into the frames, the edges of the plastic table were blunt and rounded, and the only light came from high overhead, too high for anyone to reach the light fixtures or electric sockets. There was nothing in this room that someone could use to hurt themselves or anyone else. And Ambrose too, although he looked normal enough, Rainey did think that there was something strange. His dark blue trousers had a loose elastic waistband, and his shoes were like slippers, soft-soled with no laces. He wore no jewellery, carried nothing in his pockets, had nothing in his hands. *In a way, he is strait-jacketed,* she thought sadly. *Only they've managed to do it without his noticing.*

'How is your life?' he asked her. 'How bad is it for you?'

'The days are fine,' she answered, biting her lip. 'But the nights are hell – I think I've inherited your bad dreams. I wake up in the middle of the night sometimes, terrified for no reason. But I'll survive,' she added quickly, nodding her head. 'I made up the exams I missed, and I might be able to start Northwestern in January, at the beginning of the second semester. I've got a job scrubbing floors to pay back the money I took.' She paused. 'Working isn't so bad; not starting college isn't so bad. What hurts most is the way Grandpa Garth and Mormor look at me now – like they're so, so disappointed. There's nothing else they could do to me – that look alone is punishment enough.'

'I'm sorry,' he whispered. 'It was all my fault.' He reached out a hand to her, and she took and held it, saying nothing. Yes, this was it. She knew now; he was Ambrose again. They sat like that for a long time, until both their hands felt weightless, and Rainey couldn't tell where his hand ended and her own began. She felt only the soft thrust of blood, streaming beneath the skin. Whether it was hers or his, she didn't know, and it didn't matter. *If I have to spend the rest of my life visiting him in mental institutions, I will do it*, she promised herself.

'Why did you take those pills?' she asked quickly. 'You broke my heart.'

'I know,' he whispered, bowing his head. 'I'm sorry. It's torture, knowing what I did. Can you ever forgive me for hurting you so much?'

'Yes,' she said.

'No, don't answer so quickly. I want it to be real,' he insisted. 'And if you can't forgive me, I'll understand.'

'I do forgive you.' She closed her eyes, watching the words form in her mind as she tried to explain. 'You probably don't know this – you were pretty out of it after you took those pills, but they kept me in the hospital overnight for observation. Then the next day, Grandpa Garth and Mormor came to take me home. On the drive back to Milwaukee I told them everything; everything that happened between me and you. They wanted to hate me, but they didn't. They were so damn glad I was alive. Sometimes, even now, I can see it in their eyes. How pleased they are to have me home, even though they are so, so disappointed. At first, I wanted to hate you for taking those pills. But I couldn't hate you, I only wanted you to get well. You see, Grandpa Garth and Mormor forgave me for the hell I put them through. They forgave me, and I forgive you.'

'You forgive me for trying to kill myself,' he said in amazement, repeating the words.

Rainey took a deep breath before she answered. She felt as if her heart was being lifted out of her body and cradled with kindness. 'Yes. I do. I do forgive you.' Something new stirred inside her chest – a hope that for fourteen weeks she hadn't dared allow herself to feel. Ambrose was better; he would get well. There was a future, even after all this. When she opened her eyes, he was weeping. Silent tears coursed down the sides of his cheeks. 'What's wrong?' she asked.

'My father,' he answered.

'Your father?'

'I still miss him so much. I can't believe I won't ever, ever see him again,' he whispered desperately. 'At least not in this life.'

Her first urge was to hold him, to rock him in her arms and kiss away his tears, but a voice inside her head told her, *No. Don't. Let go. Let him go.* She knew the best thing she could do for Ambrose was simply to let him be. She sensed that there was something noble in his grief, something about fathers and sons that she was not meant to come near, a covenant among men she could not enter. *He is ready to grow up now; Ambrose is a man, he is not a little boy. This is the way he must face the death of his father – and I must give him room to do it.*

She squeezed his hand and was aware again of the sensation of skin against skin, and that her hand was smaller than his.

'Rainey, I'm so glad I ended up here,' he said. 'I know that sounds strange, but I feel like I've found a part of myself that has always been missing. I feel complete. I can look over my life and ask how this happened. Why did I end up in a psychiatric hospital? Because William Schmidt touched me in a way he shouldn't have? That's all he did. Could anyone really be destroyed by something as small as that? And what does that say about me, if that's all it took to ruin my life?'

'You are able to say his name now,' she remarked softly.

'Yes,' he answered. 'William Schmidt. William Schmidt.' The words came out hard and humourless but Ambrose's voice held no malice; he *was* free. 'William Schmidt is just a man. Not a monster, a man. I don't understand what he did, or why, and I wonder how many other people had to suffer like I did. But he had a mother who gave birth to him the same as anybody else. He was once a baby in her arms, and she must have had such high hopes. I can pity his mother. I can pity everyone who ever loved him, because, no doubt, someone, somewhere did. And he was not worthy of the love, but he received it anyway. That's the key to my forgiveness. It's over now because I want it to be.' He took a deep breath and folded his hands in his lap, steadying himself in the chair.

'I used to wonder sometimes if I would be a different person without William Schmidt. And I know now that the answer is yes, I would be a different person. A better person, maybe. But I don't want that other life. I am Ambrose Torsten Dienst and I have my dignity. Even here at Sisters of Mercy Hospital, where they don't trust me with a shoelace. I still have my dignity. I do believe in God. This must all count for something in the end.'

There was a sharp knock on the door, and without waiting for a response, the attendant entered the room. 'I'm sorry, Miss McBride, but visiting time is over for today. I'm afraid you'll have to leave.'

'No, wait,' she said, surprised at the grief in her voice. 'I'm not ready yet.' Rainey reached over for Ambrose's hand, but the attendant stepped between them. 'I can't go yet,' she told Ambrose. 'I've waited so long, I can't leave now.'

'It's OK,' Ambrose said and nodded, looking up at the attendant. 'I'm tired. We'll talk again.'

They stood, unable to embrace with the attendant positioned between them. Rainey nodded. She held up her opened palm and pointed to the crease in the centre of it, the signal for the secret handshake. 'Good-bye. I'll come back soon. Maybe next week, if Mormor and Grandpa Garth will let me,' she said. She grabbed her handbag and coat, which the attendant held out to her. 'Of course they'll let me,' she added dizzily. 'They love me too much to say no.'

'Rainey, do me a favour,' Ambrose asked urgently, craning towards the door.

'Anything,' she said.

'Remember me. Tell everyone. Tell the truth about all the things inside me,' he pleaded. 'About how I really felt.'

'I will,' she said, and stepped through the door, feeling the rush of wind as it swung closed behind her. She didn't dare turn around; she didn't want Ambrose to see her face, and remember her crying.

Rainey left the hospital and followed the winding path down the hill towards the street. But halfway to the bottom, she remembered the baseball card still in her pocket. She ran back to the hospital's front door, but it was locked. She pulled the handle, banging the glass with her fist. 'Can I help you?' A disembodied voice said, rattling out of the loudspeaker beside her.

'Yes. I was just inside visiting my cousin, and I forgot to give him something important. Please let me back in.'

'Sorry. The hospital is closed to visitors now. You can call tomorrow morning and make an appointment for next week.'

'No, I need to see him. Please,' Rainey said. She pulled the handle until she heard an alarm sounding on the other side of the door. 'Damn it,' she said to herself, and as she saw a dark figure moving through the corridor, she turned quickly and ran back down the hill.

Rainey had a few hours to wait until the train to Milwaukee, so she walked around Lake Forest. It felt strange, after the bright quiet of the hospital, to be back in the world of cars and birds and newspapers. The trees were dropping leaves and changing colours while layers of smoky clouds drifted across the crisp autumn sky. She watched a hot-dog vendor on the street corner, and listened to the noises of airplanes and jackhammers, following the stream of people with cruel faces and worn-out old hands. She didn't miss Ambrose; she didn't miss him now. She didn't feel that sense of desolation which used to accompany their parting. *He is in his world now; a place where he is safe, and he is free. Thank you, God. Because I don't have to worry about him any more. As long as he's in there, I know he'll be OK.*

For a moment, she thought she'd like to go see Woody Stern, just to hear his voice. She hadn't thought of him for weeks, but suddenly he took hold in her imagination. She remembered his voice sneaking inside her; itching, tickling beneath her skin. 'No, I shouldn't,' she scolded herself. But the thought of Woody stirred something else inside her that she couldn't so easily nudge away; she saw his pale blue eyes, his sallow cheeks, his long, narrow, elegant fingers. *I'm sorry we left him the way we did,* she thought, surprised at the depth of her regret. *If only we hadn't left him like that, I'd be able to see him again; I'd be able to go back.*

FIFTEEN

18 September, 1988
Milwaukee, Wisconsin

It wasn't the look on her grandparents' faces that would haunt her forever, it was the title of the *Sportsweek* magazine article in her hand. 'Cal Ripken Jr, Oriole's Star Slugger Speaks Out'. She had just finished reading the first paragraph. She was drinking a Diet Coke and thinking about baseball. It would occur to her later, much later, that she hadn't heard the phone ringing a few minutes before.

'Come in,' she said, responding to the sound of knuckles rapping against the wood. The door opened slowly and Grandpa Garth and Mormor entered her bedroom side by side, looking pale and nervous. Their hands trembled, and they pressed against each other for support. Her first thought was that she should run to them; she should help to hold them up.

'Rainey, something terrible has happened,' Grandpa Garth told her, exhaling heavily. The sweat was visible on his temples, and his neck shook. 'The hospital just called. Ambrose died.' He paused and took a deep breath. 'Ambrose . . . killed himself. This morning.'

Rainey's eyes jumped down to the magazine clutched in her hand. 'Oriole's Star Slugger'. The words seemed to burn themselves on to the backs of her eyes, seared into her retina, from where she would never be able to blink them away. 'No he isn't,' she said, looking up at her grandparents and half smiling as the blood drained out of her limbs. 'I saw him three days ago and he was fine.'

Grandpa Garth and Mormor quickly sat down on either side of her. *As if to pin me in place,* she thought. *Where do they think I am going?* 'Rainey, this morning. They found his body this morning,' Grandpa Garth emphasised. 'He is dead.'

'Can I see him?' she asked. She felt dizzy; loose and unconnected as the room started to spin.

Grandpa Garth and Mormor looked at each other. 'Rainey, he killed himself at the hospital, in Illinois. It happened in Illinois, child,' Mormor said carefully, squeezing Rainey's hand in her cold, bony, quivering fingers. 'It didn't happen here, so of course you can't see his body.'

'But I want to see him!' Rainey shouted. She knew if she could see him, everyone else would realise he was still alive.

'Rainey, honey,' Grandpa Garth said, putting his arm around her shoulder. 'I know it's hard to understand, especially after he seemed to be doing so much better—'

'No,' she said, pulling away from his embrace. 'Stop it! Stop lying to me! Why are you lying to me? I'm going to call him right now and tell him what you said.' She reached across her bed and grabbed the telephone. Her fingers dialled the number without thinking, and in a few seconds she heard the phone ring.

'Hello?' a young man's voice answered. Rainey quickly slammed down the phone. She had telephoned Ambrose's room at Essex Academy. Wherever he was, he wouldn't be there. The hospital, what was the phone number for the hospital? She had never called him at the hospital. *He doesn't have a phone in his room,* she thought. *So I can't talk to him there. Where is Ambrose right now? Why can't I remember? He wouldn't have done something like this without telling me first.*

'Rainey, honey,' Grandpa Garth said softly, stroking her shoulder. His grey eyes were moist and full of kindness. Suddenly she felt a wave of nausea rising up inside her. Her throat tingled and ached. She jumped off the bed, out of reach of her grandparents' arms, and ran into the bathroom. She leaned over the toilet and threw up, three times very quickly and with such force it seemed to rip the muscles in her jaw. Her stomach clenched and burned as she sank to the bathroom floor. But just as her head touched the tile, she felt the next wave of sickness, and she struggled back to her knees. She tried to throw up again, but her stomach was empty, and she began to cough up a sour white liquid that burned her lips and tongue. She grabbed a handful of toilet paper and wiped her mouth, but the more she wiped, the more the sour, burning fluid worked itself into her skin.

Grandpa Garth came into the bathroom and knelt beside her, placing his hand on her back. She heard him breathing heavily. 'I know,' he said. 'I know.' Mormor came into the bathroom behind him.

'Leave me alone,' Rainey said, pushing them away and knocking them off-balance. Something about their kindness was too final, too polite to be endured. 'You never liked him anyway, don't be sorry now.'

Grandpa Garth looked shocked. 'Rainey, you know that isn't—'

'Just shut up,' she said to him. 'It's true.'

Rainey sank back to the floor, grateful for the coolness of the tile, which soothed her burning forehead. She wrapped her arms around herself and tried to stay very still. If she didn't move at all, they might go away; this all might go away.

'Rainey,' Grandpa Garth pleaded, his voice near tears. 'Come on now. Look at me, please.'

'No. Don't,' Mormor told him, holding back Grandpa Garth's arm. 'No.' She sighed and spoke quietly. 'It's OK. Leave her be for now. She needs to be alone. Let's let her be.'

'OK,' he said softly. He reached out and put his hand on Rainey's leg, touching it with a lightness she found unbearable. Her skin had started to hurt, as if she had been bruised from head to toe. 'We'll just be downstairs, if you need us,' he said. 'Come downstairs when you're ready.' She heard his knees buckle and crack as Mormor took his arm and helped him stand up.

Rainey felt herself nod, felt the movement of her forehead on the tile, and heard the tiny ripping sound as the skin lifted up and stuck back down.

Now that they were gone, she was glad to be alone. She closed her eyes and pulled her knees close to her chest. She was trying to disappear. If she could disappear, it would all be over. She held her breath. It would be easy to let go of life, easy to let go now. *Let go. Just give up. If Ambrose has done it, you can too.*

She remembered that time on the playground when Carl Muller had locked her in a full-Nelson. He had wrenched her head backwards and, for a second, she had stepped outside of her own life and seen huge black stars with many arms, dancing all around her, pointing her the way to another world. If she could let go now, she could disappear forever. *You've waited for this moment – now is the time. There is no Rainey; there never was. Never was.* She emptied her mind of all its contents, let her thoughts pour out as swiftly as sand from a bucket. *OK. OK. I'll fly away.* She had almost done it, had almost achieved that freedom, but then she felt her heart, felt it moving in her arm, her neck, her chest. *Dead.* The word was inside her now; she had accidentally let it rush in and fill that empty space. *Dead. Dead. Dead. Ambrose. Dead.*

She rose slowly to her knees, and then lifted herself to her feet, dragging herself up by pulling on the sink, which rattled in its frame behind the wall. She closed her eyes and pressed her hands to her face, afraid to look at herself. But then suddenly she did want to see her face, wanted to see it in every detail. She leaned as close to the mirror as she could. She looked at herself, made note of every detail, every feature: the shocked depth of her eyes, the pupils small and startled, the irises shattered like glass, floating slivers of grey and blue. She marked the paleness of her cheeks, the pale thinness of her mouth, and the red crescent of skin where her forehead had rested heavily against the tile floor. She memorised every inch of her own face, and then she spoke aloud the words which would stay with her forever: *This was my face on the day that Ambrose died.*

Rainey staggered back to her bedroom, and saw the issue of *Sportsweek* splayed on the side of the bed, open to the article 'Cal Ripken Jr, Oriole's Star Slugger Speaks Out'. She started to panic, her hands shook and she couldn't catch her breath, she couldn't remember how to breathe. She started to choke with a dry, hard sobbing. She grabbed the magazine and crushed it into a tiny ball, but then she felt a stab of regret, and she unfolded the magazine carefully, smoothing out every single page. This was a part of Ambrose too; from now on, everything she touched would be a part of Ambrose.

She turned towards the closet and pulled out the clothes she had worn three days ago to visit him at the hospital. She threw them on the bed and began to tear at them with her hands – *His touch, his breath, his essence; his cells are in here somewhere, why can't I find him?* she screamed to herself. She pushed the clothes to the floor and she stretched out on the bed, burying her face in the sheets, trying to slow down her frantic heart. *OK, Ambrose, if you are really dead, then tell me. Let me know. Come to me right now, speak to me as a ghost.* She remembered his promise – *'There's a place inside your head where you can go and no one can touch you. Go there and you'll find me. I'll wait for you, I promise.'*

She took a deep breath, closed her eyes, and waited. A million faces began to fill the darkness inside her head, crowding out one another, fighting for space. It was as if every person she had ever seen in the world was there above her, gazing down, benign as stars. But nowhere, nowhere in that vast sky of faces was Ambrose. She began to panic – how could she forget his face after only three days? This was Ambrose, whom she loved so much, and now something in her own soul had done away with him, something had erased his image from her mind. Maybe he hadn't killed himself; she had killed the part of him in her. *Please,* she begged, *please let me see you. Show me your face.* Her head spun and she started to cry. She still couldn't see him, but from somewhere deep inside her, she heard his voice. Not the voice he had had three days ago, but his voice from a long, long time ago; a sweet, gentle, childish voice. *'And do you know what happened then, Rainey? Do you know what happened next? Everybody clapped.'*

There was no public funeral for Ambrose Torsten Dienst. His mother had decided against a memorial service, so soon after the death of Holger, and with the family scattered across so many lands. Sissel Svensen Dienst said good-bye to her son quietly, allowing him to be buried in Denmark, beside his beloved father, in a corner of the Løgumgårde churchyard where the overturned dirt was still warm. Rainey felt the precise moment when Ambrose was buried; she felt him lowered into the ground, and felt the deft pressure of the first clumps of earth scattered across the top of his coffin. That night, for the first time in the five days since he died, she dreamed of Ambrose, but it was the eight-year-old Ambrose who inhabited this dream. He was pale and crying, dressed in the long white nightshirt that left his knees exposed. He stood outside the great stone tomb of the Niehlesen-Diensts, pounding his fists against the rock and begging to be let inside. And in this dream, Rainey, the eighteen-year-old Rainey, strode up to the little boy Ambrose, grabbed him by the shoulder and spun him around, asking, *'How could you do this to me? How could you die, and leave me behind? Didn't you love me, not even a little?'*

Every day from then on, Rainey woke to know the brutal truth: Life did go on. *It does go on, does go on, does go on.* The words pounded through her, pounded through her head and chest. The whole world was painful, both painful and numb; sometimes dead to all sensation, sometimes alive and wailing with grief. Even to take one breath seemed unbearable, and yet she kept taking them, one after the other after the other. Rainey tormented herself by trying to remember every last detail of Ambrose – the way he cocked his head, the way he chewed his food, how he pronounced the word 'Colorado'. If she lost these things, he would be gone forever. She would have failed him again, failed him one last time for all eternity; dooming him to nothingness by her own lack of faith.

'Rainey, I'm coming into your room now,' Mormor said carefully, knocking on the door. This was the day after the funeral; this was when Rainey was still waiting for some proof from Ambrose that he was free of this earth. *Now you can come to me, you can give me a sign. At least let me know you're OK.*

'Rainey?' Mormor asked. Rainey was shocked by how tenderly her grandparents were treating her, and also shocked to find that their tenderness brought her no comfort at all. Rainey listened to the uneasy silence of Mormor standing in the hallway, debating with herself whether to come in. 'I've brought you some lunch, and I need to set it down,' Mormor said.

'OK,' Rainey answered, just loud enough for Mormor to hear.

Mormor came in, carrying a big plastic tray. 'Look what I've got here,' she said, forcing a smile, and showing Rainey a plate piled high with macaroni and cheese, and a glass of 7-Up fizzing over lots of ice. Mormor put the tray down on the bedside table. She looked at Rainey for a long moment, her eyes crinkling at their corners, making Mormor appear almost kind. 'Mind if I sit down?' she asked.

'Go ahead,' Rainey told her, sliding over to make some room. Mormor sat on the edge of Rainey's bed, pitched slightly forward, looking stiff and nervous. She seemed afraid of Rainey; afraid she might explode, might do something shocking, or suddenly scream out in grief.

'It's sunny out,' Mormor offered unconvincingly, folding her hands in her lap.

'Uh-huh.'

'Margaret called. Your cousin Barry is getting married.'

'Great.'

'Just after Thanksgiving. I think we all should go.'

'OK. Remind me closer to the time,' Rainey asked quietly.

'You should eat something,' Mormor told her, nodding towards the overloaded tray.

Rainey peered over the edge of the blanket. 'Thanks, but I'm not hungry,' she said. In fact, she did feel hungry. She hadn't eaten a thing in the six days since he died, but she refused to give in to her hunger. She couldn't allow that; it wasn't right to feel hunger or thirst in a world without Ambrose.

'Even if you don't feel hungry, you should try to eat a little something,' Mormor insisted, reaching for the tray.

'Why?' Rainey asked.

'Why? What foolishness,' Mormor answered, shaking her head. 'You need to keep up your strength. We don't want you to wither away into nothing.'

'Don't you?'

'Don't I what?' Mormor asked.

'Want me to wither away into nothing. Is that really possible, to wither away into nothing?' Rainey asked her.

Normally, talking back in this manner would have made Mormor angry, but today she seemed willing to indulge Rainey in conversation. 'Oh, I think it probably is possible,' Mormor said.

'People used to starve to death when there were famines in the Old Country, you know.'

'Oh, I guess they did.' Rainey sat forward and pushed the pillow beneath her shoulder. She stared at her grandmother for a long time, taking in her every feature. She looked at Mormor's plait of thinning grey hair; her pale eyes, which were nearly the same colour as her hair; her pointed, precise nose; and the series of wrinkles fanning out from her jaw and chin. Mormor was dressed in a blue denim workshirt, with the sleeves rolled up tight to her elbows, and a pair of dark blue polyester knit trousers. Rainey could count on two hands the number of times in her life she had seen Mormor wear a dress. Even at the age of sixty-eight there was something powerful and intimidating about Mormor, though her back wasn't as straight as it used to be, her shoulders were rounded and her arms were growing weak. *Still, if you met Mormor on the street, you wouldn't want to argue with her,* Rainey thought. 'Mormor, where do you think people go when they die?' she asked suddenly.

Mormor looked shocked. 'To our heavenly Father, of course,' she said, stroking her long, thin neck. 'That's what the Bible tells us.'

'But what's heaven like?' Rainey asked urgently, leaning forward. Rainey realised that in all the eighteen years she had lived with her grandparents, they had never once discussed dying, or death, or what might happen after. They rarely discussed anything beyond the weather, or family gossip, or news from the Sons of Norway.

Mormor shrugged uncomfortably. 'I don't know. I don't dare ask, and you shouldn't either. It isn't right – who are we mere mortals to question the will of God? We are nothing, we are like ants or termites, compared to His greatness.'

'Greatness?' Rainey asked angrily. 'What's so great about it? It seems cruel of God to put himself so high above us, leaving everyone else so far below.'

'Blasphemy. It's a sin to talk this way . . .' Mormor said swiftly, standing up. 'I won't—'

'No,' Rainey replied, grabbing her arm. 'I want to know. I really want to know what you think. It matters to me. Do you think heaven is a real place?'

Mormor sat down again, still looking uneasy. 'I don't know. I suppose it could be.'

'Do you think dead people can talk to other dead people, the way we do on earth?' Rainey asked her.

Mormor took a deep breath and held it quietly. Something – an idea, a statement, had taken hold behind her eyes, and Rainey saw her fighting hard to rein it in. 'I remember, after my son passed over, I was so worried,' Mormor said slowly. 'I didn't believe he was dead, I thought he was just sick, or hurt. Like he got lost in a foreign country. He didn't speak the language, he couldn't read the signs, he was hungry and thirsty, and had nothing to eat. I couldn't stand to think of him, lost that way. But then one night I had a dream about my little sister, Astrid. She was only seven when she died, but in the dream, she was a grown woman, and she came to tell me that she was with my son. I watched her take his hand and lead him into heaven. She promised she would take care of him, and she told me not to worry any more about my poor little boy.' A pale smile rose to Mormor's face; a smile not for the brightness of the memory but for the relief of finally letting it go.

'That's so beautiful,' Rainey whispered. She felt herself shaking beneath the sheets. 'That's a beautiful idea. I hope it's true.'

Mormor sighed and looked up towards the ceiling. From the set of her hands, she might almost have been praying. Rainey saw the shadows clouding her grandmother's corneas; saw the growing, milky gloom of cataracts, blossoming inside her eyes.

'Even after all this time, I sometimes remember that. I wonder if they're up there in heaven together, Astrid and Michael, looking down on me,' Mormor said softly. 'I sometimes think they wouldn't be too happy, if they could see me now.'

Rainey reached out her hand from under the blankets. 'Mormor . . .' she started to say.

'What is it, child?' Mormor's face was open now; willing to let a little light creep inside.

'Nothing,' Rainey said. 'Forget it.'

'All right.' Mormor rubbed her face and blinked quickly. Her lips were pale and trembling, and a set of muscles tightened in her temple. *Mormor hates me now,* Rainey thought sadly. *She resents me for making her talk about her dead sister, her dead son. Now she has given something away, something she can never take back. Her words are out there, loose in the world.*

'Rainey, eat your lunch, OK?' Mormor said wearily, rubbing her hands. 'I want to wash those dishes.' She stood up and left the room, carefully closing the door behind her.

Rainey turned back the blankets and looked at the tray on the bedside table. She felt a deep ache inside her, but this was not grief; this was not hunger. This was longing; a longing for Mormor. Rainey missed her grandmother in the first few seconds after she had left the room, she missed her even before Mormor's feet had time to touch the top of the staircase. Rainey wanted Mormor to come back and tell her everything; everything about the Old Country, everything about her parents, her best friends, her heart's secrets, her children. Rainey wanted Mormor to describe what Michael and Mary Jane were like as babies, how it was to watch them grow up, and, yes, even what it was like to lose them, to lose both her children, within a year of one another. *Come back here and be for me what I have always believed you could be; come back and be the woman who loves me,* Rainey pleaded. *It's not too late if you come back now. There are so many things we need to say to each other, and we need to say them right away, before it's too late.* This sudden longing for Mormor far exceeded all the grief she felt for Ambrose. *Nothing makes sense any more. The world is full of strangers; we are strangers to ourselves.*

No one mentioned Ambrose's name in the days after his death. And by not mentioning him, they gave him such power – he was every-where, he was everything. He was now a thing too great, too overwhelming, too sacred to be spoken of in simple words. He was sound, he was voice, he was silence; his death was every last and little thing, the black space at the back of the cupboard, the rattle of the kitchen drawer opening and closing as Mormor grabbed a handful of forks and knives, the desolate moment of silence just before the telephone rang. The house on Sandstone Avenue became a temple, a kind of church devoted to his death, and Rainey had to walk outside around the block to say his name. Ambrose. Ambrose. She had to walk fifty yards in order to pro-nounce those syllables, to remember how to say the word.

Rainey left the house and walked down the street to the phone booth outside the Stop-N-Go. She stepped into the booth and picked up the phone, pretending to call Ambrose. She listened for a long time trying to make sense of the hum on the other side of the line. She thought if she listened long enough, the silence would turn itself into words.

'I will never call him "Ambrose" again,' she said into the phone, and flinched at the sound of her voice. 'I will never look into his eyes. He will never be the Ambrose who lived and breathed, instead he'll just be some dead body, rotting away in a grave. Every day that I move forward, I will leave him further behind me, until he's so deeply lost, I won't remember him at all.'

She could suddenly see herself much older; a grown woman of thirty, forty or fifty years old. She would have a life, maybe even a nice life; a career and a home and children, and friends; maybe some friends. But as soon as she mentioned his name, whenever she said, '*Ambrose. When I was a child and my cousin Ambrose and I . . .*', and then always these future friends would roll their eyes and look away, or purse their lips and look uncomfortable, or nudge her gently and say, '*Hey, Rainey, you're talking about him again*', or '*Rainey, we've heard that story a thousand times before. Rainey, that's so long ago now . . .*'

She glimpsed the terrible, barren loneliness of her future life. *I will never have another Ambrose, not ever again. Never, never, never. How cruel it is to be young; to have so much of your life still in front of you. And all of it as awful as this.*

Rainey finally came home at supper time. Grandpa Garth was already sitting down to eat as she entered the kitchen slowly, letting herself absorb the atmosphere. She looked at everything intently, as if she had never seen any of it before: the round wooden table, the ceramic dishes from the sixties, the red and white check curtains hanging over the windows. For years they had eaten the same simple food, ten or twelve recipes in constant rotation. If it was Tuesday, it was liver and dumplings; if it were Thursday, chicken à la king, or in summer, tuna casserole with shoestring potatoes, and green beans beneath. *This is my world; my little, little world*, she thought sadly. *I have sometimes felt love. But not now. My life is a foreign country.* She sat down and nodded to her grandfather, who, seeming shamed, looked away.

Mormor filled Rainey's plate with heaps of beef stroganoff, while

Grandpa Garth hastily poured her a tall glass of milk. Her grandparents were quiet for a time, then carefully began a conversation. A few dropped words to begin with, then the words turned into sentences, which progressed into talk.

'I got the phone bill today,' Mormor said gently.

'Oh? How was it?'

'Wasn't too bad. I shouldn't have called Torgrim in Florida, I suppose,' Mormor said wistfully. 'I won't talk so long next time. So what's new with the boys?'

'Ralph Schlicter is back bowling again,' Grandpa Garth answered, speaking through his food.

'How's he doing?'

'Oh, pretty good.' Grandpa Garth swallowed down a big sip of milk, then licked the residue from his silver moustache. 'Says he's been real busy, with his daughter and grandkids coming around.'

'It'll be worse after they leave,' Mormor warned.

'Yeah. I guess it will.' Grandpa Garth looked down at the stained tablecloth. 'He won't notice how lonely it is, until after they've gone.'

'I'm glad we sent flowers,' Mormor said. 'Maybe next week I'll send over some stew.'

'Yeah. Bet he'd like that.'

'Uh-huh. At least he learned to cook a little bit. After Marge first got c-a-n-c-e-r.' Mormor's voice was reduced to a whisper. 'That should help.'

'Hmm. No doubt,' Grandpa Garth agreed.

Rainey started to cry. Slow, silent tears coursed down her face and fell on to her plate, leaving a long wet furrow upon each cheek.

'What are you doing?' Mormor asked her, stopping suddenly and looking up.

'I guess I'm crying,' Rainey said, watching one of her tears billow into the dark pool of gravy.

'Well, stop that foolishness. Tears won't bring him back,' Mormor snapped.

'I'm not trying to bring him back,' Rainey answered. 'Ambrose is dead. This is what people do when someone dies – they cry about it.'

'Save your tears, he doesn't need them,' Mormor told her, grabbing a piece of bread.

'How can you say that?' Rainey asked, flashing with anger. 'Even if you didn't like him, he was your nephew. He was your flesh and blood too, as much as he was mine – how can you not care that he's dead?'

'Oh, I care, Rainey. I care,' Mormor said bitterly. 'He's the one who didn't care. He didn't care about his mother, doing this to her so soon after she was widowed. Sissel's the one I feel sorry for. She's the one who deserves your tears, not Ambrose. He didn't care about your feelings, to hurt you this way. Remember that, Rainey, he did this to you. He chose to die.'

Mormor's words stung her deeply, cutting straight to the bone. Rainey wondered if her grandmother knew what power she had to cause pain, and wondered if she was in some way proud of that fact.

'I know,' Rainey said, nodding emphatically. 'I know he did. Don't remind me. Ambrose wanted to die. I have to remember that every single minute of every single day.'

'Rainey, it isn't your fault,' Grandpa Garth offered, reaching out a hand to her. 'Ambrose was sick. He had a disease, and he should have gotten better. He was only eighteen years old and it's a terrible loss that he died.'

'Oh, for shame,' Mormor said. 'Let's not discuss this any more. The trouble with Ambrose was that he was spoiled. That's the only disease he suffered from. He had too much; he was given everything and he didn't appreciate it. People like that go soft in the middle. They don't know real suffering the way we do. They only think they got it bad.'

Rainey was shocked, shocked nearly out of her grief. *Is that what you really believe?* Rainey thought to herself. *Do you think your nephew killed himself because life was too easy?* Ambrose had been their grandnephew but they hadn't known him at all. The little they knew of Ambrose Torsten Dienst could have been gleaned from the newspaper article reporting his death.

This is my fault, Rainey thought suddenly. *I never let them know Ambrose. He was a huge part of my life but I never shared that at all.* She had kept too many secrets. This whole family had kept far too many secrets. Astrid. Michael. Mary Jane. Now add Ambrose to that list. There would be no photos, no mementoes, nothing. Even the names themselves became forbidden, taboo. *'Just pretend it never happened, and*

– 262 –

everything will be all right.' This is no way to live, Rainey thought. *This is no way to die. I could die just like Ambrose, never letting anyone, even my own family, know me at all.* But even as she thought these things, another idea came into her head – *It doesn't have to be this way. I can change; it's not too late. I can change it now.* Hope; yes, hope, mingling with her grief, soared up like a flame inside her chest.

She laid down her knife and fork and took a long, slow sip of water. She swallowed hard and took a deep breath before speaking. 'I know you've suffered in your life, and I love you for that,' she said carefully, calmly looking both her grandparents in the eyes. 'I love you but I can't stay here. I can't live with you, I can't live this way any more. I'm leaving. Right now. I'm going to go upstairs to pack my bags and leave forever.'

Mormor looked stunned. It was a few seconds before she could speak, before her anger had fully taken hold. 'Don't go threatening us, young lady,' she said. 'The last time you ran away it took fifteen years off our lives, I'll have you know. If you want to leave, if you don't appreciate everything we've given you, then go right ahead. Only this time, don't bother coming back.'

Rainey nodded. Feeling surprisingly calm, she stood and left the table. She went upstairs and grabbed her backpack, then took some clothes off the hangers and stuffed them into the bag. She took her purse and her wallet, and the little packet of cash she still had hidden in the bottom of the bureau drawer. She went downstairs and grabbed her coat out of the closet. Grandpa Garth hurried out of the kitchen towards her, brushing his mouth with the dinner napkin still in his hand. 'Rainey, come on, why don't we—'

'Pa, don't indulge her,' Mormor yelled to him from the kitchen. 'She thinks she can take care of herself, then fine, let her go. She did a great job last time, ending up in some hospital in Iowa. Shows you how capable she—'

'Shut up, Sonja. Shut up, you've done enough,' he shouted back at her. 'Rainey, come on,' he pleaded, standing before her, his face fiery red and his hands open and pleading. 'Let's not make an issue of this. We know you're upset about Ambrose, no one blames you for that. Why don't we all sit down and—'

'No,' Rainey told him, fighting her arms into her winter coat and grabbing for the doorknob. 'No. I'm sorry, but I have to leave.'

'But you'll come back, right?' Grandpa Garth asked softly, his eyes spinning in disbelief. 'You do plan on coming back.'

Rainey turned away from him. 'I don't know.' She paused. 'Look, I'll call you soon.' She opened the door and stepped outside, letting it slam behind her. She began to run as fast as she could, her feet turning up piles of brittle yellow leaves, even though she knew Grandpa Garth would never follow after her. But she heard him calling, standing on the porch and speaking into the wind.

'Rainey! Come back. Come on, come back. Rainey!'

She would go to Woody. She didn't even think about it; didn't make any sort of decision. She just knew she had to go to Woody. She rode the bus through heavy rush-hour traffic into the city and got off at the Greyhound Station. She bought a one-way ticket to Chicago and stuffed the dollar bills of change into her pocket. Then she stood out on the street corner, waiting for the bus.

She rubbed her arms for warmth, and rocked back and forth on her heels. She felt intoxicated and strangely free; as if a stone inside her had been dislodged, and now all her hard, impacted sorrow had been suddenly and dramatically set loose. She could almost see it, streaming from her limbs like flying ribbons. It was still autumn, she realised, the autumn when Ambrose had died. She watched the stream of dirty cars sliding up and down the crowded street, their headlights gleaming in a parade of gold and white. The sky smelled good. Like maple syrup and burning leaves, and the tree tops ringed with colour. There was a stiff, cool breeze, and piles of leaves like papier-mâché tumbling over street corners. 'Ambrose Ambrose Ambrose,' she said, making music of his name. It was easy to say his name out here. 'Ambrose Ambrose Ambrose. Ambrose Torsten Dienst. Torsten Dienst. Tor-sten-Dienst. Torstendienst.'

A woman with a little girl beside her walked over and stood next to Rainey, also waiting for the bus. 'Do you want a piece of Juicy Fruit?' the woman asked Rainey, holding out a pack of gum.

Rainey shook her head and turned away, facing into the wind. But then she turned back to the woman and forced herself to smile. 'Yes,' Rainey said, her voice quivering. 'Thank you. I will have that piece of gum, if you don't mind.' As the woman handed her the

stick of Juicy Fruit, the metallic wrapper flashed in the woman's fingers, catching the last of the day's draining light. 'Thanks so much,'
Rainey said, swearing to herself that she would never turn away
from kindness again.

The little girl stared at Rainey for a long time, cocking her head,
scrunching up her nose and studying Rainey's face intently. 'Look,
Mommy, that lady is crying,' the little girl said, tugging on her
mother's sleeve. 'D'ya see that, Mommy? Why is she crying?'

The woman leaned over and peered into Rainey's face, squinting
a little, then nodding her head. 'Are you all right, darlin'?' she
asked. 'Are you OK?'

Rainey smiled and drew back her tears. 'I'll be OK,' she told the
woman. 'Once I get out of here, I'll be fine. I'm on my way to getting
better.'

SIXTEEN

September 1988
Chicago, Illinois

The hope that Rainey had felt while sitting at the dinner table died quickly. An hour and a half later, she was desolate again. She found a seat on the bus and sat down heavily, pushing her shoulders into the back rest. She looked through the darkened, grease-smeared window and saw the reflection of her face looking back at her. She was shocked at how old she looked, shocked and strangely satisfied. She wanted to look the way she felt; old, hard and dead inside.

She let herself think about Woody, imagining his impassive, mysterious face, his pale blue eyes and his sallow skin. *What if he's with a woman?* she suddenly thought. *What if he is making love to her right now, and I ruin everything? How can I possibly expect him to offer me anything, even a place to stay for the night, after we stole all that stuff? Ambrose stole his ashtray, for God's sake, how stupid was that? If Woody has any sense, he'll slam the door right in my face. That's what I deserve. I hope he slams the door in my face.*

She felt firm, even righteous, as the bus pulled out of the station and down Sixth Street. Going to Woody's was a foolish thing to do, she knew that. *Why am I burdening him with my problems? I'm no one to him;*

he's got no reason to care about me. I should be ashamed for asking for help from someone I hardly even know. What if he asks why I've come? I don't have an answer. Nothing makes sense to me now.

By the time Rainey reached Woody's apartment, retracing the steps she'd taken with Ambrose, it was past midnight. She felt angry and frustrated as she climbed up the creaky steel staircase and knocked on his door. She was glad for her anger because it prevented her from being afraid. She half hoped he wouldn't be home or, better yet, he may have moved, and the flat might be inhabited by a gang of gun-wielding drug dealers. *Good. That would serve me right,* she thought. *I might get killed. Or at least have to sleep out on the street tonight.* She wanted so badly to be hurt; to feel a sharp, abiding, bone-deep pain. She wanted a hurting inside her body to match what she felt in her mind.

After she knocked a third time, the door inched open. 'Yeah?' a thin voice said.

'Woody, you in there?' Rainey asked softly. She let her backpack sag to the ground as her knees buckled beneath her with relief. Suddenly she felt tired and weepy, like a child longing for comfort. 'Woody, let me in,' she pleaded.

Woody stepped out on to the landing, rubbing his arms. His pale, watery eyes took a few seconds to focus, then grew wide with surprise as he recognised her. He wore a stained white T-shirt and the red bandana tied around his head. 'Well, if it isn't Rainey McBride,' he said slowly, scratching his chin. 'Come on in, girl. You're just about the last person I expected to see this time of night. It must be close to one.'

He opened the door all the way and guided her into his apartment, which was dark and humid, and still smelled of incense and dope. Damascus came loping in from the kitchen, struggling to bark, and tripping over his own ears. The dog landed at her feet and began sniffing her shoes. Rainey turned around to face Woody, opened her mouth and burst into tears. 'Woody,' she sobbed. 'Please, Woody.' She couldn't speak, couldn't catch her breath. She tried to hide herself, holding her face in her hands.

'Hey, what's wrong?' he said, gently pulling her hand away and studying her features. 'What's happened, hon?'

'Ambrose,' she said, choking out his name.

'Where is he?' he asked.

She shook her head, unable to answer.

'Oh Lord,' Woody said. 'Oh no. Don't tell me . . .'

'Yes,' she whispered.

'Is he?'

'Yes.'

'Dead.'

'Uh-huh,' she said. Now the worst was over, now he knew.

'Oh, honey, I'm sorry. God, I'm so sorry. What happened?' He knelt beside her, gently stroking her back.

'He, he . . .' She couldn't say it.

'He killed himself.' Woody said it for her.

'Yes,' she answered. 'He's dead.' She looked up at him. 'Woody, help me. Please help me. I feel like I'm dying too.'

'It's OK. It's OK. You're not gonna die. We'll take care of you, won't we, Damascus?' he said, glancing down at the dog, and leading Rainey gently by the hand into the living room.

He sat her on the sofa, pushed the ottoman beneath her feet and folded the scratchy yarn quilt over her shoulders. 'It's going to be all right. Just you wait and see.' He turned on the radio, a soft music station, and began waving a ragged copy of *Rolling Stone* magazine to disperse the stale, sweaty air. 'Sorry, I haven't cleaned for a while,' he apologised.

'No really, it's OK,' she said, leaning back and closing her eyes, burying her face in the quilt.

He went into the kitchen and came back with a Coke. 'I'll defrost you some soup. You must be starving,' he said, placing the Coke on the table in front of her.

She nodded. 'Yeah, OK. That sounds great.' But she wasn't really hungry. All she wanted was to lie down for a long time and let the world turn without her while she disappeared into the gaping pit of grief. She leaned back and looked at the poster on the wall across from her: *Come unto me, all ye that labor and are heavy laden, and I will give you rest* Matt 10:28.

She heard Woody singing in the kitchen, and she listened closely, following the rhythm of his voice. *I'm three times an exile, an exile from the promised land. I first went down, with Abraham, many years ago . . .'* He stopped suddenly. She wished she could ask him to please, start singing again. *Right now that would make me almost happy,* she thought. Rainey glanced at Damascus, touched by the way the dog looked up at her with his sad, wrinkled face pressed against her knee. 'Good boy, good boy,' she whispered, stroking his ears, appreciating how stoically he accepted her love.

When the soup was ready, Woody brought her a cup of it, placing it carefully next to the Coke. 'Go on, sip it,' he said, sitting back in his chair. 'It will do you some good.'

She lifted the cup and tasted the soup. It had a strange flavour, thin and bitter, with dark little seeds floating on the surface. 'It's very . . . unusual,' she offered, taking another small drink, and then a third, larger sip, finding the soup improved the more she drank of it. 'I don't think I've ever had anything quite like this before.'

'It was my grandmother's recipe,' he said proudly. 'It came over with her, on the boat from Russia. This was the first thing she made in America. The smell of this soup always reminded her of home.'

'Do you make it often?' Rainey asked him. She noticed he hadn't prepared a cup for himself.

'No. Not really. I keep a jug of it in the freezer, just in case of emergencies. But I hardly ever make it for myself.'

'Why not?'

He shrugged. 'I dunno. I guess because it was my wife's favourite. She asked for it the day before she died.'

After Rainey finished the soup, Woody took her to the guest room, which hadn't changed since Rainey and Ambrose were there four months earlier. Ragged cardboard boxes were still strewn across the floor, opened and half-unpacked. 'I'll just fix this up a little bit,' Woody offered guiltily. He grabbed the blankets and began to make up the bed, which was still covered with the same crumpled, dirty sheets.

'Don't bother,' Rainey told him, exhausted. 'I just want to sleep.'

'All right then.' He seemed uncertain but dropped the pillow back on the bed. She sat down on the edge of the mattress, too tired to move. He reached towards her forehead and pressed it gently with the palm of his hand. 'I'm sorry,' he said softly. 'I know that never really helps a whole lot, but I'm real, real sorry that Ambrose died.'

'Thanks,' she told him, managing a weak smile. 'You know, you're the first person who's said that to me.'

'I guessed as much,' he told her. 'Child, you've got a look like you've been starvin' for comfort.'

'Yeah. I guess I have been,' she said, trying not to cry.

He seemed to sense that she wanted to be alone. 'Well, good night now. I'll be in the kitchen if you need me. Otherwise, just make yourself at home,' Woody said.

'OK. Thanks.' Rainey slumped into the mattress. As she buried her face in the sheets, she realised that Ambrose was the last person to have slept in this bed. *I feel close to him again*, she thought, breathing in his scent, his dead skin cells, his essence. She clutched the sheet and dug her fists deep into the mattress, where she could hear the coiled springs creaking and singing beneath her ear. *I'm holding on to Ambrose, he's with me now. I can remember him, as long as I lie here.* She cried until the pillow was damp and squishy; and then she prayed into the spot that smelled like Ambrose's hair, into the soft cleft of pillow that still held the shape of his skull.

After she had had her fill of tears, Rainey turned over and lay on her back, staring up at the water-stained ceiling with its bare light bulb and streaks of peeling paint. *I'm glad I came here*, she told herself. *This is the place. I'll be able to understand what Ambrose has done.* She listened to the noises outside – the bass of a distant radio, trains sailing over the 'L' tracks, and hungry children crying, several rooms away. She listened long and hard and deep. She was separating, considering and then discarding each individual sound that filled the dark and fretful night, until she was sure she could hear only Woody, sitting alone at the kitchen table. She could allow herself to sleep knowing that he would sit at that table for an hour or more, offering up his prayers both for her sake and for the lost, tormented soul of Ambrose Torsten Dienst.

Woody gave Rainey several days of patience and space, allowing her to sleep all afternoon if she wanted and wander the flat by night, watching cable TV, listening to music, swinging the refrigerator door back and forth. He never asked her to contribute anything to the cost of food, he never suggested she wash the dishes, do the laundry, or pick up after herself. He went about his quiet business, humming or whistling to himself, engaged in the busy little tasks that filled his life.

'You must really hate him,' Woody said softly, early one evening. He was so quiet, so matter-of-fact, Rainey hardly noticed what he had said. He was sitting at the kitchen table, reading the newspaper and drinking an Old Milwaukee, tipping his cigarette ash into an empty tin.

'What?' Rainey asked. She had been rocking back and forth, but she suddenly sat forward, eyes fixed on Woody's narrow form.

'Ambrose. You must really hate him for killing himself.' Woody paused, turning down a corner of his paper and looking at her over the rim of his bifocals.

'No. I don't hate him. Maybe I should, but I don't.' She coughed and felt a squeezing deep in her lungs. A sickness had settled inside her; the thick green phlegm of grief. She pulled the quilt over her shoulders, fighting the chill that ached through her bones. 'What I can't understand is how I didn't see it,' she said evenly.

'Didn't see what?' Woody asked, taking a sip of his beer and sucking it between his teeth.

'I went to visit him at the hospital three days before he died. He had already made up his mind to kill himself, I'm sure of that now. He said, "Remember me, tell my story. Tell everyone the truth about what was inside me." That was a message. If I had understood, I could have stopped him. It's my fault he died.' She tightened the quilt in her fists, not allowing herself to cry.

'No, Rainey. You couldn't have known,' Woody said sadly, shaking his head.

'Yes, I could have,' she insisted. 'If I had looked hard enough, I would have seen it. Seen what he was trying to say. Sometimes I think maybe he was testing me; he wanted me to save him, just like I did at the motel in Harper's Ferry. If I had paid attention, Ambrose might still be alive.' Rainey sighed deeply, letting her words settle into the dark corners of the room. She was surprised she had said it; this was a secret, midnight thing, not meant to be spoken of in the light of day.

'Oh, Rainey, honey, that's a heavy burden,' Woody said, whisking off his glasses and rubbing his eyes. 'No matter how much you loved Ambrose, there were things inside him you could never know.' Woody folded the newspaper and placed it in his lap. 'The way I figure it, everybody has a second heart, hidden inside the first one. That's the heart only the Lord sees. We don't truly understand ourselves, so it's impossible to fathom all of someone else. No one knows the truth. Except for God.'

Rainey shook her head, dropping her chin to her chest. 'That's easy for you to say, but my beliefs are different. I used to have faith, like you do. When I was a child, God was everywhere, He was everything – a red wagon in the driveway, an air rifle beside my bed. God was the ecstasy of mittens that fit. But you see, I gave up that faith for Ambrose. I gave it up for Ambrose, and he chose death instead.'

After much coaxing, Rainey convinced Woody to let her listen to his songs. In a cabinet beneath the television he kept a box of records and tapes, which he said she could listen to while he was at work. She liked all the music, but her favourite was the vinyl LP he had made in the seventies, titled 'The Songs of Woody Stern, Vol. I'. The title struck her as somewhat sad – 'Vol. I', as if there was no doubt about the eventual appearance of volumes II, III and IV.

Rainey thought the whole album was intense and exciting, full of country-folk tragedies and restless laments that revealed more of themselves each time she listened. She particularly loved the two baseball songs – 'The Ballad of Heinie Manusch' and 'Tinkers to Evers to Chance'. *'Tinkers to Evers to Chance; doin' that double play dance . . .'* Rainey hummed the tune over and over, admiring the jangly melody which incorporated snatches of the National Anthem into the background. 'Woody is a genius,' she told herself. 'I wonder why he doesn't write new music any more?'

Behind the last row of Woody's record albums Rainey found a battered old shoebox sealed with tape. The box was so well hidden that even Ambrose hadn't found it during his exhaustive search of Woody's apartment. She knew she shouldn't open the box, but curiosity got the better of her. She slid off the cardboard cover to reveal a cassette tape and some letters, along with a dried rose, a handful of seashells, and a simple diamond ring, its tiny chipped stone loose in the setting. Rainey popped the tape into the tape player and listened to the slow, gentle music which filled the room. *'Emelita Rosalita, the dark-eyed lady from Santa Fe. I met her in Tucson, where she done stumbled straight into my heart . . .'*

The box also contained a stack of photographs of Woody with a young Hispanic woman. The woman was about twenty-five years old, with long, black hair, dark eyes and a soulful smile. 'Emelita,' Rainey whispered her name. Woody looked ten or fifteen years younger in the photos, with his dark, tight curls cropped close to his head. His face was soft and rounded, with a broad, dimpled grin. She hardly recognised him as the man she'd seen that morning, visible evidence of how sorrow took its toll.

At the bottom of the box Rainey found a mass card:

Emelita Rosalita Stern
30 November, 1946 – 8 April, 1981
'The Lord is my shepherd, I shall not want. He maketh me
to lie down in green pastures, He leadeth me beside the
still waters, He restoreth my soul. Yea, though I walk
through the valley of the shadow of death . . .'

Rainey closed her eyes, chanting the psalm as a prayer. 'The valley of the shadow of death. The valley of the shadow of death.' She said the phrase over and over, listening to Emelita's sweet music still playing above her head. She listened and listened, letting the tears stream down her cheeks. This was easier than crying for Ambrose. Emelita was more deserving of grief; after all, she hadn't chosen to die.

The music stopped with a screeching jolt and Rainey looked up to see Woody standing square-shouldered in the doorway, his face pale with anger. 'Get away from that,' he said evenly. 'Get away from those things right now.' His hands shook and his chin quivered, his whole body racked with tiny tremors.

'But, Woody, it's beautiful. The music, it's . . . beautiful,' Rainey said.

'Get away,' he whispered. 'Please just leave me alone.' He shook his head, burying his face in his hands.

'Sorry. I'm so sorry,' Rainey mumbled, burning with shame. Rainey quickly replaced the cover on the box and stood up, afraid to look at Woody, afraid to touch him as she brushed past. *Now I've ruined it*, she thought sadly. *Woody was my last friend in the world, and he'll never forgive me. What a mess I've made of everything.*

The next day Woody left early for St Adalbert's, and was supposed to return by seven o'clock. Rainey didn't start to worry until ten pm, and by eleven she was frantic. 'I should call somebody,' she told herself. 'But who would I call? As far as I know, he has no family, and I've never met any of his friends.' Every time she closed her eyes, she had visions of Woody's slender body lifeless in an alleyway or stretched out on a metal table in the morgue. 'He's got to be OK,' she said over and over. This was the closest she had come to praying in weeks; the first time in a long while that she had cared about anything.

Damascus, who had been asleep beneath the table, stirred suddenly and started to whine. He lumbered to his feet and waddled into the living room, where he began scratching the door. 'What is it, boy?' Rainey called after him. 'What's wrong?' She heard the door knob rattling in its loose metal holder, and then Woody stumbling into the apartment.

'Woody? You're back,' she started to say, but stopped when she saw him in the doorway; pale, dishevelled, covered with blood. 'My God, Woody, what happened?' she asked, running to his side. He had a long crescent of blood on the front of his T-shirt and patches of blood on either side of his denim jacket. Rainey started to shake. 'Woody, what happened?' she asked. She patted him up and down, searching through layers of clothing for his elusive wound. 'Who did this to you?'

'A fourteen-year-old boy was shot outside St Adalbert's this afternoon,' he said in a hushed, crackly voice. 'We drove him to the hospital. He died about an hour ago. Father Rick gave him last rites while I held his head. Rainey, I watched him die; I held him as he took his final breath.'

'But at least you're OK,' she said, turning him around and around, still fearing he was injured. 'At least you weren't hurt.'

'That boy belonged to someone,' he said with reproach. 'He was someone's son.'

'I know. I'm sorry. I'm really sorry,' she whispered, examining his pale, shaking, blood-stained hands.

'His friends – these big, tough gang kids, just stood there crying for him to wake up,' Woody whispered. 'What could I say? What could I do?'

'Don't go out. Not ever again,' she said quickly, pulling his jacket off his arms and letting it fall to the floor. 'Stay inside here. With me. Where it's nice and safe and warm.'

'I can't,' he said. He let out a great breath, as if he might faint. 'I can't do that.'

'It's OK, I've got you,' she said, motioning for him to rest against her arms. 'Leave everything to me.' She began undressing him, pulling off his T-shirt and undershirt, unbuttoning his jeans and leaving his clothes in a bloody pile on the floor. Woody stood before her, thin and shivering. Rainey noticed the bony notch at the base of his neck, the cupped hollows of his collarbone. Her heart ached for his knobby elbows, his pimply shoulders, his sunken chest and each visible rib. He was pale and shaking, arms damp with sweat. She saw every part of him and was not embarrassed, not ashamed. 'Come on,' she said. 'Come with me.'

She led him into the bathroom and filled the tub with soapy water. With a wet cloth she washed him off, dabbing at the spots where the blood had soaked through to his skin. Woody's eyes were dull and heavy-lidded, as if forced to observe a horror unfolding deep inside himself. 'Come on,' Rainey said softly. 'Just a little bit more.' He nodded as she squeezed the cloth against his chest, watching the thin rivulets of water trickle down his skin, disappearing into the tight folds of his stomach. He was beautiful to her, but this was a love above lust or desire; her duty here was simply to take care.

She helped him up and dried him carefully, buffing some colour into his sallow skin. He swayed back and forth, barely able to stand. He looked as if the life had been drained out of him as he blinked slowly, rubbing his tired eyes.

'It's all right, follow me,' she said, taking him by the arm and leading him into the bedroom.

'Rainey, I saw him,' he whispered, sitting down on the bed. 'I saw the fear of death in his eyes.'

'What did it look like?' she asked anxiously.

'What?'

'Death. What did it look like?' she asked, needing to know. 'Was it terrible?'

'Yes,' he said, nodding quietly. 'Yes, I think it was.'

'OK. At least we can say it. Death is terrible. We can say those words.' Rainey searched for some clean clothes, finally settling on a pair of shorts and a long white T-shirt, which she helped slide over his head, pulling his arms through the sleeves.

'I'm cold,' he whispered, settling into the pillow. 'It's so cold now.'

Rainey touched his forehead, his colourless cheeks and, even in the muggy heat, he was shivering. 'You do feel chilled. I'll close the window,' she said. She got up and moved the chair against the wall, using the yardstick to push the window up the frame.

'Be careful, the chair's unsteady,' Woody warned. 'Mind you don't fall.'

'I'm OK. I've got it.' She pressed her hands against the glass to steady herself, locking her wrists and knees. She looked down into the bleak, deserted street, stretching out beneath her. She couldn't remember what it was like to be outdoors; the smells and dust and particular odours, all were lost to her.

'I can't close my eyes,' Woody said as she stepped off the chair and moved back to the bed. 'When I close my eyes, I see his face. I see that boy's face and, Rainey, he is so, so scared.' Woody's skin was taut, pulled tight against his cheeks and bony chin. She stroked his forehead, let her fingertips touch the ridge where his skull had been broken.

'I need to pray for him. I need to pray,' Woody said suddenly, clutching her arm. 'I can't go to sleep, not like this. Not while his soul is still out there somewhere, wandering loose.'

'It's OK. I'll do it for you,' Rainey said, surprising herself with the offer.

'You will?'

'Yes.'

'Promise?' he asked.

'Yes.' She nodded. 'Cross my heart and hope to die, stick a needle in my eye.' She leaned down to kiss him, but instead pressed her face to his, hoping some of her warmth might sink into his body. 'You just rest, I'll take care of everything else.'

'Thanks, Rainey,' he said, closing his eyes. 'Thanks.' She sat back and watched the movements of the tiny muscles in his face; the flutter in his temples, the twitching in his eyelids.

Once she was sure he was asleep, she gathered up the bloody clothes and carried them to the kitchen. She filled the sink with soapy water and started scrubbing Woody's jacket with a pad of steel wool. The dried blood billowed out of the jacket, giving the water a soft, pinkish glow. The window was open, but it was humid and close for October, and her head started to sweat. 'Poor Woody,' she whispered, rubbing the thick denim back and forth, trying to loosen the deeply set blood. 'Poor Woody.'

She scrubbed and scrubbed using slow, even strokes, gradually becoming aware of the quiet, steady rhythm of her hands. Her mind emptied itself of everything except the warmth of the water and the clean, lemony scent of soap. She felt almost happy in a strange, unexpected way. Everything *was* terrible, she couldn't deny that. But she had reached a kind of settled level, she had found a resting place inside herself, like the hollow of a maple tree or the palm of an invisible hand. Yes. This was it, this was the thought that had been hiding at the back of her brain; this was the thought that had fought so hard to reveal itself since Ambrose's death: there was sadness; sadness at the centre of everything.

She lifted her hands out of the water and watched them turn red and swell. She thought about Mormor's hands; strong, callused, immune to heat and cold. She wondered when, if ever, she would see those hands again. She knew she could never look at Mormor's hands long enough not to miss them eventually, some day in the future, after Mormor was gone. *Pilate washed his hands of the blood of an innocent man. But we're all implicated now,* she thought. 'This boy, how can I pray for him?' she said aloud, remembering her promise to Woody. 'I don't even know the boy's name. He is no one to me. I never even met him and now I never will – he's gone from this world forever.'

'No. It will be OK; don't worry, it's OK.' The words that came to her were words of comfort: *'He is known to God.'* *Jesus will know which one I mean. The kid who died this afternoon. Tomorrow, he'll be joined by another; maybe two more. And more after that. There is no end to death. But death.*

When Woody's clothes were clean, gleaming dark with moisture, she hung them on clothespegs just above the bathtub and listened to the soft ping as the water droplets struck the floor. She went quietly to Woody's bedroom, and was pleased to see that he was still asleep, the blanket under his chin. 'See, I told you it would be OK,' she whispered to him. 'You just have to trust me, I guess.' She leaned over him, hovering closely with her hot face, her red and swollen hands. She heard him breathing and saw the slight movement of his chest beneath the sheets. She looked at him for a long time, just watching, and noticing everything; not willing to let any detail slip away. His eyes were set back deep in their sockets and a set of wrinkles lined his forehead. *Woody looks so old*, she thought, and her heart filled with tenderness. 'Emelita.' She whispered the dead woman's name. 'Emelita Stern.' Her whole life had been relegated to a tiny cardboard box. 'A woman once loved this man,' Rainey said to herself, looking down at Woody. 'What do I know about anything at all?'

Rainey went back to the kitchen and drained the water out of the sink, spraying away the last droplets of blood. Then, for good measure, she got down on her knees and scrubbed the stains off the tile floor – chilli, ketchup, mustard, Coke; the blurred muddy footprints of boots. She wanted everything to gleam, everything to be clean and shiny. *Tomorrow the sun will come up on a world without sin.*

When she had finished cleaning, she sat down at the kitchen table and prayed, prayed without awkwardness, without hesitation, beneath the bare light bulb in the utter darkness of two am. This she did for Woody, not for herself. The words came easy now. 'Please God, Oh please, take into your kingdom the soul of the poor boy who was killed this afternoon at St Adalbert's . . .'

After she had finished praying, she sat on the windowsill, bare feet pressed against the warped wooden frame, drinking a Colt .45 and smoking one of Woody's Marlboros. The nicotine made her hands quiver, made her head dizzy and her heart start to pound. She looked down into the empty, barren streets beneath her, stained by dirt and burned rubber, with spray-painted graffiti spreading like a pox across the sidewalk. Her eyelids felt heavy, her body cried for sleep, but she was determined to stay awake, at least until the sun came up. She vowed to keep watch all night if she had to, to keep watch and pray, while Woody slept quietly in the next room, mercifully free of dreams. She looked at the apartment building across the street rising up before her, the tall brick tower of The Sheffield Arms. There were bars on every window of the first three floors but no bars any higher, which meant you could feel safer, four floors up. Every window had a dull and darkened pane of glass, a crossed wooden frame and some kind of sash or curtain, a private veil of grief. *That boy was killed today, and somewhere, in this city, a mother and father and brothers and sisters are weeping, preparing for a funeral. Tomorrow night, it will be someone else. And the day after, the day after, and the day after that. Until someday, again, it will be my turn to cry. Until then, I must watch, wait, and pray – these are the acts of faith. Brazen belief exists against all reason. Yes*, she thought, for the first time since Ambrose died, *I do belong to this world.*

When morning came, Rainey woke up still perched in the windowsill, with the sun beating hot against the top of her head, and she knew, absolutely knew, that Ambrose was gone forever. He had chosen to die and leave her behind, and nothing she could do would ever change that fact. 'He must not have loved me as much as I loved him.' *No, that isn't quite right.* 'He loved me, yes, but he loved death better. He chose the cold, iron grip of eternity over the chance to lie warm in my arms.'

Rainey stood and stretched, feeling the stiffness in every inch of her back. And since there was nothing else to do, she made some breakfast, which she took to Woody's bedroom, carrying it in on a makeshift tray. 'Morning,' she said gently, setting the tray down beside the bed as his creased eyelids slipped open. 'I hope you slept OK.'

That afternoon Rainey and Woody took a walk through the small city park, where the trees were greyish and stunted by pollution and most of the wild birds were really pigeons, and even in the middle, in the woodland's deepest heart, she could still hear the traffic, wheezing and whining down the expressway.

'I guess I should be moving on soon,' she told him tentatively. 'Find a job, a place to live. I can't imagine going back to my grand-parents, after everything that's happened.'

Woody nodded. 'You're welcome to stay as long as you want. But I guess it's up to you.'

'Before I go, I want to buy a place. In a graveyard. You know, a cemetery,' Rainey said carefully.

Woody stopped and turned towards her, shocked. His usual calm evaporated. 'Why would you want to do that? You're only eighteen years old.' His voice was sharp and edgy.

'Because I need to know where I'll end up someday,' she explained. 'My life seems so aimless now, like I'm just drifting. I need to know I've got a date with eternity; that there's a place waiting for me, a stone somewhere with my name already carved into it.'

Woody's eyes were small and watery, floating deep in their sockets. 'Rainey, have you thought about killing yourself? Is that what this is about?'

'No,' she answered. 'Of course not.' She could feel the pain she was causing him, and that awareness was like a match suddenly struck inside her, scorching the skin around her heart. 'I want to buy the plot, but I don't plan to use it anytime soon.'

'Then why think about it now?' He gritted his teeth and squinted into the sunlight. 'What's the point of doing that?'

She shrugged. 'I dunno. I need to see the dirt I will return to . . . the earth I will become.'

He held her elbow tightly and let out his breath. 'But you would tell me, right, if you were thinking about—'

'Shh. Poor Woody. I wouldn't do that. Not to you.' She tried to smile. *You really imagined I was going to kill myself?* she thought. *How could you think that? Don't you know me better by now?* She felt a wave of dark despair. But then something else flickered at the edge of her awareness – a word or two; then a certainty. *But you know what? I can forgive you for this.* She wrapped her arms around his shoulders and kissed his face. Woody grabbed her tightly around the waist.

'Damn it all, you scared me there,' he said hoarsely. 'I was scared.'

'Hey, I'm sorry. I won't do it again.' As he pulled her closer, she felt him trembling, felt his heart fluttering behind the pocket of his denim jacket. 'I didn't mean to scare you,' she said. She loved holding him in her arms, feeling the ridges of his spine, his narrow hips, the burned smell of his hair. 'I promise not to say things like that any more.'

'Good. Make sure you don't,' he warned, whispering in her ear.

As she hugged him, her skin seemed to come alive. And then, just as quickly, she felt a hollow stab of pain. 'Oh fuck this,' she said. 'Damn it. Damn Ambrose.' Ambrose's face was all around her now; pleading, reaching, begging for her help. 'Ambrose. Damn it. I can't stand it,' she said, biting her lip. 'You were right, I do hate him sometimes,' she admitted. 'But then I'm glad for hating him, because I know then he'll never leave me. I'm willing to hang on to him, even if it means having to hate.'

She felt dazzled, everything around her was brutally alive with her hatred. The sky was filled with sparrows, masses of dull-coloured birds who sang so sweetly, a well-orchestrated song. The music was clear and simple, completely without meaning. 'Stop it,' she said, 'just stop it.'

'Stop what?' Woody asked, his face creased and confused.

'It's them,' she said, raising her arms. 'Those damn birds.' She couldn't explain it to him. The birds sang so sweetly that she wanted to kill every one. She wanted to squeeze each bird between her fingers, crush their tiny hearts and smother their lungs. How dare they be alive in a world where Ambrose was dead?

'God loves his creatures more than he loves us,' she said. 'Look at these birds – they live, they eat, they fly, they die. There's no suffering for them. They sing for no reason. All their eggs might get crushed, all their babies could fall out of the tree and die, and that momma bird will still sing just as sweetly. She doesn't know what's happened and doesn't feel anything. God loves the sparrows more than he loves us, because he lets us suffer so much more.'

Rainey tossed her head back. The sky was more blue than she remembered it, and the late afternoon sun was a disk of brittle gold. She took a breath and tasted the late autumn sky, a beautiful sky in a world where nothing was right. The air was food and drink to her; rich and smoky, like meat and red wine. The taste of the air filled the emptiness inside her, filled her when she wanted instead to stay empty. *No*, she pleaded, plunging her hands into her jacket, *don't do this to me.*

She leaned against Woody to steady herself, trying to catch her breath without tasting the air. 'If I could stop breathing right now, I would,' she said. 'If I was brave enough, I would have killed myself to be with him. But I don't think I could have done it. If only for my grandparents' sake, if nothing else. They raised me the best they could, and I've already hurt them so much.'

She buried her face in Woody's shoulder and felt his thin hands against her back. 'I'm not sure it's brave to kill yourself,' he offered, stroking her hair. 'Sometimes, I think it takes more courage to live.' They stood pressed together for a long time. Woody didn't flinch, even as the sun moved behind the clouds and the wind changed direction. 'I'm with you now,' he said, 'and I promise I won't let go. Not until you want me to, anyway.'

After what seemed like an hour, but was probably less than ten minutes, she began to tire. Her legs were cramping, her head ached. She felt the pain subsiding, withdrawing to a dull, gnawing ache. The violence ebbed away, flowing out of her like liquid. Woody took a step back and she swayed dizzily, as if about to fall.

'Come on, let's go home,' Woody said, holding her up.

'I can't,' she said quietly.

'You have to.'

'Why?'

He sighed and scratched his head. 'Because the rest of your life is waiting for you? That might be reason enough. Let the dead rest. Let them rest. As cruel as it sounds, your life is somewhere else.'

'But I can come back here, can't I?' she asked, clinging to his arm. 'This will be my place, here in this park, where I can come to think about Ambrose. To think about what he did to me, and to remember that I loved him anyway.'

'Of course you can come back here,' he said. 'Whenever you want.'

'Promise you won't ever let me forget him,' she pleaded, grabbing his hands.

'You won't.'

She nodded, letting her gaze take in the park's rough grasses, the stunted trees, the rusty iron fence. 'OK. I believe you. Then something here is finished. And this will be my punishment,' she said. 'Punishment enough.'

That night she went to see Woody in his bedroom. As she entered, he was sitting cross-legged on the bed, his ear cocked, head bent towards the long fringed string of beads that made a kind of make-shift curtain. He held his guitar tenderly on his lap and stroked the strings, gently, too gently to make any music. A cigarette smouldered in the ashtray beside him, and a beer can was balanced on the table's edge with another beer can crumpled up next to it, flattened to a small tin disk. His eyes were glassy and far away, and his mouth was firm, almost as if he might be humming, but humming too soft for her to hear. She came in quietly, slipping through the door. He didn't move except to acknowledge her with a narrowing of his eyes and a slight nod of his chin. She moved to the end of the bed and sat down. He said nothing. After a few moments, she lay down, knowing that her head was near to his bare feet.

He picked up the cigarette and took two short puffs. 'Today was tough, wasn't it,' he said, not as a question, but a statement.

'Yes,' she said. 'It was.' She spread out her hands into the folds of the bedspread, and pulled her knees towards her chest. 'There'll be a lot of days like this, I guess.'

'No doubt.'

'Days, weeks, months, maybe years of all this pain and unhappiness.' She drew in a deep breath and held it.

'Yep. 'Fraid so.'

'I wonder when I'll start to get over it.' She rubbed her scalp into the bedspread, buried her nose in the folds of fabric, felt it brush against her lip. The bed was soft and lumpy, and smelled of stale tobacco and old tennis shoes, an odour that seemed to rise up and wreathe her head with its warmth. And something in it smelled of solace.

'Your wife died in 1981,' she said carefully, studying his face for a reaction.

'Yes,' he said, closing his eyes. 'It was seven years ago.' He spoke quietly, as if addressing a voice inside himself. 'It was the week before my birthday.'

'Do you think about her a lot?'

'Oh yeah,' he answered. 'All the time.'

'Do you remember what it was like, right after she died? Do you remember how you felt then?'

'No. I don't think so,' he said. 'Not exactly. I'm sure I don't remember the worst of it.'

'Do you ever wish you could remember the worst parts; you know, as a way of not having to let her go?'

He shook his head slowly, pursing his lips. 'No. It's better this way. It's right that some things stay shrouded from ourselves. It's like our deeper halves are hidden, even from who we think we are. There's a blessing in there somewhere, I guess. I'm glad I don't remember the worst of it.'

'Did you ever think about getting married again? Have you ever said to yourself, yeah, now I'm ready, now I could fall in love with someone else?'

He shook his head. 'No. That hasn't ever happened.' His voice was confident, free from self-pity and despair.

'Then how can you stand it? How can you handle the thought of being so totally alone forever and ever?' She rolled on to her stomach and lifted her head, balancing her chin on her fists.

He smiled at her, a smile which seemed to open depths of his face which were usually hidden. 'Who says I'll be alone forever? I'm not so old. To myself, I'm not half as old as I must seem to you. It might still happen, even to me.' He shrugged. 'There's still time. There's always plenty of time.'

'So you might fall in love someday?'

'I might. I just might.' His pale eyes glistened behind the veil of cigarette smoke. 'Rainey, you might not believe it, but I have such faith.'

'Really?' she asked him.

'Yes,' he answered, bowing his head. 'Oh yes.'

– PART V –

1 9 9 2

SEVENTEEN

Thanksgiving Day 1992
Milwaukee, Wisconsin

Rainey McBride, twenty-two years old and eight weeks pregnant, stands at the living-room window, watching the dizzy whirl of falling snow fill the front yard of every house on Sandstone Avenue. Aromas from the other room assault her; turkey, stuffing, gravy and pie, a medley of smells designed to overturn her insurgent stomach, to make her poor head spin. 'God,' she whispers, her prayer visible against the frosty glass. 'What if I'm a terrible mother? What if, once I have my baby, I want to run away?' Rainey listens to the brittle kitchen music of knives and forks and spoons; a medley of voices, and the warm, comfortable bustle just beyond the door. 'Every time I think about my mother, it's a punishment. To know how much I might have loved her, and how much I have truly missed her, all along.'

Rainey presses her hands flat against the glass and stares out at the landscape. She uncovers the old path to the bus depot, and focuses on the derelict swing, its rusty chain frozen solid, icicles hanging from the split wooden seat. *I want to show my child all these things; I want my child to know everything about life. About my life,* she thinks. *Except the loneliness, I don't want him or her ever to know anything about that.* Rainey steps back an inch and sees in the window the mirrored reflection of her own face. She is pale from the pregnancy, from the daily bouts of morning sickness that leave her on her knees and weeping for relief. The skin is slightly darkened beneath her eyes, but her hair is full and glossy, a dense reddish-brown. Suddenly her mother's face rises like a moon behind her; looming high and ghostly above her own. Rainey studies Mary Jane's long, black hair, her vivid green eyes, the little gold earrings that catch and reflect the light.

'Umm, Rainey, honey, it's time for dinner,' Mary Jane says softly, twisting a silver ring around her little finger and nervously chewing gum. 'Do you want to join us in the dining room?' Rainey turns away from the image in the window to face her mother in real life.

'All right,' Rainey answers, swooning for a second and steadying herself against the icy glass.

'What's wrong, Rainbow?' Mary Jane asks. She pads across the room on stockinged feet, arms open wide, anxious to clasp her daughter to her chest. As Mary Jane grabs hold of her, Rainey smells the odour of peaches and incense, feels the uncertain caress of slim fingers against her sweaty head.

'I'm OK, I just felt a little dizzy,' Rainey says, catching her breath. 'You go ahead, I'll be there in a minute.' Mary Jane bows and retreats to the dining room, her long gauzy skirt swish-swishing with her steps.

All those years, I missed her so much, Rainey thinks, hand sliding absently over the round softness of her stomach. *And now, sometimes I find myself wishing she'd never come home.*

In the dining room, the others await her arrival with impatient eyes. Rainey scans their faces quickly – Mormor, Grandpa Garth, Aunt Ingebjorg; the solid, unwavering survivors of the old guard. Across from them sits Mary Jane; nervous, girlish, eager to please; her husband, Joe, with his gap-toothed smile and beefy arms; and their eight-year-old daughter, Rebecca, a solemn, wide-eyed child, with a stubby nose and round, clumsy hands. 'Sorry to keep you waiting,' Rainey apologises.

This is my family, Rainey thinks to herself. *I belong to them.* But she sees in the faces of those present the reflected absence of those who aren't here. She knows this table will always be partially empty, even though the names are never spoken, and the places never taken of those who are gone. A television plays softly in the den, a football game, late in the third quarter with the Badgers down 17 to 3. Rainey can hear it in the silence, but no one rises to turn it off.

'Rainey, guess what? Uncle Woody's going to teach me how to play the guitar,' Rebecca says, rubbing her wide hands together and wiggling in her seat. Her dark eyes shine like headlamps behind her heavy glasses.

'*Utmerket!*' Aunt Ingebjorg exclaims, beaming a broad smile. 'That would be wonderful. There's never been any musical talent in this family before. Well, Margaret's daughter Agnes was in the marching band, but I'm not sure if that counts as music or not.'

Rainey shifts in her seat and feels the spread of her hips over the chair's round edges. She slips her hand into Woody's, feeling his long, thin fingers curl around her own. She leans close to him, smells Old Spice and cigarettes, sees the overhead light shining through his mass of grizzled, greying curls.

'How about Amos?' he asks in an urgent whisper.

'No,' she answers quickly, shaking her head.

'Amos Stern? C'mon, it has a nice ring to it,' he insists. 'I'm still in favour of something biblical.'

'Let's just wait,' she whispers. 'Let's wait a few more weeks, just in case.' Rainey is afraid to name her child, afraid that if she names it, some stealthy and seductive force will be able to lure it away from her, to tempt it out of this world by kidnapping it before birth. Rainey told the doctor of her fears – 'The first twelve weeks are critical,' the doctor explained, glancing at her chart. 'Once you've passed that point, the odds are excellent for a healthy, full-term birth. Of course,' she had added ominously, 'there are never any guarantees.'

Ingebjorg nods to Mary Jane and they rise, slipping into the kitchen to get the food. 'So, Rainey, I hear you passed all your exams,' Joe says, leaning back in his chair. 'Mary Jane says you might graduate this coming summer.'

'Well, I'm still not sure,' Rainey answers, looking down at the table. 'I might only take one class next semester. Being pregnant does change a few things.'

'*Uff da!* At this rate, you'll be in college for the rest of your life,' Mormor says, shaking her head. 'I can't believe you're still only a sophomore.' She cranes closer to Joe. 'You might not have guessed it, Joe, but she used to be so bright. When she was a child, we had high hopes that one day she'd do great things.'

'What could be greater than having a baby?' Woody asks angrily. 'She's bringing a new life into the world.'

Mormor sighs. 'That's fine for some people, but Rainey was never like other children. She had such fire, even at the age of six or seven. It all might have turned out so different. But now . . .' Her voice trails away. 'Married at twenty, a baby at twenty-two. You've ruined everything.'

Rainey bites her lip, surprised at the depth of her hurt. 'I will finish college eventually,' she insists. 'I just don't care about *thinking* the way I did when I was a kid. There're so many more interesting things in life.'

Mary Jane and Ingebjorg struggle into the dining room balancing plates piled high with a butter-browned turkey, mashed potatoes and candied yams. Everything looks hot and shiny, stewing in its own juices, except the cold cranberry jelly, which seems unnaturally vivid and quivers like mad. Rainey holds her napkin to her mouth, fighting the burning at the back of her throat. *This is Thanksgiving*, she tells herself. *You can't throw up now.*

Grandpa Garth sits solemnly at the head of the table, presiding over the meal. His moustache quivers, but his posture is perfect and his shoulders straight, in contrast to Mormor, who is hunched in the chair beside him, humbled by the illness she still won't admit.

'Rainey, would you like to say grace?' Grandpa Garth asks, folding his hands.

'Of course,' she answers. Rainey takes a deep breath and bows her head. Woody squeezes her fingers, and she feels a hot little pulse squirt straight into her stomach. '*I Jesu navn, går vi til bord, spise og drikke, på dit ord* . . .

'Amen,' Rainey says and pauses, letting her head fill with the echo of 'amens'. For a moment she thinks she hears a rumble in the distance, rising voices and the dull, mad stamping of snow-covered feet. She imagines figures silhouetted through the window, and a sharp wind throwing open the door. 'No,' she tells herself, 'no,' and the image disappears that quickly. She opens her eyes and gazes at the table before her, heavily laden with food, but still modest compared to the Thanksgivings of years ago.

'Are you OK?' Woody asks, squinting with concern. 'You looked a little shaky.'

'I'm fine,' she replies quickly. 'Just fine.'

'So, Joe, I thought your brother and his wife were coming to town for the holidays,' Grandpa Garth says, helping himself to a ladle full of gravy. Mary Jane and Ingebjorg trade furtive glances. 'Well, weren't they?' Garth asks.

'I thought we told you,' Mary Jane says softly, twisting the napkin in her lap. 'You know, about Frank's . . . a-f-f-a-i-r.'

'Oh that's right,' Garth says, wiping his moustache. 'Sorry.'

'With his secretary,' Joe says proudly, thumping himself on the chest. 'Well, give him credit for this, she's one hot little number.'

'Joe,' Mary Jane reprimands, shooting him an angry glare. 'Not in front of R-e-b-e-c-c-a.'

'Mom,' Rebecca says cynically, pushing her glasses back up to her eyebrows, 'I am eight and a half. I think I know how to spell my own name by now.'

Rainey smiles, remembering the old house in Owauskeum, which was sold two years ago, after no one in the family could afford to keep it up. *Some other family lives there now, and they are having Thanksgiving dinner tonight, most likely. But they are not us, they don't remember those times. Our family's past is lost on them. There's nothing in that house to show that's where I met him, that's where everything that happened afterwards began. I am Rainey, and these thoughts belong only to me.*

'How are Anna and the others?' Grandpa Garth asks. Anna, Torgrim, Christina and their families had all moved to a leisure village near Delray Beach, Florida. Rainey and Woody went to visit them at Easter, driving down from Chicago when Rainey's truck was new, and new too was Woody's enthusiasm to drive across the country. Their grand plan was sabotaged by the tingling in his hands; by Chattanooga, he was losing the feeling in his feet.

'Honestly, you would have thought they were still living in

Wisconsin,' Rainey explains, laughing at the memory as she helps herself to a third serving of mashed potatoes. 'They've brought as much of home with them as possible.'

Anna, Torgrim and the others had emigrated to the land of fuchsia and sea foam, of exotic plants and key lime pie, but instead of venturing out into the glorious warmth and sunshine, they stayed indoors, pulled their curtains, turned down the lights and played canasta and sheepshead with people who came from places like Detroit, Minneapolis and Sault Ste. Marie. Their furnishings were plush and heavy; dark wood panelling, smoked mirrors, ceramic beer steins. They painted their walls plum and burgundy, and decorated them with heads of deer and pheasant hung on lacquered plaques. Anna and Torgrim seemed so out of place among their neighbours, who were tanned and fit, and whose cool houses had white Venetian blinds and matching rattan porch sets. 'We don't mix with their sort,' Anna told Rainey, referring to her neighbours. 'They walk around in their swimsuits, even though she's got that big old scar on her stomach. And we saw him go outside once wearing only a bathrobe, and when he bent over to pick up his newspaper, you could see his manly pieces hanging out clear as day! Shameful! That's what happens when you spend too much time in the swimming pool. It's the chlorine, you see, it seeps into the brain.' Anna continued to knit chunky wool sweaters in her spare time and cook lefse, lutefisk and thick, hearty stews, keeping the memory of cold weather inside her, glowing like a light. 'The sunshine's nice, but we miss home sometimes,' Anna had said sadly. 'You wouldn't think of missing a place like Blue River Township. I guess you never appreciate home until you leave.'

'This is the first Thanksgiving without Ervald,' Ingebjorg says sadly, twirling her fork above her empty plate as the meal is nearly finished.

'No it isn't,' Mary Jane corrects her. 'Last year. Remember. It was July. When he . . .'

'Oh yes, you're right,' Ingebjorg says quickly, dabbing at her lips with a well-stained handkerchief.

'Shame.'

'Yes.'

'Such a shame.'

'Oh, foolishness,' Mormor interrupts, eyes cast downwards and chin pressed to her chest. 'It isn't right to dwell on such unpleasant things.' She pushes her food in circles around the plate, clutching the tablecloth as she breathes deeply through her nose.

'Mama?' Mary Jane asks, leaning over to Mormor, reaching with her hands. 'Mama, can I get you one of your pills?'

'No. I'm OK,' Mormor replies, steadying herself in the chair.

'Maybe, Sonja, you should go and rest a little bit, eh? Mary Jane and I will bring you up some coffee and pie,' Ingebjorg offers, her broad, flushed face and rotund body a stark contrast to Mormor's pale and weathered form.

'She'll be OK,' Grandpa Garth insists, reaching over to cover Mormor's hand, giving it a gentle squeeze which seems to irritate her even more. 'It's just been a bad week. But she'll get better. The doctor said, didn't he, Sonja? Just wait until next year. Then we'll see who makes the best pumpkin pie.' Mormor nods, her jaw set with resignation, accepting the pain. A shadow falls across Grandpa Garth's face as he straightens Mormor's knife and fork. The shadow darkens the wells beneath his eyes, but this shadow does not fall on Mormor; she will take whatever comes.

Ingebjorg, with a heavy sigh, pushes her plate away. 'That was delicious. But, as usual, I ate too much. Åh, jaså, it's OK, because I wasn't going to start my diet until New Year's, anyway.' Suddenly she plunges her hand in her apron and takes out a pack of well-thumbed photos and passes them around the table. 'I almost forgot! Take a look at this little lady. It's my grandniece, Emily Ingebjorg. Six months old, and an absolute angel. Emily Ingebjorg – isn't that pretty? They named her after me.'

Rainey smiles as the photo comes to her. 'She's beautiful,' Rainey says, feeling a gentle surge inside her stomach, a phantom kick of what is to come. 'A lovely little face.'

How can I wait another seven months, Rainey thinks, her mood suddenly darkening. *That seems like forever. I want this child now, while my grandmother is still here to see it. Even though I know what she'll say – 'Oh, the baby's got curly, dark hair, just like Woody. She doesn't even look like one of us.' Woody has a chart which he keeps beside the bed, and every night before he goes to sleep, he pores over it, squinting deeply behind his bifocals. 'Our baby is now* this big,' he told me yesterday, putting his arm around my shoulder. He held up the nail on his little finger, which was cracked and yellowed, bitten deep-down to the quick. 'See,' he said proudly, 'Only this big. But he already has a spine and a heart and everything.'

Ingebjorg beams, resting heavily on her fleshy elbows and releasing a great sigh. 'See the outfit Emily's wearing in that picture?' Ingebjorg asks. 'I made that for her. I knitted it myself.'

After dinner they sit down to watch football and gaze out the window at the seeping twilight, the last blue brush of snow.

'That was a wonderful turkey,' Mary Jane says, relaxing on the sofa and patting her flat stomach. Joe, beside her, puts his arm around her shoulder, pulling her close to his barrel chest.

'It was so juicy,' Joe offers. 'The sweetest darn turkey I think I've ever tasted.'

'It *was* juicy,' Ingebjorg agrees. 'The trick is to rub the whole thing with butter an hour before it starts to cook. That's what seals the juices inside.'

'Delicious. Not dry at all,' Grandpa Garth says, clenching a toothpick between his teeth and stroking his fine, silver moustache.

'Not at all.'

'Hmmmm.'

'I think I'm going to go upstairs,' Mormor announces, rising stiffly from her chair, fist jabbed into her waist. 'My back is killing me, I need to put up my feet.'

'Let me help you,' Rainey offers. 'I'll bring your back-rest and some water, if you want it.'

'I can manage,' Mormor says edgily, holding Rainey in a steely-eyed gaze. 'I don't need any help.'

'I know,' Rainey says quickly. 'But I was going upstairs anyway.'

'Oh. That's OK then,' Mormor says, relenting.

They go upstairs, Mormor hiding the fact that she's clinging to the handrail for support, as Rainey moves, slightly breathless, behind her.

Rainey follows Mormor into the bedroom and waits patiently while her grandmother settles into the bed, adjusting the support pillows beneath her feet, and fiddling with the television remote control.

'Rainey, aren't you glad now that it's over with?' Mormor asks softly, sinking back in the bed, letting the blankets billow up around her.

'What's over with?' Rainey asks, draping the quilt across Mormor's knees.

'All that terrible business four years ago. Those things that happened . . . oh, you know.'

Rainey takes a deep breath and says nothing. *It's not over with*, she thinks. *He's with me all the time now, he can touch me whenever he wants. He won't ever leave me alone. Until I'm dead too, I guess. And then we'll be together.*

'What's wrong with you, child? You look a little peaked,' Mormor says, cruising through the channels on the remote control.

'I'm OK. It's nothing.' Rainey shakes her head, trying to clear her mind. 'Do you want me to get you anything else? A glass of orange juice, or a magazine or something?' Rainey asks. She glances at the bedside table, heavy with desperate little things: a comb and brush, a nail file, an empty glass and a bottle full of brightly coloured pills; the Norwegian prayer book, the *Bønneboken*, which Mormor received at her confirmation, the leather cover now more deeply creased.

'No, that's all right. I don't need anything else right now,' Mormor says wearily, shaking her arm.

'Well, let me know . . .'

'Rainey, I'm just having a little rest,' Mormor insists, sitting upright and suddenly angry. 'You don't have to fuss so much.'

'You're right. Sorry. Good night,' Rainey says. She leans down to kiss her grandmother, but instead only takes her hand. Rainey feels the cold, bony knuckles slip through her grasp as Mormor's hand drops back to the bed. 'See you in the morning,' Rainey says softly. 'Good night.'

'Rainey?' Mormor asks in a voice that quivers through the room, bringing up the hair on the back of Rainey's neck.

'Yes?'

'Remember to drink a little ginger ale before you go to bed. That way you won't throw up in the morning. When I was pregnant, that always worked for me.'

'I will,' Rainey answers. 'Thanks for the advice.'

*

As Rainey slips back downstairs, her ear catches wisps of the continuing conversation.

'We should have made *rømmegrøt*,' Ingebjorg says, sounding surprisingly morose.

'Do you remember how?' Mary Jane asks, leaning forward with interest.

'Sure. Well, the recipe is in the back of the cookbook; you know, Sonja's old book?'

'The one with the casserole on the cover?'

'*Ja.*'

'*Åh, javisst. Selvsagt,*' they say. '*Åh, jada.*' The old language is remembered at twilight, the past creeps up under cover of dark.

Rainey sits down on the sofa next to Woody. 'Woody,' she says softly, nudging him gently, pressing her elbow into his side. 'Woody honey, come on.' He nods, but doesn't look at her. He's drunk a beer when he shouldn't have, and now he's dull-eyed and sleepy, not really listening to the conversation, listening instead to the music she imagines he hears in his head. She watched him take the Old Style out of the refrigerator and she ached to stop him; his doctors have told him not to drink, and she wanted to grab the bottle and put it back. But then again, it was only one beer, and he had wanted it so much, she could see that; she could feel his pleasure as he tipped the amber liquid down his throat, licked his lips and caressed the long, thin neck of the bottle as he swallowed, softly tossing back his head.

'Hmm?' Woody asks, half roused from his reverie.

'It's nothing,' Rainey tells him, wrapping her arms around his shoulders and nestling her chin against his neck. 'It's OK. I'll tell you later. You can just stay quiet.'

'What's wrong?' Woody asks, leaning forward. His eyes are glassy; a softness plays about his lips.

'Nothing,' she reassures him, her earlier sadness suddenly past. 'It was nothing at all.'

It is well past midnight when Rainey, driven by hunger, pads down to the kitchen. She opens the fridge and pulls out a plate piled high with slices of cold meat, tearing off thin strips with her fingers and pushing them hungrily into her mouth. She samples the pie, the corn pudding, the silver bowl of whipped cream; even the cold, solid gravy, the surface of which she skims with her finger and presses onto her tongue. Food is so unbelievably delicious now, and tastes as intensely as if she's never eaten before. She's gained eighteen pounds, way over the limit for the first eight weeks of pregnancy, but she doesn't care. There's no sign of the tomboy in her now; she's full-figured and womanly, a brand new Rainey McBride.

At first, Rainey doesn't hear the soft footsteps behind her. 'Oh, sorry,' Mary Jane mumbles, rubbing her eyes. 'I didn't know you were here.' She is dressed in a long, flannel nightgown, dark hair in a loose knot over her shoulder, fuzzy slippers covering her long, narrow feet.

'That's OK.' They look at each other awkwardly, neither knowing what to say. 'You know, the pie was good,' Rainey offers. 'The pecan pie – the one you made.'

'I made the cherry one,' Mary Jane answers, scratching her chin.

'Oh, that one was good too,' Rainey says.

'Thanks. I like baking,' Mary Jane says, reaching for a glass and filling it with tap water. 'I just wish I was as good at it as Mama is.'

'You *are* good at baking,' Rainey insists. 'Very good.'

'Not really.' Mary Jane shakes her head. 'I'm not good at anything. I was a total idiot when I was a student. But you're good at lots of things. And so is Rebecca – she does real well in school, especially science and geometry. And building things! You should see those fat little hands get busy. Last month she made a laser death-ray machine; that's what she called it. She said she was going to use it to vaporise the kids who stole her lunch money.'

Rainey smiles. 'Is Mormor still awake?' she asks, nodding at the glass of water in Mary Jane's hand.

'Oh? No, no,' Mary Jane says quickly. 'It's Rebecca. She had a bad dream and I'm trying to get her to settle.'

Rainey imagines with envy a soft and sleepy Rebecca snuggled into the pocket of warmth beside her mother, huddled in the crook of Mary Jane's arm.

'Rainbow, I just want you to know, it's OK if you hate me,' Mary Jane says carefully. 'I wouldn't blame you at all.'

'I don't hate you,' Rainey says wearily. 'It's nothing like that. It's just that after so long it's hard to get used to having a mother. Especially now that I'm going to be a mother myself.' Rainey can never explain that after years of constructing an imaginary mother, the real Mary Jane was bound to disappoint – she was only a woman, after all, with a nervous habit of tugging her ear and a soft drawl from the ten years she'd lived with Carlos in Texas.

'I was missing my brother so much when I ran away. That's no excuse, I know, but I was sixteen, I had a baby, and I just couldn't think straight. I meant to come back, but the more time passed, the harder it got. I was so sure you'd hate me, I was afraid to ever come home.'

'I understand,' Rainey says. 'I know how you must have felt. I can imagine how hard Mormor and Grandpa Garth made everything. It was a confusing time, I'm sure.'

'Thanks, Rainey,' Mary Jane says. 'You're a better daughter than I'll ever deserve. It's my punishment to know what I missed in you all along.' Mary Jane reaches out and hugs Rainey. Her slim fingers sink into Rainey's solid back; the strands of her shiny, black hair stick to Rainey's lips. *I haven't forgiven her*, Rainey thinks. *Not yet anyway, but someday I will. The potential to forgive is within me; I can feel it, buried deep beneath my skin. But until that emerges, it is right to keep this little secret, to let her believe that all is well. She doesn't have to know the truth. She came back to me in the end, and that was more than I dared to hope for.*

Rainey goes back to her bedroom, the bedroom of her childhood, which is still full of stuffed animals and other toys; baseball cards wedged into the wooden frame around the mirror. The walls are decked with awards and ribbons, which seem to rebuke her with their accusations of lost promise, signs of something once so bright, now tarnished and past.

Woody is asleep and snoring softly in her old bed, curled up tightly with his hands beneath his cheek. She looks down at him and marvels at the depth of her love. It splits her open like an axe, cutting straight through to the dark, wet pulp beneath her skin. As she crawls into the bed, he lifts his arm an inch or two, allowing just enough space for her to slip in next to him. She rests her head against his body, listening to the noises in his chest. She hears the thin, papery flutter of his heart, seeming somehow so close and yet far away. She pulls back an inch or so. She is too aware of how easily delicate things can be destroyed; delicate things like Woody's heart, or her own, or even the microscopic heart of the tiny child inside her.

Woody wakes up a little, smacks his lips and sighs. He slides his hand around her waist and over her stomach, nuzzling his chin into the back of her neck.

'I'm getting fatter,' she confesses. 'A lot fatter, and pretty fast.'

'Uh-huh.'

'What do you think about that?' she asks.

'I like it,' he replies sleepily.

'You do?'

'Sure. Now there's more of you to love.'

'You don't really expect me to buy an old line like that,' she replies, laughing in the dark, but something about what he's just said touches her, and she starts to cry. *What I don't understand is how I ended up happy*, she thinks to herself. *That's the last thing I expected. I sometimes think this isn't right; this isn't my life. There's another life, one characterised by grief and sorrow, and it's waiting for me just around the corner; huddled just behind the next unopened door. And when that other life arrives, all this will seem like a strange and distant dream, more beautiful because it's ended. I can't hang on to what I have here; I can't be sure of this, or anything, no matter how hard I try.*

Woody's sleepy fingers touch her cheek; he feels the wetness and wakes up again, rising to his elbow. 'What is it, honey? What's wrong?' he whispers urgently.

'It's nothing,' she answers, turning her face away.

'Hey, darlin', I know you're worried about the baby, but he'll be fine,' Woody insists, stroking her shoulder. 'Or she'll be fine. What about Corrina? Corrina Stern? That's a pretty name for a girl.' She hears him sigh in the dark. 'I hope it is a girl and she looks exactly like you. Rainey, you're a wonderful wife. You'll be a wonderful mother. I know it will all work out for us in the end.'

'I want to believe you,' Rainey says, 'but I don't have faith any more, not the way I used to when I was a child. Now, it's so much harder.'

'That's OK, Rainey, because I believe for you,' he says firmly, his voice like a beacon splitting the night. 'I reach out my hand, and when we touch each other, I fill up the distance between you and God.' He wraps his arm around her body, presses his chin into her side. She can feel his breath, moving back and forth across her ribs.

He thinks I'm worried about the baby, but that isn't really true, she thinks to herself. *As I lay down beside my husband, with our child no bigger than the size of an idea inside me, I have not told him everything. I still grieve for a boy who loved death more than he loved me. And Woody, although I don't think he knows it, sometimes calls out his first wife's name in the middle of the night. Sometimes he cries in his sleep for the slim, tan-skinned lady with long dark hair and fiery black eyes. I haven't told him this but I will, someday. There's time. There's always plenty of time. I am Rainey, and these thoughts belong only to me.*

As Rainey drifts to sleep, she isn't thinking about Ambrose any more, or Emelita, or even the child inside her. Her thoughts turn instead to Aunt Ingebjorg, red-faced and sweating, passing around photos of her six-month-old grandniece. Ingebjorg is tired from the heat of the kitchen, from lifting and positioning the heavy pots and pans. She's too old for such intensive work, but she has no intention of quitting now. 'This is my new grandniece,' she says, mopping her forehead with a damp handkerchief. She leans on her fleshy elbows and points to the photograph with pride. 'Isn't she an angel? Emily Ingebjorg. They named her after me.'

Rainey knows all about Ingebjorg's secret grief; she can hear her weeping in her other heart. *But no one else can sense this, and your sorrow is safe with me. I am Rainey, and I recognise pain at the centre of everything.* In her dream Rainey is about to go in to dinner, but she stops for a second to steady her stomach and clear her head.

'Are you all right?' Woody asks, pale eyes tight with concern. 'You look a little shaky.'

'Yes, I'm fine,' Rainey answers, taking his slim little hand and cradling it in her own. 'I'm perfectly fine. And I am ready to enter this other room, where a table is waiting,' she tells him. 'I will sit down when my name is spoken, in this place where I have always been known.'